The World a Moment Later

By the Author

Our Holocaust

Amir Gutfreund

The World *a* Moment Later

TRANSLATED BY

Jessica Cohen

The Toby Press

The World a Moment Later

First English Edition, 2008

The Toby Press LLC
POB 8531, New Milford, CT 06776-8531, USA
& POB 2455, London WIA 5WY, England
www.tobypress.com

First published in Hebrew as *HaOlam, Ktsat Achar Kach*
by Kinneret, Zmora-Bitan, Dvir
Copyright © Amir Gutfreund, 2005

The right of Amir Gutfreund to be identified as the author
of this work has been asserted by him in accordance
with the Copyright, Designs & Patents Act 1988.

Translation copyright © Jessica Cohen, 2008

Cover photograph copyright © Kluger Zoltan,
Israeli Government Press Office

ISBN 978 1 59264 251 9, *hardcover*

A CIP catalogue record for this title is
available from the British Library

Typeset by Koren Publishing Services

Printed and bound in the United States

"The Jewish people, logically speaking,
have no future. Still, work must be done."

(Yosef Chaim Brenner)

Contents

vii

ix

Characters
(in alphabetical order)

Chaim Abramowitz: Son of Leon Abramowitz; comes to Israel as a young boy and builds an estate

Leon Abramowitz: Father of Chaim Abramowitz; a journalist sent to cover life in Palestine in the nineteen-twenties

Rivka Abramowitz: Sarah's daughter

Sarah Abramowitz: Chaim Abramowitz's wife and Rivka's mother

David Bonhoeffer*: A nomadic, righteous man, engaged in finding housing and work for the needy

Meir Glop: A forester who pioneers tree planting in Palestine

Greenhaus: A member of the same political party as Yehezkel Klein (together with Tadek and Tzipkin) and Lev Gutkin's friend and mentor in Palestine

Günter (Yeshaya Tarhomi): Hans's father; the first head foreman of the Abramowitz Estate

---

* Author's note: The character of David Bonhoeffer was inspired by the German pastor Dietrich Bonhoeffer, a courageous resister of Hitler's regime. He was imprisoned and hanged on Himmler's orders roughly a month before the final defeat of Nazi Germany. Some of David's dialogue in the book is based on Dietrich Bonhoeffer's statements and writings.

I

Lev Gutkin: A handsome Russian Jew who plans assassinations of Stalin and Ben-Gurion; joins the Abramowitz Estate and becomes Rivka's confidant

Hans (Shaul Tarhomi): Günter's son; a foreman on the Abramowitz Estate

Genia Klein: Yehezkel Klein's wife, Romek Paz's sister

Shmuel Klein: Son of Yehezkel and Genia Klein; a gifted electrician and a pyromaniac

Yehezkel Klein: Shmuel Klein's father; an admirer of Jabotinksy and member of a small radical underground during the British Mandate

Stefano Lerer: A Holocaust survivor from Italy who takes revenge on the Nazis and their collaborators; comes to Israel and institutes an army of avengers; joins the Abramowitz Estate and becomes a foreman and bodyguard for the Abramowitz family

Major John Manors: A British Mandate intelligence officer, in charge of investigating the affairs of Chaim Abramowitz and finding cause to imprison him

Romek Paz (Pozowski): Genia Klein's brother; a tireless party hack who enlists in Chaim Abramowitz's Testament Army

Ricki: A prostitute, Shmuel Klein's love

Doctor Meshulam Riklin: A naturopathic physician from Ness Ziona, specializing in helping women conceive; later joins the Abramowitz Estate as head foreman for Chaim Abramowitz

Naomi Riklin: The late wife of Doctor Meshulam Riklin

Chronology

1909   "Hashomer" organization founded by members of the Second Aliyah

1910   Chaim Abramowitz born

1914   Lolek Abramowitz born

1915   Yeshaya Tarhomi (Günter) born in the Kinneret agricultural collective (*moshava*)

1920   "Haganah" organization founded

1921   Author Yosef Chaim Brenner murdered

1923   Albert Einstein visits Palestine

1924   Leon Abramowitz commits suicide

1927   Handsome Lev Gutkin born

1929   The 1929 Riots, August 23 (Av 17, 5689), massacre of Jews in Hebron
Huge fire destroys the newly planted Hulda Forest
Chaim Abramowitz's first marriage

3

1930   The Yemenites of Kinneret are expelled and housed in the
        Marmorek neighborhood of Rehovot
        Chaim Abramowitz founds his estate, Rivka Abramowitz
        born

1931   Yeshaya Tarhomi (Günter)'s first marriage
        Lev Gutkin's father is taken away

1932   Chadwick discovers the neutron
        Hans born

1935   Günter arrives at the Abramowitz Estate and is appointed head
        foreman

1936   The Arabs rise up against British rule in "The Great Revolt"
        and the 1936 (5696) Riots occur; the first "tower and stockade"
        settlements are built (through 1939)

1938   July 10—watchman Alexander Zaid of Hashomer is
        murdered

1943   Final defeat of the Germans at Stalingrad

1948   Establishment of the State of Israel and the War of
        Independence
        June—Günter's second marriage
        September—Stefano Lerer joins the Abramowitz Estate
        October—Sarah dies
        December—the first "Operation Magic Carpet" airplanes land
        in Israel

1949   April—beginning of the "austerity" days of rationing
        June—Yehezkel Klein and Genia marry; the War of
        Independence ends
        September—Herzl's remains brought to Israel; Chaim's second
        marriage
        October—Hans arrives at the Estate

4

1950 March—Levin the Citrus Grower is murdered; the remains of Hannah Szenes are brought to Israel

1951 A split in the Kibbutz movement, the kibbutzim divide into Ichud ("Union") and Meuchad ("United")

1952 The remains of the paratrooper Haviva Reik are identified in a mass grave and brought to burial in Israel
The remains of David Wolffsohn are brought to Israel
Günter moves to Safed, Hans and Lerer appointed head foremen

1953 March—Josef Stalin dies; handsome Lev Gutkin makes aliyah; the remains of Naftali Herz Imber are brought to Israel
Chaim and Rivka meet Dr. Meshulam Riklin
First official appearance of Bonhoeffer at the Abramowitz Estate

1954 Remains of the Baron Edmond de Rothschild and his wife are brought to Israel

1955 Albert Einstein dies; Shmuel Klein born
Remains of Etzel leader David Raziel transferred from Iraq to Cyprus
Hans leaves for Europe; Riklin arrives at the Estate and becomes the new foreman

1956 Remains of Nahum Sokolow brought to Israel

1961 Remains of David Raziel brought to Israel
Remains of Moshe Hess and his wife brought to Israel
David Ben-Gurion announces his resignation, wins the elections and returns to the post of prime minister
Handsome Lev Gutkin arrives at the Abramowitz Estate

1963 Hans returns to the Estate

1964 January—Arab summit convenes, PLO is established
June—National Water Carrier inaugurated
July—remains of Ze'ev Jabotinsky brought to Israel
Romek Paz, Genia's brother, begins working for Chaim Abramowitz

1965 Israeli spy Eli Cohen hanged in Damascus

1967 The Six-Day War; Hans is killed
Rivka Abramowitz declares the construction of a separate house from Chaim Abramowitz

1968 Romek Paz collapses and is hospitalized

1973 The Yom Kippur War; Shmuel Klein wins a Medal of Courage
December—Yehezkel Klein dies

1974 Motti Ashkenazi begins his protest over the Yom Kippur War

1976 Shmuel Klein completes his military service and takes a job at the Museum of Prehistoric Man
Handsome Lev Gutkin dies in his sleep

1977 The remains of Marzouk and Azar, hanged in Egypt during the "Unfortunate Affair," are brought to Israel
Egyptian President Anwar al-Sadat visits Israel

1978 Shmuel Klein arrives at the Abramowitz Estate

Part One

Chapter one

Leon Abramowitz   1920

I

"Our crisis is the crisis of a nation that lacks the aptitude to live decently."
(Yosef Chaim Brenner)

n the pioneering days of 1920, as the road from Tiberias to Tzemach was slowly being paved, the tragic figure of Leon Abramowitz—part journalist, part new immigrant—could be seen trailing behind a group of laborers as he scribbled his impressions of the burgeoning country.

The laborers hammered noisily, some singing, others engrossed in their work. Leon Abramowitz, in a sky-blue suit, listened closely and tried to salvage a newsworthy item from the commotion. Once in a while he approached the workers to share a drink of water, at other times he kept his distance from the horde. Not infrequently, during the midday hours, he would sit down heavily on a rock by the side of the road and allow the Zionist enterprise to proceed without him. His hollow eyes would linger on the horizon and his mind would fill with thoughts.

It had been two years since Leon had found himself living in *Eretz Yisrael,* and his life was on hold. It was unclear whether he had finally emigrated to this beautiful land, or whether he was first and foremost a journalist, an emissary, delivering the country's maiden offerings to his excitable readers like bouquets of flowers, rather than mere fragments of paper deposited at the post office each week. He related his contemplations and misgivings to the genteel ladies at the Flomin Hotel, in Jaffa, where he discussed the hardships of journalistic work in Palestine and managed to wrest from them a few ponderings and sighs of their own. Alone in his room, he examined these contemplations and misgivings as one scrutinizes one's own body in the mirror.

Two years had passed since his editor, the accursed Klemitz, had sent him here with the promise of handsome rewards. But since then—upheavals. At first Abramowitz had supported Zionism ardently, winning frequent praise from Klemitz. Despite the air of dismissiveness he adopted whenever compliments were given, as befitted a European journalist, Abramowitz kept Klemitz's missives for further perusal, and they often served as his loyal friends. Here a piece of advice, there a gem of an insight. Quite simply, the communiqués were an invaluable treasure. As he traveled the hot and dusty roads, Abramowitz kept the letters in his pocket like a rose on a gentleman's lapel. At moments of exhaustion, or to distance himself a little from the pioneers' sweat, which wafted all the way to the surrounding hills, he would remove a letter from his pocket and study it, leaving behind the banging of the hammers, the quarriers' din and the insufferable clatter of stones being pulverized.

My dear fellow,

Your monograph on the topic of roads is, of course, perfect. Kindly explain, however, why there is a need for a road to Tzemach? If possible, divert the road to Jerusalem. How thrilled could our Zionist readers possibly be to learn of the paving of a road to Tzemach? Jerusalem, my dear man, Jerusalem! Please, as they say, stoke the fire with logs, not with splinters. In short, steer the monograph toward Jerusalem, and if the pioneers do not follow, woe unto them. Pursue your path and may you prosper.

Awaiting your minor revisions, whereupon the monograph
will be sent to press and the author's fee on its way to you.
Your friend, Herman Klemitz.

Said author's fee—namely, a livelihood—had progressed from marginal to essential. Since the very first days, it was only when Leon Abramowitz grew angry enough to drop a demanding letter into the mailbag that he received anything from Klemitz: a penny, a note or an accolade. By and by, these too dissipated. The truth was that even when they had worked together, side by side at their desks, Abramowitz had utterly disliked Klemitz. Now he had no choice but to wait for his letters, for he was the salary giver. When Klemitz had grasped Abramowitz's shoulder one evening and said, "You, we will send to *Eretz Yisrael,*" Leon had felt a surge of love for Klemitz, who, weasel that he was, had promised him the earth. "If you need anything there, you have only to write," he had assured Abramowitz. But since arriving in Palestine, it was as if the words had never been spoken. Abramowitz traversed kibbutzim and *moshavot* and *kevutzot,* surveying the life of action and the life of the mind and the various trends of thought. Driven by a desire to experience Jewish toil, he even tried his hand awkwardly at a little hoeing, some harvesting and fruit-picking, until his fingers were practically broken.

Each time Abramowitz met a laborer, he would tell him, "I am a journalist, a small-winged Jew, who wishes to learn of the goings-on in *Eretz Yisrael.*" The workers liked what he said and took time to talk with him. They told him stories of the land, and also asked how things were in Europe—beautiful, snowy Europe. Abramowitz steered the conversations to the fields, the vineyards, the guards and the crops, but their minds stubbornly filled with familiar village squares and bronze statues of horsemen. They could scarcely be dislodged from their nostalgia. Some turned grave—Life is hard here—and Abramowitz would say cheerfully: Together, we will overcome. Some were curious about Abramowitz himself: had he joined the Jews dwelling in Palestine, or was he only a temporary envoy? Abramowitz would explain that this was precisely his dilemma, that things were as of yet unclear even to himself. In his meager hotel room in Jaffa he would labor over his articles for those readers longing to taste the honey of Israel. He would also dispatch hurried notes and telegrams to Klemitz—send the money! For a man cannot happily reside in Palestine without a penny in his pocket.

This much he also made clear to the ladies in the Flomin Hotel. They liked to listen to him, and his resolve to stay in Palestine hardened when he spent time with them, sipping pale tea in the parlor. The ladies agreed: Palestine was lovely, but even here a person needed money. Sometimes Abramowitz experienced the very same desperation he encountered among the settlers of the wilderness. Every day he had to enquire: anything from Klemitz? Even a paltry few words? One evening he experienced a quarrel with Flomin, the hotel proprietor. Abramowitz accused him of hiding Klemitz's letters because of his debts, and the two men almost came to blows. In his first days here, such behavior would have been inconceivable, but the wild nectar of this land had encroached upon his manners such that he no longer found it surprising that, in times of fury, a man might even resort to his fists.

That evening, Abramowitz retired to his room in a torrent of emotions. Sitting on his bed, he studied his clenched hands as if they might offer some explanation of the event, and he found himself blaming Flomin and Klemitz and the Palestine heat, which could drive a person mad even if he did have his own vine and fig tree to sit beneath. Besides, how could they have given him a room without so much as an ocean view through its tiny window? In the evening hours the air stood still and thrust itself down one's throat. And Klemitz, what did he need Klemitz for? He sent no author's fees, and his advice was flat. Go and speak with the greatest of our Hebrew authors, Klemitz had advised. Yosef Chaim Brenner would be easy to find, either teaching Hebrew to the Labor Battalion, or around Tel Aviv and Jaffa. Go and listen to his blistering rebuke of our Zionist enterprise and draw some honey from the rock.

The meeting was arranged and the two men spoke. But

Klemitz's advice was as the counsel of Ahithophel: it was not honey that emerged from the rock, but some barely intelligible yet nonetheless hostile statements, tired and bitter proclamations that could never be turned into an article. A few days later, Abramowitz read Brenner's column in the workers' newspaper:

> *Our crisis is the crisis of a nation that lacks the aptitude to live decently... Our farmers are farmers in quotation marks. A Hebrew intellectual who comes here seeking a different life, a life replete with physical labor and the fragrance of the field, discovers within days that he himself is unskilled for any work...*

Such a thing. Why was the author carping at our farmers? Abramowitz had visited the agricultural settlements and witnessed farmers with calloused hands turning meadows of thistles into fields of wheat, swamps into furrows, brambles into fig trees. Why were they farmers in quotation marks? After all, Abramowitz had seen with his own eyes the hardship and suffering endured by the settlers. He had found men plagued with illness, their spirits broken. He had seen people living on the crooked paths of mountain tops, grasping the inclines and settling any piece of land, all for the sake of building our country. Why, then, had Brenner seen fit to torment them with his words? But the great author's utterances haunted Abramowitz and he began to see quotation marks strewn throughout Palestine: in the "national leaders" who derided all that was holy, the "senior officials" who learned corruption from the most lawless of nations, in "the philosophers" and "the workers." Quotation marks everywhere. And although he did not introduce his new thoughts into his articles, he occasionally found that while his hand penned a song of praise for a leader, his heart murmured, "leader."

On the second of May, 1921, Yosef Chaim Brenner was murdered. Leon considered writing a great article in the author's memory, but he could not steady his pen. His hand hovered over the page and found nothing to grasp at. He had no desire to write this monograph. That evening, his fellow journalists crowded into the post office to hurriedly submit their articles on the terrible murder, all recounting how the Arabs had attacked and how the British police had refused to help, and how one body, that of the young Yosef Luidor, was still mysteriously missing. They competed against one another in their reports, their pens so light, and Abramowitz fumed—what did they know about Brenner? He felt an urge to grab their pages and rip them to shreds, but he stifled his sorrow within his overcoat, sighed, and suddenly, with stark heaviness, felt like a stranger, an utter stranger to it all. How, he wondered, had he come this far? And why had they sent him here at all?

Abramowitz left the post office and felt barely able to breathe. He looked at the street, at the mosquitoes buzzing around a dim lamp, and wondered if perhaps he had been forgotten here, like Robinson Crusoe. He shut himself up in his hotel room to write an article, and a new spirit seemed to envelop his own, sweeping him away in a determined desire to write about things that had no quotation marks. Things as they were. In the mailbag he deposited descriptions of limp souls and sorrowful hearts and the shattered paths of so many men. His pen insisted on chastising the work of those wheelers and dealers and public leaders. The trivial financial transgressions of a respectable idealist, the bribery breathing new life into a business. The country was spoiling while its innocent strayed and its villainous made speeches. Every day Abramowitz completed an article or two and hurried to the post office to dispatch the truth.

One day there was a letter from Klemitz.

My dear fellow,

Please do not send more and more tragedies about which-ever of the pioneers has put an end to his life because of the hard-ships. You are depressing the spirits of our readers and weakening Zionism itself to no end, and I fear you are bringing about the collapse of our newspaper. Let go, my dear friend, let go. Send us general tragedies, those which are of great interest to the learned reader and do not depress his spirits. Perhaps, for example, a ter-rible plague has spread among the Arabians in Jaffa, and there is

*fear that the outbreak might reach the Yishuv and afflict our camp?
Or perhaps there are further conflicts among the various factions of
settlers, pioneering ideologies or some such thing? Elaborate upon
the opposing positions, and do not protect us from the harshness.
After all, it is said that the Land of Israel shall be bought with
suffering, and it is suffering that we await.*

With brotherly friendship, Herman Klemitz

Abramowitz was surprised: was he really writing so extensively about
the broken-hearted? About those who took their own lives? He did
not think so. If truth be told, there was much devastation here, but
there was also a reluctance to malign the country. One took pen to
paper in order to write about the valor, but onto the page leapt por-
trayals of deception and despair.

Abramowitz's fingers dug around inside the envelope: could
there be any money? It occurred to him that perhaps his articles were
no longer being published. But whether they printed his articles in
the newspaper or tossed them in the wastebasket, he did not care.
Abramowitz hastened back to the anguish. He wrote of the calami-
ties and the dead and the émigrés. Here a young man committed
suicide, there a tragic fire, here a father of two took his own life. In
his imaginary quarrels with Klemitz he asked defiantly: Whither
Zionism? Wherefore has this endeavor come about? Why should we
uproot hills and level rocky terrain, turn everything into roads and
farms? Why are the Jews standing in the way of history? Why must
we, too, have a homeland? We would do better to relinquish and
leave history to take its own natural breaths.

Abramowitz's life was not an easy one. In his room he ate carobs
gathered on his travels, barely able to cobble together enough pennies for a cup of tea. Flomin treated him cautiously, only delicately
reminding him of his debts, for there was a measure of warning in
Abramowitz's unshaven face, and his clothes carried the unrelenting
scent of wanderings. Abramowitz had no time to dwell on Flomin's
nonsense. The country was full of bitterness, and with a bursting
heart he scurried among the sufferers.

Gripped by a sudden idea, he sent for his young son, Chaim, from Europe. He wanted to show him the country, to plant him here as a seedling, to strengthen him. Life here was not easy for a fourteen-year-old boy, he warned himself, holding both his hands up as if to stymie his own plan. But the boy was nonetheless sent for, and one cannot say that it was a mistake. No sooner had Chaim stepped off the boat than it became apparent that this land was not foreign to him. He was a Jew returned to his homeland, and he would soak up its nature as intended—unlike many pioneers, who gritted their teeth and stomped their feet and remained unwelcomed by the harsh land.

Chaim spent a week in the Flomin Hotel with his father, listening to his overview of Zionism and the directions in which it was spreading its wings, but he very quickly began to evade the lectures and instead joined up with a group of young ramblers. He roamed the country with them, reaching as far as the Gilead. From the first, he gave his father no financial trouble. He allowed Leon to pull the yoke of journalism, and for himself he found odd jobs—a hauler for trucks, an apprentice to artisans, even a peddler of small goods. Abramowitz never ceased to be amazed. Here was Chaim's young body, caressed by the sun of Zion, his muscles rapidly strengthening and his shoulders broadening. It had been wise to bring the boy over. This much he made clear to the ladies in the Flomin Hotel, who liked to listen to him, unlike Mr. Flomin, who did nothing but demand money over and over again. Abramowitz told the ladies he had another son in Europe, and that at times he missed him so terribly that he thought he might suffocate.

"Another son?" They marveled, as if Abramowitz were a magician pulling sons out of a hat. "Give us another son!" they urged him.

Abramowitz maintained equivocal relations with the unmarried Eskiner sisters. He replied that his second son, young Lolek, would be better off staying where he was. He was a superlative student. Abramowitz had considered sending for him once or twice, but his teachers had begged that he not be taken from his studies, lest the future of a rare scholar be wasted. And so his hands were tied.

Abramowitz further whispered to the Eskiner sisters how distraught he was. He had been roaming Palestine for years now, and he did not like everything he saw as he journeyed in the heat to witness the construction of the country. Sometimes he believed he should return to his comfortable position in the cultured world, where at least the weather was cool. What, after all, was he? No great leader. No Moses.

The Eskiner sisters protested: He was an important Jew, and if not for him, they did not know how they could even take another breath. During all their difficult hours, they knew that a gallant Jew was standing at their side, and their burden was lightened.

Abramowitz enjoyed being called a "gallant Jew," and they all giggled, and things seemed lighter. More tea was considered, despite the heat. But a moment later, there in the entrance of the hotel stood Theodor Korman, a journalist from Abramowitz's newspaper, a senior figure who surely knew everything that was going on among the editors. Abramowitz rushed to the doorway, wishing to draw Korman in and introduce him to the Eskiner sisters—they were friends, after all. But Korman recoiled somewhat from the embrace, as if he had heard unpleasant rumors, and shook Abramowitz's hand limply. Abramowitz would not let go, putting his arm around Korman's shoulders and standing close to him, almost trying to absorb him, entreating him to recount everything that was happening in that faraway office. He was beside himself with eagerness to decipher all the events that had transpired since he had been sent here to rot away.

Korman, alarmed, shook him off and said dismissively: "There was a whole business over there at the paper. Seniors were dismissed, heads rolled. And your man Klemitz didn't waste any time. He is accused of a large embezzlement, half the paper's fortune. Who knows where he is now? I must tell you, sending telegrams to the newspaper at a time like this, addressed to Klemitz, asking for money…"

And then Korman was gone, taking his suitcase with him; he had heard that the Danziger Hotel was no less comfortable.

Leon Abramowitz was left behind, knowing that he had been abandoned on this desert island. And so the matter was settled: he had emigrated.

But not just emigrated. He had been thrown out. The villainous

Klemitz, who was now walking around with suitcases full of money, had intentionally sent him here, and it was clear that there was no one to write articles for now. He would never find work at the local papers. There were thirty men jumping at every miserable job. Moreover, he was disliked for the terrible things he had said about the journalists in Palestine. True, all true, every word of it, but now he felt remorse—why had he been so quick to pluck the feathers of these geese? Now he would have no way to make a living under any circumstance.

In the evening he met with his son, Chaim, which was a rare occurrence. Weeks would go by without seeing him as he roamed the *moshavot* and worked the lands. There were rumors that he was leading gangs of Jewish orange-pickers who forced their way into jobs all over the country, Jews who could find work anywhere. There were rumors that his gang had beaten Arabs and broken the legs of a wealthy citrus grower, and that Chaim carried weapons now. He was so young, only of high school age. What did they want of him?

Abramowitz attempted to start a conversation. "There are those, they say, who think about leaving. It's hard here, not everyone makes it…"

"No one's being held here against his will," answered Chaim. His Hebrew was already excellent, and his gaze was dark. He spoke in grave tones, as though he had matured prematurely, perhaps excessively.

"No, no, they're not," Leon chuckled, "but still, making a living is hard. Maybe there are those who would be better off going back to their countries. There is loneliness here…"

"Here there is unity, Father," Chaim explained, "together we are strong."

"Yes, together…but still, there are those who are deprived of a livelihood. Not everyone, but some…and what is such a person to do?"

"Together, Father, together there is strength," Chaim insisted.

Leon knew that his son attended political rallies, congresses, national gatherings. It was odd, as he seemed to have no attachment to theoretical notions. He was a man of action.

With a firm hand, Chaim pressed a bundle of paper money on his father.

"No, no," Leon said, his hand fluttering.

"Father, take it. I have more."

Leon Abramowitz took the money and as he did so, a thought popped into his mind: he should write an article about the young people here in Palestine. This was a matter to be glorified. But by the next morning he began to feel uncomfortable, and he set about frittering away the money by making frivolous purchases. He had to find a new source of income.

An opportunity soon arose. One of the ladies asked if he might be willing to accompany her on a tedious journey from Jaffa to Zichron Yaakov. Abramowitz agreed, and word spread quickly among the ladies, who handed him around from one to the next with praise and heartfelt recommendations. He busied himself with these excursions for many days, entertaining the ladies with jokes, arousing their curiosity with tales of mystery, offering political analyses of Katznelson and Theodor Herzl. When the ladies tired of words they told him to don their hats to make them laugh, they slipped their gloves onto his hands and tied their scarves around his neck, asked him to sing operettas, mimic jackals and monkeys, anything to make the hours go by.

Not all the ladies remembered to reward him for his efforts, and a few did not believe they were obliged to pay. But Abramowitz needed the money—he could not accompany a lady without a tailored suit, shaving water, oils for his hair, and men's eau de cologne, which was not yet commonly used in these parts of the world. He needed shoes, and at least five shirts, and various other small items. If not for his son, he would not have been able to maintain a presentable appearance.

Sometimes, when one of the ladies sent a messenger to knock on Abramowitz's door and ask him to accompany her on a journey, he would shout out in his heart, No! He did not wish to go! He was a journalist, a journalist! But the knocks came again and again, and he relented, almost collapsing to the floor, whispering, "I'll be right there…"

In the hotel parlor he informed the Eskiner sisters with a

chuckle, "This is how things are done in Palestine. Father and son working together. Sometimes the son gives, other times the father." When the sisters announced they were leaving Palestine, as their father the banker had decided after years of great deliberations to permanently tie his life with Zionism—he had taken a position as manager of the London branch of the Anglo-Palestine Bank—Leon noted an improvement in his own condition. From then on he was free to devote to his articles the time he had previously wasted on conversation with the sisters.

In between trips he shut himself in his room and labored over articles that ran the gamut of the national enterprise. He was increasingly of the opinion that someone should endeavor to collect his writings, for the national good. He feared another writer might be quicker than he was and reap all the glory by publishing similar articles. Someone like Klemitz. At times he glanced at the Palestine newspapers with alarm: from the headlines it was clear that the entire Zionist enterprise was continuing in complete contradiction to his positions. Not even a single Abramowitz view was reflected in the press, and he might soon be considered behind his time. He pursed his lips and determined to try harder to influence the country with his writing. After all, the world could not ignore the truth! A pleasant wave of wellbeing suffused new life into his tired limbs as he confined himself to his room to author another opinion, and another, weaving together the articles. But not infrequently he was troubled by stifling fear and a pain in his head. He locked his door against thievery and shut the windows to keep out disease. He did not diminish his efforts. Justice would surely come.

One evening Chaim came to visit Abramowitz in the hotel. Abramowitz led him to the parlor, where he ordered a good meal and two cups of tea. He secretly showed Chaim his collection of articles, and the characters on the pages trembled before his eyes as he whispered, "If anything should happen to me, treasure these."

"What is there to be afraid of, Father? We are Jews with weapons," said the son, a cigarette in his mouth. Flomin, who ferociously combated the odor of smoke in his hotel, did not even peek out of his room. One evening, when he had threatened to call the police and have Abramowitz thrown out because of his debts, young Chaim had gone up to him and the two men had exchanged some words, and since that time Flomin had not come near Leon, and Chaim smoked cigarettes openly, despite an article his father was writing, entitled, "The Jewish Capital Squandered on Tobacco." Chaim had grown so much. He attended different political rallies and selected his leaders, and his language patterns were borrowed from their speeches: the powerful, raw idiom of street placards. The son knew nothing of the dangers facing the young nation. In fact, he was a complete ignoramus when it came to Zionist political processes, but he grew bored with explanations, plainly avoiding any conversation on the topic. All he wanted was to hang placards right beneath the noses of British officers, or guard Jewish buildings all night long. How worrying it was to send him into life this way, unequipped with any comprehension of processes.

Now, in response to his son's question, Abramowitz whispered, "Of Klemitz." As soon as he disclosed the name, the real danger, the threat to Zion, Abramowitz felt a sudden ease in his mind. Relief, clarity.

The son was restless, ready to leave. He told his father he had some business far away, but soon, in ten days at most, he would visit again. Where was he going this time? A secret. A private affair. Not to worry—Chaim's business partner, Mordechai Barkha, was in charge of everything. There was truly nothing to worry about. When he returned, he would have lots of money instead of worries. He handed his father another bundle of notes and left.

Abramowitz sat alone in the parlor. The night was quiet, as though all the other people had cured themselves of their desire to sit together and chat. The bills of money poked through his fingers. He had no desire to move his hand and put the money in his pocket. The Land of Israel was a harsh land indeed. He was just dozing off when a devil emerged in the parlor of the Flomin Hotel: Klemitz, a new immigrant, stood in the doorway swinging a suitcase bursting with money from either hand.

"Here I am," Klemitz smiles.

"No," Abramowitz insists.

"Yes," says Klemitz, and although this likeness of Klemitz does not exist at all, although he is a mere ghost, still he knows everything, even the smallest of rumors. "I hear your son is the leader of a gang of orange-pickers. I hear that if you do not let his gang work in your orchards, he'll pick your ears off. Well, what a delight."

Abramowitz smiles at Klemitz. "Indeed. Not a man of the pen."

"And he makes a living for the both of you, I hear," Klemitz's figure says impertinently.

Abramowitz does not remove his smile. "See, a father and son making their living together. The ideals of socialist cooperation have permeated the family unit."

"No, it is not so," Klemitz chuckles. Bills begin to drip from his suitcases and flutter in the air, and he goes on his way, flying out of the hotel with his suitcases hovering like two balloons.

Abramowitz ponders his circumstances as he heads to his room. One son a true Zionist in Palestine, the other a scholarly genius in Europe. His treasures are safely deposited, one here and the other there. Europe and Asia are his, like Alexander the Great in his day. He climbs up the stairs, drawn to his room. Between the four walls he finally completes his article on "The Jewish Capital Squandered on Tobacco," and a warm sense of comfort spreads through his limbs. He thinks back to being borne on his father's shoulders, and marvel stirs within him—how faraway are those days.

Then comes a knock on the door, and Abramowitz finds Flomin and four hotel employees outside his room. At first he believes they have come for his advice, but Flomin is a simple man, he is here to demand his money. Abramowitz chuckles and good-naturedly promises, "Tomorrow, tomorrow I shall repay the entire debt." He looks at Flomin's face, somewhat regretful that he had not struck him that evening.

The next day, Flomin had the privilege of finding Leon's body sprawled on his bed, both hands holding out his final letter with seeming impatience. If not for the letter, his deed would not have been disclosed—not by the still room and the curtains fluttering in the breeze, nor by the few objects Abramowitz chose to take on his final path—a basket of Jaffa oranges, a bottle of *kiddush* wine, and a deed of ownership for a desolate plot of land.

Flomin stood silently above him and gingerly reached for the letter.

Let your hands be strong, my working brothers, let them be strong.

I depart now to my chosen path, but there is no fear for our country. I have considered and reconsidered my decision, chosen the time based on scientific standards, and calculated it with mathematical precision. Our country shall be founded and built even without me, and you must grasp it as a precious jewel clutches at one's heart. In the glory of days shall we live, in our land enrobed in concrete and cement. To my two sons I leave my entire estate, modest as it may be, and they shall be blessed. May Satan also be blessed, if he resides in Eretz Yisrael, but my young son Lolek, keep him afar, do not allow him to come to Palestine. Though no lovelier land than ours exists, still the younger son is best kept where he is. Since my arrival here I have seen nothing but goodness, and if for brief moments my longings pained me, recall that the greatest intimate of our pain, Yosef Chaim Brenner, said, "Here we must stay, there is no reason to wander, for this is the final station." Do not fear, my country, that you have caused me sorrow. On my first day here I kissed an orange on its branch, and since then, like a bashful youth, I have been in love, in love. I have not lived one day here that was not entirely graceful, that was not entirely sanctified. Much delight have you given me, my land, and all the treasures of creation cannot compare to a clod of your earth. There is not a moment in the theatre of Berlin that brings laughter and tears to one's cheek like a sunrise viewed from the plateau of Moab. Worry not, my land, for I have seen your laborers, I have delved into their hearts, and well do I know that they will not forsake you, the most precious of all things.

Chapter two

Yehezkel Klein   1948

> *"My country has forsaken me…It is not for me to manage this state, which apparently cannot be managed without adventurism and deceit"*
> *(Moshe Sharett)*

The spring of 1948 was a sweet and wonderful time for Yehezkel Klein. The State of Israel, dreamt of by generations, was founded. And he met a woman. In the bowels of the earth—namely, in a basement at 6 Broock Street—he saw her for the first time. She was a typist for the Etzel underground, and although Yehezkel identified with a more radical, more intrepid underground bloc, their paths met in the course of a correspondence between the two factions. Political discrepancies receded, until eventually they found themselves taking an evening walk along the sea.

Everything was in turmoil in those days. The state had been founded, but whither the underground movements? What was to become of their splendid heritage? Unite? Divide? Yehezkel Klein conducted an apolitical discussion with his walking companion, the affairs of their hearts still so secret that they were regretfully afraid to let anything out.

She said, "There's a strong breeze," and he replied, "I studied at the Hebrew Gymnasium." The wind whistled, the sea did not relent, and their hearts churned in a manner that was pleasant and yet not.

They spoke of this and that, until she asked: "What do you like most, Yehezkel?"

"Being a Jew in my people's country," he answered.

Within a week they were a couple, and they were married by year's end.

Throughout their days together, every time Yehezkel assessed his life with Genia he found it good and decent. He was very careful to treat her with the proper respect, to laud her political inclinations, to praise any opinion she offered. But he slowly began to observe that her interest in national politics was waning, and that at times she interrupted him just as he was coming to the crux of his position.

He himself could not live without his opinions. After the establishment of the state the undergrounds had evolved into parties, and his tiny faction, too, had taken on flesh-and-blood form by registering as a parliamentary party. A building with a large auditorium was rented in the center of town. Flags on the outside walls leaned into the street, radiators and fans on the inside walls heated the air in winter and cooled it in summer. The auditorium was surrounded by offices with interconnecting doors, and only the senior members had the privilege of using these chambers. But the center of it all was the auditorium, where opinions were exchanged and speeches erupted.

From the very beginning, Yehezkel told Genia that he would not be able to deviate from his custom, and that every afternoon, until evening fell, he would continue to serve at the party headquarters. "All right," she said.

And so every day Yehezkel hurried to the headquarters, where he enthusiastically joined the constant clashes between camps, as each tugged on its end of the rope. Sometimes a cord snapped and a man dropped. Every conversation was filled with fiery reversals. An opinion would spring forth, somewhere in the auditorium it would be formulated in words and would hurry off to roam among the comrades, changing directions, being underscored and denunciated, held up as a banner to live by—or to trample on—and once again turmoil would be everywhere and hearts would seethe. How nice it was to be a member of the headquarters staff. How nice and important, every evening, just this way, in a sovereign Israel.

In the heart of the headquarters, in his chambers, sat The Leader.

During the underground days, The Leader had been at the forefront of every initiative and attack. He had a narrow, almost melancholy face, and a pair of spectacles that clung to his nose. If you did not know who he was, you would not be impressed, but as soon as one of his speeches grazed your ears, as soon as one of his commands cut through your flesh...

He was pale-faced, and often silent, but when Yehezkel Klein looked at him he saw fire and steel, embodying the might of both rabbinical master and noble landowner. Yehezkel Klein had outshone all of The Leader's followers by choosing to live in the very same building where The Leader had hid during the underground days. He was unable to make his home in the actual apartment—an unknown religious man by the name of Fishman was already living there and refused all offers—but even living two stories above the coveted apartment elevated Yehezkel's spirits. Only to Genia did he whisper the secret charm of their apartment, which made up for the lopsided balcony and tiny kitchen. But more than once, in the auditorium at the party headquarters, he longed to shout out his secret to everyone.

The Leader was rarely seen in the auditorium. From his throne in the chambers he dispatched urgent instructions, errands and demands. Yehezkel Klein was at the ready to carry out any order, whether paltry or vital, But in actuality it had been a long time since he had been given any errands. Ever since the discovery of his talent for effortlessly repairing electrical appliances, he had been continuously showered with lifeless machines on which to work his miracles. He even performed the occasional resuscitation on The Leader's radio, receiving it barren and returning it steadfast, worthy of use by The Leader.

The headquarters were a second home for Yehezkel. This was

where he felt the greatness of life, the courage, the force. Upon returning to Genia for dinner with some device or other tucked beneath
his arm, his home felt confining at times. Genia was an agreeable
woman, but she was often sad. Almost every evening she lit memorial candles for relatives lost in the Holocaust. She read a lot. She sat
quietly for hours. And from all the books she read, she never extracted
a single topic for conversation with Yehezkel. If only she would agree
to accompany him to the headquarters once in a while!

Although Yehezkel determined that his marriage was a great
success, he sometimes longed to talk with someone, to ask a question pertaining to the deeper intimacies of married life. But who
could he ask? Whenever he tried to speak privately with a comrade
at the headquarters, intending simply to ask, for example, how the
comrade's wife responded when he approached her for nocturnal
intimacy—even if he pleaded gently and attentively, with a tenderness
truly worthy of the Song of Songs—Yehezkel's mind tended to wander, and he found himself once again debating the list of flag-bearers
at the annual parade. This was how it went. He found it difficult to
let his difficulties out, and in fact he dismissed them altogether. His
marriage was good and decent.

Besides, an individual could not linger on the minutiæ of his
own life while the entire state was in the throes of battle. How could
the history books record the doubts of simple Yehezkel Klein while
Jews were being murdered on the borders, Kibbutz Ein Gev was
besieged by the Syrians, and thousands of new immigrants housed
in tent-camps were begging for a livelihood?

Yehezkel Klein buried his misgivings and enlisted in the fight,
belittled all sorrows and buried the gnawing doubts in his heart. He
busied himself with any matter that could prove useful for the nation.
Any mission, any act. And who could say how far his Zionist activity
might have gone if not for the incident, the terrible incident, which
engendered the vow.

Shortly after his marriage, Yehezkel Klein came to the headquarters to
receive his wedding gift; the gift had long been promised, but the pre-
sentation was repeatedly postponed because of a secret the comrades

refused to share with Yehezkel. They would slap him on the shoulder and insinuate that the gift was worth waiting for, and so he did not wrinkle his nose when he was eventually presented with what was clearly a book, though he had hoped for something valuable. Spurred on by his comrades, he ripped the wrapping paper off and his soul leapt—it was a book about the underground days as experienced by the faction, with an inscription in The Leader's handwriting that read, "An eternal memory for partners in the cause."

Yehezkel Klein sat down with burning cheeks and began to read.

The chambers of his heart throbbed as he leafed through the tales and the miracles and the intrigues, and his pride did not subside until he had consumed every last page. Only then did he allow the thought he had kept pushing away to enter his mind: where was he? His image was absent from the photographs, absent from the stories, absent from the notes. As if it were not he who had crept through the streets on all those bitter nights, not he who had been given important secrets scrawled on notes that he delivered to the underground members in hiding! In darkness as deep as the shadow of death he would set off on his missions, shrugging off followers and would-be enemies, sneaking into buildings and delivering the notes. With his own eyes he would see the man in hiding, or his delegate, and a shudder would pass through his body. Sometimes, in the mornings, he would revisit a scribbled address and find a grey house in daylight, its balcony adorned with laundry, ropes and buckets, and only he would know, with a fluttering heart, that a diamond was hidden in the house.

And now what? Where was his story?

They apologized. They also hinted that he himself might be to blame—perhaps his deeds were too secretive?

"But you knew…I was sent…I was sent with the note…"

"Well, this is how it turned out," they said cheerfully, searching for surrender in his face—after all, this was no catastrophe but a trifling foolishness. They would discuss the matter at tomorrow's meeting, everything would be remedied in the next edition.

Yehezkel muffled his sorrow. They would discuss it tomorrow…

it would be revised. On his way home that evening, as the sadness erupted again, he quickly quelled his emotions.

The next day he came to the headquarters with a rapidly beating heart. And the comrades? They chattered with Yehezkel as usual, consulted with him about the imminent dismissal of Berger and praised his response. He offered his position on the Berger scandal with true passion, never one to recoil from grave matters, but he slowly felt his soul bubbling up—why all this talk about Berger? He restrained himself for an hour, then for two. He waited for them to come to their senses and remember. After all, his issue demanded public resolution too. Finally he burst out, What about his issue?

The comrades remembered: indeed, there had been a mistake. Haste is of the devil. They smiled to themselves: who knew, perhaps other comrades had been omitted? It was just their luck that the most sharp-eyed of them all had noticed the error.

But bitterness was rising in Yehezkel's throat. He did not like their smiles. "This must be remedied at once!" he shouted, although he did not mean to. What was there, after all, to shout about? What could these little men change? It was The Leader who should be addressed. He would instruct that the error be corrected, and heads would roll. But then Yehezkel began to recall all sorts of little deeds that had been suppressed, and insults from the years of activism came rushing to the surface, with echoes of disrespect, humiliation, grief, pain. Yehezkel Klein was burning now, he thought he might soon jump up and strangle someone. Strangle! He demanded to see The Leader immediately. But The Leader was traveling. Ever since the state had established its independence he traveled frequently, taking care of negotiations and troubles in all the local party branches.

Yehezkel Klein waited for The Leader one whole week. Every day he was told: as soon as he hears your problem he will handle it, you do not need to come. But in the afternoons, Yehezkel would disobey the supreme command of obedience and turn up outside the chamber.

"Gone," they would tell him.

And every day he observed the stack of glossy books growing shorter. The books were being distributed, an iniquity.

One day he cunningly found out The Leader's schedule, lay in wait, and managed to catch him just as a black taxi was about to whisk him away. Only The Leader's coattails were still outside of the taxi, and Yehezkel Klein grasped the door handle and waved the book around. He placed the book on The Leader's lap and leafed through the pages trying to pour his heart out, but stutters came out of his mouth instead of the words he had planned, and the more he kicked away the redundant words the more they multiplied, and only his fingers remained confident, turning the pages, pointing to the heights of injustice, lingering on a photograph captioned, "The Founding Group," at which point Yehezkel found his poise and demanded, "Where am I? Where am I?"

The Leader looked down at the book on his lap. "Come on, Klein. In Hadera a whole branch is about to fall into the hands of Karpin's gang, and you're here with the photographs…"

Weakness congealed in Yehezkel's innards. What about the notes he had relayed? Those tempestuous, fiery days…What did Hadera have to do with anything?

"What do you want, Klein?"

"I want justice to be rectified," he blurted.

"What?"

"I want you to give an order now!"

The Leader looked at him with murky eyes. "Come on, Klein, find yourself a purpose…"

He pulled his coattails into the taxi and motioned to the driver to move on, without even looking back at Yehezkel Klein. Find yourself a purpose. Just like that. With that beautiful Hebrew of his, not like the vernacular of the young men from the small towns. A learned man from Warsaw. But so what?

Yehezkel turned away, and all sorts of ruined structures tumbled in front of his eyes as he walked, piling up, a plethora of dying thoughts, and he was tempted to collapse on the side of the road and allow his heart to give way. Find yourself a purpose…What else could he do? For shame! He would teach everyone a lesson. But how? He had believed them all. The tempestuous days. Those miserable men. What was this state anyway? Evil. Corruption. It was all just words.

He went home to Genia and felt an overwhelming longing for her embrace. But at home two memorial candles were lit, and a romance novel lay open on the table—*A Woman's Secret*—and Genia was preparing cucumbers with yogurt and hot tea for him. If she only asked, he would tell her everything, let it all out. But without even her usual "How are you?" she went to bed with a throbbing headache.

Yehezkel ate alone, staring at the candles. What was this state anyway? It all seemed so feeble, so pointless. They declared rations and issued food vouchers, but secretly gave out eggs and white bread and rich cream to their cronies. A state was emerging without any goodness, where people like Yehezkel were forgotten. His brother had written to him a decade ago: Come to America. But he had allowed himself to be swindled and led to this place.

He had no desire to belong to these people who would ridicule their own allies. He had no desire to belong to people at all. They were all swindlers here, black marketeers, lobbyists looking for favors, money dealers. Unworthy. Unworthy. He tried to look at The Leader's words from a broader perspective, hoping they might seem clearer. Perhaps he would see that there was no need to be insulted and it had simply been a misunderstanding. The book, after all, had remained on The Leader's lap, and on his way to Hadera he might have leafed through it and seen for himself. He might come back and apologize. It was his duty to do so! But no. There was no other way to comprehend the phrase, "Find yourself a purpose." No. A trickle of hatred crawled up Yehezkel's throat. If The Leader did not apologize to him, he would never leave his home.

Yehezkel Klein stood up. Facing the two memorial candles as their tiny flames flickered, a resolution arose and was sanctified within him: He would not leave his home if The Leader did not apologize. Ever. Ever! He could barely wait until the next day to inform the world of his vow.

At breakfast he announced to Genia that he intended to besiege himself.

"Besiege?"

Yehezkel explained that until they came to apologize, he would not leave the apartment.

"All right," Genia said.

Yehezkel Klein stuck to his vow for three months, and all the early difficulties—curious friends, bills to be paid, difficult questions from neighbors—gradually died down. Everything fell into place with a new tranquility. The world shifted a little to make room for the vow until it was no longer in the way.

Three months.

Yehezkel did not want for livelihood. He sat in his home and friends came up the stairs, dropping in for heartfelt conversations with the odd electrical appliance in their hands. They would ask Yehezkel to repair the machines, politely requesting a special rate for veterans of the underground, reaching into the past for affairs, moments of comradeship, and if the repair was for a lonely uncle or a retired neighbor, the negotiations were accompanied by sympathetic mumurings—our state was not founded so that a man should sit in his room and suffer.

In Yehezkel Klein's heart there was no room for vengeance. He no longer needed the party, nor the headquarters. The business of Zionism was thankless and bitter. He could have been living in America now, among Jews, living the good life. Soul murderers!

The memory of "find yourself a purpose" had not weakened. Every time Yehezkel Klein revived himself and found some encouragement, the insult would rise again and spread inside him like an ink spot, indelible. Every time the sense of cold injustice crawled up from his innards with that "find yourself a purpose," he restated his vow, reminded himself of it, enveloped himself in its warmth.

For three months this went on. But when the headlines declared that the remains of Theodor Herzl, the state visionary, would be brought to Israel, Yehezkel Klein imagined the most beautiful of burial plots, on the peak of a mountain, and all the people of the country making their pilgrimage to beg forgiveness for the injustice, the deceit, the exploitation, the lies. On that solemn day he rose from his chair and traveled to Lod airport to view the coffin. Even a vow that was steady as a rock had to allow for an event of such national import.

On the long journey to the airport, Yehezkel's eyes did not fail to take in the views of young forests and red-roofed townships and snaking roads and factory chimneys. Everywhere he turned he saw wondrous beauty enveloping the country, and then when he arrived at the airport he struck up some pleasant conversations standing in the long line of people waiting to see the coffin. He began to think that perhaps not all of the country was malicious, but then when the ceremony began he recognized The Leader's bespectacled head and his heart was crushed with sorrow. Everything was corrupt. Everything.

He returned to his vow with renewed vigor. They were all hateful, these people who lived their lives in tranquility while others' hearts were burning. But in March 1950 there was news that the remains of the courageous paratrooper Hannah Szenes would be brought to Israel. This virtuous woman had been tortured and murdered trying to save the Jews of Hungary, and in her honor, Yehezkel Klein left his home. He did not deprive himself of participation in the moving ceremony. When he came home he told Genia emotionally, "People were different once." For many days afterwards he found himself reminiscing about the ceremony, missing the roads, the fields, the highways, the sea he had glimpsed here and there before it emerged in all its beauty. The speeches had been so patriotic. Sometimes Yehezkel Klein would scribble down fragments he recalled, regretful that there were words he could not remember.

The days went by, and his vow became his confidant. From the people who flowed into his apartment—to deliver an appliance for repair, to drink a cup of tea, to have a few non-party discussions—he could clearly deduce that his boycott was not going unnoticed in certain circles. Why, then, did they not come to ask his forgiveness? Although he no longer believed there would be an apology to rescue him from his vow, he nonetheless felt somewhat bolstered.

He explained to Genia, "And if they do come to ask my forgiveness—what is so bad about my life now?" He found his life to be pure, a paradigm for his former party comrades. They came into his home, deposited broken appliances and sat down to talk. Sometimes two or three would crowd into his workshop, seething with anger, pouring their hearts out, soon quarrelling among themselves.

"Find yourselves a vow," Yehezkel advised.

Throughout 1951 and '52, turbulent years in every way, as history hammered out affairs both distinguished and detestable, Yehezkel sat happily at home. The first Knesset collapsed and new elections were called. Two Zionist leaders were hanged in Baghdad. A decision was made to accept reparations from Germany, and the country filled with rallies, riots, and heart-wrenching speeches. But in Yehezkel's own heart—complacent silence.

From all the comrades' conversations, from all the secrets they revealed to him and over which they made him swear with his hand to his heart, one conclusion arose: it was unbecoming to go out and mingle with the people of this nation, who crowned vain leaders. Nothing but corruption and arrogance everywhere. If only Yehezkel were to reveal what he knew, what lay hidden in his heart, the country would be in an uproar. All those characters whiling away their time at the public's expense would be ousted. He wished he could disclose what he knew, but it was not in his nature. He viewed it as a real biological trait, that once he took in a secret, it never escaped.

Sometimes Yehezkel tried to reveal to Genia how difficult his vow was, how he would like to go out like a normal person, walk along the streets, sit in a café, listen to street musicians, sip a drink with friends. But he was always quick to stress that it was the duty of man to protest, not to ingratiate oneself with those who lined their pockets by running the country. Then he would look longingly at Genia until she said, "You're right."

During the High Holy Days he found himself occasionally longing to retire from his vow so that he could visit a friend with a modest gift, or spend a few days in another town, perhaps in the company of people who would lift Genia's spirits. He himself had no family, and Genia had only one brother, Romek Paz, born Pozowski, a member of Mapai whom Yehezkel found arrogant and boastful and who openly publicized his connections with those who sat on the throne of power. Romek saw nothing wrong with corruption. Every citizen, for example, was allocated ration coupons for fifty-six grams of chocolate, but Romek would reach into his pocket and pull out real chocolate truffles with mocha and almonds. He gave Genia pralines, chocolate shells, cocoa and vanilla drops; he brought them crates of oranges, export-quality vegetables and sometimes even a smuggled chicken. He would produce the chicken in Genia's kitchen, kiss her on the cheeks and say, "Rationing surplus. It would be a shame to throw it out." As if Yehezkel did not realize that black market business was being conducted in his kitchen, cooked up nicely with some potatoes, celeriac and salt.

Once Romek even invited them to a resort usually reserved for state luminaries. Yehezkel could not partake because of his vow, but Genia went. She came home extremely happy. She had gained weight. And she had bought herself a purple scarf and a new romance novel.

"What did you do there with Romek?" Yehezkel wanted to know.

"I saw a movie."

And the rest of the time? Yehezkel wondered to himself. How much more would he have to endure due to his blood relations with this dubious relative?

At the cost of countless quarrels, Yehezkel's rage and resentment, and weeks of him swearing to himself every time he saw Romek that he would never-ever-speak-to-him-ever-again, Romek helped them "settle" a few small issues. Here and there a favor, a word put in at the right ministry. Yehezkel accepted reality—Genia needed some peace and quiet, after all—but he fumed. Why should he be thankful for every single jar of jam? It only gave him a stomachache anyway.

In 1952 Romek himself informed Yehezkel that he had learned from associates that the remains of David Wolffsohn, Herzl's successor as President of the World Zionist Organization, would be brought to Israel. For Wolffsohn, Yehezkel left his vow at home and hurried to the ceremony. When the crowd left, after the prayers and the speeches, he stood alone by the grave in utter silence. He had learned about Wolffsohn's life story—how he had lived in poverty as a young man, selling matches in the market, and had ended his life as a wealthy but lonely merchant—from The Leader himself. But The Leader was not there now, and Yehezkel stood by the grave enumerating his troubles, telling the wreaths of flowers how difficult his vow was. Wolffsohn did not reply, but a breeze rustled the flowers and Yehezkel's nostrils filled with their sweet perfume, and a single tear crept out of his eye.

Not long afterwards he had another occasion to travel to Jerusalem, when the remains of the paratrooper Haviva Reik were identified in a mass grave in Slovakia and extricated to be brought to Mount Herzl. Standing at the fresh grave, Yehezkel wept bitterly for the fate of the daring paratrooper, who had planned to rescue all of Italian Jewry from the clutches of the Nazis. She had swiftly parachuted down, only to be swiftly captured and swiftly murdered. He found some solace looking out at the youthful Mount Herzl and its abundant plots of the nation's dignitaries. The children of this land were gathered here in Zion, the true notables, those worthy of the people's respect.

Yehezkel stood on the hilltop. Where were the bones of Ze'ev Jabotinsky? Where were the bones of the first Etzel commander, David Raziel? Where were the finest and most deserving of the children of Zion?

And then came a surprise. Remains he had never even considered—those of the poet Naftali Herz Imber, author of the national anthem—were brought to Israel in 1953. Yehezkel shot out of his home like an arrow and arrived at the ceremony in Haifa, where he joined the convoy that accompanied the coffin all the way to Jerusalem for the burial. He wrote down all the speeches that were made, which he continued to peruse for many days at home, on his own, laboring under the vow, and he barely made it in time for the reinterment of Baron Edmond de Rothschild in April of 1954, because that same year Yehezkel's entire world turned upside down: he was going to have a son, a true firstborn, and Genia said: "You're done with the vow."

Genia's pregnancy came as a complete surprise to Yehezkel Klein. One day she approached him and said, "I went to see Doctor Medinik today, my brother got me an appointment. Yehezkel, you're going to have a child," and she kissed his forehead.

A son!

For three days and three nights Yehezkel could not sleep a wink. A son! Theodor, he would name him. Or Ze'ev, like Ze'ev Jabotinsky. Or after his father, Avraham, may God avenge his blood, or perhaps David, for David Raziel, may God avenge his blood. And then there was Yair, after the leader of the Lehi, may God avenge his blood.

Yehezkel could feel the sanctity throbbing in his stomach, but Genia tolerated her pregnancy as if it were an exhausting illness. A son was coming to life in her belly, but she was grumbling, sullen and pale. In fact, her entire pregnancy was a source of irritation. She was frequently nauseous, and in the mornings she vomited into the sink. She choked and cried and had chills. Her body shook and contracted, and at times Yehezkel believed she wished to expel not only her guts but her entire body, everything that was inside her, and then he would chastise himself for having such thoughts.

During her pregnancy, Genia's brother began to appear in their home more and more frequently. He never refused a single request from Genia, and competed with Yehezkel for her favors. But he also enabled Yehezkel to keep his vow by avoiding trips to the doctor, the store, the pharmacy.

Yehezkel was annoyed. He turned a blind eye to Romek's impertinence, but his pampering of Genia gave Yehezkel no peace. How could a decent, law-abiding man such as himself compete with one whose pockets overflowed with chocolate, and who always kept chickens and potatoes hidden in the recesses of his car—for that matter, with one who even had a car at all? It was black and spacious, fit for the streets of London, bought and paid for with flattery. The endlessly shrewd brother made himself available to ministers, Knesset members, mayors, rabbis, string-pullers of all sorts. His vehicle was always at the ready for them. When they called on him to volunteer, they never encountered a delay, a rejection, or a postponement. Never did he ask for a reward, rushing to obey any request that came from anyone of the appropriate rank.

Yehezkel was forced to listen to Romek's stories and hear his boastful secrets, knowing he could never reveal them. A married woman he had slept with, another he was considering. A secret account he maintained for a political patron, a fiscal discrepancy he must quickly get rid of in one of the savings accounts before the questions became too probing. Yehezkel had known for some time that Romek's ascent up the party ladder was a result of his treacherous dealings. He would be appointed treasurer of a sleepy little town somewhere, and his misappropriations would suddenly breathe new life into the cash flow, whereupon demands would pop up from dormant accounts to cover the deficits, urgent meetings would be called, more discussions, disagreements, provisional guarantees for short-term loans. Frequent commotions over interest and accountability arose, and the little town would be drawn into the eye of the storm, calling the attention of the heads of Mapai, who took the matter seriously. They would put out the fire with a grant but demand a thorough investigation, and usually Romek was appointed to head the investigating committee. How did Yehezkel know all this? Romek himself proudly told him, recounting detailed minutiæ that no decent man wished to hear. Up and up the Mapai ladder he climbed, every deed situating him in an increasingly comfortable position in life. Even during the abysmal days of war in Europe, while his parents and siblings were being annihilated and murdered, he found himself a cushy position, dispatched to Istanbul on an official mission for the Jewish Agency to lay the groundwork for rescuing Jews, so he boasted over and over and over again.

"Six months I was posted there. Magnificent episodes in the history of the struggle could be written. One day I will write them. I burned the midnight oil, did not sleep a wink...anyone who might have been able to help, we met with. We knocked on every door. Discussions into the night. And the respect I garnered! When in fact I did nothing. And the spying! We followed Germans, and sometimes we knew we were being followed—shivers! Was a single Jew saved thanks to me? No. Glorious episodes! And what was the use? Nothing. I did nothing. Nothing at all." Whereupon a very unmanly sort of sob would lodge in Romek's throat as he bellowed at Yehezkel with a few quickly extinguished wails, soon replaced with his usual arrogance and an account of his relations with a certain woman, the wife of a high-up personage, who was Romek's lover at his whim, and who disappeared just as quickly when he wished her to.

Yehezkel burned with fury. He did not wish to hear these things, but still, he did not rebuff Romek. Sometimes he would remain captivated by Romek's stories for hours, all the while silently denouncing him for the corruption, the flirtations, the frivolity with which he treated communal resources. There you had it: this was the state.

How bitter and distressing it was to Yehezkel that even many days after the telling he could not rid himself of the stories. He sat in his workshop fixing an appliance, or gazed out from the balcony at night, and all the while his mind dramatized Romek's tales. He could not understand it. Every so often, for just a moment or two, Yehezkel experienced a consolation of sorts. At the end of a victorious tale about some foolishness over money or women, Romek would sit quietly next to Yehezkel, focusing inwards. For hours, he would just sit there in silence as though pulling out a cup of poison from the dark depths of his heart. Yehezkel would sit silently with him and feel strands of happiness gathering in his heart—here was a villain, here his reward.

Only once was Yehezkel himself transported in Romek's blacker-than-black vehicle. It happened when the remains of the Baron de Rothschild were brought to Israel, and so he had no choice. Romek, as if he were the charitable Baron himself, made his services available to his brother-in-law. "I have something important to tell you, and we can talk on the way," he said to excuse his generosity, but in the end he simply recounted a trivial affair, adding nothing to it, and looked at Yehezkel as if his story had been earth-shattering. Yehezkel grumbled silently—why was this sort of man coming to the ceremony? He probably hoped to profit from standing among the country's nobility. As he listened to the lofty speeches, the glory and the exaltation, so that he could later copy them down in his notes, Yehezkel watched Romek insinuate himself into the chatter. Nothing of the speeches' grief penetrated Romek's heart, and on the way home, in the blackness of his car, he once again regaled Yehezkel with reports on donations, long columns of compound interest, investments and profits. How could he continue to tolerate this man?

One exciting benefit did come to Yehezkel thanks to Romek. His all-knowing ears enabled Yehezkel to closely follow the attempts to bring David Raziel's remains to Israel. They had finally remembered the distinguished Etzel leader, a courageous man who had died in Iraq fighting for Jewish national revival. Once in a while Romek punctuated his stories with details of the negotiations and diplomatic developments. The Iraqis refused, the Iraqis came around, the Iraqis presented yet more demands. Yehezkel's soul was in turmoil. A suspense story from the life of the country had been revealed to him, and this entirely inferior brother was a harbinger of the wonderful news. Yehezkel found himself almost looking forward to Romek's visits, patiently sitting through his endless chatter to find out if he would say anything about David Raziel. Had he heard any news on the complications between the British and the Iraqis?

Eventually the die was cast. The British—curse them—gave in to pressure from the Arabs—curse them—and the coffin was sent from Iraq to Cyprus, where it would be buried in a modest ceremony near Nicosia. Perhaps as compensation, the following year the remains of the great journalist Nahum Sokolow, who had translated Herzl's book into Hebrew, were brought to Israel, and Yehezkel went to the burial ceremony. Sokolow had died in London in 1936 and was all but forgotten.

When he came home, Yehezkel sunk into deep contemplation. It occurred to him that there might be many more notable Zionists buried overseas, who merely because of fate happened to have died not in Palestine but in London, Paris or Berlin. Someone must instruct the government to gather them all. There should be one such person—a redeemer of bones, just like the famous "redeemer of land," Yehoshua Hankin. Within hours Yehezkel had made the decision: You, he told himself, You will be the redeemer.

With help from Genia's brother, Yehezkel got hold of a decrepit typewriter whose faltering body rattled noisily in its housing; half the keys were handed to him in a separate bevy. He set about teaching his ten fingers all the parts of the typewriter until he was able to bring the machine to creaky life, and ever after, it served him loyally, with the exception of one defect that never left it: the R had a tendency to produce, only sometimes, a letter that looked more like a D. Yehezkel discovered this defect when he wrote his very first letter, which he carefully worded on handsome notepaper so that it beautifully illustrated his arguments and wisely summarized his conclusion. But his face fell when he discovered that the heading, which should have read, "Dear Government of Israel," in fact read, "Dead Government of Israel." Nervously envisioning scenes of a police investigation, an arrest, agents of the General Security Service, Yehezkel discovered that the machine had produced several more D's where he had intended R's. His letter lay before him like a corpse.

The arbitrary replacement of R's with D's was a predicament he was utterly unable to solve. Countless times he believed he had fixed the problem, and once he even allowed Genia's brother to take the machine to Mr. Tzeller, an expert repairman in Haifa, but the machine rejected all pleas and boldly defended its singular flaw until Yehezkel grew accustomed to denying himself the letter R and checking every letter with eagle eyes in case he had forgotten the prohibition in his excitement. Because the letter R, infuriatingly, was an extremely common one. How could a proper letter be composed without employing phrases like "the cursed Germans" and "the brutal Arabs"?

The matter of the R sent Yehezkel to battle with every single letter, and through compromises and concessions he managed to produce some fine correspondence full of clear intentions and no small amount of pride. True, he was unable to promise his adversaries that they would "rot in hell," and when he was once tempted to urge a letter recipient to use "brains not brawn," the typewriter played a cruel trick on him like a cat with a mouse between its paws. But his letters were usually salvaged and made their way to safer shores.

They were not of much use.

He wrote to the government about Sholom Schwartzbard, the assassin of the Ukrainian oppressor Petlyura, demanding that his remains be removed from their burial site in South Africa and brought to Israel. But he received no reply.

He wrote on the matter of the wondrous Rabbi Shmuel Mohliver, who had been buried in the Diaspora since 1898. No one but he was demanding the reinterment.

He wrote about Moses Hess, one of the heralds of Zionism,

author of *Rome and Jerusalem.* He had died in 1875 in Germany, where his remains still lay. How much longer?

He wrote, with the requisite caution, a letter that was part request and part reminder, about the martyrs Doctor Moshe Marzuk and Shmuel Azar, who had been hanged in Cairo after that unfortunate business. They should not be forgotten if there happened to be an opportunity to bring their remains, but although Yehezkel bravely mailed his impudent letter, he was extremely fearful of the General Security Service's wrath.

He wrote on the matter of Ze'ev Jabotinsky too, though he knew it was hopeless. Jabotinsky's remains would not be brought to Israel as long as David Ben-Gurion was in power, and his followers' pain would remain unhealed. Yet Yehezkel kept writing, both out of stubbornness and a perception of the nation's needs, and because, after all, there was no R in the deceased's name, which gave Yehezkel free rein.

His letters were never answered. But Yehezkel did not stop writing and sending them, although deep inside a vague suspicion was growing—a fear of sorts, in fact—that the General Security Service was already looking into his case. That they were waiting for one small misstep. For an errant R to slip past. Yehezkel's anxiety grew stifling, but still he continued his letter-writing campaign.

On April 18, 1955, precisely at the time the world learned of the death of the genius Albert Einstein, Yehezkel's first son was born, and Genia decreed: "Shmuel."

Shmuel.

That would be his name.

Her brother immediately joined in with Yehezkel's joy, holding the baby, rocking him, effortlessly changing his diapers. But what, in fact, was his role in the household?

The vow became burdensome. The duties of a new father constrained Yehezkel. Every morning he parted the Red Sea on his way to the grocery across the street, or to the pharmacy or the market, and when he came home he quickly settled in his chair and proceeded to divide his time between his vow and his firstborn and his wife. In fact, he expected that his vow would be undone, that people would come and say, A father cannot sit at home and wait for an apology. He also expected that justice might prevail and that The Leader himself would appear to give his blessing and ask for forgiveness. Yehezkel would have liked to conclude the vow with great splendor. But instead, his comrades from the party came to him in a panic to inform him that The Leader—such calamity!—had left the country and settled in America. Everything had fallen apart. There was no political future for any of them.

Yehezkel's home became a sort of hub for the desperate. Yehezkel should have refused, should have remained aloof. He should have maintained his home like a fortress surrounded by mountains. He was a father, after all, with a newborn at home, and he had no leisure for the crumbs of political business. But turbulent events were taking place in the country that was once his. The Kestner trial began. Elections were held. The hostage Uri Ilan committed suicide in his Damascus prison cell. David Ben-Gurion left his shack in the Negev to return to the Ministry of Defense.

Every evening, arguments rang through Yehezkel's apartment, while he himself sat silently. He looked at his friends from former days—Greenhaus, Tadek, Tzipkin—and felt no longing for bygone days. None whatsoever.

What was the state to him?

One evening, Greenhaus came to see Yehezkel alone. He talked and talked, from the bottom of his heart, and listening, Yehezkel felt a sudden surge of disgust. Disgust with his words, which he had heard over and over again. Disgust with every word in and of itself and disgust with every word because it was spoken by Greenhaus. Disgust, disgust, disgust. What was the point of all this talk?

Yehezkel waited for Greenhaus to leave and then sat quietly in his armchair. What were all these conversations? Political and social speeches with no end. And what did Yehezkel recall of everything that was said? All of Greenhaus's excitable speeches—who would remember a word of them ten years from now? And all the others? All the speeches, all the sermons, where were they leading? Even Jabotinsky, the greatest of them all, what did he say? And the things he did say,

did they make even one evening in Yehezkel's home more pleasant?
What was all this? What were all these words? Oh…

Yehezkel drank tea with lemon, sighed deeply and went to
bed.

Over the next day his disgust subsided, and when the old gang
of now-desperate comrades turned up in his home, he hosted them
willingly. For if not they, who were his friends?

Yehezkel examined Greenhaus and Tzipkin from his aloof
position. Those of the party members who had found themselves a
new political entity to latch onto had stopped coming. Now only the
homeless fluttered around Yehezkel's apartment, seeking advice, forgotten, holding onto each other. Oddly, a new young man soon stood
out among the old-timers. He came with Greenhaus and left with
Greenhaus, and seemed unaware that he had joined a dying political faction. They barely knew his name. Something like Lev Gutkin.
Yehezkel found the young man utterly indecipherable. He always sat
at the edge of the conversation with his hands clasped between his
knees. His body was shrunken and his eyes burned. A handsome
man, but one day he would turn up with a shadow of a beard on his
face, and the next day he was smoothly shaven as if he had pulled
out every whisker individually. On rare occasions he intervened in
the conversation, sprinkling a few words and quickly retreating into
his silence, but those who looked in his eyes saw that as far as he was
concerned, the argument should have ended after he spoke. What
was it about him that gave Yehezkel no peace?

Finally the secret was deciphered.

Greenhaus came to visit Yehezkel alone one evening. He placed
a broken lamp on the table and said, "I've come to you with a secret,
Yehezkel. There's no one else I can trust. Here is the lamp, if you could,
it's not a big repair, I'll come for it on Friday. But that's not the thing.
I can pay you up to fifty percent of the usual price. But that's not the
thing either. Here is the thing. Do you remember the young man who
trails after me to our gatherings here? What a treasure! I met him for
the first time two months ago. After a fifteen-minute conversation, he
announces he is willing to assassinate Ben-Gurion. Assassinate. Kill.
He has no problem. Just imagine! Ready and willing to assassinate

David Ben-Gurion—an utterly forbidden act, of course. Completely unimaginable. Along comes a man, we've barely met, and he's already implicating me in an affair that might be fleetingly attractive in terms of 'we may one day need it,' but one that is dangerous and forbidden, practically speaking. What does one do? The issue of German reparations is still burning in our bones—how long will the nation's dignity be trampled like dirt and the victims humiliated, bribed into selling the memory of millions? How long can the protectors of human dignity restrain themselves? Just remember this. Lev Gutkin is the young man's name. If he ever comes to you, give him shelter. No one will check here. They'll search us all, but you, officially, are outside the camp. Don't ask him anything, just hide him! If he comes, give him shelter. For the sake of the flag. And the lamp, don't forget, I'll come on Friday, our supporters need it…"

For many days Yehezkel anticipated a knock on his door. What if the young man—a criminal by any standard—were to come? Shooting the prime minister…such an invalid avenue for expressing political protest! Yehezkel built up a strong opposition to the young man's acts and prepared himself for a sharp internal polemic if the knock came at his door. Eventually, he thought he would be better off forgetting the whole business and concentrating on the electrical appliances that needed his attention.

Yehezkel went back to his painstaking work. He repaired lamps, switches, fans, radios. But every so often, for a moment or two, he thought maybe he could do with a gunshot that would come in the midst of routine, as a contrast to the mundane, a blast of sorts—the murder of the prime minister.

Never, to the end of his days, did Yehezkel hear from the young assassin again. In any event, not a hair on Ben-Gurion's head was harmed. But in Yehezkel's dreams the evil-faced young man would appear repeatedly, startled, seeking a hiding place. Dreams distort everything, and once the young man shot the president, Yitzhak Ben-Zvi. Another time he shot the Chief of Staff, Moshe Dayan. Once he shot Genia's brother. He shot Greenhaus one night too, and he never stopped, appearing in another dream, and another.

He shot the Minister of Finance, Levi Eshkol.

He shot the Minister of Education, Ben-Zion Dinur.

He shot the Chief of Staff yet again.

And the Minister of the Interior.

The Minister of Postal Services.

And on and on.

Yehezkel did not speak of his dreams. They were all but criminal.

One day, when he began to type another letter about Ze'ev Jabotinsky's remains, to keep his fingers nimble, he felt a noose tighten around his neck. They would send him to the gallows. Perhaps not because of the dreams, they could not reach those, but generally speaking, when they took his scolding letters into consideration, they would not be forgiving. They would accuse, and convict. That is what would happen. And why? He had done nothing wrong. But there was no logic...

Chapter three

The Big Transaction   1924

*"Economic hardship further increases anti-social
tendencies in the average worker...After a certain period
of work, bitter rebellion attacks people and dismantles
groups. Indifference and emptiness prevail."
(Meir Yaari)*

From the moment he set foot on the bustling dock and was
steered through the narrow streets by his business partner Mordechai, Chaim Abramowitz found the city of Beirut to be a wonderland. The bay with its floating silhouettes of boats glowing through
the darkness. The stifling market. The women hanging out colorful
laundry to dry. Every lane was redolent of delights and frying food
and vegetables.

Before he came to Palestine, this was precisely how he had
imagined it would be—a patchwork of the postcards sent by his father
Leon, fortified with his handwritten explanations: "The sublime scene
in this etching is Jerusalem," or "That glimmer of life among the rocks
is the port of Jaffa." At school Chaim would spread the postcards out
on the floor, and with his brother Lolek he would contrive the adventures of their father the pioneer. Then he would put all the pictures
in a box and wait longingly for new ones. Each postcard that arrived
built another city and another village in Palestine, and the emerging

49

country mingled with beloved memories of mountain resorts and villages near his hometown, and an estate he once visited as a child. Then his father sent word—"Join me in *Eretz Yisrael*"—and shortly thereafter Chaim found himself being lowered into a boat at the Jaffa port amidst frothy waters dotted with barrels, and the wonderland faded away with the masses scurrying through the heat.

But now it came to life again. In Beirut.

Mordechai crisscrossed the lanes with a lustful stride, as if returning after a long absence to his city, his neighborhood, his childhood home. Chaim watched Mordechai's light steps. They had never been on a business trip together, and throughout the journey he had been unable to shake off the faint sound of alarm bells. They had been partners for more than a year now, and he was well acquainted with all of Mordechai's personas; this time, in honor of the "big transaction" they were undertaking, Mordechai was gushing and excitable.

The "big transaction," as they referred to it in conversation, was like a queen who could not be discussed in any detail. Yet still Mordechai mentioned it in every exchange, his eyes filling with darkness. "If we get caught, twenty years in prison," he mumbled admiringly, and then quickly reassured Chaim that there was no problem. The British soldiers, the French soldiers, and the Arab allies had all been bribed, and there was no danger at all. Only profits. They would spend a few days in Beirut, tourists by all appearances, then they would each go home. No danger, none at all.

Chaim's chest had burned with uncertainty, but Mordechai had enticed him with promises of the huge profits he would reap, and asked Chaim for nothing but his presence, which Mordechai needed like he needed fresh air. Every morning he rushed over to wake Chaim, promising there was no danger, none at all. His entreaties added fuel to Chaim's fear, but also an enjoyable sense of daring.

He had to believe Mordechai. He had to. They had been inseparable for more than a year, conducting all their business together. Mordechai planned and executed; Chaim was partner and assistant. During that year, Chaim had learned that a pioneer could make a living doing things that did not include picking oranges or hauling loads. He had been accustomed to breaking his back like any laborer, sometimes living alone, friendless. But then one day, when he stopped to listen to a political leader's speech in the workers' center, Mordechai had approached him and latched on ever since.

He declared to Chaim at their very first encounter: "I am Mordechai Barkha, seventh generation to a Jewish family living in Hebron." Then he watched Chaim to see how impressed the young boy was. He promised Chaim he would teach him everything about business, as if Chaim had requested it. "Learn from me and you will get rich. What the blessed Lord has not given you, I will teach you." He winked. "I have ten brothers in Hebron, all studying Torah, and I, as the Lord's aid, support them. My skill is trade."

Indeed, there was no commerce that Mordechai could not conduct, no transaction he could not squeeze a profit out of. People came to him asking for help with their business affairs, but he was only willing to help a chosen few.

Chaim could not explain why, but he saw strength in Mordechai. He was pale and emaciated, thin as a nail that had sprouted limbs. His hair was a dull red. "Like King David am I," he liked to boast. But often, even when a successful transaction had just been completed, Mordechai's face fell and he turned to Chaim for merciful judgment: "This is my talent, may God have mercy. What shall I do? If here someone is offering, and there someone is wanting, and all that needs to be done is unite the two, my heart is quickly on the move. If a man wants to sell a goat and another wants to buy a lamb, why, I persuade and mediate, sharply but subtly, until the first comes around to buying a kid and the second rushes to his pen to sell a yeanling."

Mordechai did not spend much time on goats and lambs. He traded in money and land, managed the modest affairs of the wealthy, burst into stores and infected the proprietors with enthusiasm for a chance business, or politely approached the owner of an orchard to offer a proposal on behalf of well-respected clients. Always drop by drop, always one single profitable business into which he could delve deeply and see it through.

"Not like you Zionists. Everything with you has to be completed as though a train were about to run you over. You redeem a whole valley of land and bring Jews there to build endless settlements. You anger the Arabs, and it will eventually bring a great disaster upon us all…"

Once Mordechai started fulminating against Zionism, he could not stop.

"You come here from Europe, and in your suitcases are the pogroms you're escaping…"

"You Zionists, more than anyone, you hate us God-fearing Jews. You come to this land with a hoe on your shoulder to build a new Jew, and to your surprise you find that Jews of the old kind have been living here for generations, and they have no interest in changing…"

At first Chaim tried to argue. He had his own opinions. But he quickly realized it would be better if Mordechai talked and Chaim listened.

Zionism was constantly on Mordechai's mind, at times threatening and at others threatened. Like a gray expanse of seawater, waves rising and falling. "What is Zionism? A crumb picked up by the wind to scratch one's eye. We are the eternity. Us. The God-fearing Jews. True, not all of us are eternal, and as for us Hebronites, the world will come tumbling down upon us yet. But you—who are you?"

Once he spat out: "You have wreaked havoc on the price of land. It's a good thing the English came along and conquered the land from the Turks, 'cause the land registrations got a little muddled up and now the *effendis* are so afraid they're willing to make reasonable sales."

He cautioned Chaim not to be satisfied with the way things were going in the country. Even though the British had come and the Turks were gone, and the Zionists were already waving around Lord Balfour's declaration, the days of Zionism were not long for this earth. From ashes it came and to ashes it would return.

"The way the English see it, Arabs and Turks are alike, and they hate the Arabs just as much as they hate the Turks. But you Zionists should not get too hopeful. The mighty Lord is guiding the British, and to them you are all like the Russians, who are their new fear. They look at you in your *kolkhoz* shirts and they see hoards of

Communist revolutionaries, which turns their delicate stomachs. Soon they'll regret the Balfour Declaration, which they gave in the throes of war, and they'll absolve themselves of it in the English way, just like a duchess brushes off a few cake crumbs, and every one of you who tries to get into the country they will try to kick far away. They'll prefer the Arabs, who are more like their old fears, which they've already defeated. The English are still seduced by the appearance of the Arabs, they look at them and see dark-skinned savages, a stampede of whinnying horses, swords and clouds of dust. The English are hugely seduced, but you, you Zionists, what pleasure can you give them? Coughing up tuberculosis from your lungs and staggering around with malaria, waving ideas and demanding ownership of the land. Who would want you?"

From Mordechai's hatred, Chaim learned more about Zionism than ever before. Mordechai was proficient in the statements and teachings of each of the leaders, and he knew the dates of conferences and meetings. He argued the objectives, the intentions, the plans. He made his way among the benches at every congress or political gathering, voicing his passionate hatred of Zionism. From the day he met Chaim he promised the death of every Jew in Hebron, himself included, because of the Zionists who brought so many Jews to Palestine—how could the Arabs ignore it?

"A massacre. There will be a huge massacre," he warned.

"The Hagana will protect," Chaim replied.

A peal of laughter erupted from Mordechai. "The Hagana will protect…This is decreed from above, and you think the Hagana will protect…" He promised Chaim: "We will all die…All the Jews of Hebron. Believe me."

"And you?"

"Me?"

"Will you die?"

"I am Mordechai—I live and I rebel, just like my name says. Do you understand? Heh, heh, you probably don't. You have strong muscles, like the giant King Og, but your wisdom, if there is any, is a dry well."

Chaim did not understand. After meetings with Mordechai his

thoughts were assailed by new words, new opinions. Even his father in the Flomin Hotel responded with surprise and resistance. Chaim was pleased—he could learn from Mordechai.

In his primary persona, Mordechai was a great chatterer, talking twice as much as any other man. When he missed his wife back in Hebron, he would talk about her for an entire day without stopping. If they happened to pass a synagogue, Mordechai shivered and filled with remorse—"Perhaps I should have stayed in Hebron to learn Torah like my brothers."

But no subject riled him more than Zionism.

In the alleyways of Beirut he skipped among the passersby, without stopping to make sure Chaim was keeping up. His boots thrust forward, his tongue hung out, and there was no telling where his thoughts were. All of a sudden he stopped, his blood boiling from the rapid walking, and turned to Chaim. "What is this momentary spark of Zionism? A mosquito with singed wings." Then he turned and continued on his way. Chaim hurried after him, the midday sweat dripping down his face. People bumped into him, their packages collided with his own. The incline grew steeper, the sidewalks now had little steps, stone banisters, posts. Chaim struggled on. They passed stalls selling beverages, blocks of ice, colorful cups. But Mordechai would not stop to rest. Usually he spoiled Chaim, stuffing him with food—"Take, take, eat. If you don't keep kosher like a Jew should, at least enjoy yourself." But now he charged ahead, and Chaim persisted, as if it were not Mordechai he was chasing, but the big transaction itself, which beckoned him mockingly from up the crowded road. The walls of the houses above them glowed white, and the window shutters were painted in peculiar colors. The dim alarm bells grew slightly louder inside Chaim. Where were they going?

Then, at the top of a hill, in a square fed by alleyways from every direction, the journey came to its end. On a bright blue veranda stood a bulky man in a suit and golden spectacles, waving at them.

"That is our innkeeper," Mordechai told Chaim. "Morris Alakani, one of the good Jews of Beirut."

Chaim soon found himself inside a large Arab house, shaking the hand of the innkeeper, who smelled like perfume and had a bald, bronzed head. From the depths of his suit pocket the man pulled out a small gold watch and showed Mordechai the time. Mordechai whispered to him in French and the innkeeper summoned two servants. He sent them out, and Mordechai grinned—all was to his liking.

He turned to Chaim. "Everything is taken care of. The transaction is going ahead. We will wait here for six days of creation, and on the seventh day, God willing, *and the heaven and the earth were finished, and all the host of them.*"

Chaim swallowed. "How much will we make?"

Mordechai recoiled. "Shhh…You Zionists." His face turned grave and he cloaked himself in silence.

Chaim sighed. Mordechai's persona was always changing, turning, producing secondary characters and opposing characters and replacement characters. One could never tell which character was emerging and which was disappearing, but patience was rewarded. Something always came along to pull Mordechai out of his silence, a promising transaction or some other incited passion.

At dinner he was talkative again, whispering with Chaim endlessly—Herzl, Nordau, Hebron—but Chaim was looking at the innkeeper's daughter. She served the food with her head bowed and quickly left, but when she approached Chaim, her body leaned over his shoulder.

Mordechai leaned in close. "You like her, the daughter, yes? She is your age, and she is a woman, with ripe hips…"

Chaim felt a surprising sense of shame, a painful pall. "What about the transaction?" he demanded. He felt like punching Mordechai's face. Suddenly the big transaction seemed uncertain. He could not continue to trust Mordechai without any grounds—where was the transaction? They had spent so many days traveling here, and now they had to wait even longer. He had to know what was going on.

After dinner the innkeeper appointed a special servant for Chaim. The servant took Chaim to his room, where he found a comfortable bed with soft sheets. Before falling asleep he wondered where Mordechai was. He awoke to a silverish-yellow light coming through the Beirut window, and ran from his room like a trapped creature. Where was Mordechai?

Chaim was led out onto a small balcony shaded by vines, where Mordechai sat in the first light of day, huddled in his chair, coiled like a snake. On the table before him were coffee, bread, olives and marmalade—a table set for Europeans. Mordechai stared at the food with a befuddled look and weakly confessed, "Woe unto me, such delights…"

As he looked at Chaim, his eyes danced and his tongue trembled, tasting the mud of memories. He clapped his hands. "But my wife is a jewel, why would I want another woman, you ask, why would I want another woman?"

Chaim sat down. The big transaction was in danger.

"It's the city," Mordechai wept, "the city is to blame. All night, out on the streets. What could you understand? A youth, a boy. What could you understand? Evil inclination. Straw and fire. I shall tear my clothes in mourning for my own self."

"Our transaction, is it going ahead?"

"Believe me, my wife is as white as marble, but in the depths of my soul I long for dark-skinned women. Sometimes I watch her leaving our house, and she, the pure white of an angel slipping away. Praise be *Hashem* who has created such sweet, sweet angels, and from above He granted wisdom, and down below He imparted courage, and where do I go? I abandon my body, forsake my soul…But before my eyes the women appear…their skin the woven hue of dates, the embers of their hidden depths ablaze, and I am captivated, my gaze weaves. And they, the women, like *challah* on the Sabbath table— carve yourself a piece of them and say a blessing. Believe me, a woman is goodness. Like a vine abutting your house. And my wife, never do I detract from her pleasures, for when I return I am King Solomon, and my thousand wives are one. That is how *Hashem* created me: a creature with desires. I travel here and I find women, and they are like the berries of a briar, forsaken for all men, and were I not a sinner, I would spend all these hours of longing for them moored instead in the Beirut congregation's study hall learning pages of Gemara and studying the rabbi's teachings. And at night, by candlelight, I would further study Torah, immerse myself in the sweet honey of life, distance myself from evil. But here, in Beirut, women of all kinds are housed in glorious harems. Like the fruits of the Garden of Eden, confections. Berber women of savagery, Maghreb women of the Sahara, Halabi women as noble as a lily, Baghdadi women like sweet apricots, and Armenian women of Christian modesty, and blue-black Sudanese women, and Indian women with tongues like a tiger's back, and masculine women of Gaza, and Istanbul women whose bodies laugh like a candle's flame. Everything here is at your disposal, the women will delight you and all they will say is, Come back to me. Even European girls are here, if you should thirst for women of the ruling peoples, and though your soul may cry out, even Israelite women you shall find. Yes indeed, you will find them in the brothels, broken-spirited pioneers. And with them, of all the women, I long to delight, to shout out in Hebrew, Rachel my beloved, I shall toil for you for seven years and seven more. But I am a reverent Jew— how could I corrupt a daughter of my own nation by love-making?"

Mordechai was lost in his words now, and Chaim looked over his shoulder. The city was awake, smoke and commotion and peddlers shouting. What about the big transaction?

Mordechai slumped over toward Chaim and put a feeble, trembling hand on his shoulder. "Believe me, in the alleyways you can find special places too, where they keep defective women for those who desire such things. Women with crooked limbs and burned skin, ailing women and women who cry when a man touches them. Pleasure with them can break your heart. And women who let you do with them as you wish, all they do is murmur. May God protect us from men who go to those women…"

Chaim felt the urge to hit Mordechai again. Women…Just like his father in the Flomin Hotel. Why all this talk of sick women and crying? What about the transaction?

"Go to the city," Mordechai commanded. "It is not hostile. Go and wander. I will crawl into bed. I will direct my head to strike the pillow before dreams can come to me."

Then, as though his innards had been wrenched, his usual lament thawed. "Perhaps I would have been better off being born in

Beirut. Then I would not run to this city. I would be a respectable public figure, like some of my uncles. Or perhaps I would have been better off as a European merchant, then I could have done anything in this world." He yawned. "We, the Jews of Hebron, we will die soon, all of us. The Arabs will rise against us, by the sword, all of us…"

In the evening hours, around the inn, people of many nations and varying occupations gathered. Morris Alakani's daughter, Rachel, walked among the guests serving food, her body leaning close to them, too. Modest and shy, she did not look up from the platters bearing little dishes, yet she did not flinch at the guests' laughter and polite greetings—which, for some reason, Chaim found irritating.

Every night after dinner Mordechai's persona changed; in the mornings he returned lifelessly to Morris Alakani's inn. Every night Chaim remained alone in the compound, which was fortified against the rest of the city by thorny hedges and the light of damascene windows. He was not bothered by Mordechai's absences. In the evenings, when they dined together, a thought began fluttering on the edges of his mind—after the big transaction he no longer wished to be Mordechai's partner.

When Mordechai left, Chaim would stand with his back against the wall near the window looking out onto the luminous city, and watch silently as business was carried on in the dining room. People, commerce, all manner of affairs conducted among men. The big transaction was veiled somewhere in all this, but Chaim did not know what it was, what it comprised, what risks it posed. Only a few weeks had passed since Mordechai had begun to plead, "Come with me to Beirut," hinting at miracles, warning Chaim not to ask any questions. And now here they were in Beirut. Chaim recalled how Mordechai had giggled when he asked how much they would make in the transaction. He had whispered mysteriously, "You might as well count the stars in the sky, if you can," and refused to answer any more questions. Each time Chaim attempted another probe, Mordechai pulled back, but still Chaim journeyed with him, and there were many frightening stops along the way. It took them three days to get to Beirut, traveling by car, by horse and on foot. Mordechai had arranged every detail of the journey and it was executed flawlessly, but at every moment Chaim felt trouble brewing.

They took the train to Haifa. Mordechai had bought first-class tickets, and as though harboring no fears about what was waiting for them in Beirut, he proceeded to chat with the tea-servers and read newspaper headlines over other passengers' shoulders. His first interlocutor was a French mandate officer, a startled young man whose pregnant wife had fallen ill with lung disease. Mordechai introduced himself as acquainted with excellent pulmonologists in Jerusalem, offered to help and mediate—a good doctor, after all, was half the cure—and showered promises upon the Frenchman, assuring him that he had known the nature of the disease even before the man had spoken. Although a full diagnosis would require a physical examination of the Frenchwoman, the situation was clearly not dire.

What did the Frenchman know? A Jew from Hebron sat before him, the son of a rabbi, all ten of his brothers Torah students. But how could one detect anything about Mordechai when he tossed out a series of medical terms, and his clothes held no hint of his Hebronite roots?

After he tired of the Frenchman, Mordechai tried in vain to strike up a conversation with a learned-looking man holding an iron box on his lap. Mordechai looked at the box with a glimmer in his eye, and like a cat, tried to brush up against the scholar in conversation. He made some archæological pronouncement, reported news he had heard regarding the British crown jewels, expressed his esteem for the holy relics, and enquired whether the scholar was aware of the current price of grey pearls. But the polluted, damp city of Haifa turned out to be the man's destination, and there he went on his way, his box still shrouded in mystery.

Mordechai consoled himself with an almond beverage, skewers of grilled lamb, and sugared fruit. "Just wait until you see Beirut. Food fit for kings on every street corner," he promised Chaim as grease dribbled down his chin and his lips glistened with sugar. They almost missed their ride to Beirut because Mordechai insisted on finding a street vendor he had once visited, who served copper bowls of lentils and peppers. They roamed among the shouting peddlers in the grimy Haifa market until they found the stall with its bubbling oily odors, clanging pots and unappetizing dishes. "How things change," Mordechai observed.

From the moment they reached Beirut, Mordechai's personality transformed and they parted ways. Chaim set off alone every morning, to wander the city and the market, taking occasional odd jobs and exhausting himself for a few pennies. He carried crates of silvery-pink twitching fishes. He loaded his back with sacks of flour, rice and coal. He hauled wood and chopped vegetables. Everywhere he went they recognized his strength and offered him work. He found it incredible that they did not wish to know where he was from or which political faction he belonged to. Before meeting Mordechai he had worked in the orchards, forging unions with likeminded young men, and whoever refused to employ them, employing only Arabs instead, was visited by the gang at night. Levin the Citrus Grower, a wealthy man, complained to the police. They arrested Chaim and put him in jail, but they eventually let him go. Chaim went to Levin's house, and in front of his family, forced him to give money to the labor coffers. But here, in Beirut, people lived with one another, fewer ideas were voiced, and there was no shortage of work in every lane and every courtyard. This was all very peculiar, requiring consideration, but it was complicated and difficult to comprehend.

Since coming to Israel, Chaim liked to listen to speeches at political rallies. Every speech convinced him that all the speakers were right. The citrus growers' power must be broken, the workers' power must be broken, the bourgeois' power must be broken, the British Mandate's power must be broken. He had always liked to listen, but now he was a thinker too—he had his own opinions. His father sat in the Flomin Hotel writing political articles about complicated things that Chaim did not understand, while on the streets everything was simple. Everyone was trying to be strong. He too. Soon he would have his own property, he would come back rich from Beirut. He would build a home for himself and his father. Perhaps he would start a newspaper, or a business. He liked it there, in Palestine. In his class back in Europe he had been a champion runner on the course around the park, but he would gain power here too, and status. Maybe he would join a party. Maybe he would start his own. But in fact, he had no great desire to join any parties. A man should be on his own. As soon as he had set foot on Palestinian ground at the Jaffa port, party delegates had fought over him. They fell on him as if he were a treasure, and though he was momentarily impressed by the attention they paid to every immigrant, he soon felt stifled. "I am the son of the journalist Leon Abramowitz!" he exclaimed inexplicably, and they left him as though they had touched a rotting fruit. Within seconds they were gathering around another immigrant, a short fellow who was still vomiting, and as he doubled over he was forced to listen to the names bandied over his head—"Workers of Zion," "Labor Union," "The Young Worker."

Chaim decided that when he returned to Palestine with the profits from the big transaction, he would always remain independent.

On Friday evening, two candles were placed in a small room in Morris Alakani's inn. Rachel lit the candles, held her palms up in front of her face and recited the Sabbath blessing. "*Shabbat Shalom*," she said, and smiled at Chaim.

Mordechai and Chaim dined at Morris Alakani's table, and although not a word was said about the big transaction, tension lingered and the conversation was tight-lipped. When the meal was over, Morris Alakani went on his way and left them sitting in the candlelight. Rachel served little cups of coffee and sugared biscuits studded with fresh and dried fruits, and left. But on her way out of the room she passed by the window and allowed the curtain to lightly rustle her dress.

Chaim felt that he could not sit any longer in this comfortable room, in the soft darkness of a Sabbath eve. He would have liked to haul sacks of coal in the market, or chop wood, chop and chop until his entire body was exhausted.

"In this world twisted with evil, only the Sabbath reaches out to us with rays of light," said Mordechai sprawled in his chair. "You know, when I was your age I did not think I would go off like this to trade in faraway lands, to earn the keep of all my brothers and their families. I was a boy, an excellent student. But I had a dream, one night I had a dream..."

He stood up to survey the city.

"I dreamed that Zionism redeemed the Jews...indeed...in contradiction to everything the rabbis said. And not only that. In my dream I too was a Zionist, and I hated the proud Hebronites, who believe they are perfection itself. King David left Hebron to found his kingdom in Holy Jerusalem, but the Hebron dwellers proudly count their generations in the city and require nothing but themselves. In my dream, angels coronated me with a beautiful crown on my head. It was good to be a Zionist. But then? At that moment the dream stopped—a group of Arabs who reside in the city passed by my father's house and woke me with their chatter. Alarmed, I sat up in my bed and for a moment I was not sure whether or not I was a Zionist. I rubbed my eyes until my wits returned—why would I be a Zionist?"

Chaim looked at Mordechai. He was framed in a damascene window that revealed the glimmering city through a veil of smoke, lit by blunt streetlamps. Down there, he thought, in the lower city, live the women Mordechai goes to. And up the hill, alleyways with steep steps. How he would love to climb those steps now, with sacks on his back, lugging more and more cargo until he fell asleep from exhaustion.

Mordechai took a handful of biscuits from the platter. "For us, all we desire is that things continue as they have since our forefathers' day. But you Zionists bring dust and commotion to the land. What can a little Jew like you, with muscle and muscle and more muscle, contribute? You are only one man, and you know how to work. But the rest of the pioneers? They pave a road, they build a house, then they run to the mirror to see if they've changed. It is all foolishness. What is a Jew? A Jew does not know how to work. Hoes and rakes are a decade-long adventure for you, nothing more. The day will come when you drop your hoes and bring over workers for yourselves. The Arabs won't do it, so the Cypriots will come. The Cypriots will leave and you'll tempt the Maltese. The Maltese will go home and you'll take Italians, then Germans. From India to Ethiopia, you will bring yourselves laborers…"

"If they created jobs, everyone would work," Chaim argued. "It's hard to work in our country. The capitalists insist that the Arabs are better-suited, and that is not true."

"You do not understand, child, it is not economics, it is fear."

"Why fear?"

"The Jews living in Palestine know it will be bad for them if more and more Jews keep coming, that eventually the Arabs will lose their patience and slaughter everyone. For now, in the meantime, the Arabs let us be. But if there are too many of us, we will be lost."

"Just the opposite," Chaim insisted, "the more there are of us, the stronger we'll be."

"The weaker we'll be."

"The stronger."

"The weaker. Look at who comes to Israel: Engineers? Capitalists? Why would they come among the throngs of poor pioneers who adhere to workers' views? The pioneers are only looking for someone to blame, so why would the capitalists come? And the old-timers, believe me, they would leave too if they could. Look at the ships, every day families leave, pioneers leave. And those who are afraid to leave will die at the hands of the Arabs."

"That is not how the leaders describe things."

"Dangerous. Zionism is very dangerous. My rabbi preaches against it, and his sermons are wonderful, but only I, who live among you, know how dangerous your beliefs are. A few years ago I was invited to the city of Haifa on an urgent business matter. There, in the Hebrew Technion on Mount Carmel, a founding conference was convened, another of the workers' organizations, which other than its name you know nothing about, whether the organization is living or dead. Three hundred young people gathered to hear speeches and discuss their difficulties. They talked about your overseas lands, about how they miss the foreign landscape, the church bells. I felt my own nostalgia, the devil knows for what, perhaps for the diaspora that was never mine, perhaps for a purity I found there. Longings caress the Jewish soul like a feather. And suddenly, despite my own will, I got up and spoke. I stood there in front of the young men and women and talked. About the settlements that must be fortified, and the resources that should be equitably divided, and about demanding more from the leadership. *Nu*, such things. But somehow my words touched them. They stood and cheered. Wild enthusiasm. Ha! So I talked some more. About the need to unite and the importance of diligence. Principles. And as I stand there waving my words about like swords, a leader rises from within me, and from my insides emerge true workers' ideals, words I had never said and yet were not foreign to me, uttered with ease, persuading with ease. After the speech a group formed around me and began talking at me. They wanted to start a new settlement based on my ideas. For a moment I felt like collecting membership dues and leaving, but my heart was not so quick. Their eyes were good and innocent, glimmering with the brilliance of redemption, and their hands had such a strong desire to dig the earth, to build, to redeem. *Nu*, for a moment I was not sure how to get away.

"Then I realized what a nice idea Zionism is, and that such an idea should have its head chopped off even before its first smile, because that is how ideas are—if they are allowed to beam their baby smiles, they quickly buy over people's hearts and lead to disaster. Zionism must be destroyed from the foundation. Only Jews who await divine redemption, lawfully and acceptingly, should settle in Israel. Not pioneers who hop around the hilltops like fleas. All they will bring is disaster. But what power do I have? All I can do is await the destruction. My wife wants children, and I reproach her—it is forbidden, thou shalt not spill thy seed in vain, because we Hebronites are doomed to be slaughtered. All the newborns, babies celebrated by entering the covenant of Abraham our Father, they are seeds spilled in vain, which the holy Torah forbids. Believe me, they will all die, the day is near. My father had eleven children, as if it were a blessing to him, and all of them, all of them will die—all of them!"

"There will be no destruction."

"Destruction, vast destruction…"

On Saturday evening, when the Sabbath was over, Morris Alakani took the two young men hunting in the Shuf mountains with his brother. Chaim roamed the land for three days with the strong men, and fired the rifle they gave him, but all he shot was a badger, a fairly useless creature. When he returned to the inn he gave it to Rachel. "Take this," he said as he laid it on the table, and a band of tension spread through his stomach.

"Tomorrow we leave," Mordechai whispered to him.

In the morning the sky was overcast, a storm brewing. The city was not visible through the damascene window, only a pale-blue fog thickened with smoke from the houses.

They left Beirut through the hills to the east of the city, mounted horses in one of the villages and climbed to a high hilltop. From there they moved south, between the sea and the mountains. At night they camped in an empty field. Two Arab escorts, Morris Alakani's men, lit a fire and cooked food. Chaim was silent. He was thinking of his father and his articles.

Mordechai chattered indolently, and his sentences removed themselves far away from him, from his prohibitions, fluttering every which way. All his facets took part in the soliloquy, talked and recited and protested and declared, and a mass of words penetrated Chaim's ears. For many years these words would continue to ramble furtively among his thoughts, until regimes weakened within him, and in his old age more and more words would emerge, roaming in gangs, invading his opinions and troubling him, their origins often unknown to him, as they lacked the familiar voice of Mordechai.

A mist began to roll in from the sea, over the hills, seeking its place in the open field and thickening over the stalks. Battalions of clouds gathered around them, recoiling only from the fire.

"...and what is Zionism? A flea that managed to jump up high for a split second..."

Chaim wanted to answer Mordechai, but he suddenly realized the Arab escorts were gone and a company of French soldiers was emerging from the mist.

Chaim leapt up. Mordechai slowly stood and started walking.

The soldiers shouted something—probably "Stop!" Their rifles were aimed, but Mordechai turned around for a moment, standing ten steps away from them, waved his arms in dismissal, laughed softly as if turning down a polite invitation, and walked away. The soldiers shouted again, bullets were fired, and Mordechai kept walking and the soldiers kept shooting. Perhaps the bullets missed him, or perhaps they punctured him. Everything was blurred in the mist. But Mordechai kept walking as if lost in thought, and the soldiers looked at one another, slightly afraid, then looked at Chaim, whom they'd already captured, and hoped their commanders would consider him sufficient loot, as it seemed best to stop shooting.

Mordechai stopped briefly, turned around, and called out to Chaim, "Do not worry—castles will yet be built in Judea!" The soldiers were encouraged, as if Mordechai's promise increased their own chances of hitting the target. One by one they aimed at him, holding their rifles up to their shoulders, but in vain. Their hands filled with fear—he was a devil, they were shooting at a devil—and their fingers faltered as they pulled the triggers, each hoping the other man would shoot. The shots died down and Mordechai's image disappeared into the mist like a vapor.

They led Chaim on a tortuous journey, handing him off from one guard to the next. Eventually he was delivered to a group of British soldiers who took him to Jerusalem and placed him in custody. They arrived in the evening, and it was the first time he saw the city his father had dreamed of. In the twilight it looked like the etchings on the postcards, a dark, crisscrossed gray of hills and walls. From the window in his cell he could see the walls and a tower, and from that same window he smelled a strong scent of apricots, distinct from the stench of buckets of excrement and disinfectant.

He sat in the cell for three days. Once they beat him, and twice another prisoner was thrown in beside him. Most of the time he was held in confinement, without being interrogated, as if they did not know what to ask him. His captors seemed to know nothing of the "big transaction." Or perhaps all questions were simply beside the point—he belonged in jail.

On the third day he was taken to a hearing. They sat him down in a dark hall that smelled like wax. An appointed attorney spoke from the stand. He had red hair and his robe billowed as he waved his arms. "An innocent boy!" he declared. "He does not know what crime is!" A hum went through the room, English and Hebrew entered through the windows and the cracks beneath the doors like a slow sweep of dialogue. Chaim was bored. Across from his lawyer sat the prosecutor, who had a massive face with dark bags beneath his eyes. With that man, Chaim thought, I would do business.

Two guards stood by the doors, tortured by the heat. One of them had a rifle resting on his thigh. Chaim could hear the shots of the hunting rifle. He remembered Rachel, the innkeeper's daughter, and felt angry. He would like to get up and examine the rifle, but there was talk around him, and another guard was dozing off right next to him.

The door opened and the court clerk brought in a note for the judge. The judge glared at Chaim, then summoned the prosecutor and the defender. They whispered and looked at Chaim. Then they appointed his redhead lawyer to face him and say, "Well, the thing is, you're an orphan."

They took him in a British car to a dark warehouse in Jaffa, where they handed him a bundle of items and the last letter written by Leon Abramowitz, his father. They led him to the door and announced, "You're free," as if shooing a hesitant bird out of its cage.

"I have no money," he ventured.

The soldiers and the clerks and the warehouse officers dug through their pockets and gave the new orphan a few bills and some coins. One clerk took his coat off and put it over Chaim's shoulders. "It almost fits," he said, grinning.

Chaim rifled through his father's belongings. "You didn't happen to find in my father's things...any articles?"

"Articles?"

"Yes, for example, 'The Jewish Capital Squandered on Tobacco,' or 'The Botheration of Smiling.'"

They told him all the belongings had been carefully wrapped up out of respect for the deceased, and that whatever was not in the parcel probably did not exist. Then they sent him on his way.

For a week or more, Chaim wandered the outskirts of the settlements. When he was thirsty he found water. When he was hungry he stole unguarded food. In the mornings he could not remember the previous day's deeds, and by evening he could not recall the morning. He roamed far away from people. He thought a lot. I will need to be stronger, he told himself at times.

One day he spotted a donkey munching on weeds by the side of the road. He approached the donkey and nearby, beneath a eucalyptus tree, he found a man shot dead. A shiny gun was still in his hand and a note protruded from his pocket: "I have tired of it all," it read.

The only sound was the buzzing of flies swarming around the pool of blood. The red trickle had turned black, and the sun breaking through the eucalyptus leaves illuminated a face that was determined at the moment of death, but was gradually losing its confidence, as though upon death the man had encountered new doubts.

Chaim Abramowitz took the pistol from the dead hand. "Another weakling," he thought, and was about to hide the gun in his clothing, but he stopped. The donkey stood chewing weeds in the empty field. Chaim's arm lifted angrily. He shot the pistol with a deafening thunder and hit the donkey. He shot again, and this time he was ready for the blast. The donkey's front legs collapsed. He shot another three rounds, and then the gun made a clicking sound. There were no more bullets. The donkey lay on the ground.

Chaim tossed the pistol aside. He wanted to run, get away from this country, go back to school, be a star student, a champion runner. He picked up the pistol and put it under his coat. The swarm of flies abandoned the dead man and moved on to the new corpse, and their buzzing bothered Chaim, like the echoing sound of the shots just fired.

Years later, when he would own many guns and lease firearms to the fighting factions in the War of Independence, he would still keep that pistol, the first one, on his body. He would forget its origin over the years, and rid himself of any memory of the event itself. No questions would come to his mind—who the man was, or what he should have done. He would simply forget the incident and not burden his memory even when he would hold the gun. But on rare occasions, for no apparent reason, the phrase *I have tired of it all* would steal into his thoughts and dreams, out of context, spoken by dream-characters with no relation to that man, nor any reason to say *I have tired of it all*. Inexplicably, a dream would bring forth, *I have tired of it all*. Offer it up unexpectedly and then remove it. Sometimes his thoughts would rise from the distance, *I have tired of it all*, just like that, for no reason, as though plucked out of that event that still wanted to live.

He needed oil to clean his new gun, and he needed bullets. He thought he might be able to meet people and enquire discreetly whether they could sell him any bullets for his gun. On the main street in Rishon LeZion he met the wife of Meirson, the banker, and she asked him to help her with a nail that needed to be hammered. She led him to her home, took his hand and walked him through rooms with drawn curtains. She showed him her crystal from Vienna—real crystal, it was hard to get hold of here—and the embroidery she had been working on since coming to this country. One could not find such threads here, such refinement. All they thought about here was food. To relieve her boredom, truly out of mockery, she had learned to make marmalade—here, taste some, although things here did not taste like they did over there, it was too hot here, bad for the fruit, blinding, boring, no culture. She invited him into her room—he should take some marmalade—and in her room she would show him her pictures from Vienna, from her childhood home, she would show him real beauty. In the dim, lazy light of her room, she showed him a picture that had fallen off the wall, a loose nail, there was no one to fix it, and she burst into tears, "Everything is madness...everything here is madness," and fell to the bed in her dress, grieving with her hand over her eyes. Chaim took a paperweight from the writing desk and hit the loose nail, his back turned to her as she sobbed, and he

Chapter four

Find Yourself a Purpose
1964

> *"We do not have a life—not one of our own.*
> *That is the sum of our tragedy,*
> *and a life we must seek."*
> *(A.D. Gordon)*

Until 1967, Yehezkel Klein did not encounter a single day that was different from the previous ones. He worked silently in an alcove on his balcony. When given a broken radio, he would eagerly repair it and allow himself to turn the dial to the British occupiers' station, the BBC. The sounds of the English language on the radio still excited him, prompting him to groan, *"Ach…the British. If they were still here we would force them back to the gate with our onslaught! We would never surrender."*

But apart from the BBC, nothing caused Yehezkel's heart to ignite with fire as it had in those faraway days of the youth movement, in his little village in the Diaspora, the days of young girls and incessant debates, the days of *aliyah*, the underground, the days of The Leader.

In 1961 the remains of David Raziel were finally brought to

Israel. His coffin was transported by plane to Sde Dov airport in Tel Aviv. Speeches were made. Betar members accompanied him to the party headquarters at Metzudat Ze'ev. After remaining there for a day, he was taken in a convoy led by policemen on motorcycles, horses, and jeeps to the great synagogue on Allenby Street in Tel Aviv. Speeches were made. Then, in an even longer motorcade, the coffin was carried to Jerusalem. Speeches were made. Finally, David Raziel was interred.

Yehezkel Klein sat silently in his room.

Later that year the remains of Moshe Hess and his wife were brought to Israel and buried in the cemetery at the Kinneret *moshava*. That day, Yehezkel repaired three old Czech radios and an electric Olivetti.

In 1964 the remains of Ze'ev Jabotinksy were brought to Israel.

Jabotinsky!

That day Yehezkel sat on his chair fixing a double-horn gramophone with an electric arm. He trembled a little, but did not move. He looked at his son Shmuel working beside him. Not even at *barmitzvah* age yet, and already this son of his was quietly handling a broken Ampa radio. It would soon come to life in the son's hands and Yehezkel would turn it on to test it, and perhaps, by chance, from there, from the ceremony, they would broadcast the speeches. Perhaps the radio would emit the cantor's prayer over Jabotinsky's bones. *Ach*, better not think about it. The radio was working now, placed back on the shelf, no need to even test it, everything worked when Shmuel fixed it. A real wonder boy. *Ach*, Jabotinsky…Better not to think.

*

Although he was only nine, Shmuel was already known for his talent at fixing electronics. He barely knew what this or the other device was used for, but he could always identify the source of its defect. Neighbors from all across the political spectrum came to admire his work. Some visited from far away to test his knowledge, handing him appliances with subtly hidden flaws, and Shmuel would immediately reach for the damaged component.

Genia kept a careful watch over Shmuel's hours. More than once she chided Yehezkel when he worked the boy too hard in between homework and dinner, after which a growing boy's time was to be completely devoted to rest and hygiene. Except when her brother Romek came to visit, whereupon all rules were forgotten.

Romek came and went as he wished, trampling the household silence, merry and boisterous, recounting for Yehezkel this or that juicy piece of trivial news from the corridors of power, things a decent man did not need to know. Then he would turn his attentions to the boy. There was always a gift for Shmuel—a toy solider, a little Indian, a cavalier, an Eskimo with a dog, an African elephant, a Zulu warrior, a dwarf with an axe. Shmuel was allowed to handle the gift for a few moments to assess its merits, then he was sent for the big war chest. With the contents of this chest, an upholstered trunk packed with fighters of every kind, Genia's brother maintained a whole world of life and death. Each time he visited he conducted an all-out battle on the carpet, seeing the conflict through to its bitter end.

Yehezkel was pushed into a corner of the room.

Shmuel was only allowed to sit and stare.

The groups were lined up facing one another and each one's advantages were enumerated before they were set upon each other. Eskimos hurled tiny harpoons at their enemies, the Zulus of Africa, while the black savage warriors shot deadly arrows at the Eskimos, their arrow-tips laced with deadly black mamba poison. The jungle trees sheltered the archers while the Eskimos hid in holes carved into the ice. Japanese kamikaze pilots helped the Children of Israel cross the Red Sea and defended Masada against the evil Crusaders. Arab *fedayeen* attacked Vikings, and Indians aided by a yellow bus battled soldiers from the Jordanian legion in Stalingrad.

The only outcome of these battles was mass death for all fighters, although sometimes one survived. This victor, usually moments from death, whom the uncle eulogized before he knocked him to the ground with his thumb, remained true through life and death to Zionist ideals.

"What did the last Eskimo say before he died?" Romek would ask.

"It's good to die for our country," replied Shmuel obediently, quoting the legendary Trumpeldor.

"Or, 'I did not betray,'" added Romek, in turn quoting the heroic Israeli soldier's final words to his Syrian captors.

Every week in this sporting league an encounter occurred between two ethnic factions who met to settle a blood conflict. Yehezkel looked on in bitter silence. He considered protesting once, when instead of Avraham Stern—God avenge his blood—the Lehi fighters were led by a giant bulldozer. But the familiar noose tightened around Yehezkel's throat, urging him to be quiet, to say nothing, to give up on it all.

Yehezkel had long ago abandoned hope that the day would come when fate would deal a just blow to Romek. This brother, miraculously, had never had a single failure in life, not even when he tempted fate by acting rashly against his own best interests. For these many years he had cunningly calculated every step, and now he had built up a solid array of civil service positions for himself, with all the public coffers at his disposal and dignitaries' wives defiling their innocence in his company. He would tell Yehezkel about jobs he had obtained and jobs he would soon have, with not a shadow of conscience in his expression.

But suddenly, one day, Romek abandoned all his aspirations. With a flushed face he announced to Genia: "I met a man… What a man!" and declared that he would be cheerfully resigning from all his positions, as if to cleanse himself of his sins. In one moment he resolved: he would work solely for the benefit of this man. "A saint…he's practically a saint. He has no fear, I tell you!" Now he was addressing not Genia but Yehezkel, forcing him to hear about his new employer, a wealthy and secretive man by the name of Chaim Abramowitz who owned an expansive estate, and businesses and land. He had twice been imprisoned by the Israeli government, and before that by the British, and his strength was unrivaled! Such wonders!

"Chaim Abramowitz demanded that I keep all my positions. I am letting you in on a great secret! It was my desire to leave them all, to declare out loud—I resign! But Abramowitz ordered me to keep silent, to keep toeing the line. A great secret…"

From the time he began working for this Abramowitz, Romek was a changed man. His cheeks were always flushed and his voice climbed frequently to a shriek. He had lost his repose, it seemed to Yehezkel, and his body seemed to contort with the effort to please his new master. The frequency of his appearances in the apartment diminished, as did his inclination to speak at any length.

In August 1966 the new seat of the Israeli Knesset was dedicated, and Genia's brother appeared with invitations to the ceremony. He explained to Yehezkel that many people were kicking up a fuss to get hold of just one ticket, waving military commendations, handicap status and glorious pasts, but he himself had four invitations and Yehezkel could be one of the lucky recipients. "I myself shall not go," Romek clarified, "because Abramowitz is opposed to the Zionists. They are the ones who killed his brother. And besides, what would I do at a ceremony dedicating the Knesset of Israel?"

Yehezkel refused. He stayed at home. He objected to the Zionists, too. What was the state to him? But he kept two invitations in his drawer as a souvenir. It was not every day that the Jewish people got their own parliament, a real modern-day Sanhedrin.

In June of 1967 the Six-Day War broke out.

Even before then, for many days, Yehezkel could sense fear spreading. People came to him with flashlights, radios, gramophones, speakers, medical devices, wanting them fixed in preparation for sitting in bomb shelters. Genia began lighting memorial candles every day, for her parents, her brother, all the relatives she had lost in Poland. Yehezkel's brother wrote from America—"Come, it's peaceful here." The thread of fear wove its way through the people. In the cinemas, before the movies, audiences anxiously watched newsreels depicting the Arab armies' parades, Nasser's speeches, and the Arabs' pledges to throw the Jews into the sea.

Yehezkel fixed the appliances for the usual rate. What did he have to do with the war against our Arab enemies?

Genia's brother, who was all but forgotten in their home, began appearing again.

"I've enlisted," he boasted, but gave little explanation. He walked around their home without a uniform, but hinted at a new position in the security apparatus. He showed Yehezkel a map with canons marked on it.

"Abramowitz has permitted me to contribute to the war effort. He himself is helping out."

Under suspicious circumstances, while Shmuel was still at school, Romek would kneel on the floor in the guest room, alone with the war chest, and conduct battles among the toy soldiers. He groaned and muttered and his face turned red, and after every victory his eyes were torn with fear. He spoke only briefly with Genia. Shooting a glance at the memorial candles, he would say, "I'll get you some of those for cheap," and dart away.

On the fourth of June, half a day before the war broke out, Yehezkel went outside to buy some yogurt and white bread, and was approached by a man with a grave but decent expression. The man asked Yehezkel if he would answer a few questions. When he meekly agreed, he was flooded with a torrent of enquiries. First there were questions of a general nature, such as the extent of his concern over the situation and whether he estimated the city would be badly bombed from the air. Then he was quizzed on practical questions, namely, his knowledge about the location of the nearest bomb shelter and how much contact he had with the Civil Defense representative. Terrified, Yehezkel answered all the man's questions. As a guiding light, he asked himself how Ze'ev Jabotinsky would respond if this man were to stop him on the street. Finally the man informed Yehezkel that he had just participated in a pioneering survey, the first of its kind, conducted by the Institute for Practical Social Research. His opinions would help shape the government's policy on handling citizens' concerns.

And of what concern is this to an isolationist like myself? Yehezkel wondered. But he consoled the man, "Don't worry, we will win."

Not many hours later, the war broke out. Six days of victory, boundless liberation, salvation. A multitude of emotions galloped through Yehezkel. Courage, glory, persistence, joy. The justness of his chosen path was not undermined—it would be best for him to remain isolated from this entire country. But he was overcome with a desire to celebrate, to be redeemed, to be a Jew who was proud of his people. He took Shmuel and hurried to the Western Wall, where a good many people were already gathered. They walked the streets of Jerusalem. They promised themselves they would tour the entire liberated country. Yehezkel bought more and more victory albums. He bought all the newspapers and assembled his own private scrap-book of clippings. He did not entirely reject the new politics. He was not drawn to the remnants of his own party, a faction cobbled together by Tzipkin and Greenhaus out of the last few followers, but he reexamined Menachem Begin's party, though it was unwelcom-ing to people with strong opinions such as himself. He would sneak into congresses, go to different cities and insinuate himself into local branch meetings. Would they recognize him?

He wanted to renew his great enterprise, to bring the remains of important figures to Israel, and he invested his money in a set of encyclopedias.

"What for, Yehezkel?" Genia sighed, "you're not going to find anything about either one of us in there."

But Yehezkel scanned every entry, running down the pages with his finger: perhaps one of the country's worthy personages had been forgotten somewhere in the Diaspora? Because now even an eternal resting place on the Mount of Olives was once again possible. The country was being redeemed, as in the days of David and Solomon, prophets and kings. Yehezkel perceived that happiness was possible, that it would be good to live in this liberated country. But then news came—in the midst of these days of victory, Genia's brother Romek had fallen ill, a spiritual matter, bottomless sorrow. He was hospital-ized somewhere in the hills near Jerusalem.

Genia told Yehezkel, "You go, I cannot…"

Yehezkel dragged himself on three buses to an enchanting green oasis in the Jerusalem hills, a corner of the homeland unrivaled in its quietude and beauty, where Romek lay, straining to open his eyes, clutching Yehezkel's hand and whispering, "Genia."

Yehezkel did his duty. He went to see Romek once a fortnight and gradually managed to breathe some life into his bones. Holding his arm, he would encourage Romek to get out of bed and walk around a little. By summer's end he had taken him all the way from his room to a bench in the garden. The two men would sit silently facing a glorious landscape of fresh green colors, trees bustling with joyous birds, and in the background the hills of Jerusalem, soft and grey. Romek's lips would move, murmur, perhaps in anger—once they had uttered words of pride and arrogance, the women of the nation had left the taste of their lips on his own, but now they were like torn sails, mumbling syllables and fragmented complaints.

On Independence Day of 1970 they spent the whole day together. Romek rewarded Yehezkel with a complete sentence: "I was a soldier in Chaim Abramowitz's Testament Army."

And back to his splinters of mutterings.

Genia never went with Yehezkel on his visits to the sanatorium. She did not go to visit her brother alone, either. But every time Yehezkel left, she kissed his hand and said, "Thank you." She asked him to be the one soul who tended to her brother in his time of illness.

Yehezkel kept a secret from her: from the devoted nurses he had learned that there was another soul, a woman, who visited Romek once in a while. Her name was Rivka Abramowitz. The nurses urged Yehezkel to see the rose garden that had been planted thanks to her generosity, and the olive tree grove she had donated, and the new wing, and the air-conditioning system for the welfare of all the patients.

Yehezkel never saw the benefactress, although he tried to time his visits to coincide with hers. Why did he wish to see her? It was unclear to him. Why would he want to see her? What connection did he have with this anonymous donor? But he was gripped with suspense every time he made the journey, and at every stop along the way, between one bus and the next, the tension would climb, pulling his nerves tauter and tauter. When he asked at the gate and was told she was not there, disappointment would course through his blood and not leave him for many days, replaced only by the glimmer of hope that arose in anticipation of the next visit.

Once a nurse said, "She left just this moment."

"Just this moment?" Yehezkel stammered.

They often encouraged him—she was here yesterday, she will be here tomorrow, she hasn't been here for two weeks.

In his little workshop at home, Yehezkel sat hunched over his work and imagined an encounter with Rivka Abramowitz. He thought of what he would say and what she would say. These imaginings began to supercede his thoughts about bringing bones to Israel. In 1971 he heard that Eliezer Shalit, a founder of Rishon LeZion who had died in Berlin in 1915, was finally being brought to Israel. On the day of the ceremony Yehezkel calmly got up from his chair, took two buses, and walked with hunched shoulders until he arrived at the cemetery in a dusty condition. But as soon as the burial was over he went home and sat in his chair on the balcony, and his lips murmured, "A proper resting place...A proper resting place."

He leaned on the balcony railing and looked down at the bare yard in the moonlight, with its silently swaying bushes. Something bad was present in his life, something ongoing. Here in *Eretz Yisrael* he had been given a new name, Yehezkel, and he had also acquired his underground name, Ben Avigdor. Women had called him Ben Avigdor, too. Then the state was founded. He wanted to be an underground fighter again, a young boy, a dreamer. He wanted to hear his mother calling his real name, Bonjek. To feel her fingers running through his hair...

In early 1973, Yehezkel's only son, Shmuel, enlisted in the Israel Defense Forces. The Yom Kippur War broke out. Shmuel fought on the southern front and earned a citation.

At the end of that year Yehezkel fell ill. He was rushed to the hospital and kept in for observation. They told him it was heart failure.

"This is the end," he told himself.

Genia came in the afternoon.

"I am sad, Genia," he said.

An hour later the monitors began to indicate something wrong, and by evening his heart rate had plummeted. A doctor was called. It was futile. Yehezkel Klein died that night.

Chapter five

In Fact the Heat is Maddening 1929

> *"How weak we are! How miserable! From whence shall our help come? Perhaps this abysmal tragedy is worth something in human life, but it cannot be used to conquer a land, nor to redeem a nation."*
> *(A.D. Gordon)*

Greetings, Mr. Chaim Abramowitz, Mr. Chaim, Chainek—greetings! Yasha Yosedorf, that is I. And what a joy! You have agreed to meet. *Nu*, well and good. For I have sent three people to see you already, and all returned alike, twins of a gazelle, bearing the same black circle around their left eye—a personal mark, your own Solomon's seal. Well and good. *Nu*, it is Jews such as yourself that we need here. Stalwart. But how did you arrive at this sort of conduct, answering a business inquiry in such a fashion? You were merely called upon to respond with a simple 'yes,' and yet you chose to use fists of steel.

But now you have come, yes, you have come. One final emissary I sent, before appearing before you myself, and me with these damn legs, I do not walk much these days. Outside of this café, may it be blessed of all the places in Zion, I find no rest, and I was at a loss as to how we might settle our little matter, seeing as you marked my emissaries with your seal as though they were epistles sent to a distant land, lacking only stamps on their faces. Well and good.

Indeed you seem to be a man of ideology, no mere brute. I have certainly heard of your heroic deeds. Throughout the *Yishuv* you are talked of. Last summer a British officer drew his pistol at you, and you replied with your own in his face. A pistol! Drawn against a British officer! *Nu, nu.* Two men stand facing one another on a town street. Each with a pistol at his forehead, but the two could not be more different. The one backed by a great empire, a Goliath, and you—what is your heroism? Just like young David, pure and ruddy, "Though comest to me with a sword and with a spear and with a shield, but I come to thee in the name of the Lord of hosts, the God of the armies of Israel..." *Oy*, these heroic Jews. And they say the officer dropped his gun and surrendered, yet that very same day you were taken in by seven police officers. I understand your honor spent six months in prison. A shame. And I heard that the whole dispute was over a Jewish tailor whom the Arabs treated cruelly, and that you would not abide by his suffering, while the British officer would not abide by the beating you gave the Arab thugs. This is what I heard. But perhaps there is another truth to the tale?

Look here. Yasha Yosedorf, that is I, an officer of territories, I trade the lands of our mother *Eretz Yisrael*. This café in which we are meeting has witnessed some of my transactions in the past, the handsome signing of documents and the reaping of profits for all concerned. There are those among us, the land dealers, who rob the weak and the meager, and cause documents to be signed and then throw them to the wind. But I—let me now offer you the entire truth, from one decent man to another—I purchased a cluster of lands in a far-flung spot from the great land merchant, Emil Azar, a scion of the famous Tian family, who conducts his business from Paris. But it transpires that in some circuitous way, in the very core of the territory, right in the midst of the hills, lies one small piece of land that was acquired by an unknown man, and this man, you see, was your late father, Leon Abramowitz. How and why did he make the purchase? Emil Azar's memory had no room for such miniscule transactions, and he was not one for keeping papers, the Arab. So I am here before you now with this news, every word of which is the truth, to inform you that you, your father's heir, own this sliver of land. I might have continued to conduct my business and sell the lands, ignoring this most trivial fact—after all, any sorcery is possible in the land registrations of our beloved country. Your name would have disappeared, the land would have been sold, and I would have reaped a handsome profit. I am more than a merchant, however: I am a Zionist, a lover of this country, and once I was a real pioneer. I came here in 1905 from the Mogilev region in the Diaspora. And what was my heart's desire? To build agricultural collectives, to march with a hoe on my back and a song on my lips. I fancied myself a poet too, and poetry is still dear to my heart today. Incidentally, a poem of mine was published in *Hamagid Hachadash*.

But look here, what use are remembrances now? This meeting was called for business. And so, my young boy, I shall offer you a handsome sum. You could have no use for this piece of land, and I have buyers interested in the entire plot. I shall buy your portion, my conscience shall be clear, and I shall be happy to have given a monetary gift to a young man. Being, as I am, a land merchant—an officer of territories in the army of *Eretz Yisrael*—I shall sell the lands. Settle in them I shall not, on account of my tired, sickly legs. I once believed my Herculean strength would never subside. I had fists and brawny shoulders like your own, and courage, and a beautiful bird danced in my soul, producing poems for me to write. I published a poem in *Hachavatzelet*, perhaps you read it? I am no great poet, no great talent—talents I have none at all, with the possible exception of the talent to have been born at a time when even the talentless may lead an adventurous life. But look here, today my strength has abandoned my body, and building settlements is not for me. This is what happens to a man. Heed my advice, dear boy, strength is not forever. Take the money, build your world. Strength is not forever. A man believes he will always be strong and successful, and does not plan for days of despair, and then how bitter is his end, how very bitter. I shall tell you a fable.

Observe that woman, in the corner of the café. Sarah, née Blum. Her boundless beauty is a snare for one's eyes. You may gaze and gaze and never have your fill. And there are not, after all, many beauties among our women. Agreed! They are not to blame. Our women, ideologically speaking, are most lovely. But fatiguing work and hellish sun take their toll. Sit with them to debate the issues, look at them, their nails are hard, their faces sharp. They speak of the purpose, the way, the dangers of disunity, but their faces reveal terrible exhaustion. Yes this Sarah, here in the café, although one cannot detect a thing on her face, has suffered great tragedy, greater than she has the strength to bear, like all of our nation's sacred women who take on greater and greater burdens until they can bear no more. A short while ago her husband fell ill and died. He was one of the great men of Hashomer, one of the founders. A young man, scornful of property and the inconsequentialities of merchants like myself. He would look at a man such as me and spit, and ask scornfully, Have we come to this land to build a national home for people like this? But the man lived and died, and it is a great, great sorrow. As you see her, one moment a proud woman, the wife of a hero, a soldier, and the next, a martyr's death, the husband gone, the pillar lost. What will become of her, this beautiful widow? I shall tell you another secret: she is with child. Still concealing her pregnancy, perhaps even from herself, hiding her body, for so bitter and so sad is her fate even without a babe to take the last piece of bread from between her lips. Look at her, such a beauty, a woman of such charm, and some say a wild woman. She rides horses and can handle swords and guns, and she roams the forests, disappears into the desert. Some say they have seen her bathing in the streams, her body as silver as the moon above her. Any man would want her, you see, but who would provide for her with a child not his own?

Now, avert your eyes from Sarah, she is merely an example, a parable. Avert your eyes, and we shall discuss the moral of the parable. You are a young man, strong, the world is at your feet, and here an exceedingly wealthy man comes to you—that is I, Yasha

Yosedorf—and offers a fair price for your land, does not cheat, does not steal your poor man's lamb, even though it would be possible. Take your remuneration, and I shall add a gift, and perhaps we may yet work together one day. Business is plentiful in Palestine, it is not all poverty and disappointment and disease. Take the compensation for your land, go, build your future so that disaster does not befall you and your strength is not lost, and enemies do not surround you.

Young friend, you must cease looking at the woman, at Sarah. She is older than you, and she bears a great weight on her shoulders. She is simply a parable—a parable of human life. Now is the time for you to peruse an offer from a trader of lands, a former poet, a former pioneer. I was a young man like you, and I ran away from my father's house to join the pioneers. In the Galilee mountains, land of the ancient prophets, we settled on a hilltop. What can I say, the terrain was rocky, there was no majesty and no glory. Arabs all around, their villages built around wells, while all we had was a vehicle that crawled down the hill once a week to bring back contaminated water. Money for shoes we had not, nor for agricultural tools. On the hilltop we sat and suffered, clinging on day by day in the sun, the desolation, calling ourselves the holders of land, pioneers. Fruit of the earth we did not produce, the cattle grew thin in the barns and pens, suffering like us. From morning to evening we yielded no produce, but we were pioneers, having stood in the sun for another day without dying.

Do you know, there were times, in the evening hours, when my mind would strain with empty thoughts, desperation, and the foulness in my heart. Then my memory would call up lucid scenes of the way we used to be in the Diaspora, when we were still active Zionists burning with vitality. Back then we dealt in such trivialities, always scheming among party factions on how to elect so-and-so as a committee representative, how to add another man to the delegation, and we would think: in Zion it will be different. In *Eretz Yisrael* we shall live among king and messiah. Everything will be momentous and pure and soaring. Yet there we sat in our huts, downtrodden, grumbling over a couple of hoes.

A life of culture there certainly was—after all, we had not come to Palestine to lose our culture! It soon transpired that almost every one of us was a poet, and after work, in the evenings, though our heads were dropping with exhaustion, we knew that repose was for the bourgeois, for our parents in the Diaspora, and so to the culture room we would hobble. In truth it was half a room, borrowed from the kitchen, with only a tin sheet separating us from the stovetop. But our voices were modern as we sang songs of the soul, fresh off the press—Mandelstam, Bialik, Marinetti. Imagine the scene: five people sit in a room reciting poems of snow, cherry branches, *oh my beloved, oh my soul*—when in fact the heat is maddening.

And so we sat, pioneers with hearts of stone. Our bodies were empty, our souls were empty, and on we went for another day and another, malaria, desperation. But one day—reinforcement. A young boy arrives. He has come to Palestine and wishes to be a pioneer. But his appearance? Gaunt, pale-faced, his cheeks sinking into his mouth, seeking shelter. But all eyes are drawn to his hands, dove-white hands of muslin with long, pale, polished fingers, each nail carefully shaped. A pioneer. We welcomed him politely and asked his name and where he was from. The young man grew startled and tried to evade our questions as though they were probing at the depths of his soul, invading, uncovering secrets. He barely managed to give his name, and it was Yasha. The name of his village he did not disclose, it was too much to bear.

We let him be. The next day we sent him out with a hoe, and by five in the morning he had fainted away. We carried him inside to cool his body and decide what was to be done with him. He awoke shouting like a slaughtered calf, "I will not go back! I will not go back!" Recovered, he was sent to the pen to help clean and learn how to milk. By evening he collapsed in the middle of the pen, bleeding, waking and shouting only when he believed we were discussing sending him to a sanatorium. He was miserable. His look was so refined, an Abel who sees all the world as Cain come to kill him.

A week later, a mail vehicle ambles up the path with a telegram. Imagine to yourself—a telegram arriving at our little place! It transpires that young Yasha is no mere dreamer, but a prodigious musician, a gifted pianist, his fingers worth their weight in gold. How could we have known, embedded as we were in a wilderness, a land of hot coals in the summer and swamps in the winter? How could we have recognized his name as being famous in all the capitals of Europe? We learned that the boy, a true Zionist, had slipped away from his agents, teachers and coaches. Slipped away from his mother, Alicia Fidlée, a noblewoman from an affluent family of known Zionists, and she was sending us this telegram to the desert sun. Send the boy back! she demanded, as if we had taken him hostage, as if we were Ishmaelites and he Joseph.

The telegram informed us that her envoy would be coming to collect her son on the sixth of April at precisely nine o'clock, at which time we must bring him to the fence for delivery. And indeed, on the sixth of April a vehicle made its way up the hill again, conveying Attorney Felix Shokef from Haifa. Scanning the wasteland of our settlement, he enquired whether he had reached the right place, and asked to see the boy.

Yasha does not flee. He goes out to the attorney and faces him. Attorney Shokef wipes his brow with a handkerchief, looks at the boy and forms his impression. Then he looks this way and that at our garden of Eden, and stares into our faces. "Who is the leader here?" he asks, and we have an urge to pour forth a torrent of explanations on this bourgeois man, this urbanite—for we are a group, we are equals, we have no need for leaders. But Attorney Shokef silences us with his hand and says dryly, "I shall speak with one of you. Then the rest shall listen to my terms pertaining to the grants we shall award in return for attention shown to Yasha, for so long as he lives here."

He looks at us scornfully while the dizzying concept of grants dries up the refusal on the tips of our tongues. And I, who have recently been appointed treasurer, and who often look down from our hilltop to the valleys and see empty wallets, I announce: We shall talk! The group makes way and Attorney Shokef looks at me and makes his proposal.

And what did he propose? He informed me that the whole pioneering business was a passing fad for Yasha. His future was in Europe in front of a devoted audience. But since this was Yasha's desire, and his nerves were known to be fragile, and he himself had no intention of forcibly removing the boy lest roots were injured, he would reach an agreement with us. Every week Yasha would write a letter to his mother. This was the first term. Every two weeks Attorney Shokef himself would arrive to examine Yasha's welfare. If the mother was pleased with his letters, and if Attorney Shokef was satisfied with Yasha's general condition, the mother would bestow a grant upon the group, as well as a personal grant to me, the leader. If Yasha was not well kept he would be removed immediately and the grants would cease. If his spirits were good—the grants would increase. Attorney Shokef then began to list numbers, advance fees and premiums. I was seized by a sweet sense of horror. How could we refuse? Attorney Shokef suddenly leaned in close to me, dwarfish and flushed with perspiration, his glare penetrating my depths, and warned, "Keep his fingers from all harm!"

A few days later a large package arrived from Europe. Inside, for Yasha, were a beautiful set of work gloves, a nice little hoe, a couple of rakes, a colorful funnel and several hats. There were also dishes, and a fork and knife, and napkins. But we were busy with our own gifts—excellent boots and work shirts and dress shirts and kettles and pots and pans and pruning shears and forceps and a tool for gathering dates and baskets for gathering fruit and various other agricultural devices for crops we did not even grow. How could we possibly have orchards? How could we have vineyards? We had barely a bunch of goats and two cows and a donkey who produced nothing but pitiful neighs, as if he too had left behind his father, mother and sister in Mogilev.

This was the beginning of an enjoyable era for us. All our efforts, both of body and soul, were concentrated on Yasha. He was the main crop. We had to protect his body from any hazard, and his fingers—twofold. We had to preserve his good spirits and allow him to amuse and befriend the women. We did not pressure the girls, we were not engaged in any dubious sins, but we hoped that one of them would grow especially fond of Yasha and would allow him to unbridle his sadness.

Each one of us oversaw Yasha's letters. Every week, with

astonishing precision, a package arrived with a letter from the mother that overflowed with happiness and sorrow. The lovelier Yasha's writing, the greater the package. We were soon able to build a new pen and barn, restore the decaying coop, enquire about additional lands, and purchase new clothes and shoes. But there was a fly in the ointment—Yasha. He had complicated issues with his mother, we could not understand them. On a crate in the communal room he would sit begrudgingly, place a sheet of paper before him, and we would all stand around him, waiting. But Yasha? His letters were dejected. Barely letters at all. We encouraged, badgered, warmly patted his shoulders, brought him a pitcher of water, some dried figs, an apple. Allowed him to take a short walk for inspiration. Put our arms around his shoulders again. But Yasha let out a trickle of words here, a trickle there. Not enough. We urged him, explaining that her packages were extremely helpful to the enterprise. We wanted her to send more so that our yields would grow, but Yasha would say, I don't want to…I cannot…leave me be…it is impossible…

Once a fortnight, like the great eagle, Attorney Shokef comes to visit. He places the money in the cash box, explains to me how the sum was calculated, with premiums and supplements and fines and subtractions and management fees and so on and so forth. He examines Yasha, talks with him, and asks again, "Won't you go back to Mother?"

This arrangement persisted for four months. The group was blossoming, there was plenty of money, and every corner of our home was handsome. Only Yasha, woe unto him, was wilting. His face grew bronzed, but in the crack of his eyes lay a plea—Release me from myself, from my bonds. What ill did the boy's soul suffer? I will never know. A poor boy, a small fool. And then one day we were in a playful mood and took a majority decision that was senseless—to use the gift money to hire a bus and go off for a good time in the big city. Singing loudly, we set off on our way, knowing that the next day Attorney Shokef would arrive and our budget would be replenished. After all, a little enjoyment does no harm to anyone. We reached the city and had a wonderful time. A spirit of comradeship.

Yasha was with us too, reticent and sullen, but when a hand patted his shoulder a smile would come to his lips. As we looked through a window into an inviting café, we saw a piano on a raised platform inside. The idea came quickly: Yasha must play. Yasha evaded us, refused, lost his voice, tried to disappear. But we could not let it go. He lived with us, a member of our group, a supporting pillar—how could we never know the pleasure of his music?

We sit him at the piano and he stutters, "The piano is not tuned." The café proprietor is called: It certainly is tuned, he retorts, Batsheva Fried plays her beautiful music here every Tuesday. Finally Yasha accedes and places his fingers on the keys. Silence surrounds us. His music is familiar, a light melody, well-known, easily played on a harmonica. But what can I say…you would not understand. It is his fingers that we watch. Like ten white plows they drive on, injuring—injuring the soul. At a certain moment all you desire is to bury your face in your hands and weep. Weep over the ways of the cruel world. Your distress has no remedy, and there can be no peace. You wish to weep because the beauty of the world lives beyond the mountains, and beyond the mountains is your old father's house, and there sits your mother at the window, longing to see you, her son. Perhaps you will understand…

That evening Yasha went home with us, but he sat alone. The bus carried us all along in utter silence. Where was the day of rejoicing, the day of foolish happiness? Yasha's playing had taken its toll on us and shown us how very, very low our lives were. The bus climbed up the hill and we sank lower, and did not turn to Yasha…a saint… an angel about to be taken, Yasha…

His name was Julian. Julian Fidlée. And 'Yasha'? His own invention. But never mind. With that name he lived among us, and by that name I shall call him longingly.

The next morning was the day of Attorney Shokef's visit. Yasha lay like a corpse, sickly, seemingly claimed by malaria. He raised his head and asked, When is Attorney Shokef coming? We responded in a merciful chorus, "At nine." And we prepared, wanting to bathe Yasha, refresh him, stuff him with medicine and food, give him hot tea. But Yasha refused and took to his bed. At ten minutes before nine the car appeared and we called for Yasha, but the poor boy's body was already swaying lifelessly on a rope, with no hope of resuscitation.

What did we do? We ran. We simply ran. Each in a different direction. We left everything behind in the flourishing settlement. One man loaded a goat on his shoulders and took off downhill, another grabbed a till and a woman and left on horseback. Catch as catch can. I fled on foot. For three hours I walked, I almost died by the time I reached a side road. The whole way I carried with me the communal funds in a heavy box. I waited for another twenty hours, almost a whole day and night, until a vehicle from Kibbutz Kotshim came by and picked me up. And here I am before you today, two decades later, a land dealer. All my initial capital was from that cash-box. Twenty years have gone by, and the conscience? Shall we enquire as to its state? Well, life has turned out this way and not another.

But enough, enough stories. You are better off not listening to an old merchant who is neither one of the best nor one of the purest. Among our Jewish people there are those who pave roads through the wilderness, fight malaria, build brick houses. We are a healthful nation to have so many of these people. And then there are those like me. There are also those like me.

Here are the papers. Sign them, just sign them. One signature and your future is assured. Or perhaps you will not sign. Perhaps you will wish to persist, to settle the land. Perhaps you will choose to be among the pure men who end their lives hanging on a rope. I do not need to remind you of the parable, of Sarah, who sits there. For all the while I have been talking it has seemed to me that the parable is superseding its moral. You are looking at her, at Sarah Blum, looking and looking, as if you do not understand that she is a parable, merely a parable. Sign the papers, please, sign and save yourself. Do not be Abel—be Cain.

Do not linger, my son. I am a businessman, with ailing legs, and I must hurry. I was a pioneer. *Nu*, even dreams are gone now. Sign, we will shake hands, and we will be off. Our conversation has brought me sorrow. Perhaps it is regrettable that our meeting occurred. It has brought me only sorrow and self-pity. For I was a Zionist, young and excited in my little town, so excited when I left for Palestine, excited to settle the land, to give life to the Zionism in my heart, and what... dreams...I look at you and I recall things long forgotten. Perhaps your eyes are those of a child, an innocent boy.

Listen, I will tell you something. When I was a child I had a beloved uncle who brought gifts every time he visited. One day he gave me a little compass and taught me how to find the north. I took the compass with me everywhere I went, and the first thing I did was find out where the north was. In every place the needle showed the north. At school, in the playground, in my room, in Father's store. On his next visit, my uncle asked me a riddle: If you stand right at the north pole, where will the needle point?

His question stumped me, and he rejected every answer I could think of. Then he told me: There, in the north pole, the needle will go mad. It will point up, down, sideways, every which way. The compass is good for indicating the north in every place on Earth except for the north itself.

That is what my uncle said. And the moral?

How easy was Zionism when all it consisted of was longings for Zion. In all the corners of the Diaspora, in Poland and Russia and Yemen and Morocco, the needle pointed the way, showed us what must be done. But from the moment we came here, to Zion, the needle went mad. Here is right, there is right, everything spinning around.

And now, my son, do not linger. Sign the paper and we shall leave.

*

In 1929, a few days before his twentieth birthday, Chaim Abramowitz married Sarah Blum. Five months after their wedding Sarah gave birth to her daughter, Rivka. They began to build their house on the small plot of land inherited from Abramowitz's father, Leon. The surrounding territory was sold to Chaim Abramowitz, at full price, by the land dealer Yasha Yosedorf.

Chapter six

The Abramowitz Estate
1936

I n the 1930s, a Tel Aviv photographer with a fondness for taking
portraits of men had to hastily leave town in the wake of a scandal.
He packed up his camera and hired a driver to take him away. The
pioneer landscapes of the country did not speak to his heart, and he
spent most of the journey hunched over his lap, composing a letter
of love or farewell or apology. Three times along the way he had to
get out of the car to vomit. During one such stop, while the driver
was checking the engine and wiping dirt off the headlights, the
photographer noticed the tiny figure of a house some distance away,
leaning sideways on a hilltop. He was moved by a sudden urge to
photograph this lost, lonely house extinguished in the desolate wilderness. He went back to the car and dug through his equipment,
and managed to put together a combination of lenses that could
capture the structure. The Abramowitz Estate, for the first time since
its construction, was immortalized in a photograph. The picture was

slightly blurred, with Chaim and Sarah's house framed in the center like a small flame from a candle.

The photographer left the lonely estate behind as he sat down in the car and feebly asked the driver to continue the painful journey. He looked back at the house once more. It sat frozen on its hilltop, indifferent to the photographer's arrival, indifferent to his departure. A few days later he lost the roll of film and it was never found.

*

Chaim Abramowitz's name was becoming known in the *Yishuv*. Among the café-frequenters and the politicos, and in various organized movements, an assortment of stories were exchanged about him. There was also talk of his house, built in a remote spot bordering two Arab villages whose inhabitants silently respected the tradesman. Here and there the house appeared in official documents. The Mandate government's land bureau filed registrations for the lands Abramowitz had insisted on purchasing so that he could expand to the south and to the east, all the way to the border of the two villages and the range of hills in the west, where the orchards were the last to come into Abramowitz's sight when the sun rose every morning.

The people of the *Yishuv* learned to recognize Abramowitz's figure on horseback when he appeared on the doorsteps of faltering factories, at the gates of neglected farms, and in the yards of semi-abandoned warehouses, naming his price. Abramowitz the tradesman slowly expanded the radius of his travels, showing up in more and more distant places, releasing industrial pioneers from their nightmarish debts, redeeming lands from frightened settlers. Sometimes, after the exchange was complete, a seller would offer up himself, too, and follow Abramowitz to join his board of trustees on the estate.

In the private sector, which was groaning under the economic crisis and the ideology of collectivism, Chaim Abramowitz was considered a savior. But in the public sector, among the labor movement, his financial offers were sternly debated.

"Every penny he brings in to the coffers—we will pay back twice as much," warned men in work shirts.

"We are aware of the dangers," replied the men's adversaries gravely.

"We will know how to get close and we will know how to keep our distance," said the movement leaders.

"Collaboration with Abramowitz is irreconcilable with most of our moral dictates," determined others.

There was not a single organization or movement that was refused a meeting with Chaim Abramowitz to ask for his support. Though he avoided doing business within the organizations, averse to the fiery intrigues and the elbow-jabbing, his influence silently anchored at the port of every association, never too close yet never absent. At the end of 1935 the Abramowitz Estate was mentioned for the first time in a key speech in one of the movements' congresses.

"This matter proposed for the agenda, the proposals made by the tradesman Abramowitz...Our discussion of them must not overlook the heart of this scandalous issue. I have been sitting here for an hour listening to speeches by the esteemed members who spoke before me. And what do my ears witness? The 'Abramowitz Estate' here and the 'Abramowitz Estate' there. And I, if the members will be so kind as to clarify to a knowledge-thirsty comrade, I stop and ask, What is all this talk of an estate? When I left my father's house I innocently thought I would never again hear that feudal word, not here! Yet now, in the heart of our country, an 'estate owner' rises up to exploit the economic security crisis that rocks us all, and offers us all sorts of commercial proposals. In fact, he offers money. Charity. No less. And instead of denouncing the man, repelling him in every practical way and asking whence this 'estate owner' has emerged, I hear of comrades rushing to take shelter under his wing. I am aware that our camp is splitting into two. On the one side are those eager people, whom I condemn, and on the other side are those vehemently opposed to Abramowitz, members of the fanatic type, who trample any ties with people outside the movement. And I tell you, comrades in both camps: I would be happy to stand here before you and tell the 'estate owner' Abramowitz that I wish to take neither his honey nor his sting. I would like to join the camp of the proud fanatics who are not plagued with nightmares of our empty coffers. And why should they be? For they are men of vision, prophets. And the budgets? The finances? Other people will take care of that. However, I now must drop a bombshell. For it transpires that in the opposing political camp, and you know full well to whom I am referring— to those who dispute our way—there too, wonder of wonders, the tradesman Abramowitz's offers have been made. Are there no morals? No shame? Moreover, it is clear that if we utterly refuse, the pennies we reject here will be dropped into the coffers over there. This ugly fact must guide each one of us. Our 'conscientious people' and our 'prophets' must not ignore their knowledge of where the money will flow if we refuse it ourselves, even if we do not approve in any way of this 'estate.' Indeed, I urge every member to think before voting.

"I would desire so very much to step down from this podium now, to join you there in the audience as you contemplate what I have just put forth. But I am forced to examine one more matter that disturbs my peace. According to the regulations it is clear that the decision regarding Abramowitz's offer must be made solely and exclusively by a full quorum of the party convention, no less. Under no circumstances any less. Unfortunately, the next convention is not until March, and yet we face a proposal that is good for only thirty days. What my heart says, I know. Do not confound me with your emotional pleas. I know, I know. But at the end of the day, comrades, there is no real choice—not for me, not for you. We must accept the offer, comrades. With a heavy heart we must accept it and be done with the matter."

At first the estate was only a rumor, a name, a registration on a document. No one visited it. No one saw it.

From his estate Chaim Abramowitz would set off on his travels, and when he returned he would chart his course through one of the larger communities, staying for a few days in this or that town, where he would eagerly consume all the movies screened in all the cinemas, sometimes staying to watch the same film over and over again. Deals within a hair's breadth of being signed were left hovering in the air, fragile and vulnerable, until Abramowitz had sated his hunger for magnificent stories and adventurous lives.

First he tried to buy the "Ophir" cinema. Then he badgered Chaim Fleishman, the owner of the "Chaf" cinema in Hadera, incessantly. Finally, he insisted on meeting with Mograbi from Tel Aviv and making him excessive offers. All in vain.

One afternoon, after a three-hour meeting in the heat of the day, Mr. Mograbi trembled and asked Abramowitz, "In the end, if I don't sell, will you kill me?"

When Abramowitz asked where he had gotten such an idea, Mr. Mograbi pursed his lips, wiped the sweat off his brow and murmured, "They say…"

Rumors came and went about Abramowitz.

Sometimes the *Yishuv* leaders sighed as they pondered the man. "In all circumstances we are peace lovers, except when it comes to a war of survival. Yet now we have such a Jew amongst us. But perhaps it is not a bad thing to have a ruffian Jew, just one…"

Abramowitz continued trying to purchase the "Mograbi" cinema until the winter of 1942. Every time the negotiations hit another dead end, Abramowitz would pierce his interlocutor with his gaze, pin him to the chair with fear, then leave the room without a word and go straight into the auditorium to watch a movie, once, twice or three times, to revive his spirits with dramas and faraway tales.

Sometimes he would come home from a two-week trip comprised of an adventure on the plains east of Damascus, or a secret visit to his friends in the Mahajna tribe, or a deal struck with industrialists, or a riot encountered along the way. Yet when he came to Sarah he would regale her with an enthusiastic description of the dramatic scenes from the movies he had seen. Sarah would interrupt him with a caress, saying, "And the man you brought home on your saddle today? You have not told me who he is." Abramowitz would stop to introduce another man he thought looked useful and might be a candidate for joining the estate, then steer the conversation back to the movies.

Sarah never found fiction to be of much interest, and with the exception of one night at the outdoor cinema in Tel Aviv, she did not watch movies. Once in a while she would read a book, giving herself over to some story or other, but she was rarely affected. Her own travels on horseback were dedicated to the barren seaside, where she collected little treasures to bring home for "her orphan," Chaim. "For you," she would say, even when the gift was something as peculiar as a crate full of wigs that had washed up on shore. Once she brought an antique armchair she found on the beach. Another time it was the empty shell of a giant turtle, and one day she found a pair of illegal immigrants who had been lost in a smuggling operation. And one day she came home with Günter.

She found him passed out on the beach and brought him to the estate. Even when he regained consciousness and was closely examined, he still looked useless. Why had she brought him? But Günter, like a market trader unpacking his wares and calmly displaying them on a counter, gradually revealed his virtues until eventually Abramowitz appointed him as his head foreman, the man responsible for managing, supervising and overseeing the estate.

"When we are gone you will be in charge of everything," Abramowitz explained.

"When you are gone?" Günter asked worriedly.

Every time Chaim or Sarah returned from their trips, Günter was the first to sense their approach and quickly limp to the gate to welcome the weary travelers. His heart would beat with a little excitement and a lot of anxiety. "It is dangerous, what you are doing. Jews alone on horseback?"

"Why worry?" Abramowitz would answer. "Alexander Zaid also made his journeys alone."

"But you…you…I worry about you," Günter persisted.

"Even our Harkin, when he was in Hashomer, he rode alone," Abramowitz reminded him.

"Our Harkin, if you'll forgive me, I have heard that no one wanted to be on guard duty with him. And here too, if you'll forgive me, with us, the workers come to me with complaints, they cannot tolerate it, and matching Harkin with a shift partner is harder than mating a speck of sodium with a drop of water in my test tubes. But not to worry, everything falls into place, and Harkin is nicely matched with work. You, sir, should concern yourself only with your important affairs. Leave the daily matters of the estate to me. But why do you ride alone? And what about Sarah? How can you allow her to ride like that, a Jewish woman on her own?"

Sarah then began taking Günter on her trips, and he sat unsteadily behind her on the saddle.

In between trips Günter approached Chaim Abramowitz and whispered, "Because of my limp, I may find it difficult to protect Sarah against a large number of rioters, but against one or two I will give my soul, never fear."

In 1936, once the riots erupted and groups of Jews were frequently assaulted, the empty roads leading to the estate filled with fearful travelers seeking protection and shelter. No one was allowed to enter the estate itself, so as not to disturb the residents' peace, but visitors were received on a little common outside the fence, and from there they could observe the house on the hilltop.

Hospitality was overseen by Moshe Harkin, a veteran of Hashomer, who was strict about where the carriages and carts and cars could park, and examined the horses to find out if they were stolen, and initiated his own interrogations of the travelers. More well-liked was Günter, who would welcome the travelers politely, limp among them and ask each one as to his profession so that they could discuss a topic in which the guest was proficient. If an enjoyable conversation developed, Günter would even be bold enough to ask if the guest happened to have a book or some papers that might clarify the issues of his expertise.

From time to time people from the estate disturbed the conversations, coming to Günter with all sorts of questions:

"What percentage did we offer Lember last year in Hadera? And what did it go for?"

"How much hay is left in the warehouses in Petach Tikva?"

"How much of Kantor's commission has been paid? With which bills?"

Günter patiently answered every enquiry, dictating columns

of numbers and adding footnotes. Then he would send the enquirer on his way and turn back to intelligent conversation.

"And so, first one adheres the damp sheets and then one presses?"

"Has the price of zinc truly fallen that much? And here I was thinking that in modern times the value of this metal would sky-rocket!"

If the disturbances persisted and business prevented Günter from devoting himself to the conversation, he would apologize and bow his head. "All these questions. You must forgive me. You see, I am the head foreman for Chaim Abramowitz..." and his gaze would pause on his interlocutor's face to see whether he believed that this man limping among them was conducting all the affairs of Abramowitz's house on his own.

If one of the travelers returned to the estate a few weeks or months later, Günter would amaze him by renewing their conversation at precisely the point it had left off. Indeed, he would assail his interlocutor with a plethora of questions that had needled him since he began studying the respective visitor's topic.

"I have truly been unable to comprehend how one calculates property and land tax since the laws were updated."

"And this brass alloy, if we decrease the rate of zinc to twelve percent, will it still be useful for welding?"

"But what, in fact, is the essence of the argument made by the acclaimed Ephraim Hareuveni regarding the classification of grasses according to their botanical species?"

If Günter took a special liking to one of the guests he would be taken inside the estate, and if he showed evidence of a scholarly nature, Günter would excitedly lead him to his own residence at the edge of the estate, a small cluster of huts he had built for his scientific research. There, oblivious to the guest's dubious looks, Günter would introduce a bold new experiment.

Günter was often accompanied by a little girl of about six. He would limp around her worriedly, taking time between conversations to answer her questions and consult with her on topics that seemed, from afar, extremely significant. The girl's face would twist into a sob or awaken with a smile or fill with mischief, and Günter would navigate their exchange until the face once again filled with contentment.

The guests conjectured that this was Rivka Abramowitz, the daughter of Sarah, mistress of the estate. They watched her with deference even as she shamelessly skipped among their parcels, dug through their belongings, and pried into their destinations. They were preoccupied with fear and exhaustion and rumors of murderous incidents occurring along their travel routes, and did not imagine that Rivka was using their answers to hide an array of hedgehogs and tortoises and worms and flowers and fruit and weeds in their bags, so that the flora and fauna of her estate would be spread throughout the country.

Rivka Abramowitz's love of animals inspired Günter to build her a little zoo on the estate. Its main residents were a confused fox with a missing leg, two ever-trembling hedgehogs, a songbird with a broken beak, and a one-winged crow. Rivka found all of these on her walks with Günter, and the two agreed that there was no choice but to gather up the miserable creatures and take them to the zoo, where they would be adorned with the necessary bandages and splints. She employed an exacting precision beyond her age in her care for these animals, even though sometimes, with childish weakness, she forgot to feed one of them, and Günter would hurriedly do her work. Günter also did his best to feed Rivka herself whenever he could, and would dance around her with fruits or bread or sweets, hoping to cajole them into her mouth.

When he reported his successes to Sarah Abramowitz, she would sigh. "How do you not tire of it?"

Almost every day the sounds of fighting cut through the estate—Rivka and Sarah in one of their arguments. Their voices would rise, take flight, and eventually reach Abramowitz's ears. If Günter did not show up to make peace and Abramowitz sensed the fight would not die down of its own accord, he himself had to gingerly approach, support one side or the other, and eventually volunteer a solution, which was invariably to take Rivka for a ride on his horse. With one motion he would sweep her up and sit her on the saddle in front of him, place his hand on her little stomach, and gallop off.

More than once Rivka joined him on his longer journeys too, a fact Günter found intolerable.

"Take guards with you," he admonished.

"Do not go far," he begged.

Abramowitz would turn up with Rivka at business meetings, on visits to his Bedouin and Circassian friends, and even on his tours through the weapons factories he was secretly setting up. Adding her own character to the meetings, Rivka would finger the moustaches and beards of Abramowitz's friends, appease angered adversaries with her laughing face, or put on a girlishly polite expression and pinch Chaim under the table. Abramowitz did not always have the power to overcome her, and at the end of their journeys together he would have to face Sarah and shamefully admit, "She stained her dresses. Both of them." Or, "She did not eat a thing. Only tasted spices in the market." And once, "She got away from me in Petach Tikva. I found her an hour later sitting with a circle of women in mourning."

When Rivka was five she disappeared from the estate. She left on her own one day and marched on her little feet to the Arab villages to the east, to find herself some friends of her own age. After a few hours, by which time a panicked search party had been dispatched, she was brought home by some villagers. Rivka took her punishment courageously, defended herself against all of Sarah's castigations, and burst into tears when Sarah herself wept. But the next morning the success of her excursion was apparent: in groups of three or four, the village children emerged along the estate borders, their questioning eyes staring at the gate, waiting silently for it to open and signal that they were allowed to go and play with Rivka. A few months later, when the 1936 riots erupted, Rivka found playmates to amuse herself among the children of the travelers seeking shelter in the estate.

Only with Günter did Rivka choose to show her genial self. The two could be spotted around the estate, he limping and she skipping, engrossed in one another like a pair of doves, examining their discoveries together, sitting down for storytelling or singing. As soon as Rivka appeared before Günter's eyes in the morning, his heart grew anxious and his worrying drove all his actions until evening time, when he would read her stories, insisting to Sarah Abramowitz that it was no trouble at all. When night fell he sung her lullabies in a distant language.

"You're a natural father," people said admiringly, and Günter filled with embarrassment. He let the guests examine fabric ducklings that felt like hardened whipped cream to the touch, or glass tractors that could fit in a child's hand, produced in his laboratories, and he boasted of his method of molding toys for little Rivka—an endeavor that did not befit his declared propensity for pure theory, for hard science without any practical application. Yet he found that it lifted his spirits more than anything else.

Chapter seven

The Sanatorium 1971

> *"The natural landscape of Eretz Yisrael is: depth of sky, brightness, clarity and clouds of purity."*
> *(A.D. Gordon)*

Every two weeks, with no acceptable pretext for cancellation, Yehezkel Klein made the tedious journey on three buses to visit Genia's brother Romek in the institution. In winter he worried that snow might swiftly cover the Jerusalem hills and prevent the last bus home from leaving. In summer he wore his glum expression for a whole day before the trip: by the time he gets there he's practically passed out, the journey is hot and disagreeable, in any case the doctors say there's no hope for improvement, Romek's soul is shattered, and what does he need these trips for? His back aches for two days after every visit. But Genia begged him, "Go." The young nurses at the sanatorium pestered him too, flocking to him the moment he arrived, as if no other visitors had stepped off the bus with him. They would surround him in an overbearing group to inform him of improvements in Romek's condition, demand that he see them, that he notice them. They would tug at his arm and lead him to Romek's bed—See, here is the improvement—and not let go until they wrested from him an enthusiastic nod of agreement.

The head nurse would soon scatter her staff, scolding loudly, and take hold of Yehezkel's arm with her own pincer-like hand. "But you know, of course, this is his condition…" Then she would spur the giggling nurses on to their work and lean over Romek as he lay in bed. "Truly, there is no hope."

There was a smile on her face, and no malice. Rather, she displayed the candor of an experienced worker. Yehezkel looked at her hands and saw healthy resolve. Her uniform hung impeccably on her body, and she projected a majestic appeal. The institution she directed impressed Yehezkel too, bright and shiny as it was, surrounded by woods. He sometimes found it hard to go home. Since Shmuel had gone off to boarding school and it was just Genia and him at home, the apartment seemed oddly less spacious, more stifling. But here in this house of the wretched, there were great expanses for everyone, huge windows, clean beds.

Still, all the traveling was a nuisance to Yehezkel. Why him? He had never even liked Romek, had not even wished him well. True, he had not intended anything like this misery, but why every fortnight? Through heat waves. Through cold spells. It was exhausting.

He came with plastic bags. One contained Genia's dishes, although Romek ate nothing except the occasional spoonful of the institution's insipid food, fed to him by the nurses. The other bag, which accompanied Yehezkel there and back, held crumpled photos of Genia's family, salvaged from the devastation.

The nurses prodded Yehezkel. "Show him the pictures, tell him, point to people he liked."

Yehezkel obeyed. And for what? Romek's face was impervious, with only the occasional twitch passing through like a cavalry in the mist.

The nurses were undeterred. "His condition improves every time you visit. You must come more often."

But what would he do there? Romek did not recognize the pictures. Only rarely did a thin sound erupt from his mouth, a frightened syllable like an animal's cry.

The nurses urged Yehezkel, jabbing their fingers at him. "Talk to him. Don't give up. With your help he will get better, stronger."

But what did Yehezkel have to say to Romek? What did they have in common? He evaded the issue with some inconsequential chatter. Genia. Shmuel. Tidbits of news from the Suez Canal. Sometimes he experimented with news from his own world: "I've started going to synagogue a little. No, I haven't become a believer, but it's near the apartment…Sometimes, to pray…" Or, "I raised Shmuel to stay out of trouble, but now he's away at boarding school…" And, "*Nu*, children bring happiness…"

The nurses persisted. They spied on him from behind the curtain and peeped into the room. "Why don't you talk to him? Talk!"

But what would he talk about? Yehezkel was not a man of speeches. Hard-pressed, he explained to the nurses, "There are personages who give speeches. Ze'ev Jabotinsky, once appeared in our village when I was a youth, and then the skies parted and fire raged—"

"The skies parted?" repeated the nurses joyfully. "Fire raged?" Yehezkel was a true orator!

"Not I. That was what the newsletter said," he whispered. "They wrote in the papers about Jabotinsky's visit to our village, and there was a photograph, and my father, wearing a brimmed hat, was just beyond the corner of the photograph."

The nurses enthused. "Tell him about your village, about your childhood."

"Is that of any consequence?" Yehezkel asked dubiously.

"Yes, yes," the choir urged him, and left Yehezkel alone with Romek. What could he tell him?

But it happened that the spirit moved him, and he began to talk. About the street by his house. The little village square. Mr. Schliesl's barbershop, which smelled like vinegar. And soon Yehezkel was making his trips to the institution in the hills of Jerusalem to talk about his childhood. Summer. Winter. Three buses. He was determined, talking and talking and talking and talking.

One day the nurses ran to him when he arrived. "A miracle! He woke up! He woke up!"

They encircled him, crushed him, as if at any moment they might pick him up by his arms and legs like a cockroach. Genia's brother was sitting up in bed. He did not look quite human, but his expression revealed a change, even his impious smirk had almost returned. He was not quite awake, and appeared to be looking beyond Yehezkel at a distant horizon. But the nurses were overjoyed. "He is awake and speaking, not at this very moment, but speaking, and thanks to you, thanks to you!"

"Thanks to me?"

"Well, who else? Who else visits him? Only you!"

Yehezkel cast about. "There is that benefactress, the lady... Rivka Abramowitz...Such a shame, I never manage to see her. Perhaps it is thanks to her?"

"No, no," the nurses bubbled, "thanks to you, thanks to you." They continued to chatter until the head nurse arrived and sent them away.

"Mr. Klein, I am deeply impressed," she said.

Yehezkel felt weak, as if his knees might buckle. What was all this honor for? The room felt stuffy, he had not yet recovered from his journey. His throat was phlegmy, heavy, dry. A glass of water would help.

"What exactly did you do?" asked the head nurse admiringly. Her strong features and polished appearance drew Yehezkel's gaze even more than usual.

"Nothing..."

"And yet?"

"I talked," Yehezkel said softly.

"You talked? If everyone in here could be helped by mere talk, well...What did you talk about?"

"Jabotinsky."

"Jabotinsky?"

"The greatest man of our generation," Yehezkel said, squirming.

"Oh..." said the head nurse, disappointed.

Yehezkel could tell, as he always could, that she did not belong to his political camp. She was with them. The majority. The system. And what of this well-kept institution? These funds? She was not from his camp. He could not overcome the sudden urge to cry out,

"I am still a follower of Jabotinsky! And I always will be!" So that the nurse would know. So that there would be no doubt.

She nodded, a gentle smile on her lips, and did not mock him at all.

Yehezkel explained fervently. "I am still a follower of Jabotinsky, but in the school of Katznelson. Not your Katznelson, Berl, but our Katznelson, Yosef, who was known as the Black Prince. He also died, but there are no streets named after him. The Black Prince, he was called! A hero! He called for liberty! Better a dead lion than a living dog!" Yehezkel sat down silently on a chair in the corner of the room, as if the head nurse had asked him to.

"Better a dead lion than a living dog," the head nurse repeated, as though she wished to memorize the saying. Yehezkel thought he could hear the musical voice of Katznelson the Prince in the room. A voice of flames, a sword of fire, blood-flushed spears, hot coals glowing in the heart…

It was a pity they did not belong to the same camp.

Once every two weeks the head nurse would appear at the front gate to welcome Yehezkel ceremoniously and walk by his side to Romek's room. Every time he visited she tried to draw him into an intimate conversation. She no longer wished to talk about innovative rehabilitation techniques, but about herself. She was a widow, more emotional than one would have guessed, and she related bits of gossip better left unsaid, about doctors and staff members and nurses, embellishing all the characters Yehezkel had come to know, even the lowliest of them, even that skinny redhead nurse who gave the impression of being nothing but a frightened girl.

Yehezkel was barely able to extricate himself from the head nurse's whispered colloquies. Sitting down by Romek's bed to talk with him, he found his own topics of conversation more fluid. "I, with women, I was always tempestuous yet decent. But you…all sorts of women, even the wife of a minister, while he was hard at work for us all…" He wiped away a strand of saliva from Romek's lips, fell silent for a moment, and then his anger burst forth again. "You did not have even the slightest bit of stateliness!"

Yehezkel felt sad. He thought about Genia, about how they had met. The basement at 6 Broock Street. He turned to Romek again. There were many things to say, he had only to arrange them in his mind. In truth, this brother had helped them out, and now they were thinking of treating him with electric shocks, so unpleasant. Without him, *nu*, things might have been difficult…dangerous. To be ill now, of all times, when things were good in the country. He had lived to see the Six-Day War in good health. He had witnessed victory, the greatest victory ever. If only the illness would leave him he would get along quite well. People just like him were getting rich on all sorts of deals now. *Nu*, that was the way of the world. There were people, and there were people. But Yehezkel, his whole life had been difficult. Genia too, things were not easy for her, but a person needed happiness. Yehezkel could complain, but he did not. After all—what a country! What victories! His father in his little store, so afraid of the drunken *goyim*—would he have believed this? That the Temple Mount would be ours? And Sinai? And Bethlehem? And Hebron, the City of David? How could he have guessed that his son, Yehezkel, would live to see not only a state, but a victorious state. There was nothing to complain about. Now there was a war of attrition, and our forces at the Canal were striking the enemy every night…every night…and Yehezkel was so angry at what they had done to him that he took barely any part in the affairs of his own state. But how fortunate that the Six-Day War had occurred—it had opened his eyes. He had said to Shmuel when he went away to the Air Force's technical school, "You must study well, at least about the wars of Israel, because in the army they'll want you to know about the victories." A good boy, Shmuel, but he took an interest in unimportant things. He liked to play with fire. Electronics. Perhaps it was not only the boy's fault. Indeed, others were also to blame a little.

Yehezkel kept up his visits to Romek. There was still a long way to full recovery, if that was even possible. Romek started to walk and mumble, and some degree of logic began to echo through his speech. Not language, not meaningful words, but a hurried, nervous chatter that spewed from his lips like the patter of raindrops on a rooftop. Yehezkel listened, detecting a few phonemes, syllables, words and names within the torrent.

Once Yehezkel arrived moments before a big storm began. The rain lowered a screen over the buildings and lawns. The head nurse invited him into her private room, where they sat drinking hot tea. The raindrops banged and banged on the windows.

"And Romek?" Yehezkel asked.

"What about Romek?"

"Well, I came to see him…"

"He is well, and you will see him soon."

They sat and talked. Suddenly a man appeared in the room.

"Hello, Gutkin," said the head nurse demurely.

This Gutkin seemed not to notice Yehezkel. He walked up to the nurse, soaking wet and expressionless, and clumsily handed her an envelope. Yehezkel trembled. Did he know this Gutkin? He felt he knew him and yet he did not. No, he had clearly never seen this peculiar man before. How could he have? Impossible. But a noose tightened around his neck. Who was this Gutkin? His face was handsome, there was no denying that, but it bore a pained, indifferent look. No, he did not know him!

After Gutkin had delivered the envelope, he seemed exhausted by the effort. Breathless and bewildered, he turned to the door.

"Thank you very much, Gutkin." The head nurse rose to see him off.

Gutkin walked slowly out of the room with his back to them.

Yehezkel stroked his neck. Was it possible that he knew the man after all?

The nurse explained. "That was handsome Gutkin, a wonderful man. For seven years he planned to assassinate the Russian dictator Stalin, but then Stalin died on him."

Assassinate? The dictator? Yehezkel shifted in his chair. He imagined a shot. But it was not Stalin, rather Greenhaus, his friend… for some reason, it was Greenhaus…Then another shot rang out. The

Chief of Staff. Yehezkel felt his strength coming back to him. He shook himself off and asked for a glass of water. He was quite certain he had never seen this man before. And yet...

Next, the nurse amazed Yehezkel by saying, "Now he is Rivka Abramowitz's head foreman. Her most senior confidant. And why she herself has not come for two months? Who can say."

Yehezkel peered at the path down which Gutkin had disappeared. It was spotted with mud and glistening puddles. The head foreman of the benefactress Abramowitz? Something choked him again—he had seen the man somewhere. Indeed he had. But how could such a man be on the Abramowitz Estate?

The nurse sipped her tea. "*Nu*, sometimes she comes here and shuts herself up in a room for three days. As if we're running a hotel. But with the donations she gives, everything is allowed."

Yehezkel felt compelled to keep listening.

The nurse continued. "What does she do in the room for three days? Who knows...*Nu*, never mind. The main thing is, when she arrives she is sad, and when she leaves there is a smile in her eyes. And she has patience for everyone. She leaves a donation and goes back to the estate. One day I will retire from my work and perhaps they'll take me in there. A good, quiet place. Heaven." The nurse put her two swollen feet up on the chair opposite Yehezkel and sighed.

On Independence Day in 1970, because of a disrupted bus schedule, Yehezkel spent an entire day with Genia's brother. And he heard a complete sentence. It erupted from Romek's lips in a stifled whisper into Yehezkel's neck: "I was a soldier in Chaim Abramowitz's Testament Army."

Then confused chatter and shortness of breath.

Yehezkel buried the words in his heart. Testament Army— what did it mean? This sort of utterance was best kept secret like an underground note, where it could do no harm, to be delivered when there was someone to deliver it to. He could not understand how he always missed Rivka Abramowitz's visits. Once they tell him he missed her by two days, once by a day, and other times they tell him—practically mocking—that she had just left.

"Perhaps the odds would improve if you came here a little more often," suggested the head nurse.

One day she smiled and asked, "Mr. Klein, are you the one who is always asking about the benefactress, Rivka Abramowitz?"

Yehezkel tensed. It was nothing more than curiosity, he explained.

The head nurse continued. "I will introduce you to her. Why not? You deserve it. But today, if you'd like, her bodyguard has come to deliver a package."

"Her bodyguard?"

"After everything he's been through, Chaim Abramowitz would not allow anything to happen to Rivka. When she travels, she always has a bodyguard. And not just anyone, a stalwart like Bar-Kochba. Lerer is his name."

Yehezkel longed to see this mighty Bar-Kochba, and the sympathetic nurse took him by the elbow as if half of him were already a patient of hers and only the other half were still a visitor. She led him to one of the large windows. Outside on the lawn stood the bodyguard, looking bored. He was a short man, getting along in age, slightly square in his physical proportions, with graying-white hair.

"That is the bodyguard?"

The head nurse was disappointed with his disappointment. "His name is Lerer, Stefano Lerer, and believe me, Chaim Abramowitz would not entrust Rivka to anyone who could not guarantee her safety. You have surely heard about Chaim Abramowitz?"

What could Yehezkel say? That indeed he had? That Genia's brother mumbled nonsensical things, like, "I was a soldier in Chaim Abramowitz's Testament Army"? Should he divulge the secret? Hoping to entrap her into disclosing some information, he asked, "What is it about him, this Abramowitz?"

The nurse withdrew. "Believe me, I have stories, but I have no time."

"No time…"

"Chaim Abramowitz boycotts Zionism. He has a huge estate, in the heart of the country. A great master!"

"Boycotts Zionism?"

"But his wife does not. She did not join his boycott."

"His wife did not join…"

"But who has time to stand around talking?"

"Just tell me, does he have an army?"

"An army? How could he have an army?"

She let go of Yehezkel, and only then did he notice that she'd been clutching his elbow all this time. Her steps were vigorous, manly, but her bottom swayed as she walked down the corridor and there was no ugliness at all in her gait.

Yehezkel turned away out of respect, and looked back at the bodyguard. He did not look like any Yehoshua Bin-Nun or red-headed young Absalom. Unenthusiastically, Yehezkel went to see Genia's brother.

Romek, even in the days of his recovery, remained an inde-cipherable creature. Sometimes he stood and walked and spoke in complete sentences, even mentioned Genia by name, as well as some-one named Avigail, and other times he withdrew, indulging himself once again in his comatose state, rendering Yehezkel's accomplish-ment imperceptible.

But why should Yehezkel care? Let Romek sleep, let him sleep his punishment out. Yehezkel had done all he could for Romek. Stefano Lerer, the bodyguard, was now the one taking Yehezkel on a voyage of thoughts. What went on there, in the estate? Who were its residents? And what could one man, this Lerer, do against aggressors? True, it was well known that in faraway Japan they learned lethal com-bat methods, and a single warrior could defeat five or six men, and once Yehezkel even saw proof of this in a movie he snuck into. But this Stefano Lerer, what was he? And why did the masterful Chaim Abramowitz need a man like Genia's brother? And who were these people who served Abramowitz—were they the best of the best, or the lowest of the low?

The head nurse reappeared and took hold of his elbow again. "Come, let us drink some tea in my room."

In her room, Yehezkel asked her about the Abramowitz Estate again.

"Heaven," the head nurse said, "heaven."

Yehezkel sighed. "If I could only set my son up in a place like that, I would be able to close my eyes."

The nurse perked up. "It's a shame to talk like that, Mr. Klein. You are so young, and you make such a favorable impression on us all here. But this son, does he know how to do anything? If you'd like, I could talk to some people I happen to know there…I have a few connections."

"He fixes electrical appliances. Almost as well as I do. No, better. The best!"

"How old is the boy?"

"Sixteen now, thank God, and he's in boarding school. The Air Force Technical School. He insisted. Genia wept, but it did no good. *Nu*, soon he'll be a soldier."

The nurse's gaze cooled. "What does he study there, at the technical school?"

"He's in the helicopter course."

"Helicopters? I'm not sure…They only take excellent people at the Abramowitz Estate."

Yehezkel sighed. "He's a good boy, my son. Quiet, polite."

The little room was silent. Yehezkel went on. "Ever since childhood, he's always liked fire. Lighting it, watching it. Genia used to get so angry, but it was no good. He likes fire, the poor boy. But at the Abramowitz Estate, if they take him, he won't make any trouble. He could fix any electrical appliance, and if they need him to, he can teach them how to light fire with electronics. Remotely. He has all sorts of inventions, my boy."

The head nurse said cruelly, "No, they won't take him. Why would they? A boy who plays with fire? If they need an electronics expert they can get the best money can buy. They have plenty of money there. This envelope that Gutkin delivered contains a large sum, but for them it's nothing. Whatever Abramowitz needs, he buys. Including some things he doesn't need…Look at the generosity in this place, every year they give." Her face tightened. "If you ask me? Spendthrifts. They waste and waste. Too much."

Yehezkel Klein never saw Rivka Abramowitz. He was tempted to ask the head nurse to inform him by telegram of the benefactress's scheduled visits—she had told him explicitly to ask her for whatever he wanted, anything at all. But he found it difficult to justify such a request. What if the head nurse asked why he needed to meet her? The more he labored over inventing a compelling reason for the meeting, the more his imagination began to conjure up a threatening encounter with the bodyguard, Stefano Lerer. He envisioned Lerer interrogating him with his frozen look: "Why did you ask about Rivka Abramowitz's schedule?" Then Lerer demonstrates combat methods like Yehezkel saw in the movies. "This is what will happen to anyone who takes an interest in Rivka Abramowitz's whereabouts!"

Yehezkel saw Lerer only one more time. He saw Lev Gutkin, who had planned for seven years to assassinate Stalin, twice more. But never Rivka.

One of his visits led to a partly serendipitous incident. "You, Mr. Klein, are always lucky," announced the head nurse as he was about to leave. "Bonhoeffer was just visiting here and he's driving down to the coast. Instead of taking the bus, you can get a ride with him."

"Thank you, I will pay for the trip," Yehezkel said proudly.

"He won't accept it. Bonhoeffer is a righteous man, you will see. But they tell stories about him…" She shook her head and refused to gossip any further.

Yehezkel was led to the driveway outside the storage area and introduced to Bonhoeffer, a wild-looking religious Jew wearing a short jacket he could barely zip up over his stomach.

"I'm headed to Ness Ziona," Bonhoeffer shouted gleefully at Yehezkel, and ushered him into an old brown cargo van. Moving his whole body, he grasped the steering wheel, sharply reversed the truck, and with his free hand suddenly gave a tremendous whack on the partition between the driver's cabin and the cargo area. "No pee-pee in the truck!!" he shouted, reminding whomever was back there of the rules, and jerked the vehicle out of reverse. They were soon on the road and engaged in conversation. Bonhoeffer took a great interest in the number of rooms in Yehezkel's apartment, for some reason.

Yehezkel asked evasively, "Why do you want to know?"

"Because sometimes a person has a spare room in their house, and that is worse for the heart than loneliness is. Because sometimes an empty room pierces the happiness in a house."

"And let us say a man has an empty room, what would he do with it?"

"He would give shelter to someone who has no roof over his head and can help out with odd jobs. A day or two. Two or three. If you have such a wound that needs healing, I can find you someone who will agree to stay in your room."

"No…No, I have no…In the room…Shmuel… No rooms."

As Bonhoeffer drove, he kept a broad field of vision. All the edges of the road were visible to him, and at every bend in the road, the truck's nose dipped down.

Yehezkel was uneasy.

"Pressure in the ears?" Bonhoeffer enquired. He sat up straighter in his seat to apply the full weight of his body to the gas.

Objects rattled in the back. Yehezkel turned around to look. Three old sailboat masts stuck out of the cargo area. Yehezkel thought they looked liked the war memorial on the way to Jerusalem.

Bonhoeffer was only too happy to explain his successful business to his new audience. "The masts back there, they were on boats that sailed the seven seas, and now they're going to Ness Ziona, to the industrial zone. There's a good man over there, he has a factory that makes Popsicle sticks, and he said he'd consider buying the masts. He'll use them to make the wooden part that you hold in your hand, the backbone of the whole Popsicle." Then Bonhoeffer cheerfully revealed the rest of his scheme. "I have Leonid here with me. He's having a little trouble now, nowhere to live, and he will help me carry the masts. We'll work hard, so everyone will see how useful Leonid is, and then I finish my work and leave, and Leonid stays—I mean, they're not going to throw him out, are they?"

But they did throw him out, and the next day Leonid was offered to a *moshav*, reinforced with a Betar Jerusalem T-shirt. But for now Yehezkel was impressed with Bonhoeffer's wisdom, and hoped there was also a wisdom of driving, for at every turn in the road he grew more desperately anxious—the wheels were not supposed to hug

the side of the road quite so closely, and although it might be appropriate to ignore one or two traffic signs, this driver observed none.

As they approached the coast, Bonhoeffer made one more
attempt to find out if Yehezkel would like to give temporary housing
to a homeless man who could do any odd job. Then he gave up and
asked about Yehezkel's connection with the sanatorium, and about his
childhood, and how he made a living. "The pressure in your ears will
go away now," Bonhoeffer promised. He reached out with the hand
that had been holding the steering wheel and pulled out a bottle of
orange-colored liquor from the depths of his seat. He wrestled with
the cork, defeated it with a cheer, took a swig and offered it to Yehezkel,
chuckling. Yehezkel politely refused. From behind came the sound of
urgent tapping on the partition. "None for you!" Bonhoeffer roared.
He corked the bottle and shoved it back into its hiding place.

"I also have here in the back a cargo of unkosher *etrogs*. After
Ness Ziona I'm going to find out in Jaffa what they'll give me for
them. These are the finest and purest unkosher *etrogs*! After that,
before it gets dark, I have one more trip: at the Abramowitz Estate
they want me to take a couple of guys away. They've given me the
final warning."

The Abramowitz Estate! Yehezkel's blood froze. Could he ask
to stay in the truck? They would sell the masts, and the *etrogs*, and
then, Yehezkel Klein at the estate…the Abramowitz Estate…But
what would Genia say? She would worry. Yehezkel shrank back in
his seat.

"And what am I going to do with those two? At the estate they've
been saying for a month already that the two-day probation is over,
and they're not satisfied with them, not with the blind one and not
with the amputee. No choice, I'll have to take them. But what will I
do with them? Would your honor be so kind as to remind me how
many spare rooms are in your home?"

Yehezkel shirked the matter of the empty rooms. He was confused and frightened by this whole trip, and the Abramowitz Estate.
Still, perhaps he would hear something of interest. But Bonhoeffer
sailed on down the coastal road and said nothing more. Only once
in a while he thumped the truck partition violently to ward off any

unruly behavior. Miraculously, he knew the way to Yehezkel's house, as if someone had given him the address.

Yehezkel wobbled out of the truck. He thanked Bonhoeffer profusely but he felt afraid of him, for some reason. He walked away from the truck with its masts and slowly climbed the stairs to his apartment.

In the evening there was an unseasonable thunderstorm. Yehezkel sat by the window. The sky was lit up with massive bolts of lightning, and in the distance an estate flickered, a heaven, with guards posted above the walls and a great iron gate slowly swinging open. But the gate led nowhere, revealing only darkness.

As Yehezkel stared at the lightning, a figure hovered before his eyes. It was none other than the master of the estate, Abramowitz, like a huge cloud hanging above the walls. The sky was set ablaze with a bolt of lightning, and Yehezkel, frightened, went inside and put the kettle on.

Chapter eight

Stefano Lerer, the
Italian Bar-Kochba   1948

When Stefano Lerer left the battlefield, not a single living enemy remained. He spoke Hebrew slowly, in a dry Italian accent. "Now you," he would say to the injured men as they lay twitching, and he would start slashing with a knife or strangling with a white shoelace.

Now you.

Only then would his silver-haired figure slowly detach from the battlefield with his men behind him, watched in frightened silence by their partners in victory, men from the Palmach or the Etzel or the Chish.

"Call us!" Lerer would shout back at the men whose job was to act now, after the win, constrained by political and military considerations and subject to the headquarters' commands.

Always call us.

Then the silvery hair of Stefano Lerer and his people would

melt away into the woods down the wadi paths, disappearing into the landscape of strawberry and carob trees, terebinths and white poplars.

"They left," the fighters would murmur. Through their exhaustion, they would begin to digest the horrors of the battle with a deep sense of gratitude to Lerer's people—for coming, and for leaving.

*

Stefano Lerer was a survivor of Bergen-Belsen, the only remaining member of the thirty-strong Lerer family of Rome. Two years after his liberation from the camp he still roamed through Europe seeking revenge against the Germans, the Croatians, and the Italians who collaborated. He used knives, shoelaces, barrels of water. After killing two policemen in Florence he fled to Palestine. There he tried to join the Etzel, the Hagana and the Palmach, but was thrown out of them all because he scared people with his fierceness, his persistent whispers about vengeance, and his never-ceasing threats against anyone who tried to rein him in. He continued to fight alone, joining the ranks of Palmach fighters in mid-battle, when no questions were asked, disappearing when the fight was over. He would often assign himself missions and storm enemy posts on his own. His one and only desire was to kill the enemies of the Jews in Palestine.

From time to time the organizations tried to appoint a liaison, some brave Palmach officer who would keep Lerer in check as he operated on the margin of military frameworks. But Lerer would find the liaison's home, and in front of his wife and children, demand assignments. He would frighten the officers and their families, and one after the other refused to continue handling him.

Lerer slowly built up a gang of like-minded silver-haired Holocaust survivors. They loved to be sent to any fiery battle, any stubborn enemy outpost, ambushed path, or deadly road trap. Anyone who dropped out of the standard battalions, anyone who felt he was wasting his time sitting around merry campfires, found his way to Lerer. Together they lived in the fields, traversing battlefields, seldom understanding the Hebrew spoken over the walkie-talkies, but appearing anywhere they were needed.

Although they were feared, their arrival was always welcomed. People tried in vain to forbid them from murdering hostages and liquidating injured enemy soldiers. "Only the dead are dead," Lerer would say, and they would fall silent at the sight of his figure and his ever-present knife. They would look away as his men searched the bushes for injured enemies, crouching down among rocks, tall grasses, wells—the tiny hiding places of the battlefield. "I've only just begun," Lerer would say, and kneel down holding his shoelace. For him, there were not enough battles, not enough opportunities to subjugate the enemies of the Jews. The War of Independence ambled on during the pauses between flare-ups, subject to economic constraints and the need to conserve resources, obtain arms and promote political processes. The Jewish *Yishuv* sighed and counted its victims, gathered strength, but Lerer wanted more. More battles.

"I was a chemist once," he told his men, laughing, "at the technical institute in Rome, and I had a good life."

His men laughed with him and told stories in their own languages about former professions. About families. They had lived good lives too.

One day a very short Jew turned up in their gang. He was pale and toothless, and he followed Lerer's every step, lurking like a shadow wherever he went. No one could remember where and when he had appeared, but they were suspicious. Where had he come from? They claimed he was born from Lerer himself, ripped out of his shadow. The man said his name was Mendel, and after gradually creating his own history, he pronounced his mission: to closely document and glorify Lerer's deeds. "They write histories of the Palmach, of the underground, yet no one writes about the Italian Bar-Kochba. Don't worry! I will make sure the heritage of Lerer is not forgotten!"

But one shadeless midday hour, a bullet found its way into Mendel's skull, and in his belongings they found nothing but a few poems, some political slogans decrying an activist named Tennenwasser, and the name "Lerer" scribbled thousands of times on three rolls of paper.

Where were Mendel's writings? the men wondered. For at the end of every battle he had walked among the tired fighters badgering them with lengthy questions. He had found an interpreter for every mute fighter and loudly lamented the men who had been lost, and with them, their perspectives. But as the days wore on, there were fewer men left to wonder.

The Palmach liaison officer tried to calm Lerer and put a stop to the actions that cost his soldiers' blood. When the officer denied him pistols and rifles and machine guns and hand grenades and mortars, Lerer and his gang robbed the storehouses, got into fistfights with the Jewish organization men, and threatened to shoot anyone who stood in their way. Sooner or later all his men were killed, but they were always replenished by the constant stream arriving from Europe. Each new man stood ready to revenge, to attack, to die.

Lerer himself was never injured. He reported constant headaches, aching bones and a burning body, but claimed to feel neither ill nor weak. His only desire was for more missions, so that not a night would go by idly on the starlit field.

"I've only just begun," he said repeatedly.

After seventy-eight men and women from Hadassah Hospital and the Hebrew University were slaughtered on their way to Mount Scopus, Lerer was summoned to the Palmach headquarters for an urgent meeting. The room was swathed with Israeli flags and pictures of Herzl. There were Bibles on the table. Lerer was asked to concentrate his forces on securing the convoys to besieged Jerusalem. Nothing else. He promised to take revenge upon anyone who ambushed the convoys. Among the flags and the pictures of Herzl he set forth his doctrine: "A man who stays alive without taking vengeance is deader than the dead."

Operation "Nachshon" was at its height. It was followed by Operation "Harel." Lerer and his army integrated obediently among the Palmach fighters, sometimes inside the armored vehicles climbing in frosty fear up to the city, sometimes attacking enemy posts in the woods, among the rocks, on the inclines, anywhere the Arabs lay in wait. On May fourteenth, the day the State of Israel was declared, Lerer was sitting next to the bodies of two Arab snipers in a vineyard near Beit Makhsir. After hearing news of the declaration, he went to see the liaison officer to ask for a special mission, one with many enemies. He made his way through the crowds of people stamping their feet on the streets in celebration and found the officer.

"A mission," Lerer said.

"Today we are celebrating, Lerer. Celebrating! We have a state, a state! Tomorrow we'll go back to battle."

Lerer grunted angrily. He looked at the people dancing, in danger of forgetting that their nation was being slaughtered, that there was still revenge, that they could not fade away into civic life. Soon they would decide it was time for peace and they would lay down their weapons, but he had not yet avenged so much as his father's little fingernail, not even touched his mother's murderers and the murderers of his cousin Laura. What celebration? What was there to celebrate?

His bones begged for more action. More revenge. He went off to rove the Jerusalem hills and did not rest until he found snipers preparing an ambush on the roadside. After killing them, he continued to wander alone, walking like a messiah until he reached Jerusalem on foot. It was late afternoon, a time of quiet terror, and as he walked in a daze along the road he met no enemies or friends. On the outskirts of the city, in an area usually peppered with troops and ambushes, a supply convoy passed him on its way to break through the siege. It looked remarkably different than the fire-soaked convoys he himself had managed to lead to Jerusalem. These were comfortable black vehicles transporting unruffled men who sat like sleepy tourists.

Once he entered Jerusalem, he found the vehicles parked calmly in one of the Jewish neighborhoods. They did not seem to have drawn any fire. He looked carefully at the unarmored luxury cars and went up to the man who seemed to be in charge of unloading the cargo. When he enquired about the convoy's identity he met with impudent replies. The overseer skipped among the vehicles scolding his workers sharply, granting Lerer little attention. "This is Chaim Abramowitz's convoy," was all he said in answer to every question. Eventually he spat out an impatient explanation: "No one shoots at an Abramowitz convoy." This was a slap in the face of Lerer's own perforated armored vehicles. He gradually gleaned some information from a few indifferent Jerusalemites who had gathered. They casually explained that

Chaim Abramowitz was a great tradesman who had agreements with all sides—the Palmach, the British, the Arab gangs, the Jordanian legion—to transfer select goods and people unharmed. All, of course, greased by rivers of bribery and handsome profits.

"For example, if Kahenman, one of the wealthiest men around, has a liver condition, and needs to see Dr. Balk, the well-known physician from Tel Aviv, they will either bring the besieged to the doctor or the doctor to the besieged," members of the crowd explained to Lerer nonchalantly, showing barely any interest, as if they were not the hungry and thirsty people waiting for Lerer's convoy to break through the siege so they could put food in their children's mouths.

Lerer wanted to wave his knife around, to take revenge, to restore the dignity of his fellow fighters, but he felt weak in the knees. He was tired, very tired. His feet hurt, and something, a certain sorrow, spread inside him and flooded his body. He sat limply for a while on a low stone wall. Then he stood before the convoy supervisor. "I want to see this Abramowitz of yours."

Between jumping and shouting, the supervisor found time to respond. "Abramowitz sees whomever Abramowitz wants to see. Why should he see you?"

Lerer pulled a gun from his belt and held it to the man's forehead. "Is this a good enough reason?"

"I think not," sighed the man.

The two men stood motionless for some time, considering their positions. Furrows of worry began to appear around the barrel of the gun on the supervisor's forehead. "Why don't you offer a reason?" he suggested. "Something Abramowitz might want to see you for."

Lerer put the gun back in his belt. He longed to sit down. He legs were shaking. He wanted a bed, a soft bed, like the one he used to have in his family's holiday villa in Ravello. "Where does Abramowitz live?" he asked.

Many days later, on a muggy summer afternoon, Lerer knocked on the heavy wooden doors set into the gates of the Abramowitz Estate. The guards beat him and sent him on his way. After he came back and knocked again, and was beaten again, they told him the master of the estate was away, that he was concerned with nothing but finding his missing brother, Lolek.

Lerer waited for Abramowitz. For three days and three nights he lay in the muddy weeds outside the gates. The guards took pity on him and offered him food, but Lerer refused. He drank water from the puddles. One of the guards thought he even hunted a rabbit.

On the third day, Abramowitz arrived on horseback. Lerer was granted a roadside interview. He stood next to the horse and introduced himself to the rider.

"What will you do for me?" asked Abramowitz.

"I know how to kill the enemies of Israel, and I used to be a chemist," replied Lerer.

"We kill the enemies of Israel ourselves," said Abramowitz, "but a chemist is important. And what will you want from me?"

Lerer's face tensed. "I want you to take me back."

"Take you back?"

"To what I once was, to everything…" His skin tone was grey, his eyelids were drooping.

Abramowitz looked down at him and summed up the terms of the bargain. "Don't kill any enemies of Israel without my permission."

Lerer was put on chicken-coop duty. The report from his first day was that he worked diligently and vigorously. Once or twice his nerves had to be calmed, and some of the slower chickens had to be protected, but there seemed to be no serious problems. But on the second day, when Lerer was left alone for a few moments, he got into a one-sided fight with the man they called "Psalms", whom he beat mercilessly and threw out of the coop, thrashing him with a rake.

"I am allowed to choose the egg on which I will paint the entire Book of Psalms," claimed Psalms in a trial held before the head foreman, Günter.

"He came in and started touching all the eggs, to see if he could steal them," Lerer countered.

"I told him who I was!" announced Psalms, fingering the rake-marks on his waist and shoulders.

"I couldn't understand what he was saying. He was making fun of me for being new in Israel."

"He's a Yemenite Jew. That's his accent," Harkin pointed out.

"But Günter is also a Yemenite, and him I understand."

They explained to Lerer that Psalms had an eastern Yemenite accent, and he was allowed to choose an egg every day for his biblical illustrations, to be presented as gifts to national dignitaries or sold to American Jews for a lot of money.

Lerer waved his hands in the air. "Enemies of Israel won't steal any eggs on my watch!" he roared, and was permanently barred from the coop.

Abramowitz announced that he would take Lerer under his wing, and promised to give him what he had asked for. "I will take you back."

Every day he called for Lerer, and the Italian would arrive with a bowed head and walk with Abramowitz through the fields or in the heart of the estate. The two men appeared to be conversing. Sometimes Lerer would clutch an old photograph, point and explain and talk, and sometimes he silently held his white shoelace or his knife.

During work hours Lerer was assigned to one of the trade assistants, Alkalai, to work as a porter, which calmed the body and the soul. After a short while Alkalai came to Günter and reported that the new laborer was an extremely talented bookkeeper: he could balance the accounts and reconcile long columns of numbers. When he was sent to put a stack of papers up on a high shelf, he noticed a few calculation errors as he climbed up the ladder. His notes were found to be correct, and he was allowed to look at some more papers. From then on he demonstrated a rare knack for mathematics.

"Yes, I used to put together reports in the technical institute. Numbers are easy," Lerer explained.

"You can be an accountant here," Abramowitz informed him after Günter looked into the story and found it worthy of the master's attention.

Lerer joined the other accountants and was soon put in charge of them. Günter supervised his work, and promoted him up the ranks until eventually he crowned Lerer a senior partner in managing the entire estate, except for the chicken coop area. As an act of friendship he also invited Lerer to talk about chemistry a little, and discovered that his knowledge was good, although not inspirational, and that he was able to contribute some very practical suggestions regarding measurements and weighing.

"Help me improve my experiments!" Günter said excitedly.

Lerer agreed. He took part in Günter's new trials and helped to remedy errors that had thwarted previous research. But he did not share in Gunter's enthusiasm. "I never liked chemistry," he said dryly. "When I was young I went to study chemistry in Turin because I wanted to be close to cousin Laura."

Anyone observing Lerer in those days would have found a stooped Italian Jew ambling from one task to the next. On Friday evenings he would ask for permission to cook, and if Abramowitz allowed it, he would produce Roman pasta dishes from the pots and pans. But most days Lerer kept to himself, carving on the walls of his room with a small red pen-knife.

The wildness inside him still longed to burst forth, and Abramowitz continuously observed Lerer out of the corner of his eye. Before he left on his travels, Abramowitz would invite Lerer to see him. He would scrutinize him, and if he feared Lerer's soul might ignite while he was absent, he would take him along. Once, when Abramowitz was attacked by an Arab gang near Rehovot, the dragon fire came out of Lerer and seared two of the assailants, causing the entire gang to scatter in terror. One bullet hit Lerer's hand, and while Abramowitz carried him to safety, Lerer looked embarrassedly at his wound, unsure of how it had appeared or where the shreds of human flesh under his fingernails had come from.

Abramowitz decided to appoint Lerer as his personal body-guard. Together they set off on journeys, appearing at every meeting or visit in tandem. When Abramowitz visited his weapons factories, which had operated covertly during the Mandate and now sold rifles, bullets and grenades to the IDF, Lerer would stare at the products with a frozen, alien look. What did he have to do with guns? What did he have to do with battles? He would sigh tediously and wait for Abramowitz to finish his visit so he could sit with Günter again in the evening, help manage the estate or join in one of the scientific experiments that made Günter so happy.

Rivka, who tended not to associate with the estate people, took an interest in Lerer, curious about his subdued nature. Abramowitz forbade her to be alone with Lerer, but Rivka would sneak away from the guards and instruct Lerer to accompany her on walks through the fields surrounding the estate. There in the lap of nature, she convinced him to draw honey for her from the wild beehives and pull prickly pears from the thorny branches. She would sink her teeth into the fruit, spit out the peel and seeds, and dig the flesh out with her fingers. While she did so, she questioned Lerer and listened raptly to his answers.

In those days she was already eighteen, with dark black hair and an elusive color to her eyes. When she walked around the estate people stared at her, following her young body and supple movements. Only Lerer looked at her as if behind his eyes there was no thinking mind. His gaze focused on the ground, the air, or a puddle, but whenever she asked him a question he looked up at her and answered generously, at length, as if replying to himself as well.

Günter   1934

When Günter turned seventeen he was a married father of one who cleaned latrines for a living, and his name was still Yeshaya Tarhomi.

He was born in Kinneret, a small Yemenite *moshava* on the shores of Lake Tiberias, before the Yemenites were expelled and moved to Rehovot. When he was five, Yeshaya twisted his foot in a ditch and it never healed. His limp drew mockery rather than compassion, and his happiest moments were spent alone. He used to steal the few holy books his father had brought from Yemen and study them, following neither the customary prayer times nor the books' narrative order. He loved every sentence, but found it distasteful to hear people intone the texts loudly on the holidays as their own prayers.

It was after the Kinneret Yemenites were removed to Marmorek, a newly developed neighborhood in Rehovot, that Günter's father died of malaria. To provide a roof over her children's heads, his mother married a man who took her as his second wife. This husband beat her and her sons whenever the opportunity arose, and he hit Yeshaya, the oldest son, more than all the others. During one such beating, Yeshaya's healthy foot was broken, and it never healed either, producing the gait he referred to as "my second limp."

At sixteen Yeshaya Tarhomi was married off to a widow one year older than him, and five months later they were thrilled to give birth to their first son. They uprooted to Tel Aviv, where Yeshaya rode a cart through latrines and refuse heaps, making his living by cleaning the country and contributing to sanitation for all. His supervisor, an elderly Bedouin man, used to whip him and fine him at his whim. The other workers pestered him with questions—How are your children? What is Kinneret like? We hear it is beautiful. Yeshaya Tarhomi distanced himself from them, gazing up at the sun and the sky far beyond the trash cans and the latrines, marking the passing of time, the days that slowly crawled from Yeshaya Tarhomi's mornings to Yeshaya Tarhomi's nights.

Many times after work he found himself walking to the home in which his mother was trapped by her new husband. He never dared to enter. He would wait in the dark, tensing when the door opened, his heart leaping hopefully when a shadowy figure emerged, but before the shadow materialized he would be stricken with terror by his stepfather and flee on both limping legs.

At home the widow would great him with, "We are hungry, and you, where have you been?"

"*Nigofi*," he would mutter at her, "*Nigofi…*"

May the plague be upon you…

In between his tedious hours at work and his hateful hours at home, he would think. About what? He could not explain. At night he was repeatedly visited by a dream that sometimes reared its head in daytime too. It was not a heroic dream but a silent vision of a dark, warm, mysterious place. A storehouse of sorts. And in the storehouse were thousands of books glowing like clusters of stars, their spines lined up close together like chickens crowded into a coop. No one read the books, as though the world around them had been obliterated and they were abandoned, longing for a reader. Yeshaya Tarhomi saw rows of long shelves in his dream, stretching into the darkness like rays of sun, weighed down with books that filled them all the way to the shadowy end. Though he wore himself out reflecting on the image, he could find no logic to it. Especially perplexing was the burning sense of nostalgia that permeated the dream. Nostalgia for what? He knew not.

Once while he was working, Günter's pitchfork speared a written page that called, in Hebrew letters, upon Jews to settle in a land that was all beauty and glory, an Eden for the faithful, a merciful mother for the laboring. He eagerly studied the beautiful words of the manifesto until he realized that it was speaking of *Eretz Yisrael*—the place he was already in.

The Bedouin fined him for dawdling, but worse than the fine was the disappointment, which stayed with him even at night, as he lay beside his whimpering baby. He almost cried. He so wanted to go to that land, which took mercy on its workers, but he was already in it—where could he go?

His furious wife cursed him—he had not even brought home a penny's worth of pay, and the baby needed to eat.

"*Nigofi*," he whispered, "*nigofi*."

Since the day of their marriage, Yeshaya had rarely come to his wife in bed, and he blamed himself, only himself, for not having the urge to take her. A second son was born to them, and a year later a third. Yeshaya concluded that his wife was secretly finding herself other impregnators, but instead of being angry he thanked her silently for not disgracing him in public, preferring to bring him shame modestly, as a decent woman should.

One day he found a pile of books discarded outside a shop. He loaded them onto the garbage removal cart and climbed up. As he rode, he perused one of the books, and it was as though a hand reached out from the depths and pulled him on, drowning him in the book until its very last page, spurring him on to read the second book, and the third, goading him to protect the books when the cart arrived at the refuse pit. In return for one day's pay, he took the donkey and moved the books to his family room. He sealed his ears against his wife's sobs, did not explain where his pay had gone or where space would be found in the tiny room for his books, and proceeded to sit rocking over *Hydraulics for Engineers* until the sun rose.

From that day on, Günter found books everywhere. Like a

leech he sucked them from every possible place. He wandered down sidewalks, roamed courtyards, reached into trash cans—his old acquaintances—and almost every day he was fortunate enough to bring home a book or two, the fruits of his labor. In his searches he passed by windows and gazed into cozy, warm homes serenely lined with bookshelves that filled him with lust and nostalgia. At nights he continued to dream of the storehouse filled with thousands of shining books.

As the days went by, his home—a shack built of brick and tin—filled up with a vast treasure of books. He guarded them closely, and did not allow his wife or sons to harm or even touch them. Returning from a hard day's work, he would glance at the room and know if a book had been removed or a cover creased. Until sleep fell upon him, he sat reading in a corner, and at dawn he jumped up to his books, averting his gaze from his wife and children sleeping curled up upon one another. "As for me, is there sweetness in my life?" he would ask bitterly, before escaping to the street. "Perhaps today I will find many handsome books," came the reassuring answer within moments.

One day, in a courtyard of tall weeds, he found five books in a little heap. But more than the books, he was drawn to a cast-iron frying pan that lay there appearing brand new. He happily picked it up, and in the evening he gave it to his wife. "They gave me this, a gift in appreciation of my good work." His wife reached out as if to hug him, took the frying pan, polished it meticulously and placed it proudly on the bookshelf. When she came to him that night he did not resist. In the morning he looked at her and felt sorry, but what could he do?

The more books he gathered, the more his limbs were seized by an exhausting hunger, and the same dream of thousands of books glowing in the storehouse tortured his hopes. More and more books, more and more knowledge, that was his desire. But how would he build his shrine out of the miserable findings among bushes and fences? None of the books he found informed him that there were public libraries in the world, that there was even one in his own town. When he limped beneath the balconies of this very library and found *Cotton Fertilizers* next to a potted plant, even then he did not imagine there was a place where he would be welcomed, allowed to study books, even valued for his erudition.

From the books he learned about hydroelectric theory, modern poetry, and the adventures of robbers. He learned torts law, military tactics for Jewish commanders, advanced algebra, bridge-construction methods, motor engineering, vegetable gardening, the foundations of electrical physics, and guidelines for managing institutional kitchens. But these did not sate his hunger. For the books hinted at other books, sometimes referencing them by name so that curious readers could peruse them. But where would Yeshaya Tarhomi find these books? It seemed to him that the learned authors were addressing learned readers, that every sentence concealed a tone of kinship with the well-informed, with professionals, not with uncredentialed yet studious men born in Kinneret.

He handled the books lovingly, mending their tears and treating their stains, and although after just one reading he remembered every character forever and no longer needed it, each book was awarded its place on the shelf. It did not occur to Yeshaya Tarhomi how unique his skill was, how rare it was for a person to engrave in his mind, without missing a single note, every conversation he had ever heard since childhood.

Once, as he walked down the street with his work tools, he saw through an open window a man walking calmly from his armchair to a bookshelf, scanning his books with satisfaction, plucking one from the shelf and walking softly back to his armchair. Günter's body burst into tears. They had killed his father with hard work and malaria and he had not lived to see his dreams come true, and now they were killing his eldest son, Yeshaya—killing him.

Yeshaya did not go home that night. He broke through the window into that apartment and sat on the floor until sunrise, quiet as a mouse, reading books by the dim candlelight. That year, while his own leaking house shuddered every time the wind blew, his wife's tears had dried up and his sons went hungry, he broke into houses all over town, read their books and left. When he was finally caught he tried to escape; he might have overcome his first limp, but the second limp was his downfall.

Fortune shone upon Yeshaya Tarhomi in jail. The warden, a tough British man who was usually merciless, recognized the advantages of having an assistant with a flawless memory, and he struck a bargain with the new inmate. Yeshaya held all the affairs of the jail in his memory, documented and updated every detail of the inventory, holidays, verdicts, punishments, fines, procedural reviews and amendments, and produced them for the warden upon request, without delay and without error. In return, the warden made each of the prisoners teach Yeshaya Tarhomi his native language—Arabic, Greek, Turkish, English, Italian and Russian—and ordered them to provide Yeshaya with as many books as they could. In addition, one corner of the prison kitchen was declared a scientific area for the exclusive use of the prisoner Yeshaya Tarhomi.

Yeshaya, usually a quiet prisoner, broke into raucous shouts only when he was informed that he was free to go, in the midst of biological experiments and halfway to understanding the process of metal oxidization. His ally the warden suggested a variety of petty crimes that would extend his prison stay, but when Yeshaya studied the law books he discovered that before returning to the prison kitchen he would have to go through an arrest, a trial, and a lengthy wait for the verdict. This was unfeasible considering the attention his experiments demanded.

Having no choice, he went home. He walked in through the front door, scanned his books and the cast-iron frying pan, still gleaming and polished in its place of honor, glanced at his wife and declared one corner of the house a scientific laboratory. His wife, whose sentences had by now turned to mumbles, barely protested. *"Al rijal jimal, al rijal jimal,"* she hissed, and condensed herself into an even smaller living space. Besides, she was already involved in binding relationships with two or three men from nearby neighborhoods, from whom she was to bring more children into Yeshaya Tarhomi's home.

Yeshaya Tarhomi lost no time. His release from prison had ripped a great hole through his progress, and he dedicated the new days to his tempest of science. He unwittingly imitated Galileo's experiments, labored on reconstructing Henry Cavendish's research with his modest means, and although a year went by before he found the periodic table in an introductory textbook, he was nonetheless able to draw important conclusions about states of matter, and he created the nucleus of a definition of molecular weight. He was acquainted with both pre-Galoisian and post-Galoisian mathematics, although he had never sampled the theories of the wonderful mathematician himself. He was also troubled by a gap of a few centuries between the discoveries of Carl Friedrich Gauss and the modern works of Issai Schur and Fekete, since he did not happen to come across any books that dealt with that interim period. He was further tormented by his wife's grumbles: "The children are hungry, *sirgu alaik*, the house is empty, and you with your Cavendish."

By that time the extent of Günter's knowledge in certain scientific fields would have enabled him to pass the examinations for advanced degrees, but he still turned up daily for his work in the latrines, "conquering cleanliness," as his work was described by a party man who came to speak to the Jewish latrine workers. This man urged them to unionize, to strengthen the workers' status and to strike immediately, if possible. He praised their work as a link in the nation's challenges, after "conquering labor" and "conquering land."

Günter's world changed shortly before Passover of 1934, when he dug through a pile of pharmacological books in a garbage bin opposite a pharmacy. The pharmacist, in a pressed white coat bearing the name tag "Günter Horace, Head Pharmacist," came out and offered to pay Yeshaya to clean his basement. They reached an agreement, and the pharmacist was so pleased that he hastily offered to employ Yeshaya regularly as his general assistant, doing everything he appeared able to do: cleaning, hauling, odd jobs.

After a week Yeshaya suggested to the pharmacist that he sleep in his basement at nights.

"What for?"

"To keep away the mice."

"I have no mice," the pharmacist declared.

With great pains Yeshaya gnawed at some of the books with his own teeth, and when this made no impression on his superior, he trapped three mice, released them in the basement and waited patiently for the shouts—Mice! Mice! Yeshaya, come and catch them!

In the pharmacy basement Yeshaya lived a life of glamour, utterly enslaved to happiness, excitement and hope. In the dark at night he conducted vital experiments, read through Günter Horace's library of medical books, and closed the gaps in his chemical education. In the mornings he scrubbed the floors, dusted the shelves, washed the pharmacy tools, and hurried here and there to do anything the owner asked. He did not mind, as long as his luck kept shining.

One morning the pharmacist complained of a headache and went to take a nap in the back room. He asked Yeshaya to keep watch and call him if a customer came in. Yeshaya Tarhomi stood behind the counter and the devil drove him to put on the pharmacist's white coat. He straightened the name tag and stood waiting for customers. A few minutes later the bell over the front door rang, and one of the town's most important ladies came in seeking advice and some ointment.

"Yes, Madam," Yeshaya addressed her in his cloak.

The lady glared at his white-coated figure, at his face and at his stature, and promptly issued a loud shriek. Terror had demolished all her manners, and her shouting awakened Günter Horace and alerted worried citizens who came rushing in from the street and the nearby stores. The lady shuddered, her lips trembled, and with the last of her strength she pointed at the black man in the white coat.

The pharmacist was shocked. The townspeople surrounded Yeshaya silently, trying to assess the threat. One moment Yeshaya Tarhomi did not know what to do, and the next a scream erupted from his own lips. He took his first limp, and his second, and burst out of the pharmacy flinging the doors wide open, his coattails flying in all directions, his throat filled with fear, shame, and a hard rock of sorrow. He ran through the streets all the way to the ocean, faltered and fell in the sand, got up and continued to run, limps and all, far, faraway. In the midst of this uproar, in one sudden thrust, he passed out.

Many hours later, he slowly began to regain consciousness.

"Günter, Günter, awaken!"

When he opened his eyes he was back in a world where everything was as hateful and painful as it had been, apart from the blue-eyed woman looking down at him with a kindly face and whispering. She had a wild scent, myrrh and frankincense, the smell of a herd of horses.

"Come, Günter," she whispered.

So be it. "Günter" he would be.

The woman stood up with him in her arms and hoisted him onto her horse. "I will take you with me, Günter," she whispered, and broke into a gallop across the sand. The world spun around—equations, Cavendish, Avogadro's number, Cauchy's hypotheses, Euclid's proofs, the smell of Yemen. He passed out again, but this time as Günter, forevermore Günter, and he descended comfortably into the abyss, embraced and contented in the Lilith arms of Yemen, and his name would be Günter, and that was how it would be, there was no more Yeshaya Tarhomi, he was lost forever.

Sarah Abramowitz brought Günter to the estate and placed him, frightened, at the feet of her husband, a large man with terrible eyes, a Samuel, a King Solomon, a Nebuchadnezzar.

"Who are you?" asked he with the terrible eyes.

"I am Günter," Günter replied with a bow.

They allowed Günter to rove freely for a few days without any duties, and he walked the estate like one of the geese and ducks and chickens in the yard. Eventually they asked what he was able to do for a living. They quickly skipped over the matter of the latrines and soon discovered his miraculous memory, the towering mountain dozing within him.

Within two weeks Günter had at his disposal a gorgeous library and a budget to purchase new books. Every day, workers from the estate knocked on his door when they returned from their business in the cities and villages, bearing books they had found on their travels and thought might be useful. Alongside the library, Chaim Abramowitz encouraged Günter to set up a little laboratory where he could work—perhaps he would be able to develop an inexpensive bomb, or find a substitute for coffee or tar. But Günter's successes tended to slip away from the practical. Even when the skies above the estate blushed once or twice when the lab caught on fire and Günter emerged drenched in materials, he would simply declare another theoretical discovery.

Günter's most palpable use stemmed from his memory. Every detail to do with the management of the estate and its business affairs was trapped between his ears, never to be lost.

"You really remember everything," people remarked in awe.

The days went by, and Günter grew to become part of the estate's flesh and blood, a focal point for all the activities and demands and records and reports. He was declared "Head Foreman of the Estate," and as he sat in his room every day, reviewing his new title, he was satisfied with himself and his fate. People seemed impressed by what he found so easy, and they even paid him, and enriched his library, and besides Abramowitz and his horse-riding wife, Sarah, there was also the little girl Rivka, whom he found so charming. He derived great pleasure from the encounter with her tender wisdom, from the sweet wickedness of her mischief, and from the ease with which she accepted a world entirely dedicated to fulfilling her wishes. "Günter, Günter!" she would call out, and he would happily run to her.

From time to time Sarah Abramowitz helped Günter up onto her horse and they set off for a wild ride through the fields. Terror and fear. Nights and twilights. Clinging to the back of a Russian Lilith whose forefathers grew up along the terrible Dnieper river, but her scents awakened his nostalgia, and her braided hair danced like a snake before his eyes. Sarah showed him the country, the lands of Abramowitz, the dreams of the giant. She took an interest in Günter's own dreams, his family, his plans. Sometimes she made him turn away and gravely swear to keep his eyes shut, and she skinny-dipped in a pool or a river, giggling, skipping, then stepping onto land, dressing, modest once again, her body still glistening under her clothes.

One day she told him he could bring his family to the estate. Günter was excited, but it was not his wife and children he wished to bring. He went to his mother's house in Marmorek and encountered his stepfather, who saw nothing different in Günter than what he had seen when he was Yeshaya Tarhomi. He mocked Günter's limps and drove him away shamefaced.

Günter returned to the estate and told Chaim and Sarah about the humiliating expulsion. When he next visited Marmorek, he brought an entourage of thirty horsemen. The stepfather peered out of the window, then out of the front door, then out of the back door, and in a burst of generosity invited Günter into the house and slipped away to a hiding place. Günter announced to his mother that he had come to take her away, but she protested. "This is where I live!" she cried, and warded off Günter's embrace with both arms.

Günter was taken back home, limply draped over a horse. He wanted to forget, to forcefully forget his mother. He tried to train his soul, to thrash every awakening ember of memory—being carried on her back to the shores of the Kinneret, kisses on the back of his neck, the smells of her baking—and he could not forget.

He never saw his wife again either. During "Operation Magic Carpet," which brought the Jews of Yemen to Israel, his wife gathered up all her children, took the cast-iron frying pan, and in utter contradiction to the operation's Zionist intent, took off in a plane and disappeared forever into the city of Aden.

*

By 1948 Günter had been a citizen of the estate for some twelve years. When he was taken in, Chaim Abramowitz was surrounded by a few dozen loyal citizens, and his business was in an embryonic state. By 1948 the Abramowitz Estate was serviced by hundreds, and Abramowitz was as wealthy as a king. Nowhere but in Günter's memory was there a carefully organized array of all the details and the labor and the jobs and the divisions of responsibility in the estate.

Every evening, Günter, the head foreman, would sit on his bed caressing his first limp and his second limp and warming his heart. "For I have done well, I have done well in life," he would say to himself. But a coal-sack of sadness weighed on him. Many times he used his new powers to urge Abramowitz to help the Yemenites living in Israel, the settlers in the Ben-Zion neighborhood of Netanya, the struggling immigrants in Hadera and its environs, the Yemenites in the Galilee and the Yemenites in Jerusalem and the Yemenites in the southern *moshavim*. On his travels with Abramowitz, Günter visited every community and every city, gave speeches to his Yemenite brothers, collected books, solicited donations. Sometimes he saw himself as a leader of the Yemenites—not like the politicians who were multiplying unchecked, but a great leader, distinguished, neither elected nor deposed. A great rabbi of sorts, or a Caesar. But for some reason it was Abramowitz around whom the people gathered, always happy to see him. When they knocked at the doors of the estate to ask for something, they appeared before Günter first, and it was he who determined who would be allowed in and who would be removed. But it was Abramowitz they wished to speak with; Günter was not even close to being their Caesar.

In the spring of 1948, with the War of Independence still raging and Günter reciting weapon improvement methods from memory to the Hagana engineers, dictating from Czech books he had read in 1934 on how to handle field mortars, explaining how to dismantle land mines with Russian techniques from a 1940 military guidebook, he suddenly unraveled his old recurrent dream of the storehouse with the thousands of glowing books crowded like chickens in a coop: in the abandoned Hebrew University of Jerusalem on besieged Mount Scopus there must be a forgotten warehouse with a multitude of books. That was where the treasure was buried, the secret diagram leading to the cure for Günter's nostalgia.

It was the only time in all his days on the Abramowitz Estate that he hid anything from Abramowitz and Sarah. Risking his invaluable mind, the sole archive of all of Abramowitz's business, he set off on a dangerous trek to the site. He easily slipped in among the diminishing ranks of volunteers trying to get to Jerusalem in an armored vehicle convoy, and just as easily found himself caught in enemy fire—a few infernal moments that ended not with death but with one injury, suffered by Günter. The bullet in his leg was the beginning of his "third limp." Hampered by his old limps and the emerging new one, he rolled out of the armored vehicle and his head hit the road. The entire convoy was caught in a battle of attrition until they were finally able to get Günter back into the vehicle and retreat.

He was returned unconscious to the estate, where Sarah tended to him and did not allow anyone else to touch him, and in her arms he awoke. At first he smelled the river, the Dnieper, then horses, then her neck. Günter smiled, opened his eyes and looked into the blue of Sarah's eyes. He was gripped by a corporal excitement, an erection that could not be concealed.

"Close your eyes, Günter, rest now," Sarah said and kissed him.

He fell asleep and spent a whole day and night fluttering in a world filled with darkness, and when he awoke he did not know that he had forgotten something. He had forgotten—just like a regular person might—the moment when he awoke in Sarah's arms and wanted to sleep with her.

Günter went back to his work on the estate. He slowly grew accustomed to his new body. First, his dynasty of limps—from the founding limp, inflicted at the age of five, through the third one, from the bullet. The three limps fought bitterly over the crown, and with every changing season a different one prevailed, dictating the style of his gait, until its turn came to fall behind. But more complicated and difficult than the conflict among his limps were his erections. He was surprised by this new emergence of his body, the flare of his loins that tortured and whispered beneath his skin and tried to break free with a tormented cheer. The body led the mind, and Günter began secretly collecting unscientific books in which men lay over women, and women lay over men, and there were kisses and passions, and everything was forbidden and everything was permitted.

He did not dream about Sarah and he did not look at her. He forgot their horse rides together and forgot about her bathing in the water as he stood with his back to her, his eyes closed as promised, and he forgot the saddening time when he might have briefly opened his eyes just a fraction, an eyelash-wide crack, and perhaps he saw but perhaps he did not see the magnificence of her body, her golden sanctuary, and perhaps he immediately shut his eyes tight, or perhaps he fluttered them one more time, and a tear hid the magnificent scene.

Chaim Abramowitz did not admonish Günter for his recklessness on the way to Jerusalem. When he sat at his devoted foreman's bedside, an idea came to him: if people wanted to go to besieged Jerusalem, why should they risk their lives? A monetary arrangement could be made to satisfy all parties.

He noticed Günter's erection and suggested that he take a wife. Günter vacillated, and agreed, and turned down proposals with various excuses, until he saw Ruth Mintz, a widow one year older than him. He wished to marry this golden-haired woman.

Abramowitz gave him a piece of land within the confines of the estate, and Günter built a house for Ruth.

"I will not bear you any children," Ruth warned Günter.

"It is all from above," he replied.

Besides, what did he need a family for? He had Chaim and Sarah and Rivka.

But his family soon grew in a surprising way. One of his sons took advantage of "Operation Magic Carpet," which on the Yemenite side was called "On Wings of Eagles," and returned to the State of Israel. The pilots remembered him—"the one who asked to come into the cockpit, to learn about the instruments"—and he was ingrained in the memories of all the people who helped him reach the Abramowitz Estate as a curious, inquisitive and endlessly diligent young man.

When he arrived at the estate he stood before his father.

Günter wondered if he should kiss his son. He hoped the son would initiate an embrace. They stood some distance apart from one another, smiling.

"You are seventeen years and thirteen days old," said Günter.

"And you, my father, are thirty-four and four months and two days old," replied the son.

They both stood and rocked slightly, two paces away from each other. Finally, the son leaned down to his bag and took out the cast-iron frying pan. "I brought this with me."

"What did your mother call you?" Günter asked excitedly.

"Shaul."

"Shaul Tarhomi, my son."

"Yes, but perhaps I could have a name too?" Shaul suggested.

"A name?"

"Hans, I was thinking," said Hans.

Chapter ten

A Little Black Bra   1977

I*"Man is miserable, but at times he is also wonderful"*
(Yosef Chaim Brenner)

n the beginning, after his army service, Shmuel joined the staff
of guides at the Museum of Prehistoric Man.

Since he was never able to convince the children that the prehistoric mannequins' fishing and hunting exploits were authentic,
he eventually left the museum and went back to his despised occu-
pation, repairing electronics. But even in that line of work, which
offered better compensation, he was occasionally visited by moments
of anger from his former position, leading him to lash out at no one:
"Come on, children, really, that man is not trying to see the other
man's thingy—they're stalking a mammoth together, you can see its
tail end in the bushes. I mean, really..."

Not infrequently, when he was engrossed in the delicate repair
of an electrical appliance, his memory would draw him back into
an old argument: "The woman is not naked! It's prehistoric garb!
She is not naked!!!" The irritating recollection of giggling children
would crawl up into his throat, but his thoughts would soon settle
back on the appliance, far from the children and the annoyances of
the outside world.

Every morning Shmuel awoke with the knowledge that he

would have to spend his day meeting people he did not want to meet and answering questions he did not want to be asked. In the evening, when he came home from work, he would find a mailbox full of bills to be paid, and even when he closed his apartment door behind him, Fishman the neighbor could still knock on his door with some complaint about the residents' committee or the roof tarring, and that was how it would be every single day, forever, always something unpleasant cropping up, something insistent, every moment of quiet destined to be replaced by something else.

He lived alone in the apartment he had grown up in, and although his parents, Genia and Yehezkel, had died long ago, he maintained the apartment as if at any moment they might turn up at the door, put their suitcases down heavily, and his mother would complain, "My drapes are wrinkled."

He had the entire apartment at his disposal, but he restricted his living space to the room in which he had spent his childhood. He did not invade his parents' room, and spent barely any time in the living room, which was reserved for guests. He followed his late mother's rules in the kitchen too, being very careful with the gas stove, avoiding the little flame that crept up from the stovetop like a claw. He cleaned the apartment once a fortnight, moving the furniture aside so as not to miss any dirt. He swept and mopped and battled the dust, and finally hung all evidence of his efforts on the balcony—damp rags, a thick cloth and a thin cloth. From the height of the balcony he would examine the street below, the traffic of passersby, then go back inside to indulge in a cup of coffee and a large slice of cake.

On such evenings he also opened the box in the kitchen and took out all the documents and forms and bills that he had tossed inside without a glance over the past few days, closely examined every piece of paper, made a note of how to handle it and whether he would have to ask Kalman at the electronics store for advice, and updated his income and expenses in his mother's old notebook. He kept working on the columns of numbers until everything looked in order, and once again rewarded himself with a cup of coffee and some cake.

On weekends Shmuel usually preferred to be alone, but sometimes he felt a desire to go out, sensing there might be something interesting going on. He would walk to the ocean to watch the fishermen, or just wander the streets and look at people. Sometimes he stood across the street from his old school or walked down the lane near his house to the park with the sandbox and the slide where he had played as a child. Hava, his kindergarten teacher, had liked him. But in school he was always sent to the back row, because of his height, and told to sit near the wall, perhaps because of his width. At recess he used to closely monitor the children playing, but in the afternoons he was only allowed to go as far as the yard outside the apartment building, or accompany his mother on errands. Sometimes he took the bus with her to visit a sick friend.

On Saturday nights Shmuel sat on the balcony watching the freshly bathed people going out in couples, and sometimes he went out too, to the movies or to window-shop. He liked to look at window displays, even the ones at women's shoe shops, where occasionally a woman would stand beside him looking at the shoes and their reflections would appear very close. When he ran into an acquaintance he wished them a good week, answered their questions, and silently counted the seconds before he could continue his walk. He sometimes chose one of the shabbier cafés in the center of town to sit in, halfheartedly munching on a dry pastry, but despite his height and breadth, and his bearishness, the characters who frequented these cafés taunted him, and tried to pick fights, and then he would get up and hurry back to his apartment to sit on the balcony and look at the windows of the nearby houses and eat a piece of cake. There was nothing to be afraid of, he would tell himself, nothing to be afraid of. Why should he be afraid? His father had not been afraid when he was in the underground. Why be afraid?

Sometimes he sat in his apartment and imagined a fight in great detail. He would take a few punches from a couple of thugs and then find a way to defeat them, usually with a trick like an electronic device he had designed and which had been in his pocket all along. He spent several Saturday afternoons constructing these gadgets, some of which were very good for fights, and after testing their ability to produce an electrical shock or a surprising burn or a blinding flash, he dismantled them.

He took his father's old soldering iron with him to all his jobs, and used nothing else. He would often embed one of the components his father had left in his workshop into the devices he repaired, like little gifts, hidden tips for customers he was fond of—a conduction coil for a wide-eyed woman with a broken toaster, a tiny transmitter for a gentleman with a soft potbelly and a radio that needed rebuilding. But usually the clients disappointed him, and so did his co-workers, who at first always barraged him with troubling questions but soon left him alone. Shmuel longed to find a friend, of either sex, and every time he set off in search of a new job he looked through the nearby windows and half-open doors to see who his new neighbors would be. Sometimes he experienced a thrilling hope that wilted precisely as he began to feel comfortable in the new routine, one day following another, until soon he wanted to change jobs again.

He found work easily. Employers glanced at him and knew immediately that this was a man who would know how to work, would not ask for an outrageous salary, and would be as loyal as they wanted him to be. When he started to work and his new employers watched as he resuscitated stubborn appliances, complete duds, they would thank their lucky stars. They had always said, after all, that a good employee was half the business. And so they were always surprised when he announced he was leaving. They could not dissuade him with promises of higher pay or hints at future partnerships. Shmuel would get up and leave, eager to go, as if unburdening himself of a heavy weight. When he sat down on his chair in a new workplace his heart fluttered cheerfully, as if he had set fire to the old workplace and they were looking for him but now would never find him.

Every time he switched jobs he devised a new walking route. In the mornings he was careful to stick to the usual path, permitting himself no delays even if he was tempted by an interesting scene. But in the evenings he dragged himself off the route and wound along the side-streets, not wanting to go back to his apartment. He looked for little events, even a broken traffic light or a torn laundry line hanging down into the street like a banner of blouses and bras. Sometimes his principles seemed put to the test: one morning he saw a naked woman wrapped in a blanket while two paramedics held her and tried to subdue her crazed sobbing. Another time he saw a group of Arab workers huddled on a street corner, sick with fear, while a couple of very calm policemen leafed through their papers. Although he hurried on his way and put the incident out of his mind, he often recalled the scene, as if a certain accountability was somehow expected of him. Sometimes he found himself walking back to the street corner to scan the bare, uneventful spot, hoping to decipher something in the surprising silence, where everything else looked just as it had that day, the stop sign and the green balcony swelling out into the street from above. He would search without knowing what for, stop to think for a minute—perhaps he would listen to the news and that would give him some idea. But ever since his father had died the dial on the radio was locked on the BBC, and he was loathe to move it.

Every so often some piece of news did reach Shmuel. In 1976 he completed the repair of an Ampa radio with a green backlight and learned that an Israeli aircraft had been hijacked and diverted to Entebbe in Uganda. The event aroused something in him, but he was soon given a fan and two tape recorders to repair, and it was some time before his employer burst into the workshop and announced, "We rescued them! We rescued them!" They put on yarmulkes and laid *tefilin*. In 1977 Shmuel was fixing a modern Philips radio that informed him that there had been a political reversal: Menachem Begin would now be his prime minister. Shmuel knew the man from a speech he had heard a few months earlier on a Tadiran radio with a built-in cassette-tape player. And his father had mentioned him a few times, not unfavorably.

Near the end of that year he heard that the president of Egypt, Anwar Sadat, was coming to Israel on a visit. This news did not come from a radio but from Fishman the neighbor, who opened his door just as Shmuel walked by and, wearing barely more than a pair of pants and a yarmulke, declared, "Hello, Shmuel, peace is coming!" He tried to infect Shmuel with his excitement. "History! Sadat is coming to Israel!" Then he added a sad note: "Your father, may he rest in peace, will never see this reconciliation."

Shmuel got away from Fishman and went up to his apartment, annoyed. Why had Fishman brought up his father? Did it not occur to him that this was a peace his father would not have wanted? He calmed down a little once he was in his apartment. Why be angry? He sat down in the silent living room and thought about the green-eyed woman he had seen that day for the first time, a customer at the clothing shop next to his new workplace.

He thought about the pretty saleswoman in the drapery shop, whom he had discovered on his very first day.

He reflected on what Fishman had said.

Even in his father's isolationist years, when he had stuck to his vow and seen no one, he used to go downstairs to do odd jobs for Fishman. Perhaps Fishman did know what his father would have thought after all? Every time something broke in Fishman's apartment, Shmuel's father used to run down there as though Fishman's well-being and the integrity of his apartment were vital. Sometimes, when he had a backache, he sent Shmuel to do the repair, telling him to do whatever was necessary and not rush. Fishman would stand very close to Shmuel, watching him work, and sigh. "Your father will have his reward from above."

Still, what did Fishman know?

Shmuel had no rest from the monumental peace even when he went downstairs to take the trash out later that evening. He ran into his downstairs neighbor, Alma Almagor.

"Have you heard, Shmuel? Sadat is coming. There will be peace."

He had known Alma since they were children, but had never seen her emerge from her apartment looking like that, dressed sloppily and visibly excited.

Alma had always lived with her mother in the apartment beneath Shmuel's, until the mother died and Alma, like Shmuel, was left on her own. There had never been a father. They said he had betrayed the country, that he had left, that he had been killed on a national mission. Shmuel never played with Alma or even said a polite "hello" when she walked to her music lesson every afternoon. But one day, when he was ten years old and playing with fire in the yard, a little black bra fell down from the laundry line, covering his eyes before it dropped to his hands. He looked up at the rope shuddering in the wind, and among the mother's heavy bras he saw two more black ones, lightly swaying as if they also wished to come down to him. That night he shoved the bra into the secret hole in his mattress and could not fall asleep. Over the next few days he contemplated the bra as he sat in class, worried that his mother might find it or an angry Alma might demand it back. But he did not want to give it up, and when the opportunity arose he lit one of his secret fires in the yard and burned the bra, watching breathlessly as the flames consumed the fabric and it shrank before his eyes.

After that, he used to be gripped with terror every time he came across Alma. But he grew up, and she did too, and now they were both left to live alone in their apartments.

"To me this is the absolute fulfillment of Ben-Gurion's legacy," she said to him now in the stairwell.

"Yes," Shmuel replied weakly, rattling the trash can so that Alma would realize he had no time for small talk. This was no longer the Alma Almagor whose bra had fallen over his eyes. This was a different Alma, one who seemed to be playing the part of her pianist mother, thin and stiff as a statue.

"I'd like to invite you on Saturday night to watch Sadat's arrival on television with me," she said, clutching the neck of her blouse with a soft hand.

"Saturday night?" Shmuel said, alarmed.

"Yes, come over. It will be a day of excitement for every real Zionist."

Shmuel tensed. Why was she talking about real Zionists? Why did everyone keep saying that? In the Museum of Prehistoric Man, shortly before Shmuel left, a new director had arrived, and on his first day he had walked among the employees and questioned each one: "Are you a real Zionist?" Even before that, during his military service, Shmuel had been harassed by Sergeant Adika with the very same question. In some roundabout way the guys in the unit had picked up something about Shmuel's father and his political obstinacy, the vow he had taken to isolate himself from the state. Adika, flanked by Benzi Tirosh and Shimon Alfasi on either side, used the question as yet another way of abusing Shmuel. "Are you a real Zionist?" And now Alma Almagor.

Shmuel emptied the trash can thoroughly, went back upstairs and found that the question had followed him up.

What did Alma Almagor want of him?

He closed the apartment door behind him. In the bathroom he washed his hands well and began undressing.

Was he a real Zionist?

He had answered the museum director with a simple "yes," so as not to lose his job. But sometimes the director would meet Shmuel in the hallways, back him into a corner, and interrogate him: "If a Canaanite came to you now and said, Give us back our country, which you occupied from us during Yehoshua Bin-Nun's time, would you know what to say?"

On the new director's very first day, he convened the employees and said he wanted to tell them a little about himself. He then proceeded to spend an hour and fifteen minutes asserting his absolute faith in the doctrine of Yitzhak Tabenkin and insisting that Tabenkin's strain of Zionism had been wrongly abandoned in favor of an utter poverty of courage and an infirmity of spirit. Within a few days, Israeli flags began to appear up and down the museum corridors, and informative signs were hung over the displays:

"Prehistoric man stood on guard for his people, ready to defend his property and land against rampagers."

"Prehistoric man knew that the borders of his land would be defined by the plough."

Usually, when he was not busy conducting a surprise tour or ambushing an employee, the director sat in his office trying to raise funds for the institution. In the mornings, when the employees reached the museum gates, they found the light already on in the director's office and his silhouette talking on the phone with a potential donor. In the evenings, when they closed the gates and cleaned the chewing gum and other defacements off the mannequins, the light in his office was still on. It was not difficult to surmise that the new director had no home and was living in the museum. Then came rumors of his bachelorhood, of his origins in the Jezreel Valley, his long service in the artillery corps and his eventual dismissal, possibly in the wake of a fiasco in the Yom Kippur War.

The new director gradually retreated into the safety of his office. Only when groups of Arab children from nearby schools came to visit the museum would he leave the office and inform the staff that he would be touring the museum personally with these children. He would sit them at his feet, greet them with *"Ahalan wa-Sahalan,"* and explain, "We were here before you in the Land of Israel, and as we all know, you are here too. But before all of us, our state was inhabited by prehistoric man." Standing uselessly in the corner, Shmuel watched the attentive children, who seemed to acknowledge the director's authority. They stared at the prehistoric man lighting fire, never dreaming of any impudence or mischief.

Shortly before Shmuel left, the director commissioned a new sign for the museum: "The Museum of Prehistoric Zionist Man." When Shmuel resigned, partly because of the children and partly because of the director, he thought he would never again be bothered by anyone about being a "real Zionist."

And now, Alma Almagor. What did Alma Almagor want of him?

In the evening hours Shmuel's personality unfolded like a fan. A spirit of freedom would fill him, and it usually ended in a pampering hot bath. First he lathered his head with a heavy mound of Dramafon shampoo and allowed the foam to drop into the water in little peaks. With a misty look he gazed at the islands of foam as they floated heavily around, nodding their foreheads to one another and slowly uniting, and he followed his thoughts helplessly this way and that like an insect borne by a row of ants. Then he slowly surrendered to his thoughts and dozed off. His nostalgia for things he had never lost was so great that he almost passed out. He would take a bite out of an apple he had placed next to the bathtub ahead of time, close his eyes, and listen to the sounds that disturbed the silence of the bathroom.

Dull clinks from the neighbors' apartments.

Wind rustling.

A weak fluttering of something from outside.

Distant horns blowing, perhaps from the boats at sea.

The crumbs of the day would collect before his closed eyelids, little morsels of memory, scenes recovered. The water that touched the sides of the bathtub, which touched the walls of the building, connected him with all the neighbors and with the residents of the block and with the people in all the world. His thoughts touched on things he wanted, and some difficult things, and things he had to talk about with Kalman, urgent things, and little things, tiny things, which insisted on their place in his thoughts like the peeling plaster in the kitchen, which his mother had wanted to fix and which Shmuel looked at once in a while and knew he should repair but did not. Or old Herman from the shoe shop on Herzl Street, where they had bought Shmuel his first pair of shoes. Shmuel still bought all his shoes there, sandals in summer and boots in winter, twice a year. Herman always told Shmuel to sit down and knelt at his feet with a few samples, then he thought for a while, went back to the storage area, and reemerged with a new box and an old complaint: "You, Shmuel, with your size, should have had feet two sizes larger." In the bath, always, that sentence came back to Shmuel painfully. He would look at his feet, wanting to think about something else, about women—what did he care about old Herman?—and he would shut his eyes tight, tighter, anything to change the thoughts. Sometimes he managed, but usually another unimportant picture popped into his head, like the tab at Levi's corner store, which was the only place where Shmuel was not embarrassed to buy the things he really wanted. He liked to say, "Put it on the tab!" and watch Levi add the debt to the very same card he had kept for Shmuel's mother, Genia, whose paid debts still peered out at Shmuel from the card. Shmuel did not like it when Levi sighed and said, "What will happen in the end?" because he felt that Levi was referring to him—What will happen with you, Shmuel? When will you get married? He did not like to think about Levi in the bath, but Levi crept into his thoughts, like the others did, and sometimes, to stop it all, Shmuel opened his eyes and looked at his penis peeking up among the islands of foam, and with a grave expression he held it and examined it, allowing his eyes to close and new thoughts to roll in...

Each day his memory plucked one woman he had seen on the street for this hour, and she was where his thoughts would go.

Only rarely did Shmuel trouble real women with his passions. At the age of twelve, when he first experienced the great bodily thrill, he found a solution that required no partner, and proceeded to shut himself off in an efficient form of physical existence and indulge himself almost every day.

His custom was to weave a story with a plot that began far away from any women. But then something would happen and Shmuel would meet one of the women from the street. Although things would not immediately go as he wished, the woman would eventually be seduced and the inevitable would occur. He liked to go back to the same stories over and over again, with the same women, but his recollection of their appearances tended to quickly fade until not much remained, even of the most exciting ones, apart from a speckle in their eyes or the color of a boot. More convenient than the women he picked up off the street were women with whom he had a slight acquaintance, some he knew by name, and the most convenient of all were his neighbors. In the mornings, when he opened his door and walked down the steps to the ground floor, his soul slipped behind the apartment doors to look for women.

Right across the hall from his own apartment was Tami, who had a sign on her door announcing, "Tami and Oren Halfi live here happily." Her hair was a false shade of gold and the polish on her fingernails was chipped, but the lovely mounds of her breasts clamored to peek out of all her clothes, and they were honey-colored. Every morning when Shmuel passed her apartment, he removed Oren Halfi's existence from the world and imagined Tami knocking on his door. Some minor disaster had befallen her, and with fragile emotions she stood close to Shmuel, her volition waning, and in her weakened state she tempted him to enter her.

Beneath Tamar and Oren Halfi's apartment lived Noa the

dancer, alone. On his way downstairs every morning, outside her door, Shmuel constructed a story that rewarded him with the graces of her body. It was always she who opened the door abruptly and uttered a double entendre, and it was always Shmuel who was trapped submissively and disappeared with her into her chambers. Once, when he was a boy, an older dancer named Hemda had lived in the same apartment, and the neighbors had proclaimed her a wanton. Men and women would go into her apartment and leave at times well documented and grumbled about by Fishman. When Hemda got cancer, Noa began to appear in her apartment to care for her, and when she died Noa stayed in the apartment. The neighbors complained—there would be no peace and quiet with these people. But Noa lived silently, and if not for Shmuel's occasional sightings of her emptying the trash on a Saturday morning, wearing very short shorts and a sweater, it is doubtful whether he would have had enough of her body to feed his stairwell stories.

Across the way from Noa, directly beneath his own apartment, lived Alma Almagor. Like her mother, Alma was slowly becoming a grande dame who brought no joy to any fantasies, but through no fault of his own Shmuel found his thoughts turning to her sometimes, ever since the day she came to him wearing a warm-smelling robe and asked if he could help her hammer in a nail, hammer it deep in, on her apartment wall.

Shmuel agreed. And together, his heart beating, they did the job.

On the floor beside them lay the old nail that had failed, crooked and spotted with plaster, and on the table was a picture of two angels at the feet of a maiden, against a backdrop of bluish forests and streaks of mist.

The job took all of three minutes. Alma turned her hardened face to Shmuel, but he detected the scent of her pulsating body enveloped in a blue robe that hovered around her ankles and alighted to her neck. It all amounted to nothing, and even her thanks were given curtly, but Shmuel now possessed a new pasture for fantasies, and the scene in Alma Almagor's apartment developed from simple plots through acts of coitus, at first restrained and rigid, in the way of a grand lady and a lowly man, but finally wild and hedonistic, like the lovemaking of two gods.

On the floor beneath Alma was an empty apartment, where a man named Hezi had lived until recently. He had curly hair and did not say hello. Shmuel often heard women's voices coming from his apartment, and from time to time he even spotted the owners of the voices coming and going. They were giggling, light-footed, beautiful girls, who sometimes carried artists' portfolios and sometimes flute cases, and none of them ever wandered up to Shmuel's apartment or knocked on his door by mistake even once. Shmuel did not like Hezi, but his apartment was a vital port for the enrichment of his bathtime stories. When Hezi left one day, the apartment remained empty, as it had been before Hezi, after Mrs. Midovski had died.

On the first floor lived Mr. Bart, alone, and they said of him that he was once the lover of Edith Piaf. Curly-haired Hezi's apartment belonged to Mr. Bart, and since he owned two apartments in the building he felt he deserved special privileges, and argued with the other tenants over every little issue. In the world Mr. Bart was nothing at all, but in their building—a big deal.

Opposite Mr. Bart lived the Biedermans, past whose door Shmuel walked tranquilly. On the ground floor he would come across a door that said in heavy writing, "Fishman," and behind it lived the elderly Fishmans. Shmuel avoided that door, sometimes skipping three steps at once, but the door caught up with him once in a while, leading to a stubborn and extremely unpleasant fantasy in which it was Mrs. Fishman, of all people, who asked him in, and he agreed, and despite his aversion to her folds of old age, the most infuriating of all happened there, of all places—it was there that his lovemaking reached its climax.

In the entrance to the building, one step before the street, Shmuel would lose himself in the mailboxes—miniscule allusions to the large doors. In the top right corner was an old sticker that read "Genia and Yehezkel Klein," which Shmuel could not bring himself to remove even now, and every morning when he glanced at it he would lose all his passions and leave the building.

Not many times in his life did Shmuel actually sleep with a

woman. If fate looked upon him kindly and put a woman in his path who was ready and willing, Shmuel complicated her advances so much that the opportunity died down. With Tzilla, the most senior guide at the Museum of Prehistoric Man, the opportunities ebbed and flowed. Many times Shmuel was animated by his imagined intercourse with Tzilla, although she was crude and had a thick voice and was always dwelling on some dashed affair with a man who had left her in her youth, and the remnants of insult peppered her every sentence. Eventually, during the new director's tenure, Shmuel became involved in a tempestuous interlude with her, from which he could not extricate himself without intercourse.

The affair began, oddly, just when Shmuel was beginning to think that things at the museum were returning to their old quiet state, to the tranquil days before the new director's arrival. But one day an order came down the hallways and Shmuel was called into his office.

The new director spoke decisively: "I'm going away for three days to an international conference on mortars. I don't trust anyone, so you will replace me."

Shmuel felt a three-day long shadow hover over him. Why me? he wanted to ask. There were more senior employees than him, more talented, more suitable. He thought about Avner, about Yehoram, about Tzilla, her stomach, her breasts, her thighs.

"Best of luck," the director said, ending the conversation.

"What's the problem?" Tzilla said afterwards. "When he goes away we'll put up a sign saying the museum's closed. Who's going to know? We'll reschedule all the groups and we'll have a little break. Maybe you'll take me out for coffee at the shopping center."

Despite the absolute objection embodied in his racing pulse, Shmuel went along with the idea. When the director left, he and Tzilla hung up a "Closed" sign and Tzilla made the entire staff swear to keep the secret forever.

During those three days he slept with Tzilla six times, but not before being instructed to court her, take her out for coffee, then to a restaurant, buy her presents of jewelry and clothing, and then take her by storm, with her encouragement, with her excited words, her cursing, her begging for his big, huge body, her whispered pleas that he treat this fragile woman with mercy, no, without mercy, yes, with mercy, without mercy.

When Shmuel returned to his bathroom loneliness, he cupped himself with a sigh of relief and indulged himself in ways only he knew how. No woman could ever shock him with such pleasure.

When the director came back from his conference Shmuel was called to his room. "While I was at the conference I heard a rumor about you. Is it true that you were awarded the medal of courage in the Yom Kippur War?"

"Yes," confessed Shmuel.

"Not everyone earns a medal of courage."

"No."

"Something's not right. You put in your resume that you went to school at the Air Force technical boarding school."

"Yes, the boarding school..."

"So how did you get a medal of courage in the armored corps?"

"After technical school, I enlisted in the armored corps because I hated the helicopter course, because..."

"You don't look like a case of courage to me. I have friends, they'll check your file. But meanwhile, I salute you, man of courage."

Shmuel turned pale. He smiled.

"You know, Klein Shmuel, in the Yom Kippur War I should also have been awarded a medal of courage." He plunged into a long story involving mud, cannons, a post one did not abandon, and endless casualties. "If there was anyone left to testify for me..." he summed up.

Shmuel nodded.

"Not everyone goes down in history," said the director. He turned back in his chair, opened a little cabinet and took out a small bottle of golden alcohol. "Let's drink to courage, Klein Shmuel!"

Before Shmuel could refuse, the director pulled two glasses

out of the cabinet, poured a little strip of liquid into each of them and placed them on the table. "*Lechayim*!" he proclaimed, and took a sip.

Shmuel obeyed. Fire spread through his throat, lurched down and jumped up and pecked at his ears and nose.

"See you later, Klein Shmuel."

Shmuel turned and left, but the next day he was urgently called to the office again. The director's eyes were bloodshot, his tie lay crumpled on the desk. "I want to talk to you, Klein Shmuel. For some reason, ever since yesterday…" On his desk next to the tie stood an almost empty bottle of army-issue "Rabbinate Wine," and in his hand he clutched a pen-knife. He was carving thick slices of onion and swallowing them with a sucking sound.

"I am the first grandson born to the settlers of the Jezreel Valley. Me! The first! My father was almost the first son of the Valley, just imagine. The first son! But his mother was slow, she came from a family of rabbis from Warsaw, aristocrats, snobs, always with the nose turned up, and she did not give birth to the first son of the Valley, or even the second. Five children beat my father to it. My grandfather, the famous Gershon Yechiel, hated her for it. Back when he was an assistant cobbler in Odessa, it was his dream to produce the first son of the settlement in Hankin's valley. Even before the incident he hated his wife, an aristocrat, nothing good enough for her, always making comments, wanting to go back to Europe, a woman with no Zionist awareness, only a backache. But don't think he banished her. On the contrary. He wanted at least one of his sons to produce the first grandchild of the Valley! Almost no day went by when she wasn't pregnant. Ten children, my grandfather produced, and urged them to marry young. Tragedies. He forced my father to marry at seventeen, and he managed to give birth to me, the first grandchild in the Valley. It's a shame my grandfather did not live to see it… Having the first grandchild was the enterprise he lived for. And it's me…I am his life's work. The whole Valley was thankful for the first grandchild. And what do you think, did it do me any good? Did it do my poor father any good?"

He paused his flow of chatter for a moment and Shmuel felt obliged to answer the question, but the director quickly moved on. "My father, the poor guy, one day he decided to establish a 'House of the First' on his kibbutz. Not like Sturman House, but a real Zionist museum, where they would document battles and famous people like Grandpa Gershon Yechiel, who spent his whole life recording all the first sons and grandsons—you know, like Gideon Bertz, the first son of Degania, and Amotz Cohen, the first son of Motza. It was research, serious research, and my father thought all his notes should be published. The records, the scribbles, the proofs, where the first son was born, which ones were disqualified, where there were disagreements. The kibbutz was convinced, and they decided to build the 'House of the First.' And who did they give the job to? To my father, who suggested it?" He paused again and Shmuel tensed up. The director galloped ahead. "Why should they? They gave it to the guy who had his hand in all the committees. And what did he do? He decided to focus on memorializing the settling of the Valley, just like everyone else. Just an ordinary 'House of the First.' Who needs another one? But six months ago, when the position opened up, I applied. Not for my own sake. I'm an artillery man, after all. But so they'd remember my father, who also died brokenhearted, the sixth son of the Valley, second generation to heartbreak. I wanted them to look me in the eye and not forget my father. Besides, I was out of the army and I couldn't find a good job, like the one I had in the artillery corps. I thought I'd take my revenge, avenge the three generations of the Valley! But I didn't get it. I didn't get it."

He looked at Shmuel with tears of onion in his eyes, his penknife erect in his hand. He slowly sat up straight. "Well, *nu*...Strike it from the minutes. *Ach*...never mind. Go do your work."

Shmuel was about to leave but the director held him back at the door. "That's the way it goes. Not everyone goes down in history."

And that line, for some reason, brought a deep sadness to Shmuel that accompanied him all day and only intensified in the evening when he tried to cover it up with the pleasure of a whole falafel and a double-feature.

Not everyone goes down in history.

He decided to leave the museum as soon as possible, and he started visiting appliance stores, repair workshops, labs and distributors. Shmuel had a natural understanding of electrical appliances. When he was presented with a broken machine he needed nothing more than one squinting eye and an outstretched finger to feel the pulse of an electronic component. Although he occasionally used a voltmeter or an ammeter, he did so not to measure anything but because he enjoyed holding up the tiny terminal to the component and observing the thin needle wavering in the instrument panel. Sometimes, for no reason, he clamped the voltmeter's alligator teeth on his fingers and then released them. Then he clamped them down again and released them.

Ever since being forced to do so in his military service, Shmuel had hated fixing electrical appliances. When he was fifteen he transferred from the municipal high school to the Air Force technical boarding school—"the Tech"—and completed a course in helicopter maintenance. When he was eighteen, enlistment age, he announced that he did not want to be a technician. He wanted to be an ordinary soldier and they could post him wherever they wished. The recruiting officer looked him over and, like so many others, mistakenly diagnosed a slight case of recalcitrance that could easily be cured. Shmuel contended with the recruiting officer for forty days and forty nights. He was jailed twice in the objectors' wing of the induction center, where he was interviewed by several officers with increasingly senior ranks. He did not tell them that he hated working with the helicopters' electrical boxes; that he was so good at learning their specifications that they penetrated the shell of every thought; that sometimes for no reason he recited, *an offset switch is installed in the fuse box on each of the collective poles*; that under no circumstances did he ever want to fix another A7 malfunction in an offset box; that his soul practically burst with loathing when he was called upon to repair a fault that even the teachers had trouble locating. Shmuel simply allowed the tempest to proceed and stuck to his bottom line: "I don't want to be a technician."

Eventually he was sent to the armored corps. It was September of 1973. A terrible war, the Yom Kippur War, was about to materialize in the sandy deserts where Shmuel was posted—a lowly soldier breathlessly trying to protect himself against all those who sought to harm him. At first he was harassed by Sergeant Adika, then by Sergeant Gershon and the medic Bakhtin. Shmuel had almost finished his training course, after which he would be sent to a battalion where history would introduce him to Sergeant Major Nissim, who would detest Shmuel and ignite all the sparks of evil within his introverted personality. But Shmuel never reached the battalion and never met Sergeant Major Nissim. Before his training was over, the whole team was sent to the defense lines in Sinai to relieve the more experienced soldiers for the High Holy Days.

On Rosh Hashanah, Shmuel was on guard duty, and shortly before Yom Kippur, by coincidence, mistake, accident, miracle, he was once again on guard duty. His fellow guards were merely other soldiers like him, Shmuel-look-alikes, the men who were always left behind on the holidays. During the holiday itself, on Saturday, the hours were divided up into shifts, guard duties were assigned, and the most Shmuel-like soldiers were assigned the worst shift: Saturday afternoon in the desert heat. Throughout the Israel Defense Forces, similar soldiers began their guard duties, and at two o'clock in the afternoon it was they who greeted the war when it tapped on the windows and announced, Here I am. With artillery and air strikes. With the flight of Saggers trailing their clear strand wires. Here I am.

While the other soldiers, the non-Shmuel-like ones, were called back from their homes, the war was contended with only by the Shmuels of the desert and the Shmuels of the Golan and the Shmuels of the home front. It was them and the war, all alone.

Chapter eleven

Empty Lands

1948

"In Jerusalem…lepers, cripples, the blind, and the idiotic assail you on every hand, and they know but one word of but one language apparently—the eternal 'baksheesh'…Jerusalem is mournful and dreary and lifeless. I would not desire to live here… Of all the lands there are for dismal scenery, I think Palestine must be the prince. The hills are barren, they are dull of color, they are unpicturesque in shape. The valleys are unsightly deserts fringed with a feeble vegetation that has an expression about it of being sorrowful and despondent."
(Mark Twain, 1867)

Oh, love. Oh, love!

Major Manors filled the blank page in front of him with neat little circles of ink.

Oh, love.

It was the simplest day of his life. He had already filled two suitcases with the intelligence reports on Chaim Abramowitz, along with a toothbrush, a map and an old photograph from his service days in India. Now the suitcases stood beneath the walnut table at his feet, like a pair of panting dogs. But it was not time yet. He took a new sheet of paper, wrote "Sarah Abramowitz" across its center, and began to cover the page with circles.

Major Manors had come to Jerusalem in the early spring of 1936. Colonel Larwin, his commander and friend from India, had invited him here to serve as a Mandate intelligence officer. Shortly after he arrived, Larwin left, and it became evident to Manors that Larwin had intended him all along as a replacement, not a partner. The Great Arab Revolt erupted in its full, cruel force, and Major Manors was no longer at leave to dwell on his disappointment. But he remembered full well that Larwin had not mentioned leaving—on the contrary, he had written to Manors of renewing their old friendship.

In the cities and on the roads, no one was waiting for Manors. The two peoples—Jews and Arabs—fell at one another. Ambushes, raids, murders. They aimed to do away with the British Mandate, too. Six months after his arrival, Manors was asked to author the first report concerning an enigmatic new character by the name of Chaim Abramowitz.

As the acts of hostility intensified, the figure of Abramowitz rose above it all. "There is virtually no Jewish economic or security activity in which this Abramowitz is not involved," Manors' reports stated, but he hastened to stress that Abramowitz did not fit into any known pattern. "He maintains close and friendly ties with all members of the Jewish organizations, including the radical ones, and is not a member of any organization or a known participant in any activities. The heads of the Jewish national institutions employ his assistance in a variety of ways, but he does not belong to the labor movement or to any other. He has friendly business relationships with several Arab factors, even those among them who are most hostile towards the Jewish *Yishuv*. We are also aware of his diverse ties with British Mandate officials. A series of surveillance and undercover activities has not led to any cause for arrest, although in the distant past he was imprisoned for commonplace thuggery."

Major Manors was tasked with capturing Abramowitz and supplying the Mandate authorities with a reason to throw him into jail—or better yet, to the gallows. He employed methods that had proven effective during his service in India. He had known similar fellows there, all-or-nothing sort of people who were involved in everything yet tied to nothing. Their personalities were readable, their weaknesses concealed only from impatient eyes. But Manors had patience. Eventually the truth would ensnare Abramowitz.

Manors' supervisors demanded quick results, but he operated quietly and slowly. He had been pressured in India too. And there too—the heat, the exhaustion, the fearful people. When he had first arrived in India, his predecessor, Colonel Larwin, had been reassigned to Palestine. Handsome Colonel Larwin's trusty instincts always warned him when a terrible outbreak was imminent. In India, Major Manors had been caught up in a period of terror, a sudden vigorous uprising against British rule and a complete departure of the rules of coexistence that had prevailed for decades. And it was in India that a mosquito bite had resulted in a facial tick that aggravated him day and night. "I used to be a handsome man," he would conclude as he studied his image in the mirror and observed his twitching cheek. "It's a pity, a real pity…"

He avoided the company of women. Why even try? Women could not be expected to put up with his appearance. There had been one local girl, in India, before the mosquito bite, but he had gotten rid of her. She was only a local. Nor did he covet the pleasures that men around him laboriously pursued. What was this pleasure?

In India and in Palestine, as in all such places, people around him found ways to escape the hardships of service. Constant sex, alcohol, tobacco, and various Eastern hallucinogens. He himself avoided these traps. He had only to think back to his family, his mother, their faces. He would never touch alcohol.

At staff meetings he sometimes sketched a portrait of Abramowitz's psyche, in an attempt to explain his physical wholeness, his emotional wholeness, the wholeness of his destiny. He enumerated the man's features in detail and tried very hard to convey to his listeners the roots of Abramowitz's personality—the journalist father who had committed suicide, his own battles, the women who had fallen in love with this orphan. And the principles. The principles he imposed on his estate and his spirit—rigidity, persistence, even cruelty.

"He is cruel...very cruel..."

"You've fallen in love with him," his colleagues mocked. Stupid fools. If not for these men, some of whom had ties of convenience with Abramowitz, it might have been possible to lift the mask off Abramowitz's face. And they mocked him? Very well. He would mock them too!

Work brought tranquility to Major Manors. He liked to sit in his office late into the night and look out of his window while Jerusalem robed and disrobed itself in different garbs of light as the hours passed. He looked at the landscape of houses, weak yet buttressed by one another, crisscrossed with the branches of an ancient apple tree that bore no fruit. It was all so hollow, so empty, and yet calming. Sometimes he stood at the window and prayed aimlessly, mumbling the words he had known since childhood and which, even here, provided nothing. Oh, Father Leightly, if only you had seen Jerusalem with your own eyes!

He could never understand why people loved this city so, or why they hated it. His relationships with Jerusalem's people helped him to grasp the kitchens of its soul, the chambers and the yards whence the fanatic faiths and the horrifying ideas arose. He spoke with priests, public officials, and learned archæologists. And always the same sword was drawn, the blade of steel—Jerusalem is ours, only ours. The willingness to set fire to it all, to trample, to slaughter.

He deemed there could be no peace between two peoples who were both in the clutches of such a city. He always believed a war would erupt one day, a final war, and that the Jews would lose. Their attempt to hold on to Palestine would end in another catastrophe, but their fate of continued existence would not be weakened or altered.

His internal logic sided with the Arabs. They were a truer force, more infinite. He observed the conduct of the Jews, to which they themselves were blind, the way they touched, reached out with hands that grasped and sloped, clutching trees, walls, doors; the absence of absolute faith in their tangible existence in this country, a constant reexamining of their very presence. The Arabs did not need touch. They were the true children of the land, lacking enthusiasm, lacking despair. They would win.

Major Manors did not care who won and who lost. His department's original purpose had been to maintain contacts with secret operatives, to amass information meant to support the desperate attempt to rule all classes, people, parties, factions, religions. But here, as in every colony, the crisis of manpower bred disorder, and his department was forced to engage in a range of espionage activities. There was no shortage of people: every year more and more officers and clerks arrived. What they lacked were uniquely excellent people, the kind who would not succumb to one of the poisons proffered by serving far from home, in these lands full of peoples and yet so empty.

Manors was subject to a complex organizational structure, senior supervisors, military and civilian, entwined in one another in a constant battle of authority. They were united only on the subject of Abramowitz, and despised Manors' failure to present compelling evidence against him. They wanted the gallows. They wanted a pronunciation in the name of the law: to the gallows. They found Major Manors unhurried, lifeless, even lazy. They shot their arrows of criticism at him with the aim of causing pain, insinuating that he would not be promoted, that he might be suspended, replaced.

He ignored their harassments. The promotion they worshipped did not interest him. He had been promoted far enough. And the future? There was no place that would not have use for an honest man. Besides, at the end of his days he would have only himself to support, and the little habits he would acquire by old age, the hobby that would keep him alive.

In June of 1946, as part of "Operation Agatha," the Mandate authorities raided all the hiding places of the Jewish Hagana, uncovered stockpiles of arms, captured fighters, arrested leaders. Major Manors led the military forces to the right places and the right people. His estimates were perfectly precise. He knew that in the Jewish *Yishuv* they referred to the operation as "Black Saturday," and he took pleasure in his success. It was a more meaningful compliment than the praise he received at the Mandate headquarters. For a while, after "Agatha," his detractors withdrew. But they soon resumed harassing him.

Against his will they arrested Abramowitz without probable cause. Then they let him go. This was a frequently promoted method among the Mandate authorities—a short tactical arrest meant to shake up the detainee and see who he turned to in times of trouble. Abramowitz's arrest achieved nothing.

Major Manors knew that in one of the most covert units of the Mandate authorities there had been a brief proposal to simply assassinate Abramowitz even without any verifiable justification. Their proof would be the subsequent peace and quiet. Manors could not understand it. What was it about Abramowitz that they were trying to expose? What troubled them?

His superiors made him spend more time on Abramowitz than on the devilish Fauzi Al-Kaukaji, or the Jerusalemite Sheikh Al-Husseini, or David Ben-Gurion and Moshe Shertok and Yitzhak Tabenkin. And after all, who was Abramowitz? He occupied no formal role, had no designs on the seat of power. In fact he was nothing but a skilled merchant growing richer by the day. His business was successful thanks to good instincts and a fleet of hardworking, frighteningly loyal assistants.

They wanted to hunt down Abramowitz, and Manors knew that these civil servants had developed reliable instincts over the years. Their keen senses could identify anyone who posed danger, and they would tear his limbs apart. They did not know Abramowitz, not like he did, but he nonetheless respected their animal instincts. One day he might come to see things as they did, and then he would expose Abramowitz's dangers, convict him and throw him into the pit with his own hands.

It was not easy to reach sources among Abramowitz's men. If Abramowitz were to find out about a single leak, he would strangle the informant with his bare hands. There were suspicions that he had already done so more than once. But Manors obtained his own methods. He embedded people in the heart of the estate and cannily identified those who would agree to talk—some naïvely, some with malice. He was even able to locate a few outright traitors. He sensitively deciphered the power relations in the estate, listened to every echo of complaint in the soul of an employee, paid attention to every frustration and every grumble, picked any fruit that might produce a piece of leaked information.

When he felt that real progress had been made in his investigation, Manors could feel the intoxication of joy trying to break through, but he fought to restrain it. He had tasted the results of this elation in the past, and knew that it eventually turned to a stifling sort of depression, as if his body were turning on his soul. Every such episode was followed by a string of gloomy days which nothing could quell except tireless work with late suppers of toast blending into morning cups of tea, rambling journeys through the streets, markets and courtyards of Jerusalem. He dared not touch any alcohol, nor the poisons of the East, but he sought the company of people and ideas. He hoped they would exhaust him, saddle him with the deadening weight of their unbearable burdens. He begrudgingly learned about all the ethnicities, even the tiniest and most eccentric. The deathly fatigue of pettiness, ignorance, fanaticism, hatred. In his searches he developed a curiosity about the Nawar, a tiny community of Jerusalem gypsies whose men all looked old, scarred and deformed. One day when he was meandering, he thought he might abandon it all and be swallowed up in this tribe, even find himself a woman from among them. Why not? One of his forefathers, his great-great-grandfather, had traded in tin and copper, just like the Nawar. Why not?

Eventually he would return to his office, where he stood by the window and looked at the barren apple tree. He would bind himself to his chair and desk, and continue his work. He liked being in the office, without the sight of people, the citizens of the city, the streets. Yet he often found himself imagining the people outside as he gazed out the window. In summer, on the warm evenings that hatefully lunged at Jerusalem like murderous sons of the desert, he would open the window wide. Jerusalem was a place that many people would die for. All of Palestine was such, but in Jerusalem even the tranquil, the quiet, the appeasers—even they would suddenly be caught up in hatred, their eyes aglimmer. As an intelligence officer, he would be remiss not to comprehend this enigma, the passions that bared their breasts from within the people's souls. And the people themselves— there, faraway, down in the streets. Their miserable lives, the battles they fought against one another. Jews and Arabs, all motivated by terrible powers. None of the wise officials in the Mandate headquarters knew the taste of these embers, so how could they understand Abramowitz? His people were in the throes of a struggle, desperate Jews trying to acquire themselves a state. The spirit adhered almost of its own will to principles, to ideologies, to belief, to fighting for a cause. What chance did the Mandate have? What chance did Manors have? None at all. The son of a sated empire. They did not need his great acts. In what could a man believe unto death? For a man needed something like that. Every hour, every moment, he needed something to torture his heart, something that gave life.

Only once did Major Manors meet Abramowitz face to face, during one of the tiresome receptions in honor of some holy day. As Abramowitz faced him and shook his hand, Manors felt that the hand was held out in scorn. But perhaps not. Perhaps Abramowitz was scornful, but not of him—rather of this regime, which was temporary, rotten. A whole empire trying to establish law and culture in a place where no one wanted them. Manors shook Abramowitz's hand and the tick fluttered on his face. Abramowitz looked at him. Manors felt his throat tighten.

He shook Sarah's hand that evening too. She was a tall woman, slightly heavy-set. He shook her hand and wondered if she knew how many women had given themselves to her husband. The information he had gathered created the impression that in his youth Abramowitz had roamed the Jewish settlements like a wolf, hungrily hunting women. Major Manors could have reassured Sarah Abramowitz with well-verified information that since their marriage Abramowitz had not looked at other women, nor did they constitute a way to entrap him. But Major Manors looked at Sarah and felt that she did not need his reassurance.

The reports filed by Manors' subordinates contained a cheerfully detailed account of Sarah's habits. Naked. Naked. And again, naked. His men always giggled when asked to describe her. Horseback riding. Bathing in hidden springs. A sort of Lady Godiva, but without the noble cause. Major Manors sifted out the trivialities. As far as he could verify, Sarah had been observed bathing in the nude only in the company of the strange Yemenite man known as Günter, who walked with a limp. But the reports were jovial—after all, what pleasure did intelligence gatherers have other than from reports of naked women?

I know a lot about you. I know a great deal. This was what he wanted to tell her when they shook hands.

He examined the couple intently that evening. Not the open, social behavior, but the pockets of their relationship, the veiled details that swayed the true bond between Sarah and Chaim Abramowitz this way and that. That evening Manors also understood something that had been right in front of his eyes all this time: Abramowitz was only in his late twenties, yet his associates treated him as if he were older than them, stronger. He might as well have been forty or fifty. And his power—how many people achieved such power in their lifetimes? True, he had been forced to fend for himself after his father's suicide, but this alone could not explain the annihilating power through which he had taken control of businesses and people. At a young age he had married Sarah, who was older than him, and had set up a home on the estate with her. Such peasant simplicity, such crudeness. As though he had absolved himself of life's dilemmas to focus on more important things. But what?

Abramowitz was not religious and displayed no Zionist fervor. Among the new Jews in Palestine there were many expounders of ideas, all people who had been battered by reality. But Abramowitz simply lived on his estate, purchased factories, negotiated deals, gave money to various programs and organizations that interested him. No ideas, no religion. Just crude existence. What were his aims?

Major Manors observed Abramowitz that evening—his height, his expressionless eyes. A peasant. But so different from all those crumbs of men, the Jews, little people who had come to this country, who grasped onto a store or a small kibbutz, lived their lives and married and had children, until they died, leaving no trace in history. Abramowitz was different. He was no crumb of humankind. An upright pillar among the people, searching out those who could be of use to him. And the people were not indifferent to his searching eyes. They were drawn to him, drawn to serve him. Manors watched as they went up to offer him drinks or canapés or other things, themselves unaware of why they were approaching. He made a note to himself of Sarah Abramowitz as a possible avenue into Abramowitz's world; perhaps one day she would reveal a shadow of betrayal. For there was some unease there, between Sarah and Chaim. Major Manors could sense it, secreted though extant. The true nakedness, the nakedness of the human soul—he was destined to always perceive it.

He observed Sarah Abramowitz's lines. Sweetness, the heavy sweetness of sherry. As a child his mother used to let him sip the sweet sherry in church. It was cheap. And so sweet. An arrogance that concealed fear. A wildness covering pain. He saw Sarah Abramowitz stand close to her husband while something within her recoiled, seeking distance. She repeatedly succumbed to her own inducement to lean on her husband, but was immediately overcome by the attempt to disconnect and move away. Standing and talking and smiling, completely unaware of the perpetual struggle existing within her, to distance herself from Abramowitz, to lean on him.

Manors had spent over a decade monitoring Abramowitz's employees, their yearning for his closeness, like insects drawn to fire. How much power Abramowitz had gained due to this loyalty! Only Sarah, the anomaly, displayed independence, desperately clawing her way to an existence separate from Abramowitz. Not too far away, but at some distance.

And then there was the girl. Rivka. They brought her with them to that reception all those years ago, his single encounter with the Abramowitzes, as though among all the 380,000 Jews of Palestine, no one could be found to look after her for one evening.

The girl enchanted everyone. She spoke rounded, childish English. One official ran to his office and came back with a kite for her.

"Thank you," she said with a curtsey.

But what was she doing here? The girl was not Abramowitz's daughter, Manors knew, but he treated her as kindly as if she were. What would become of her when the Jews lost this war?

Often, in front of the window that looked out from his office onto the rooftops of Jerusalem, he would conjure up scenes of battlefields, the final moments. The defeated Jews, the conquered

Abramowitz Estate. Abramowitz's wife Sarah carried away and raped repeatedly, violently, then murdered. And what of the girl?

Major Manors looked at Sarah. If Abramowitz dies, he thought, if he is sent to the gallows, I will go to Sarah and propose to marry her. And I will take Rivka in and raise her.

Major Manors never saw Abramowitz again. And yet, he did. Roaming the city one day, he wandered into Khalian the Armenian photographer's shop and proceeded to dig through old boxes of negatives, photographs and undeveloped contact sheets as he chatted with Khalian in the hopes of hearing something useful. The photographer gazed at him with his one innocent eye, and the other, more cunning one. And then he saw it: a photograph of Chaim Abramowitz. Khalian explained that he himself had asked to photograph Abramowitz, long ago, when Abramowitz was a young boy of eighteen; most of the photographs were still gathering dust somewhere.

Major Manors held his breath—how much would the photograph cost?

Khalian named a price but insisted that the photograph's beauty would be enhanced by a proper frame, if the Major would be so kind as to wait three days.

The framed photograph was delivered to the office at the end of the week. When Manors ripped open the envelope his eyes widened in alarm: a handwritten dedication had been scrawled across the picture by Abramowitz himself: *For my dear Major Manors.*

Khalian squirmed when Manors confronted him in the shop. Enlisting his innocent eye, he confessed, "He found out…Abramowitz found out about the purchase. How? Devils whispered to him…there's no way of telling." He practically got down on his knees and begged Major Manors, both eyes blinking and his face turning pale, as if the Major's pistol was drawn.

"Get up," Manors said, himself startled. After all, they were having a civil conversation and the Armenian was flailing about as if violence and death were in the air. "How did he sign the picture?" he asked softly. Did the Armenian see a menacing face when he looked at him?

Khalian stammered—Abramowitz had come to the store himself, written the dedication and left. He had paid for the photograph and the frame. Khalian had nothing to do with it. Nothing at all. Truly. Then he started to whimper. "The Major must have forgiveness..."

Major Manors took a deep breath. Abramowitz was following him.

At the beginning of 1947, Chaim Abramowitz made a mistake. Or perhaps it was made by someone else, but either way, a gun tying him to several crimes under Mandate law fell into the hands of Major Manors.

The Jews had finished celebrating Chanukah; the very last of the Christians had bade farewell to the Christmas season. A spirit of reconciliation and encouragement swept through Jerusalem, even among Manors' informants, and emboldened them. When the gun was handed over in its holster, Manors placed it in the empty top drawer of his desk. The next evening, the door to his office opened to reveal Sarah Abramowitz.

Major Manors did not ask how she had found his room, nor who had seen her coming. A look of surprise was on his face, and on hers, but more discernible still was the sense that both of them, like a pair of actors in a dress rehearsal, were about to recite a series of lines they were powerless to change.

Major Manors took the pistol out of his desk drawer.

Sarah sat down.

Major Manors looked at her. She had come to surrender. She would give herself over. All of herself. A rigid heat gripped his face like forceps. His cheek began twitching. Did Chaim know she had come?

"I want the gun," she said.

Major Manors smiled. The tic spasmed, but he did not care. He arranged his hands on the desk, leaned forward to her, then sat back again. "You are making an impossible demand of a Mandate officer."

He wanted Sarah Abramowitz to try and penetrate him with

her gaze. To stab him with her deep blue eyes. Project the reckless-ness of her decision. He recognized the scent of her body.

"You are asking me to commit a criminal act," he said, stretch-ing. He got up and closed the window so that they would not be disturbed by the evening breeze that sometimes picked up without warning, frightening the birds asleep on their branches, shocking the silence of his office. He looked at her dress. It was very feminine, too vernal.

"What would you ask for in return for the gun?" she asked.

"I know what any other man would ask for," he replied.

"And you, John, what would you ask for?"

Her voice was soft. So soft. He stood by the window, not wish-ing to go back to his chair just yet. He would sit down later.

Sarah looked down. Why did she not stare at him with her husband's deadly look? She lowered her head even more, almost bow-ing. Beneath his window he could see rooftops with rotting tiles that needed cleaning.

Manors sat down again. His steps felt clumsy and fretful, as if this woman was controlling him, when in fact she was in his hands. Her husband was in his hands. She would give in to his every desire. To all his desires.

He felt soft lashings against his cheek.

"I want us to meet. In return for the gun, in return for the risk. Who knows how I will explain what I have to explain? I will not give you the gun. It will disappear, the evidence will disappear. That is all. But once a fortnight, at least, you and I shall meet."

"You ask for very little, John," she said. Her eyes looked at him with deep calm, as if her fate were not quivering in the palm of his hand. As if he could not turn cruel. She stood up and held her face very close to his. "We will meet, as you have asked." She turned to leave.

When she was at the door he called after her. "The meetings... we will only talk...it's only to talk."

She looked back at him and smiled. Then she left and closed the office door behind her.

Why had he said that? Major Manors thought to himself angrily. Everything was spoiled now. Why had he spoken like such a child?

The next day Sarah sent a messenger with instructions for their first meeting. Major Manors was to come to a small monastery whose monks functioned as an external division of the Abramowitz Estate.

When he arrived, he was seated in the manicured garden of an inner courtyard. A table was set with almond cakes and ice-cold fig juice, and Sarah soon appeared. He wanted to listen, to ask, to know about her, about Abramowitz. He had prepared many questions, and he was excited. He did not like the monastery. The stone structures seemed to have been blackened with soot. He despised the way the rectangular courtyard was surrounded with buildings, like Satan's footprint. But he had no choice.

"This is where we shall meet," said Sarah.

He tried to talk about Chaim Abramowitz, but she spoke about her first husband, a member of Hashomer. He wanted to talk about himself and tell her about handsome Colonel Larwin, but instead he found himself embarking on tales about the Mandate government, the intrigues, the power struggles. He felt a desire to explain his facial tic, to tell her about his wonderful days in India, with Larwin, before the mosquito bite. He felt he might burst, and his thoughts drifted until she got up to go, and they continued to drift for two weeks, distractedly, painfully. Why had he not spoken? Why did he always ruin things? He promised himself he would talk more at their next meeting.

Two weeks later they met again in the same little garden in the monastery. They continued to do so every fortnight, and their conversations slowly warmed. As 1947 fumed around them—on November 29th the United Nations pronounced a partition of the country and an open war of destruction broke out between the Jews and the Arabs, with the British mandate like a living organ between them—Major Manors and Sarah Abramowitz discussed the customs of India, the early days of the estate, her first days in Israel, and his own. Only rarely did the conversation touch on the killing and the fear around them.

In their last meeting of 1947, just before a snowless and joyless

Christmas, Major Manors waited for Sarah, feeling tense and upset. He wanted to tell her about the Arab he had met, a longtime informant of his, whose recent observation had given him such clarity on the struggle between the Arabs and Jews that he had experienced a change of heart.

Sarah looked pale and weak when she arrived.

"Has your journey to Jerusalem tired you?" he asked worriedly.

"The dangers on the way are more troubling."

"You will continue to come," Manors decreed angrily. She had to understand that the ransom for the gun was not yet paid. Not yet! She did not seem to appreciate the complications he had to handle, with a gun suddenly gone missing.

They sat silently. Major Manors searched for the thread that would trail behind it an entire bundle of conversation.

"You Jews will win eventually, do you know?"

"So, the British Mandate has already decided who will win?"

Manors smiled sadly. "I only wanted to make you happy." He lowered his head.

Sarah whispered almost into his ear, and her smell, the smell of cotton that a woman's sweat has dried on, seemed to bleed into his nostrils. "I thought you English knew the Arabs would win."

"I thought so too," he said, perking up. "I thought so too…" He clenched his fists and turned to look at her. "My thoughts changed completely yesterday."

"Yesterday?"

"That is what I wanted to tell you. You Jews will win, yesterday I found out. Only yesterday!" He got up, no longer bothered by the tic burning his cheeks. "I spoke with my informant—an illiterate man, a savage with limited abilities. Money is not enough for his information—he demands conversation with the English. A wicked little man, although he sometimes surprises me with his observations. Yesterday he told me he saw a procession of Jewish children with wreathes on their heads, wearing white blouses and carrying saplings. They were walking through the fields opposite his village, in the neighboring kibbutz. When he asked, he was told the children had come from Tel

Aviv to plant trees in honor of the Jewish holiday, Tu B'Shvat. And this is what my Arab told me: people who would travel all that way to plant trees so far from home, far from their own gardens, will take this land." Major Manors looked at Sarah.

"Excellent idea. I will tell Chaim."

Manors filled with happiness. "Yes, let's see what Chaim thinks." They began walking around the courtyard together. Manors asked, "Does Chaim know about our meetings?"

"Chaim always knows what he needs to and what he can," she said smiling.

"I hope you are not using our conversations to get information out of me. I forbid myself to get information about Chaim out of you. Our meetings are devoted to us. Only to us."

Yet their conversations did concern Chaim Abramowitz, and only him, although they cautiously and silently observed a set of unwritten rules. They met every two weeks, with unfailing punctuality. In between meetings Major Manors' anxieties increased—after all, if Sarah chose to betray him and to stop coming to the meetings, he would be powerless. The wager, the gun, was long gone. How would he induce her to rescind her betrayal? Every time he reached the monastery and Sarah arrived, his heart tightened like a fist—there she was, he had not been wrong, she came willingly.

Their conversations flowed gently. He listened to her voice, to the empty spaces between her words, asked cautious questions and collected her replies into his thoughts. He spoke about Abramowitz and looked for ways to ask his questions. He was usually restrained, but sometimes burst out with crude, gossipy questions, malicious ones even—Why was Chaim installing more and more lightning rods in the estate? Why was a strong man like him so afraid of lightning? And how did he act when he was alone and the sky lit up with bolts of lightning? Manors accepted Sarah's responses respectfully, even when they were nothing more than an awkward smile, and in them he sought the true Sarah, her true life. How did she love Abramowitz? And why? For it was so easy to fall in love with such a man. His power, his arms, his shoulders. Major Manors probed for some hatred she might harbor towards Abramowitz, some remorse that caused her sorrow, but it was all buried in their marriage. He thought back to the reception, to the moment at which Abramowitz had shaken his hand, and the aversion he had sensed in Sarah toward her husband, toward the man she relied on so much.

"You know, your husband has a great power over people."

"I thought we decided our meetings were meant only for us, to talk about ourselves."

"You do not know your husband!" he spat out.

"Perhaps."

"No, you do not. You live your quiet life on the estate, bringing up Rivka, and you have no idea. Do you have any idea how many people your husband has killed? A woman should know."

"Do not attempt to know what a woman needs, it's too difficult."

They continued walking in the shade of the garden walls.

"A woman should know," he mumbled desperately. He leaned closer to her body, breathed in the hair that had absorbed the scent of the trees, perhaps trees from the mountain paths near Latrun. "Our meetings are for us, that is true, but to understand your husband… that is important for both of us. And for who else? Together we could understand your husband, what motivates him."

Sarah began talking about her late husband again. But the Hashomer man did not interest Major Manors. He was interested in the estate. He was interested in the people who had served Chaim loyally for decades.

Sarah would not speak about Chaim, yet everything she said was helpful. From beneath the scents of her body and her flowery dresses, Manors could sense her spirit, and he knew that it was saddened by the hardships, by the widowhood at a young age, and the encounter with Abramowitz. She told him a little more every time they met, and he, an experienced intelligence man, assembled the little contradictions, the repeated words, the small points of hesitation and lies. She told him about her life on the estate, the hard work. He could see her walking among the employees whose loyalty extended only to Chaim, and she the most loyal of them all. Their loyalty was frightening, they were willing to die for him, but she, though loyal, looked away from him. Manors could feel her, her compulsion. Among all the faithful people on the estate, all those who executed its very existence, only Sarah had to endure the touch of Abramowitz as a husband, the weight of his body on hers. For he did lie on her with all his weight as he penetrated her. Manors imagined Abramowitz's weight on Sarah. His power. The violence inside him. He felt pity for her, and wanted to hold her hand and kiss her.

That year Jerusalem had a stormy winter, followed by a dry, stifling spring. Sometimes they walked around the garden wordlessly, quietly enjoying their silence. Here, finally, a pair of people exempt from the need to talk. Sometimes they sat in the shade as the monks silently served them, and all they had to do was talk. Once Sarah brought her daughter Rivka. Manors looked at her, surprised to find that she was no longer a little girl. She was about eighteen, with troubling blue-black eyes. Her hair was shiny and very dark. He felt sad. Why did Abramowitz and Sarah have no children of their own? For this girl was hers, only hers, having flowed out of her like a little drop.

Manors was surprised to see one of the monks hand Rivka a colorful kite. She played with it throughout their meeting, ignoring Sarah and the Major, pulling and leading the kite strings, allowing it to fly cheerfully outside the monastery's confines.

Rivka's presence was oppressive to him. How could they talk? He found the kite distracting.

Sarah suggested they get up and walk. She apologized, "I had to bring Rivka. We see each other so little. She volunteers with medical teams nearby. Cares for our injured, she has no fear, and they fall in love with her…not a week goes by without an exciting story."

What if Rivka had a child? Major Manors wondered. But he banished the thought from his mind. After all, she was not Abramowitz's daughter, so why should he take an interest in her?

"She has grown up so much," Sarah continued, "but still a girl."

Major Manors said nothing. He did not want to talk about Rivka Abramowitz. The kite flew back and forth in front of his eyes, dulling his thoughts, irritating, teasing.

"You know," he said, "I once knew someone, someone like your husband…a great force."

He almost told her about Colonel Larwin, his friend. About the days when Larwin would burst into his room unannounced and take him on his journeys. In the infernal Indian midday sun, Larwin used to lead him to secret gathering places along the green, polluted river, whose waters were so full of insects and vapor they seemed to hover in the air. Within a few hours they would be on their own, isolated from any other humans, while the heat gnawed at Manors' consciousness. What was there? The smell of mud, the smell of many animals. As if they had left the gaping mouth of the British Empire behind and escaped it like criminals, like free men, to a place with no law, no prohibitions, alone in the scalding heat under a mantle of insects. Colonel Larwin, the handsomest of all men, would stand serene, comfortable, examining his muscles that glistened with sweat, and Manors would be flooded with panic. In the evening hours they would go back to their residences, put on their uniforms, and in the quietest hours Larwin would tell Manors his recollections of more peaceful posts, in Burma, Singapore, China, Africa. His only regret, he told Manors repeatedly, was that he had not been posted in a region of India where there were tigers. That was what he had expected when he was sent there. He had thought he would be able to hunt tigers in the jungle, to rid the area of the dangers lurking for human beings.

Major Manors wanted to tell Sarah about Larwin's merits, and about his cruelty, the indifference with which he treated others, including Manors. About the immense force that emanated from him. About the most pleasant hours that Manors had ever experienced. But he did not want to take up their entire meeting on Larwin. One day he would tell her. And for a moment, as he breathed in the scent of her body, the odor of dry sweat, cotton, trees, wine, his thoughts were swallowed up in a desire to embrace her, to grapple with her body, to exhaust her, a woman beneath a man.

If I murder her, who will punish me?

He thought about Chaim Abramowitz's revenge, murderous and frightening, and he was horrified by his own bliss.

Four days after their meeting he sent her a note:

I know that tomorrow is your birthday, but I demand that we meet. There is no other option. And to compensate you, I will give you a special gift: since our entire relationship is based on an act of betrayal, I will introduce you to a traitor.

The next day Sarah came to the monastery. Major Manors sat on a garden bench. He handed her a bouquet of flowers and wished her a happy birthday. Sarah smiled. The monks laid the table as usual, and Major Manors, impatient, his cheek twitching, began to introduce his special gift.

"Soon you shall see him. He is one of your Jews. He has already entrapped quite a number of people, and his advantage is that he is a complete idiot. It never occurs to him that after each of our conversations people are arrested, sent here and there. He has no ill will, and that is his strength. He is a forester, he belongs to your cult of tree worshippers, all he wants is to see forests in this country. He harbors a wild passion to plant trees, he dreams about a Palestine entirely covered with woods, as if he has never opened his eyes and seen how dead everything here is." Major Manors grinned at the thought. "His name is Meir Glop. I told him you were interested in afforesting the Abramowitz estate, and he has all sorts of requests. I will let him introduce himself. I warn you, he thinks I'm an advisor for the Mandate government's afforestation department, and you must not expose my true identity. Although even if you wished to, you would have to make a huge effort. I do not believe he could ever be convinced that I am not an afforestation advisor. I hope you will appreciate the gift. You know that I myself do not often smile, even the meetings with you do not bring smiles to my face. But after every meeting with him, I sit in my office and laugh. I hope you will laugh too, Sarah, and afterwards I must give you something very personal."

Manors signaled with his hand. One of the monks opened a

door and a short Jew came through hastily, scurrying over to shake Sarah's hand.

"An honor, an honor. Meir Glop at your service, Madam, no introductions necessary for yourself. Such an honor for me. Such great things we hear about your husband. He has been most helpful in the afforestation of our country. Why, Ettinger himself asserted that not many men could rival him in their contributions!"

"A pleasure to meet you, Mr. Glop."

The monks appeared briefly with a third place setting, but Glop remained standing.

"I even contacted your husband directly once, it was a great undertaking…I begged him…begged him to put a stop to it!" Glop pulled his lips back until his pink gums were almost entirely exposed. "You see, Spivak had once again determined the rules for the Jerusalem Forest plan, and once again he announced his intention to plant pine trees. Pine! And there I was, shouting out, 'But the resin! Pine-tree resin is turpentine! You are planting torches of fire! The forests will burn!' But that man, Spivak, smiled and ignored me—what did he care? I wanted to ask your husband to intervene, to obstruct the plan, but I was unable to get an audience with him. His assistants prevented me, they even hit me on the head. And now here you are!"

"Indeed I am here."

"…and Spivak, as you know, is gone now, sent to prison. I had already complained a number of times, because in the evenings he used to throw me out of my office, literally force me to leave, so that he could hold his meetings with people who did not belong to the department. But here you are now, and I am at your service— Meir Glop!"

"I have heard a lot about you, Mr. Glop, from Mr. Manors."

"And to Mr. Manors here, too, I have extended my pleas regarding the Biria forest. I have reminded him of the helplessness of the 1929 events, that terrible day when the Angel of Death stared at us with his black eyes from every which way. And I must ask—if your honorable husband agrees, and if you yourself agree, for it is of the utmost importance not to repeat the mistake, but to fortify the Biria forests with suitable trees—I ask you, what is a forest if not its trees? And the Abramowitz Estate? You have only to say the word and I shall present you with my papers, just a general outline of course, just for your approval, and then I will labor over comprehensive plans, weeding and planting, removals and thinning, each detail in its place. I can assure you that Meir Glop is nothing if not thorough."

"I will have to ask for diplomas, references," said Sarah.

"Diplomas?" Meir Glop asked breathlessly. He sat down on the bench beside Major Manors.

"Where, for instance, did you get your training? And what are your ties with the Jewish National Fund? Mr. Abramowitz works in cooperation with the Fund."

"I thought Mr. Manors had explained things..." Mr. Glop sounded disappointed. "You see, I was thrown out of the Fund..." He looked up at her hopefully.

"As an impartial observer I can testify that an organization such as the afforestation department of the Jewish National Fund was too narrow to confine the wingspan of Meir Glop," Major Manors interjected.

"Such a fate! You see, I was certified at the Imperial School of Agronomy, that is where my diplomas are from, but I was thrown out of the afforestation department. Oh, the tribulations—so mortifying! And who are they? Apart from Ettinger, what experts do they have? Of course, if your name is Weitz you have nothing to worry about. Take, for example, the afforestation directors: Sharon Weitz, Eliezer Weitz, David Weitz, Yosef Weitz. And do you think these people have diplomas from the Imperial School of Agronomy? And do they wage a war over every penny, over every tree planted? Why, of course not. All they wage is a war of arguments."

Meir Glop shook his legs out and stood up. "I hereby declare!" He stretched his hunched body up and clapped his hands. "The day will come when the inhabitants of the country shall bathe in shade, and every basket shall overflow with succulent fruits, and the nectar shall burst into the people's open palms, and yet if not a soul remembers Meir Glop, the man who planted their forests, I shall harbor not an ounce of disappointment! But if perchance they do remember, if perchance they sing my praises, and if perchance they name a monument after me, or even teach my methods in the schools—well, that will be a good thing, but I will not insist upon it."

He sat down.

"Mr. Manors here, with whom I share every matter, can certainly testify that the plan to afforest the coastline was mine, and Ettinger supported it, but then along came Kaplan and ruined it all, and the letters of complaint did no good. But did I insist? Sixteen letters I wrote, and no more. I have no need for reverence. Let the people say that Kaplan built the coastal forests—I should not care. But how bitterly things turned out for Mr. Kaplan, who is now in prison…"

"As it turns out, not all the afforestation department personnel were necessarily concerned with afforestation," Manors explained. "A few bad seeds were removed. Quite by chance it emerged that Kaplan, for example, belonged to the Stern gang, part of your Lehi movement, and was hiding ammunition and guns in the forests."

"But we must remember that we have gathered here on behalf of the Abramowitz Estate and its afforestation," Meir Glop mumbled, standing up and sitting back down. "Twenty acres of planted lands on the estate, and another seventy-five acres of moribund groves. We have come here to rectify this state of affairs, to afforest all the empty expanses." Meir Glop took a few sheets of paper out of his shirt pocket and spread them out. Sarah recognized diagrams of the estate, its borders, the hill, her square home.

"Mr. Manors gave me some blueprints, and I have already drawn up plans," Glop explained. "I wish for you to know who stands before you, Mrs. Abramowitz. To whom your budgets shall be allotted. After all, you do not know who Meir Glop is. I was thrown out from the Jewish National Fund's afforestation department, but it was merely an act of kindness. Just as it was an act of kindness when I decided to leave an abundant homeland, a good family, and the prospect of a peaceful life. When I arrived here, in bald Palestine, it was merely an act of compassion. For over in Europe, where is the effort in planting a tree? A forester is a supervisor, an overseer. What does a tree require? But here in arid Palestine a forester must penetrate the secret that lies in the roots of a tree. He must learn what makes nothing into something and something into nothing, the living into the dead and the dead into the living. And I found out! I should be given awards! I should be allowed to make speeches! But what? Out they throw me! I have discovered the secret of life. And you should know, Mrs. Abramowitz, that from the lips of Meir Glop no mere lavish words emerge. The secret of life and death is in my hands. I can grow firs in the Negev desert!"

Major Manors intervened again briefly. "At this point, with your permission, I will take my leave for a short walk. You have so much to talk about."

"You wanted to give me something very personal," Sarah reminded him.

"Later, later," said Manors. He began to circle the courtyard, leaving Sarah and Meir Glop to talk. Oh love, he thought; Oh, love! He had to tell Sarah that they were sending him home, to England, getting rid of him, in fact. But he had a plan. Major Manors smiled to himself. The time for news would come. Mr. Glop would finish his circus show and Manors would send him on his way. Then he would turn to Sarah and tell her that he was being asked to conclude his service to the Mandate in Palestine.

He slowly continued his walk.

I emigrated from Hamburg in 1920.

From the very first I could see what Palestine lacked. What was truly seething in its absence among the rocky terrain—trees!

I obtained a budget, but it was robbed and given to Kuperman...

Every time he passed Sarah and Meir Glop, Manors picked up a fragment of Glop's monologue. Pieces of proclamations, snippets of information from the present and the past, a disorderly chaos of exclamation marks.

They gave me another budget, and Halbert took it!

    Here and there, you know, the way of nature, what began as an argument became a complaint against my colleagues, that is the way things happen...You must forgive me, Madam, but when matters are burning in a man's bones...

    My adversaries in the afforestation department began to outnumber me. Spivak went and Kuperman came! Kuperman went and Glick came!

Major Manors strolled with his ears pricked up. Glop's sentences cheered him up. He could see the little man happily chatting with Sarah.

At the afforestation conferences I gave very important speeches!

    There were never very many of us, but I always believed, unflinchingly, that we would win, that we would overcome!

    My faith has weakened since the 1929 massacres. That summer... such a disaster...the young and tender Hulda forest...4,105 cypress trees burned, 17,747 pine trees burned—may God avenge them!—600 casuarinas, 145 pepper trees...a catastrophe...and the fire...

Major Manors' grin began to turn downwards. A poisoned breeze blew over him. A nervous sadness. Anger. Why was his mood agitated again? It was always this way. He could never remain calmly confident in his own joy. And what now? Everything he needed to be happy was right here. Sarah, the silence, a jovial birthday mood.

Ever since then, something sank in my heart, a fear that perhaps we would not win.

    Kuperman eventually told me that trees were not the main thing. He winked, hinting that sometimes it was important to take advantage of the forest protection budget to protect the people—yes, to buy weapons with our budget! Such a scandal!

    With my own hands I began the "Forest Headquarters." It was a real organization, just like Hashomer, but our interest was trees!

Not everyone is Ettinger, I say, not everyone is Ettinger!

Major Manors began to panic.

All these years I have been writing letters to my brother. I lied, telling him Palestine was covered with a vigorous landscape of forests, and I urged him to come so that I would not be lonely. I told him life here was easy, healthy. And now he informs me that he is planning to come and join the war for our country, but I have not had time to build the forests yet—what shall I do?

Perhaps your husband can help, perhaps they can send my brother to live and fight near Lebanon, where the woods are satisfactory.

At first I myself used to go up with the hardworking tower-and-stockade settlers, as a representative of the Forest Headquarters. But it turned out I was not one to work with trees in their plank form—instead of nailing hammers into the wood, I hammered my fingers.

It is symbolic, don't you think? I am incapable of harming a tree, so how could I drive a nail into wood?

Where was this sadness coming from? And the panic? Everything was going well. Everything was in order.

I am a man of impeccable faith. Even Ettinger himself defended me!

Myself and Mr. Manors here, we did some commendable work during the tower-and-stockade era. I would let him know in advance where and when the settlers were planning to camp, and he would make plans for the afforestation and try to help out with a small budget.

Major Manors moved closer to Sarah and Meir Glop. Panic. Two Jews, speaking Hebrew—had they already forgotten that their dead language had been brought back to life not so long ago? Now they were talking of forests, and one day their imaginary forests would be built, and the Jews would forget that there were no trees in this dead country, and the sight of a forest in Palestine would no longer excite them. One day the Jews would have a state, and they would forget that it had not always been so. That there was a Mandate here. Where would Manors be on that day?

Your husband contributed too! And we had a conference, twice!

I disbanded the Forest Headquarters because of debts and inaction, and I founded Forests of Life, an organization that exists to this day, albeit without me.

They organized an ousting, voted against me, and when they asked if I had any final words, I announced—I resign!

As if expecting the bitter news, the betrayal, Sarah waved at Major Manors. "Mr. Glop and I will go to the estate together. I've decided to let him take a few measurements," she said.

"A bond of friendship has been forged!" Meir Glop declared.

Major Manors stopped walking. "With him?"

But what about the Major? There would be no chance to tell Sarah that there would be no more chances. That he had to go home, to England, to set up a new unit in the intelligence headquarters. That he had been promised a promotion, broader authorities. He saw through their ploy: they wanted him to abandon Chaim Abramowitz. The Mandate officers in Jerusalem knew their days were numbered, that it would soon be dismantled, and they wanted to settle a few scores. The fools. He would not abandon Chaim Abramowitz. But what could he tell this woman now, Chaim's wife, who preferred to listen to this clown rather than to him. And now she was taking him home with her, trampling his plan to send Meir Glop on his way, to tell her, to clutch her hands and declare that he would not leave Chaim, that he would be as loyal to him as Sarah was, and now—

On the simplest day in his life, Major Manors got up from his office chair, picked up the two suitcases and walked out of the building. Two days later, when the search began, they found the stack of papers on his desk. Lots and lots of circles, and in the center of every page the name 'Sarah Abramowitz.'

At the Abramowitz Estate they claimed to not have seen the

Major. Officers tried to enter and look for him, but they met with resistance and left. Two detectives were in charge of the search. Rumors told of a monk in the Jericho desert who looked like Major Manors, and an English fighter among the Arab ranks in the Galilee.

In the middle of May 1948, the Mandate left the territories of Palestine—*Eretz Yisrael*. The State of Israel was declared. Arab armies invaded the new state, battles raged everywhere. The search for Major Manors was called off.

In June, Chaim Abramowitz began his own search, for his missing brother Lolek. There were reports that Lolek, a physician by training, had disobeyed Chaim and sailed illegally to the shores of Israel. They said he had been enlisted to a battle somewhere and disappeared. No one could say what had become of him, but persistent rumors sent Abramowitz on arduous voyages of desperation.

In mid-summer, while a heat wave tormented the land's inhabitants and caused them to forget their war, a car stopped alongside Sarah Abramowitz as she walked down the main street of Tel Aviv. In the car sat Major Manors—clean-shaven, calm, wearing his officer's uniform.

He smiled at Sarah. "Get in."

"John!" Sarah looked at him in his neatly ironed uniform. But the Mandate was over...

"How are you, John?"

"Get in."

"What are you doing here?"

"Get in."

She looked at his face, at his eyes. She took a deep breath.

Major Manors' eyes were sparkling. He opened the car door and urged her, waving his arms in a panic. "Quickly, they mustn't see me! I disappeared for Chaim's sake. They wanted to kill us..." He leaned over and softly held her hand. He did not pull her, but looked around in all directions. "Quickly...life and death...on the way I can tell you...everything is connected..."

Sarah got into the car.

Major Manors sped out of the city going east, toward Petach

Tikva. Sarah sat silently, examining his neat appearance out of the corner of her eye. A Mandate officer in a shiny uniform. But there was no Mandate.

"Where are we going?" she finally asked.

Major Manors smiled. They approached a T-junction. The rock wall of an old quarry was straight ahead.

"Where are we going?" she asked again. She felt for the door handle.

"We're already there," Major Manors said with a smile.

When he pressed down on the accelerator, he could feel that she was responding to him with a subtle gesture. A feminine softness. I am a coward, he thought, and the car careened straight into the rock face.

Chapter twelve

Oh, Love! 1977

In the middle of 1977, Shmuel took a job in an electronics lab owned by Mrs. Zeller, a beautiful silver-haired woman who left lipstick-stained cigarette butts in the ashtrays. Mrs. Zeller's husband lay dying in a distant hospital, leaving her to defend his piece of the family estate against his brother, who was trying to pilfer the business through trickery and deceitful accounting. Since Mrs. Zeller knew nothing about electronics, she found hope and comfort in Shmuel, and sought his protection against the brother-in-law.

Shmuel found the scarlet- and strawberry-colored cigarette butts thrilling, and Mrs. Zeller's conversational advances aroused an awkward bodily response. But every time he considered his sexual prospects with her, he quickly dismissed and condemned the thought. The simplicity of appliances was to his liking—their ills amounted to fuses, shorts and overloads. But Mrs. Zeller was more complex. Sometimes she presented him with a document, a machine or a receipt, and demanded an explanation. At times her cheeks were sweetly flushed. Other times she scolded him for no reason, and her castigations reminded him of the days when two dozen children would surround him in the Museum of Prehistoric Man, all yelling in tandem, "*The man isn't making fire—he's making doo-doo! He's not making fire, he's making doo-doo!*" Although Shmuel tried to wipe away the nonsensical image like cold vapors from a window, it insisted on reasserting itself.

Sometimes Shmuel felt an increasing desire to leave. He could easily find another job. But then Mrs. Zeller would come to him with a belated apology and ply him with tales of her hardships, her nervousness, the needs of a woman living alone. Her silver hair and lipstick intensified his resolve to stay. After all, things were good with Mrs. Zeller. Sometimes she even reached into her personal cabinet and pulled out a little bottle of brandy, which she poured into a thick tumbler for herself, and eventually, for him. Her lipstick kisses would appear on the rim of her glass, and Shmuel's heart would smolder as her radiant eyes fixed their gaze on him.

Shmuel's thoughts spent many hours of the day drifting to the silver hair, the red lipstick, the golden bracelets. Sometimes he lost his patience and considered approaching her and declaring masterfully: You and I will go to bed, like a real man and woman! Sometimes he thought he might entreat: Please, you are such a good woman.

Mrs. Zeller had an ancient secretary named Esther, with whom Shmuel's longings actually had a chance of materializing. She liked to talk to him and watch his swift fingers handle the appliances. Sometimes she sat very close and confided in him; she had been widowed at a young age, and her emotional forthrightness and self-pity drew out kernels of longing from him.

By focusing his thoughts, Shmuel was able to get through the day and repair everything he was given. In the evening, he would happily burst through the workshop doors and escape into the streets. He was not, so he perceived, a man merely taking his regular route home every day, but a man intently preoccupied with a long, fatiguing and even dangerous voyage. He liked to walk, his legs longed to walk. He would stop along the way to buy a sugarcane to suck on, or a jelly doughnut, or two portions of falafel. Every day he encountered something beautiful, sparkling, strange. One day he glimpsed a magazine with vulgar pictures, and although they were marred by an unpleasant blurriness, he devised extended itineraries that enabled him to purchase the magazines surreptitiously, far from the eyes of acquaintances and distant relatives to whom his late mother might appear in a dream.

Not all his days were good, but Shmuel had a vast capacity for assembling happiness. Every evening as he walked home, the events of the day would be gradually digested, and little cogwheels would comfort him and reconstruct the day more beautifully than it had begun.

He liked working for Mrs. Zeller.

He liked his journeys through the streets.

He liked lying in the bathtub.

But not infrequently, during his long soaks, he was troubled by disagreeable questions.

What would happen? What would happen?

Shmuel rediscovered the pleasures of fire. The great delight of his childhood days began to draw him in again, and now his methods were even more sophisticated, involving quasi-military experiments with materials he bought from Kalman at the electronics store, who whispered guardedly, "If you get caught, I had nothing to do with it." Shmuel went to abandoned lots and fields where he built fires and lit containers and tried out devices he had invented, and burned huge blazes. He was very pleased. The flames excited him. The smell of the fire. Its savageness. He liked fire. He liked it very much. Sometimes, when the flames burst up high into the sky, they reminded him of Mrs. Zeller.

After the Sabbath, one Saturday in November of 1977, the president of Egypt landed at Lod Airport, and every real Zionist watched his television elatedly. Sitting on the couch in Alma Almagor's apartment, Shmuel was excited too.

Only a small gap hovered between Shmuel and Alma. Shmuel's body assailed it with tiny shifts and covert motions, but he could not close the gap. Alma's borders were maintained, her body declared far away from his.

"This is the total realization of Ben-Gurion's legacy. I always said so!" Alma claimed delightedly.

Shmuel said nothing.

He thought about his father, about the historical peace that he had not lived to see, which may or may not be a pity. He thought of how his father's life had gone by, the childhood he used to talk about, in the Polish village of Tulna. Who would remember how he had met Mother, in Palestine, and the electrical repair workshop on the balcony, and the taxes he paid regularly, and his nationalist friends, and how sometimes, when he heard good news, he would take a little glass down from the top shelf and pour himself some 777 Brandy, and he would laugh and lift Shmuel up to the ceiling with one hand, up and down, and Shmuel would scream and scream, and his mother would scold him with admiration and laughter in her voice, "Strongman, the boy will fall if you're not careful!"

Everything was gone now, melted away.

Not everyone goes down in history.

Shmuel felt sorrow fluttering its wings inside him for a long time.

"You know, my father is dead," he said quietly.

Alma looked at him.

Later Shmuel found it difficult to reconstruct the details of their intercourse. Alma's robe fell to the ground and a cinnamon-like fragrance wafted through the room. Everything he had planned to recall in detail was swallowed up in one powerful memory—the touch of Alma's body, the first touch, the tiny fraction of time after which he would always wonder how his imagination had not dwelled more on the touch of a woman's stomach, the pleasure that overpowered all subsequent moments. Always the seduction, always the penetration, the glory of coitus, but never that one moment that emerged victoriously from the commotion of little details: Alma's stomach beneath his own.

They lay quietly in each other's arms for a few moments, then Alma got up, put her robe on, and served coffee and little sandwiches and cookies. On the television screen there was nothing but shapeless snow. Alma turned down the noisy hum and together they sat calmly watching the snow, munching and sipping politely. The apartment was comfortably quiet. It was nice to chew on the sandwiches and look at the delicate etchings and the embroidered pillows and the furniture covers, handmade by Alma. The glass shone in the doors of the heavy breakfront, which housed tiny decorative china, crystal animals, ornamental bowls, silk flowers, candlesticks. Alma's mother had started the collection, and Alma kept it going for many years, adding item after item.

Shmuel took a bite out of his sandwich.

"I should have married, Shmuel, I should have married," Alma suddenly wept. She buried her face in his shoulder and sobbed. Shmuel put the sandwich down on the platter.

Later that night, in his own apartment, Shmuel woke up, still half-lost in a dream. He got up and went to sit in the living room and allowed his gaze to wander over all the familiar items, briefly pausing on the drapes and then roaming over the floor tiles. His eyes were almost shut, but something obscure inside him fought back—do not sleep, do not sleep. As the disparate desires went on clashing within him, he felt himself slowly stagnating, awake but fossilized, as if under a spell. He stayed in this state until morning, blending in with the still shadows in the room. When he went to work that day, and when he came home in the evening, he tiptoed quickly past Alma's door.

It was after one A.M. when Shmuel heard a knock on the door. He feared it would be Alma, still weeping, but he hoped she might be coming to let him know she was all cheered up now, that she had just cried a little for no reason last evening. But when he slowly opened the door he found curly-haired Hezi standing outside. The neighbor who had left. The one who never said hello.

Hezi promptly addressed Shmuel with a pleading tone: "Listen, Shmuel. I need a little favor. I don't have anyone else, so I'm asking you. Tell me if it's okay or not, I'll understand. All I want is to put this guy who's in trouble in your apartment for a couple of days, maybe three. You have a few rooms and he'll keep to himself in his room, you won't even see or hear him. Ask whatever you want in return, you'll get it. Believe me, nothing complicated, but it will be a big help—for me, for you, for the guy. So what do you say?"

Shmuel stood looking at Hezi. Things almost never happened

to him, and now all of a sudden there was Alma, and Hezi, and the peace. All at once. "Okay," he said.

Hezi left and reappeared a few moments later with a hulking young man whose forearm was tattooed with a green tiger. "Listen, Shmuel. This is the guy I said before. He'll be here with you for a few days in the apartment."

Shmuel looked at the giant and the giant looked at Shmuel. Hezi nervously shoved Shmuel into the apartment.

"You can't let anyone find out about him. Don't talk to anyone. Just go about your business without thinking about him, and that's that. We'll put him in your parents' room, God bless their memory, and he'll just stay in there. He's leaving in a few days, and meanwhile, everything he needs his people will bring him."

"His people?"

"No questions, Shmuel. You're doing me a huge favor. Don't worry, you just go about your business, nothing out of the ordinary."

At night Shmuel woke up with a stomachache and a dry throat, but he convinced himself to go back to sleep, everything would be all right, Hezi had promised. He fell back asleep and by morning he was already getting used to the thick silence behind the closed door of his parents' bedroom. But then he heard a knock on the front door, and a short guy appeared with a meal of noodles and fish. The guy went into Shmuel's parents' bedroom as if he had no doubts about where his boss was staying, and a few minutes later he came out with a note.

Shmuel went to work without eating breakfast. He repaired appliances all day without a break, and in the evening he hurried back to his apartment to see what had become of it. He turned the key and gingerly opened the door. The apartment was cloaked in silence. Under the door of his parents' room was a strip of light, as though the giant was living in there by candlelight.

Shmuel went into the kitchen and prepared his dinner. There was a knock at the door again and he tensed up—should he open it? He looked through the peephole and saw a very pretty young girl.

From his parents' bedroom behind him came the giant's voice—"Is it the woman? Send her in, send her in."

Shmuel warily opened the door. The girl rearranged her purse-strap on her shoulder and with supple steps and no hesitation walked straight to the bedroom.

Shmuel stayed in the kitchen for a long time. He munched on a roll. Made a cup of tea. Washed the dishes in the sink. He could hear the giant's lustful cries as he pleasured himself with the girl. No need to get angry, Shmuel thought. No need to get angry. Hezi didn't know the guy would bring girls here. He went into the living room and sat down bitterly. After a minute he got up and took a volume of *Encyclopedia Hebraica* off the top shelf. When the girl came out she would see him sitting in his armchair reading the encyclopedia. How happy his father had been on the day he brought home the first six volumes, which he had bought on sale—a real opportunity, a national treasure, at a price even modest people could afford.

Shmuel paged through the book. He looked at "Julius Caesar" and tried to concentrate. The conquest of England. Caesar's wife. The despicable murder. He thought of his father again, and suddenly, sadly, faced with the daring acts and historical figures and disasters on the pages of the book, he wondered who would remember his father, Yehezkel Klein, and how he had lived out his life. But as he kept reading his sadness evaporated. The girl was still in the giant's room, and it was time for Shmuel to go to sleep, but he insisted on waiting, like a child who had been promised a fireworks display.

The bedroom door opened briefly, and before Shmuel could see anything, the girl hopped into the bathroom as if she had known the apartment forever.

Shmuel listened to the shower for a long time. He heard water running, stopping, then starting again. He wondered if there would be enough hot water in the tank. Did she know where the soap was? And the shampoo? He wished he had one of those soaps that were pink or baby-blue or pale green. He always stopped to smell them in the new supermarket, wrapped in packaging with pictures of clean women, but he bought the plain ivory-colored ones, the ones his mother used to get. The water came back on for a minute, then slowed to a trickle and stopped. There was some hesitation going on in the bathroom, which was no doubt perfumed with her scent now. Perhaps he should knock softly on the door like a good host and politely tell her where the shampoo, towels and comb were. The water came on again. Shmuel shrank back in the armchair—where did he get these ideas? He listened closely. Soft noises. A towel rubbing a fresh body. Soon she would come out.

When the door opened his heart pounded. The girl walked out of the bathroom and appeared before him in a white towel, with another wrapped around her hair. She was clutching a toiletry kit, with a bottle of shampoo peeking out the top—of course she would not use his. She walked barefoot toward him, her body wrestling the white towel as if attempting a prison escape with every step. He had never seen such a beautiful woman. Wonderful. Simple and clean in her towel.

She looked at Shmuel and a quizzical expression came over her face. "Do I have to do it with you too?" Then, whether to herself or to Shmuel, she replied, "Shimi didn't say."

A new force entered the room. Perhaps she had to do it with Shmuel too?

"I'm cold," the girl said to Shmuel, one foot rubbing the other. "Can I stay here for now?" Then she added, "until he needs me again."

They both looked at the closed bedroom door. The girl walked softly to the armchair opposite Shmuel and sat down with her legs folded under her body.

"My name's Ricki," she said. And everything about her was simple, and she seemed very comfortable.

"I'm Shmuel," he said politely. He was still wondering. Did she have to do it with him too? Who was that up to?

The room was silent. Ricki sat back in the heavy armchair, no longer interested in the answer to her question. "Don't you have a TV yet?"

"There's a telephone," Shmuel said proudly. His father had

successfully outsmarted the long waiting times, called in old favors, even contacted someone who remembered Genia's brother, and was the first in the building to get a telephone installed. Granted, most of the time it sat silently like an old chicken on the table, but it was revered among the building's residents.

"Can I read something?" Ricki asked, and almost angrily added, "I can read, you know."

She took out a pair of reading glasses from her purse and put them on. She suddenly looked very peculiar and very sweet. She got up to look at Shmuel's mother's bookshelf, and as her rear end moved around in the towel, it looked supple and small. She reached out to the romance novels, ran her finger over *The Girl from Rome*, *A Woman's Heart* and *City of Sins*, went back to the armchair with *The Girl from Venice* and huddled up again in an even sweeter position than before. She opened the book and flipped through it. The cover was stained with an ancient coffee ring his mother had left.

Shmuel stifled a sob of delight. He watched Ricki reading for a long time, the way she fingered the pages, wrinkled her forehead, flicked her tongue. When she looked up at him he fled her gaze. Once or twice he was trapped and their eyes met.

There was a knock at the door, and a late dinner was served to the giant. The guy who delivered the meal signaled to Ricki. "Let's go."

She didn't even bother to get dressed. With a white towel and wet hair she took her purse and toiletries and walked out. But at the door she turned to Shmuel and said, "Don't worry, I'll be back tomorrow." And she smiled.

In the morning Shmuel leapt out of bed for his day of work. All day the appliances felt hot between his hands. He felt like Shmuel. Yes, simply like Shmuel. It was as if not all the components of Shmuel had managed to be Shmuel before, but now he was all Shmuel. Shmuel.

Between one repair and the next he hummed tunes and aroused himself with odd thoughts. He smiled to himself and to Esther the secretary, and almost kissed Mrs. Zeller on her neck. All day long he thought of Ricki. He told himself the story of her life. A troubled childhood had led her down a dead-end path, but then she was rescued thanks to a series of generous benefactors who all looked like Shmuel. And now here she was, grown up and beautiful, a real woman, his Ricki, his very own Ricki.

In the evening they met again. They both giggled when she was let into the apartment. The tattooed giant hardly disturbed them. He used Ricki twice, and she spent every free moment sitting with Shmuel in the living room, he with an encyclopedia on his lap, she wearing a robe that used to be light-blue. She read *Freedom for Lovers* and asked Shmuel a few questions. Just before midnight they came to get her, and she winked at Shmuel. "Tomorrow…"

He spent another nourishing and joyous day. Everything he saw and heard gave him pleasure. Mrs. Zeller made him laugh and he made her laugh.

He decided to tell Ricki about his medal of courage that night.

But at times of happiness, the heart pays a price.

That afternoon he ran home. He raced up the stairs thinking only of how glorious life was. When he opened the door he found the apartment empty. A short note from Hezi read, "Thanks. Things worked out well. I owe you."

Shmuel leaned on the kitchen wall. Ricki was gone. Ricki was gone.

Chapter thirteen

Do Not Come, Father Said 1948

> *"I couldn't sleep all night because of this map.*
> *What is Israel?...One tiny mark! One spot!*
> *How will it exist in this Arab world?"*
> *(David Ben-Gurion)*

In 1914 Leon Abramowitz's second son was born and he named him Leon. "Even the ancient people named their sons after themselves," he explained. He always called the boy 'Lolek,' as if to suggest that he was a little lion, and encouraged everyone else to adopt this diminutive. Even when his father settled in Palestine as a journalist-delegate-pioneer-settler, Lolek did not regain his real name. His father was far away, but he was still Lolek.

In Leon's testament-suicide letter he wrote, "My young son Lolek, keep him far away, do not allow him to come to *Eretz Yisrael*," thus decreeing both that the boy's name would be 'Lolek' ever after, and that he would never be allowed to go to Palestine.

Chaim Abramowitz, Leon's firstborn, followed his father's testament strictly. Every two weeks he sent a letter to Lolek with some money, and cautioned, "Do not come, Father said." In 1937 he ordered Lolek to move to France before the European threat worsened.

When the war broke out, he transferred him to Luxembourg, then to England and later to Switzerland. Chaim's emissaries saw to all of Lolek's needs wherever he was, and helped Chaim keep an eye on his brother's affairs. When the war was over, Lolek was sent back home. He was thirty-one and had earned a medical degree.

Throughout the reversals of war, Chaim managed to maintain regular correspondence with his brother, so as to ensure that Lolek would not make the mistake of transgressing their father's prohibition. *Do not come, Father said*, he signed every letter. Sometimes Lolek responded with agreement, sometimes with pleas to immigrate to Palestine as a Zionist, and at other times he seemed to have forgotten the matter entirely.

During his years of medical training, Lolek's life was filled with exciting love affairs, local politics and theoretical hardships, and all his events were described on paper in crowded detail, the stories pecking at one another as if the cage of paper were not large enough to contain all his troubles. Chaim read every word of every letter, and despite being embroiled in his own war of existence in Palestine, he took the time to unravel his brother's affairs, fill in missing details, and enquire about all his travails. In Luxembourg Lolek found it difficult to adjust to the demands of his rigorous studies, and asked Chaim to move him to a more comfortable setting. "The professors are all anti-Semites. It is very difficult for me," he complained. His mood did not improve in England, although he lived in a semi-rural town that was rainy and agreeable. "You will have to buy me another pair of spectacles this winter. A ruffian beat me and there is no one to lodge a complaint with," he wrote. Only in Switzerland did he find the tranquility he longed for, and although he sometimes taunted his brother—"You cannot forbid me to come to *Eretz Yisrael*. If I come, what will you do?"—he usually reported excellent grades and launched into accolades about his professors. For two years he experienced no hardships, and his letters dwindled to a few lines of courtesy meant only to assure Chaim that he had not left Europe and was not disobeying his late father's wishes.

The war ended and Chaim purchased a medical clinic for his brother. Lolek was successful, and soon informed Chaim proudly that he had hired two salaried partners. Chaim Abramowitz's people reported that there was fervent Zionist activity going on in the clinic, where young men and women gathered every week to debate and deliberate, listen to delegates from Palestine, and expound their own arguments. Lolek's letters were touched with the passion of Zionism: "There are women who are unwilling to tie their lives to a man who intends to immigrate to *Eretz Yisrael,* and there are those who are unwilling not to. What should I tell them? Thanks to you I am lonely."

Reading his brother's letters, Chaim Abramowitz did not form the opinion that Lolek was plotting to violate their father's edict, but he spread word among acquaintances who smuggled illegal immigrants that they must prevent any infiltration by Lolek into Palestine. "My father, Leon Abramowitz, asked that his second son remain in Europe, and so it shall be."

In June 1946, as a result of "Black Saturday," Chaim was arrested for a few weeks. While in prison he asked to write one letter, to his brother Lolek. The British officials examined the letter closely and regretted that it contained only a single line: "Do not come, Father said."

Abramowitz's associates in the Mandate released him, which, in turn, facilitated the release of several transactions that had been held up or obstructed. Chaim Abramowitz's freedom was beneficial for people. The Mandate officers got their little rewards, and the Jewish *Yishuv* officials exploited his generous grants and the quiet hospitality he offered to each and every party and faction.

At night the gates of the estate would open and dark cars would glide up the path leading to the house. Prominent leaders would exit the cars, throw a hostile glance into the darkness, and enter Chaim Abramowitz's house, although they found themselves troubled by questions that persistently hovered just beyond their grasp: How could it be that a private individual in Palestine had a perennial stream running through his estate? And what sort of taxes could be levied on such a place once the state was established? Even after hours of discussions, when they got back in their cars and were escorted out of the estate by armed guards, similar thoughts danced through their minds: Such lawlessness here. Armed militias…When the state is established there will be a lot of work to do. But for now… for now we must have peace and quiet.

Abramowitz always reminded his guests of the command: "My father, Leon Abramowitz, asked that his second son remain in Europe." He demanded that they see to the matter, as if the heart of Zionism itself was at issue. The guests, as they huddled in the back seats of their cars on the way out, pondered the harsh edict and the peculiar centrality it had gained. They could not figure out this man, Chaim Abramowitz, whose estate they had just left.

Abramowitz's name often came up in party discussions. Activists beat angry fists on tables and shouted, "He sells arms to Arab gangs!"

"But he sells them to us at a much cheaper price," others pointed out.

"He's getting rich off Zionism! What would become of him if not for us, we who are fighting for a state?"

"He does a lot for the state, and the few who need to, know what I mean. He is a man of secrets, Abramowitz, and asks for no fees in return."

"Fees? Where did that concept even come from in our country—fees?!"

The private nature of Chaim Abramowitz's business did not please the collective institutions, which championed a socialist vision for the nascent state. In tempestuous debates the forces of ideology went to battle in the form of one secretary-general against another, one leader against another. Abramowitz's offers sparked glorious speeches uttered from the depths of the speakers' souls. The compromisers felt the day would come when Abramowitz would be forced to conform, but the extremists demanded immediate action. What sort of action, they could not say conclusively.

"Perhaps instead of criticizing, we should learn a little business acumen from him?" some members suggested. "It's a pity he's not the one in charge of some of our funds…"

Monumental arguments quickly sprung up, waves crashing into an ocean of bitterness, and over the screams and the anger, the silent figure of Abramowitz the merchant loomed as both paragon and disgrace.

Abramowitz did not always make wise business decisions. From time to time he succumbed to his weakness to enter into partnerships in age-old family enterprises. Rather than buy them out and purge them of ancient quarrels, he would join the existing businesses and be swallowed up in the intrigues, the hatred and the rivalries. He found himself in the midst of the strife between the Papashko brothers in their marble factories, the litigious relationship between the Eckler brothers over their metal works, and the disputes among the Cohen brothers in their hotel. He came between bitter fathers and resentful sons in two soap factories. He shared one failing glass factory with the four heirs of the Megossi family in Nahalat Yitzhak, and an oil and wax factory with the five heirs to the Paul family. Many of his profits were eaten up by these contentious transactions, bankruptcies and lengthy downfalls. He spent hours listening to family members' claims, appearing at arbitrations and trials and settlements. But Abramowitz, who was shadowed by stories of his violent method of settling disputes, revealed infinite patience towards these partners, acquiescing to every request and patiently taking part in discussions and hearings. He devoted precious time to plodding investigations into complaints rooted several generations ago, arguments between great-grandmothers and distant cousins. Even when large sums of his money melted away in compromises and settlements, he did not withdraw from the partnerships, but rather he patiently deepened his family ties.

One day a surprising letter was delivered to the estate. It was from Lolek, although it was not written on his regular schedule.

> *Imagine to yourself! I met the Eskiner sisters, who, they say, had a close relationship with Father. They lived in the same hotel in Jaffa for a long time. They are the daughters of the prominent Zionist banker Eskiner, both married, in their forties, and have no children. We met by chance, and a friendship emerged. We even spent a week on holiday together. The sisters were shocked to learn of Father's death, and during our time together we spoke*

of him quite a bit. The sisters sensed a thread of guilt deep inside, and rather than reject it, they tried to comprehend its meaning, even enlisting their psychologist to address the matter. At the end of the week the sisters came to me excitedly and claimed that they did not wish to part with me, that their sense was that I was as close to them as a true blood relative.

In particular, the older sister felt an attachment. She is an extremely noble woman, and I will confess to being most impressed by her command of a variety of languages. She wishes me to become her personal physician. She offers a generous salary—unlimited, in fact—after all, she is the daughter of one of the wealthiest Jews in Britain. What is your opinion? It would entail arduous travel, as the lady's husband is a diplomat, a non-Jew, and has many business interests in Europe. I fear for my health, as travel tends to exhaust me. But it is a wonderful opportunity. To be the private physician to Miss Eskiner, an old friend of Father's! What is your opinion?

"The Eskiner sisters were shocked to learn of my death?" asked Leon Abramowitz eagerly.

"I'm not certain of that, Father," Chaim replied. His father stood facing him, real yet illusory, an apparition of detailed precision. Leon wore an expensive tailored suit acquired after his death, and his hands rested on a wooden desk that one might expect to find in a wealthy man's home. A bountiful library lined the walls behind him, and his whole room, a study of sorts, stood murky but stable, flooded with clean light.

"How can you say they were not shocked? My son Lolek wrote that they were!"

"The Eskiner sisters toyed with your emotions during your life, and now, if you allow them, they will do so after your death. I intend to forbid Lolek to have any contact with them. He has no need to be a private physician; I send him all the money he needs."

"No, no, do not forbid it!" Leon begged. "I...you see, culturally speaking, I would like Lolek to gain a little refinement, to spend time with society's elite."

"Society's elite is here in *Eretz Yisrael*," Chaim decreed, "working the fields, building houses."

"*Nu*, as you wish. But keep the elite of *Eretz Yisrael* to yourself and leave Lolek the elite of Europe."

"There are educated people here too, and they are not afraid to work, Father."

"*Nu*, yes. And you, my son, do you keep up your reading?"

"When there's time, I read. And Günter educates us all. That's the way it is here in *Eretz Yisrael*."

"And the Bible, do you read?"

"In my home, at dinnertime, we read a chapter of the Bible every day," Chaim said proudly.

"And are you learning proper Hebrew?"

"Yes, Father."

"You must be sure to do so. Which reminds me, what is the meaning of this business with the woman from Beer Tuvia?"

"Father, the woman from Beer Tuvia…It's been twenty years already, and you go back to it over and over again. I am married to Sarah now."

"*Nu*, yes, the wife…Oh, well…But still, I would like at least one of my sons to be a true scholar. Not the *Eretz Yisrael* type. In Palestine a man reads an instruction manual on wheat-growing and calls himself a scholar."

Chaim bowed his head. "It's not easy here, Father."

"You are not like Lolek, and I say so regretfully. From the age of fifteen he was known as a genius. All his teachers said so, every single one of them."

"When I was fifteen, Father, you brought me to Jaffa. I broke my back working Levin's orchards. Legend says I worked for one whole year, day and night, never shutting an eye, to compete with the Arab laborers. And do not forget, I was orphaned."

"Orphanhood, my son, if one examines it closely, is not in fact detrimental." Leon Abramowitz settled into a comfortable position in his desk chair. "Here are some established facts for you. The father of Hassidism, the Baal Shem Tov, was orphaned at the age of five, and Ze'ev Jabotinsky at the age of six. Yosef Bussel, who would have been a leader of this nation had he not drowned in Lake Tiberias, lost his father at seven, and Alexander Zaid, the legendary watchman whom you yourself surely admire, outdid us all by losing his mother at the age of three! Were the prospects of these orphans harmed? Allow me to polish my pen and I shall present you with an article, 'In Praise of Orphanhood'!"

Leon's figure wavered a little, as if he wished to disappear and go back to one of the articles he had been laboring over since death had absolved him from the nuisances of life.

"Don't go yet, Father. Tell me, what you are writing about now?"

"Me? Much as always, a denunciation of *corruptzia*," Leon replied.

"You know, father, we have a Hebrew word for corruption in *Eretz Yisrael* now."

Leon's image began to break up like a mirror splashed with water.

"Do not go, Father."

"My son Lolek is an orphan just like you, and we must not deny him his chance for happiness. Let him become Miss Eskiner's physician. I still remember her. Such a lovely young woman. She was all of eighteen years old, and her delightful young age glistened in the spark of her eyes, on her rosebud lips, her shining hair. And you, Chaim, you too have earned the mercy of many women. I have been watching…*Nu*, well done. Not only the wife of the banker Meirson threw herself into a well. Yes, and thus a tragedy is built. But back to Miss Eskiner—she can teach Lolek nothing but virtuousness. Those poor women."

Chaim looked at his father's image. His desk was strewn with unfinished articles, political pamphlets, and envelopes full of correspondence with other deceased people.

"I knew the young lady when she was the same age as that girl, Rivka, the one with the beautiful eyes, the wild one, the sweet one… the daughter of the woman, your wife…"

"Her name is Sarah."

"Yes, that is her name, and of all the women in Palestine you took that one…pregnant, another man's wife…"

"A widow, not another man's wife!"

"And older than you!"

"We've already agreed, Father, that we will not discuss Sarah. Not every time."

Leon looked chastised, and his figure wavered. He reached out to an envelope as if he had to get back to work.

"Father, don't go! Not yet."

"Come to think of it, on the matter we just referred to…how is she, your wife? How is she?" Leon asked and gave a large yawn.

Chaim woke up. He was lying on the side of a deserted path near the slopes of the Carmel. His horse stood nearby chewing grass. *How is she, your wife? How is she…*What his father had meant to find out, Chaim knew, was whether Sarah was pregnant. He had always said, "A man who does not leave his seed in the world, it is as if he never lived. Take me: I left two sons."

Only in those faraway hours, alone on his journeys, did Chaim's conversation with his dead father emerge. After Leon's suicide his memory was swallowed up in the great flood of life, banished by the struggles, the difficulties, the women. But two or three years later he began to resurface and claim his place. At first he tried to appear in Chaim's dreams, but found them inadequate for his needs. He eventually made his way into Chaim's daydreams.

Chaim did not usually give himself leave to waste precious time, but when he was alone on his travels he often experienced a burning urge to sit down on the side of the road with his head against a tree and shut his eyes. His father would appear immediately, not as an angel armed with a sword, but sitting comfortably in his study. He seemed happy in death, and the glimmer in his eyes that he had long ago lost was renewed. The questions of Zionism that had preoccupied him in life troubled him in death too, and he would grasp his pen and sharpen his tongue on the paper. He did not look fondly on Chaim's business, which he found practically dangerous and ideologically ambiguous. Leon Abramowitz found flaws in his son's relationships with the Arabs, "who are inclined to be our enemies," and commented on his ties with the British, "whose White Paper policy publicly desecrates the memory of Lord Balfour."

Since ridding himself of the trivialities of existence, Leon Abramowitz had adopted a habit of ignoring time. He talked to Chaim incessantly about the topic of his great work in progress, the weakness of the *Yishuv*, throwing in the Baron Rothschild with the labor movement, David Ben-Gurion with Herzl. Chapter by chapter his essay took shape, fermenting and expanding, touching on every issue and all manners of trouble.

"I had scarcely completed my essay, 'Against the Bane of Electricity,' and had begun to consider the topic of my next article, even considering a short leave from my research, when I came face to face with 'The Botheration of Smiling.' You may ask, Chaim, what I mean by this. I shall explain. One day I happened to find myself in a bank, observing the conduct of the clerks. And what did I witness? As they converse with the customers, each and every one of their utterances is affixed with a contented smile. They say this, they say the other, and finally, at the tail end of their words—a broad smile. Needless to say, I was incensed. Have you any idea how many more customers could have been served by these clerks if not for their smiles? I measured the wasted time. You will never guess! Mathematics determine: sixteen additional customers per day! Imagine to yourself, another sixteen loans, sixteen grants-in-aid! Day by day, sixteen infrastructures for building a new house, a farm, a factory. And of course one must then calculate how many this means every year, and the answer: five thousand additional houses and farms! And in twenty years? One-hundred thousand! One-hundred thousand new houses and farms for Zionism! Now I ask you to consider the weight of this curse of smiling!"

Leon Abramowitz's indifference to the passage of time left him greater energies to devote to his castigations of Chaim. He fumed over Chaim's love affairs with the women of the *Yishuv*, as if he had not been married to Sarah for many long years. He spoke harshly of the marriage with Sarah, "of all the daughters of Palestine," and made insistent demands regarding her fertility. "Children are the heart of life!"

Chaim stood mute in the face of Leon's sermonizing, acquiescing to all his dead father's demands, taking comfort in the fact that there was no logic in these appearances, and that despite his apparent vivacity and lust for life, his presence must symbolize an internal dialogue between Chaim and his own conscience, which meant that all the arrows of criticism his dead father shot at him were best regarded as his own inner judgments.

On the subject of the Eskiner sisters Leon did not give up, insisting that Chaim allow Lolek to become the young lady's private physician. "Do not worry, only good will come of Lolek's time among the learned of Europe," he promised.

But in May of 1948, a few days before the State of Israel was declared, Chaim received a letter from Lolek—or rather, a frantic note:

> *The inevitable has occurred between Miss Eskiner and myself, and her husband is pursuing me. I have no alternatives, brother Chaim. I have no alternatives. His power is great and his vengefulness fierce. You must allow me to immigrate to Eretz Yisrael, and if not, I shall come without your blessing. I have heard that they need physicians in our war; since I am a physician, how could you be so bold as to prevent me from coming to care for the wounded?*

Chaim rushed a letter to his brother and sent his men to intervene with the British, who were embroiled in the chaos of their departure. He entreated Jewish military commanders, illegal immigration agents, Druze smugglers on the Lebanese border, contacts on the Syrian border, and everyone who had any loyalty to him—they must prevent Lolek Abramowitz from entering Palestine.

On the tenth of May, word came that Lolek had disappeared and his belongings were on their way to Palestine.

Chaim gripped his chair. He closed his eyes so that he could concentrate on this nightmarish development. "Call Günter," he said softly.

He dictated three-hundred and eighteen lines of instructions. Hundreds of his men set off to the Zionist establishment offices, the immigration institutions, the security apparatuses, the labor parties and the underground movements. They turned up at ports of entry, at the desks of immigrant registrars, and in all the offices where the details of new immigrants were piling up. Chaim Abramowitz himself left on horseback, but not before hiring seven detectives to operate in the Galilee, the Negev, the Sharon, the Carmel, the Jezreel Valley, the Coastal Region and Jerusalem, all charged with locating Lolek, identifying possible routes and landmarks, and monitoring them closely until Lolek himself was found.

Abramowitz galloped from trace to trace, from investigation to disappointment. Twice he crossed the border into Syria, twice into Jordan and twice into Lebanon, hunting down every witness, every rumor, every sound. Clues arose and tumbled, testimonies soared and shattered. More than sixty possible routes were drawn up, each based on reliable witnesses, steadfast hints and indestructible signs of life—Palestine was dotted with Lolek from border to border.

Abramowitz's delegates increased their pressure on the establishment. They burrowed through records, checked in the monasteries, searched among Bedouin tribes and obscure communities. Each delegate reported back with clues, each offered a decoding that put him only one step away from catching up with Lolek himself. Volunteers of all types stepped forward, the hallways of the Zionist organizations bustled with initiatives and a vague sense of worry—that, and no small amount of guilt.

In May 1948 the State of Israel was declared. Chaim Abramowitz did not join in the celebrations. His brother was not on any of the ships arriving at the shores of the new state, and the name 'Lolek Abramowitz' did not appear on any passenger lists. But people all over the country reported sightings of Lolek, including some in the battles that ensued immediately after the state was declared. Casualties who had been treated by Lolek came forward, providing dates and names of battalions. There was no trace of Lolek in official papers, but the testimonies sketched his progression. Sometimes in the south, sometimes the north, sometimes in the heart of the country.

"He seems to be missing," concluded Leon Abramowitz.

Chaim lowered his eyes. He had been disobeyed. People who had given him their word had let his brother come ashore and join the fighters, allowing him to interfere in battles that were not his. No one took responsibility, no one admitted they had recognized Lolek and allowed him to pass.

"My son is missing," Leon lamented.

"I'll find him, Father. I will find him."

Chaim Abramowitz did not allow himself to spend a single night on his estate until October. He traveled to and fro, full of wrath and despair. His people made inhuman efforts. They scanned abandoned wells, ruins, beaches, transit papers, licenses, casualty lists, obsolete posts, kibbutzim, transit camps. Lolek had been everywhere, and was nowhere.

When Chaim searched in the Galilee he was joined by a company of soldiers provided by the military authorities. Policemen, some undercover, accompanied him on his searches in remote villages, along the borders, in the monasteries dotting the Judean Desert, even in enemy territory. The Ministry of the Interior sent detailed reports for his perusal, the Ministry of Health tried to prove that someone named Arieh-Lolek Abramowitz had filed a request for a license to practice medicine. All arms of the Zionist state tried to help, to contribute, to endear themselves—it was not their fault, after all...not their fault.

"What have you done?" Chaim Abramowitz demanded.

"My son, where is my son?" asked Leon Abramowitz.

Visions of his father came to Chaim repeatedly. Chastised, he promised to step up his efforts.

At the end of October 1948, it was suggested to Chaim that his brother had been taken hostage by the Syrians in the failed battle over Mishmar Hayarden. Lolek's name was not among the dead or missing, nor was he officially listed as a hostage, but the rumor was persistent, and Chaim believed it. The assumed date of Lolek's arrival coincided with the desperate June battles that had ended in the complete destruction of Mishmar Hayarden. If someone had allowed him to disembark on Israel's shores, if someone else had taken him under their wing and brought him to a military group, it was certainly possible that Lolek had been captured in one of the houses on Mishmar Hayarden, besieged and desperate and frightened. The dead were already buried, the matter of the hostages had been concluded, but several people from Mishmar Hayarden were still missing, and the recriminations had not yet died down.

"The Zionists killed my brother," said Chaim Abramowitz.

He crossed the border in pursuit of Lolek. Two of his Druze friends took him to the tent of a Bedouin acquaintance, and at night he was rushed to a meeting with a witness. They were attacked in a wadi by a Syrian force, and Chaim was abandoned. He lay hidden by some bushy growth, ready to defend himself, when Leon Abramowitz appeared before him sitting silently at his desk, his face buried in his hands.

"I will find him, Father," Chaim promised, and before Leon's image disappeared he had time to glimpse him waving his hand dismissively.

"I will find him!" he called after his father. A burst of gunfire ricocheted through the bushes around him.

In the morning he managed to slip away from the Syrian guards. He crossed the border and lay down to rest at the foot of a tree. He leaned his head back and waited. But Leon did not come.

At midday, when he rounded the bend just outside the estate, he found Günter waiting for him. Sarah was dead.

Chaim Abramowitz settled down in the estate and devoted himself to its affairs. He did not speak of Sarah, and he stopped searching for Lolek, as if the two tragedies had somehow negated one another and vanished, arm in arm. He never again saw his father in his visions.

Part Two

Chapter fourteen

A Sad Circus Car   1948

"The 'Zionists' do well not to come here:
as one awaiting 'the fulfillment of Zionism,'
there is nothing to do here."
(Yosef Chaim Brenner)

A few months after the tragedies, an anxious and awkward Günter finally faced Abramowitz.

Every day while Abramowitz sat in his room, Günter had studied his face for signs of grief, reasoning that despite his marble eyes, Abramowitz was in deep mourning. Each day as he walked to the house, Günter's spirit gained an uncommon sense of courage, a protective barrier, as though he were being cast in steel with every step he took, and by the time he stood facing the stony glare of the master of the estate, he was able to stare back at him with equally unwavering command. It had been decreed from above that he fathom Abramowitz's great love for Sarah, and now she was dead, and everything he did was in her honor, so why should he retreat?

But now he was anxious and awkward, his strength failing him as he stomped and panted up the steps and breathlessly reached Abramowitz's room. What would he tell him?

A large shipment had arrived: the bundled belongings of his

brother Lolek. The cargo had gone astray months ago, and the shippers had made many excuses—after all, there was a war raging in Palestine. But now here it was at the gates of the estate and it could not be ignored.

Abramowitz studied Günter's face and knew. "Someone has arrived. Who?"

Günter pursed his lips. The question was a simple one, easily answered, but he held his tongue, hoping Abramowitz would guess—"Lolek?" he might ask, or even, "Sarah?" And then Günter could burst into tears.

But Abramowitz sat silently.

From outside, near the gates, came the sounds of a commotion. An altercation between the shipping agents and the guards. Abramowitz looked out. The cargo sat outside like a sad circus car, visible through the fence. He quickly turned back and told Günter curtly, "Give it to the poor."

Maybe now, maybe now Abramowitz would weep?

Günter himself almost sobbed, but he held back. He wished Abramowitz would say something to give birth to his grief.

Günter took a deep breath. Only someone as close to Abramowitz as he was could have noticed the long shudder that passed through him. His conduct. His business dealings. But why did he never say "Sarah"? Why did he never say "My brother, Lolek"?

"I am an orphan again," Abramowitz said.

"No, no…" Günter echoed. He gestured at the window, trying to encompass the landscape of the estate, to comfort Abramowitz with the many people who were like family to him, but his hand remained hanging in the air. Abramowitz was grieving. He was. Swaying this way and that in the darkness of his days. Sarah was gone. Lolek was gone.

Günter's hand briefly considered coming to rest on Abramowitz's shoulder, but it hurried back to its place. Deep inside, Günter was burdened by a profound sense of bereavement, but to overstep his boundaries, to flood the world with a grief professing to exceed that of Abramowitz himself—this was forbidden. Sometimes, even during trivial business conversations, Abramowitz would say something that evoked Sarah, and sometimes the two of them sat silently for a long time, their thoughts drifting to the same places, describing something that could not take shape. "The Zionists killed my brother," Abramowitz would finally say, his hatred taking frightening forms on his face, and Günter would shiver.

"Give it to the poor," Abramowitz repeated and waved his hand at the commotion through the window. He stood up, and did not need to explain a thing to his foreman, who recognized every one of his tones: he was leaving on one of his horseback journeys.

Abramowitz's voyages took place in a country still at war. The last of the battles dotted the hilltops and roads. Chaim Abramowitz would stop on his way to doze off alone beside trees and wells, and wait for his father, hoping to be found. But his father never came.

As he left the estate and rode past the sad cargo of Lolek's belongings, Abramowitz steered his horse far away and felt that this time his father must appear. When he stopped to rest beneath a cluster of trees, he briefly felt the familiar haze in his mind, and knew that soon he would see the study, the desk, and his father's tired, stern eyes. But instead he beheld the man who had shot himself under the eucalyptus tree, with a note jutting out of his pocket: "I have tired of it all."

Abramowitz returned from his voyage in a fury. He ordered his people to replace the fences with stone walls. Government inspectors soon came to inquire and demanded a variety of licenses, permits and certificates. Abramowitz refused to present papers to the Zionist state; he would not be held accountable to them. "Where is my brother?" he asked.

The next day police officers arrived. An argument ensued. Rifles were aimed. Günter limped among the parties and tried to mediate. "Perhaps a committee..." he suggested.

"A committee?"

"Yes, I heard there are lots of committees..."

The police withdrew. But the next morning a company of soldiers arrived and prepared to encircle the estate.

Abramowitz ordered trenches dug, barricades erected,

observation posts and sniper towers built. Another company came to reinforce the first one. The soldiers stood on guard and stared at the kites blossoming over the estate, rustling large and colorful. Beneath them stood young Rivka, who came right up to look at the men and did not seem an enemy at all. They called out to her once in a while, and tried to make jokes. She smiled and craned her neck to see them, but did not acquiesce in their joy. Let them chatter. Let them celebrate. Let them ask in vain for her to come closer, right up to the edge.

The officers fumed and shouted thunderously at the walls through megaphones: "How long can you hold out?" But Abramowitz's builders kept at their work. Finally the commander got up on a wooden crate and issued a two-day ultimatum through the megaphone. But someone in some government office soon came to his senses and ordered that the battlefield be dispersed. "One *Altalena* was enough for us. We'll handle Abramowitz yet."

The wall went up.

Chaim Abramowitz declared a total boycott of the Zionist state, Zionist acts and Zionist intent. The Abramowitz Estate was now a place with no connection to the State of Israel.

The state ignored him. Who was Abramowitz anyway?

Most of the time the state was too busy delighting in its new-found status. What could be more enjoyable than passing laws? The Areas of Jurisdiction and Powers Act of 1948. The Administration of Rule and Justice Act of 1948. The Defense Service Act of 1949. The Customs and Excise Tax (Rate Change) Act of 1949. The delights of ruling, the joys of levying taxes, the bliss of developing more and more legislation and subclauses of legislation, like tiny and precariously delicate threads. Who cared about Abramowitz?

Here and there in some government offices, old friends tried to appease him, offering the only bounty at the disposal of an impoverished state: to name a street after his father.

Abramowitz refused.

They explained that a street would be named in at least two cities, and insinuated that even a town square might be possible.

They suggested an institution, like a sanatorium or a military base, exclusively named after Leon Abramowitz.

Abramowitz's steadfast refusal ignited hostility. Why, the state wondered, were they beholden to him? They remembered his armed men, the stream running through his estate, and a handful of dubious acts to which his name had been tied. They could imprison him, after all—there were laws now.

For a while the adversaries ignored one another. The War of Independence was not over, groaning ships full of immigrants deposited their passengers on the shores of Israel, adding to the ranks of fighters and settlers. Abandoned villages and new immigrants intermingled. Government offices, municipal boards, organizations and institutions sprung up. The new and the old sighed deeply and fought on.

The state was inclined to ignore Abramowitz, and he too waved a banner of indifference. But both parties discovered they could not be rid of one another quite so easily. The state's development projects repeatedly came up against private lands belonging to Abramowitz that were stuck right in the heart of the plans. The state took fearless steps: appropriation, annexation, nationalization. But Abramowitz set his venomous lawyers on the state and they waged a war against it, vacillating between compromise and rebellion, grasping at every branch of the law and all its dark ruses. The state despised Abramowitz. How could it express the degree to which it hated this man who himself hated it?

Induction orders began to arrive for young Lolek-Arieh Abramowitz, as per the Defense Service Act of 1949. Summons as per the Compulsory Education Act of 1949. And ration stamps for the citizen Lolek-Arieh Abramowitz.

The state laws wanted Lolek. They longed for Lolek. He was entitled to assistance as per the Discharged Soldiers Act of 1949. And he was a defector as per the Defense Service Act of 1949. The Ministry of Health wanted to vaccinate him. The Ministry of Education registered him for both kindergarten and the third grade in the same year. A phone line was ordered in his name, and against all logic, instead of the customary two-year wait, technicians came twice to hook up the line.

Günter suggested writing letters of complaint to all the government offices, but Abramowitz refused. Günter sent the letters secretly, demanding that they cease to address the missing Lolek Abramowitz: they had already killed the boy once. Enough was enough. In particular, he asked to stop sending the ration stamps, as the Abramowitz estate had erased itself from the lists of recipients under the "austerity" regime.

Abramowitz fought the state. Every acre, every foot. No development plan was drawn in which some plot of land belonging to him did not emerge. The state fought back. Legal entanglements grew on every piece of Abramowitz's land. Surveyors paced back and forth among the furrows. In the shade of thinning trees, attorneys for the state and attorneys for Abramowitz gathered to present their arguments. From time to time, government representatives came to the estate and tried to levy a tax or summon someone to an inquiry. Seeing Rivka's kites hovering cheerfully in the sky above the estate, they whispered among themselves—

"What about the austerity?"

"People are hungry."

"Fire on the borders."

"People are begging for work."

They felt there was something inappropriate about the kites, which somehow seemed disloyal to the law, to the regime, to the era. But this vague sense could not be corroborated by any particular article of law, and so they let the kites be. They also allowed the taxes and the inquiries to languish at the foot of the walls surrounding the estate. Abramowitz declared he would give nothing nor ask anything from the state that had killed his brother.

At night Günter watched his master awake as if a whip had lashed against his cheek. He would sit up in bed, then rise and wander around the estate until morning.

"You," Gunter mumbled, "perhaps what you need...is a wife."

Chapter fifteen

Autumn is a Good Season: the Body Opens Up   1953

Eighteen months after Sarah's death, Chaim Abramowitz announced that he was marrying his stepdaughter Rivka.

The wedding was held on the estate with a small circle of guests and without any joy. Günter walked the orphaned bride to the *chuppa* and worriedly tended to her needs, then withdrew into the audience and stood sneezing, his eyes teary. *Al rijal jimal, al rijal jimal,* a voice in his head kept saying—*men are camels.* Günter shook his head to banish the words. *Nigofi,* he hissed at his former wife—*Nigofi.* When he looked at the bride and groom standing close under the *chuppa* he felt a lump in his throat, and all he could see was his absent wife, inflaming his hatred: *Nigofi! Nigofi!*

*

There were no great changes on the estate after Chaim and Rivka's marriage. The couple did not build a new house or revitalize the old one, nor did they fill it with new furniture and rugs. Rivka packed up her effects. She hung her kites on the walls of her old room like disused agricultural tools, and relocated to Abramowitz's room.

From time to time the employees would look up at the house as if expecting something to happen, and upon seeing it sitting silently on the hilltop they would turn back to their work. After a while, they stopped looking. The house settled back into the estate landscape and there it stood on its peak, distracting no one.

Beyond the walls the state continued its infantile mischief, experimenting with its newfound independence. There were social, economic and other domestic issues that needed to be addressed. Laws and laws and more laws. Like a puckish bear pup unaware of its colossal weight, the state trampled anyone unwatchful. In desperation, people turned to Abramowitz for help, as though unaware of his boycott, or because they were simply accustomed to his patronage. A rabble of small-time merchants, former underground members, Arab villagers, new immigrants, the unemployed, and errant politicians.

Friends from the heart of the system were allowed to visit Abramowitz despite the boycott, to congratulate him on his marriage. As they sat with him and discussed the affairs of the day, their eyes scanned the room. Products that even the black market could not boast of appeared on the Abramowitz estate—pomegranate juice, fine butter, plentiful eggs, silk handkerchiefs. These friends adopted grave expressions and discussed the conflicts, the challenges and the dangers, but what they saw tugged at their hearts. They knew their response was unjustified—for what were luxuries to them? And yet the thoughts were there. As if that were not enough, before leaving they were handed little notes with requests to help the desperate people who came to Abramowitz. Once in a while, a meeting would end with the guest stomping his feet and demanding to become part of the estate.

Every week Abramowitz took in new followers from the ranks of the Zionist state. Günter, whose life had trained him to identify any sign of bitterness, wandered among government offices, military units and security services, marking people ripe for enticement.

Abramowitz's recruiters would take it from there, enter into negotiations and extend offers until the process reached its zenith—a personal meeting with Chaim Abramowitz, whether for good or for bad.

It was known in certain circles that Abramowitz paid handsomely for betrayal, and occasionally an eager defector would appear at the gates. Phony turncoats sent by the government came too, but Günter quickly exposed them: he always picked up the absence of gripes, his heart could sense if there was no thicket of grievances, no demand for a nourishing form of compensation different from mere money, something akin to the comfort of a mother's breast.

More and more people joined the estate. To build houses, they needed more land. Abramowitz had his eye on the orchards to the west of the estate, which, in springtime, exuded a fragrance that covered up controversial dealings in the land registration office, heirs and cousins of heirs intertwined through ancient lawsuits. The walls of cypress trees and the rows of orange trees struck roots in the depths of the bureaucracy and wrapped themselves around rigid inheritance battles reinforced by the shrewd parsimony of farmers. Abramowitz's old nemesis, Levin the Citrus Grower, lorded over his associates. Abramowitz's henchmen worked hard and gave out bribes far and wide, threw Abramowitz's name into the ring, but it was all in vain. Levin was adamant: We will not sell to Abramowitz. He still remembered the young boy of fifteen who had come to work in his orchards years ago and had soon begun fighting for workers' rights and rousing other pickers against the growers. At the height of the conflict the young Abramowitz and his devotees had waged a personal crusade against Levin—not the usual sort of political dispute, but a skirmish fought with rakes and hoes. Word of the events had spread throughout the *Yishuv*. Over the years, Abramowitz and Levin had met once or twice, allowing their hatred to amass, but they did not seek out conflict. Now it seemed the adversaries were once again locked in battle.

"The orchard lands will be ours," Abramowitz resolved.

To the west of his estate were the orchards, and to the east, in his line of sight, a town was emerging. First the two Arab villages adjacent to the estate were abandoned and new immigrants entered the houses with their possessions. Then the gap between the villages was filled with a transit camp. Finally a local council was declared.

In February 1950 the estate was ordered to pay municipal taxes.

Abramowitz declared he would not give a penny to the state.

The council asked for an explanation.

Abramowitz replied that he would not give explanations either.

Every morning he watched the town springing up, pieced together from the tents of old transit camps and abandoned stone houses, laundry lines, and linens.

And to the west—Levin's lands.

"He will never get them," Levin declared.

One day while Abramowitz and Rivka walked through the field between the estate and the orchard, shots were fired, hitting a cluster of rocks nearby. Six weeks later, while attending the wedding of a friend from the Mahajna family in an Arab village, celebratory gunshots rang out. One or two bullets mingling with the festive rounds narrowly missed Abramowitz's head. He blamed Levin's men. At the end of that year a bomb went off next to Abramowitz's car. Miraculously, no one was hurt.

"Bombs are not Levin. This is the state," Abramowitz affirmed.

A shot just missed him as he walked with Rivka on the Tel Aviv beach. Another hit a tree that he was leaning on near Kibbutz Ginosar.

Chaim Abramowitz did not look kindly on the attempts to murder him. He met an old acquaintance from the security apparatus, who promised him that although the state desired very much to try him and throw him into jail, under no circumstances would it act to assassinate a citizen.

"I am not a citizen."

"Even someone who is not a citizen."

"So who is trying to assassinate me?"

"Certainly not the state. Even though your connections with

unwanted parties are known. Even though we know you had close ties with Kamal Arikat at the height of the War of Independence. Even though you helped out Muhammad Hawari on at least two occasions. Even though after the murder of Bernadotte you hid suspected Lehi members. And even though we do not like you at all."

"So who is trying to assassinate me?"

"To the best of our knowledge, our judgment, and our investigations, the assassination attempts occur without assassins. You will probably say this is illogical. But what is? Is it logical to start rounding up all the weapons that are floating around in people's hands here? There is a state now. You must have heard about the Firearms Act of 1949. These arms will have to be seized, by force if necessary."

In early 1951 the Abramowitz Estate was raided. They came to find out if Chaim Abramowitz was involved in distributing fake ration stamps. Unverified stamps had been turning up everywhere, allowing the wicked to take food from babies' mouths. They interrogated Abramowitz and searched all corners of his estate. They confiscated every last weapon they could find. For seven days and seven nights the estate teemed with soldiers, bomb-sniffers, diggers, policemen and detectives, until every stone had been turned.

Abramowitz did not resist. All week he sat in his home studying documents and working on new transactions, ignoring the state. When investigators entered his room to gingerly poke around and asked to look under the tiles beneath his feet, he let them do as they pleased. If anyone was expecting the angry giant to call in his men and put up a struggle, they were disappointed. The soldiers roamed the estate idly, stole eggs from the coop, tried to shear wool off the sheep. Seeing kites flying freely above the grounds of the estate, they longed to hold them. And Rivka.

Two days after the estate was declared free of weapons, Levin the Citrus Grower was found shot in one of his orchards. The suspicion fell on Abramowitz. But when the police came to question him they found a proud young Arab man who confessed to the murder. They took him and his two brothers to the police station, where he restated his confession. The two brothers efficiently corroborated his story, testifying to nothing but the bare necessities: a motive, a weapon and a summary of the deed. Why would the police think anyone else had committed the murder? The young Arab, a member of the Mahajna family, then began to boast of his triumph. He had always hated "Jewists," and Levin the Citrus Grower was a "Jewist." That was all there was to it. Buoyed by his feat, he embarked on a flowery political speech to prove the extent of his hatred, until his brothers elbowed him to stop and he sat back quietly.

With Levin absent, the heirs to the orchards handed the lands over to Abramowitz, who proceeded to swallow them up within the estate and cover them with houses and walls. From the highest peak, right at the edge of the estate, one could see a strip of seawater, and Abramowitz ordered a lookout tower to be built.

The state went about its noisy ways. A plague of locusts desecrated crops. The rationing worsened, the black market flourished. A rift broke out in the kibbutz movement between those who supported socialism-but-not-Stalin and those who championed socialism-and-Stalin. Pieces of kibbutzim broke away, families were torn apart, people were forced to take sides. Every community ripped in two by a knife of hatred insisted on keeping its name, but added a mark of distinction—*union* or *unified*. The two camps struggled, separated, split, and cleaved, but both stuck to their names in a decidedly un-united fashion, each insisting that it was not to blame for the other's factionalism.

Abramowitz almost took pity on the fraying state, but when it transpired that the rift would not kill it but merely cause eternal heartache and families that would grow old under the shadow of terrible words they could not take back and hatred they would carry to the grave—he withdrew his pity.

In the state there was turmoil. The *Yishuv* was gripped with poverty, terror, distress and hunger. On the Abramowitz Estate all was tranquil.

It was only Günter, ever since Sarah Abramowitz's death, who broke the restfulness. What was science good for? What was his wife Ruth good for? And work—he no longer wished to manage a vast estate using only his memory. He did not wish to remember. Damned memory.

Günter walked around the estate as subdued as he could be, but his appearance aroused unease.

"What do you want?" Abramowitz asked.

"Nothing at all. Nothing at all. What could I want? Nothing. Except…except maybe a synagogue."

"A synagogue?"

"Yes. And a rabbi."

The synagogue was built and Günter spent much of his time there. From the window, during prayer times, he looked out at the estate. Where was his passion to work for Chaim Abramowitz? Where was his determination to increase the estate's success? Where was the delight that used to burn in his bones, of aiding Chaim Abramowitz?

One evening he looked at the widow he had been matched with.

Ruth, he thought.

Moabite, he thought.

He got rid of his science books and burned his collection of erotica. He purchased holy books and grew a beard and side locks. He asked Abramowitz for permission to travel around the country, perhaps to spend some time in the Galilee, in Safed.

"What for?"

"Penance for sins."

"What sins?"

"Of a man."

"When I find a replacement you can go," Abramowitz decided.

As the State of Israel raged over the question of German reparations, and clouds of locusts rose forth from the desert to annihilate the fields, and poverty continued to take its toll, Günter roamed restlessly around the estate.

And then his son Shaul appeared, borne on an airplane, and asked to take the name of "Hans." Günter appointed him deputy and trained him to be the head foreman. Hans did not possess his father's impressive memory, but he was found to have considerable intellect, keen business instincts, and a slyness that could bend horizons.

Günter taught his two deputies, Hans and Lerer, drop by drop and with infinite patience, and they soon fought mercilessly over every role and every power.

"When can I leave?" Günter asked Abramowitz.

"Soon."

Günter waited. In the spring his first limp grew stronger and overcame the younger limps. In the summer and autumn his first limp fell into a slumber and the second rose as king. Come winter time, the third limp was awarded a short reign. And spring again. Günter waited.

Lerer and Hans spent every day stubbornly clashing over the division of authorities. They both acknowledged the indifferent superiority of Günter, who, in turn, was but an echo and a shadow of the absolute authority of Chaim Abramowitz.

Günter watched as the two men fought and the estate flourished, and he longed to withdraw from the world. One day in the fall of 1952 he was granted his exile to the town of Safed. Before leaving, he told Abramowitz, "I will pray for the fruit of the womb to be given to you and Rivka."

Günter's words lodged in Abramowitz's flesh, and he began to seek out Rivka constantly. He preyed on her body, and she submitted without complaint. In the mornings and at night and on holidays and on days of rest and in their room and on their journeys.

I will pray for the fruit of the womb...

From his marriage to Sarah he had no children.

A man who does not leave his seed in the world, it is as if he never lived...

His father's words haunted him. And Günter's arrow still hurt.

I will pray for the fruit of the womb...A man who does not leave his seed in the world...

After they were intimate, Rivka would say, "I am barren, Chaim."

"You are not barren."

"Mother was barren, too. We are a breed of barren women, Chaim. My mother conceived me with great difficulty, and her mother conceived her with great difficulty, and, as you can see, I bear no children at all. Why do you attach yourself to a breed of barren women? Cast me out and marry a good woman who will fill the estate with babies."

Chaim searched for a remedy, a way to have his child. Doctors from all over the country offered treatments, but nothing worked. There was even a letter of advice from a gynecologist calling himself Dr. Lolek Abramowitz, full of crude language, erotic and evil.

In 1953 Chaim Abramowitz took Rivka to see Dr. Meshulam Riklin, a naturopath in Ness Ziona who was known for performing miracles on women's wombs. Infertile women came to him from all over the country, and secretly from Jordan and Lebanon. They said he could give the gift of fertility, that every woman who paid him would be rewarded with the fruit of her womb. But the gossip also held that every child he had brought into this world grew up to be miserable, weary and failed. Something was always wrong with these children, something unseen but nonetheless real.

After Chaim and Rivka Abramowitz left his clinic, Dr. Meshulam Riklin took out his diary and wrote: "Rivka is not beautiful. One's body takes pleasure in seeing her, but does not tell the soul." Then he added: "And she does not look like Naomi, my poor dove, she does not. But had my little dove not passed away, would their eyes have been similar now?" As he did every time he wrote the name Naomi, he did not shut the diary immediately, but turned the pages back to read through previous entries about patients in distant times. Yet he was not thinking about his late wife, or about Rivka, but about Chaim Abramowitz. A giant of a man.

A week later Chaim Abramowitz came to the clinic to pick up an herbal mixture the doctor had concocted for Rivka. He held out the jar of herbs and explained how they should be taken. He spoke slowly, deliberately, as if reciting to a child from large print. When he walked Abramowitz to the door, he wanted to lay a hand on his shoulder and say, "I am a good doctor. I have healed many women." But silence paralyzed his throat.

When the treatment produced no results—neither a baby, nor a pregnancy, nor a discovery of the root cause—Dr. Riklin was remarkably restrained. He rallied his strength and continued to examine Rivka over and over, administering medicine to awaken the womb, herbs to purify the ovaries and the blood vessels. In his diary he wrote the name "Chaim Abramowitz." When he looked at the name his chest fluttered as if something were being born, and he was loathe to close the diary and go back to his life.

Rivka's treatments drew on into autumn. Dr. Riklin was encouraging: "Autumn is a good season: the body opens up."

He wrote letters to physicians in Europe, consulted with colleagues, and experimented with new techniques. He wanted to create a child, to liberate Rivka from her infertility, for Chaim Abramowitz's sake, for the sake of this man who looked at him with dark eyes that set terror in his heart, and excitement, the thrill of success—for this man, he threw himself into the endeavor.

"I am a good doctor," he said to Abramowitz, sighing.

In his diary he wrote: "By his side I forget myself. Only when he leaves do you return, Naomi my wife, my dove…"

He began to turn away new patients, heartlessly rejecting pleading husbands, refusing to soften. Sometimes he sloppily wrote down names of other doctors or murmured them through a crack in the door. When a patient finally became pregnant, he did not rejoice. He could barely tolerate these other women—what was their happiness to him?

For some time he felt himself growing dizzy, weakly drowning in a whirlpool around Abramowitz. "For you know, Naomi my wife," he wrote, "since you left I am a nomad. I sit in my room and I rove. But he is different…There are no others like him, my dove."

When a year had passed since the beginning of his failure, he was finally able to pour his heart out to the giant man, whose stories were known to all, and who must be given a son.

"Your wife's organs blossom like the lilies. Everything is as it should be in her garden, if I may…"

He felt that the words, though they came from his heart, added to his disgrace in the eyes of this man, whose hands could strangle him with one wring and whose fist could ram a bull. He wondered why he was speaking to Chaim of lilies and gardens, and he tried to protectively entrench himself within the fortress of medicine. In meetings held at evening time, with Rivka and without her, Dr. Riklin erected fences between himself and Abramowitz's contempt; he released meaningless words into the air—hypoesthymia, dytrosis of the uterus, surgical avrentation—that would surely impress the hulking ignoramus. But after another year of failure he himself was willing to abandon his fortress and surrender to this man, to face him in the open field of simple words. There was no point in hiding. Riklin gave up and stopped fighting the dizzying whirlpool. He shed his body and soul—let Abramowitz take what he would.

Abramowitz simply demanded more methods, more attempts, and Dr. Riklin acceded. In the summer it seemed as if a treatment from Germany might hold the cure, and a tone of intimacy was perceptible between Abramowitz and Riklin. They stood in the clinic scanning the latest test results with more than a shred of hope in their eyes.

"Soon you will be a father," Riklin wanted to promise him. For your wife—he wished to say—is as the dawn, fair as the moon, clear as the sun, while all I have is recollections of my departed wife Naomi, née Mussadof, so beautiful, so noble. You have hope—see here, in the X-ray, her ovaries are like the blossoms of a snapdragon, her womb young as a fawn curled up in its mother's lap. The entryway to her body is unblemished, and she will bear a child without shedding tears, for her pelvis is muscular and supple. What more could you ask? What is left for me? Dr. Riklin was gripped by an urge to kneel at the feet of the giant and ask for something—but what?

It was better to say nothing, to simply place the X-ray neatly on his desk. At least he would spare Naomi from the contempt with which Abramowitz regarded him. Why speak? Better to hide Naomi and shelter that one sorrow. *O my dove that art in the clefts of the rock, in the covert of the cliff.* Perhaps when he made the giant's wife fertile, then he would speak.

He felt a moment of loathing, for it was she, the wife, who did not bear him a child. She, not he. He pondered Rivka's face, always lowered, willing to undergo any treatment, obedient. And still she did not bear him a child…and was not disappointed.

As if he had been jolted and pushed down a staircase from the top of a tower, Dr. Riklin's thoughts plummeted to the always expectant abyss. There at the bottom was the pale visage of Naomi, and his heart filled with mercy and guilt.

When the German method failed and his letters received polite but fruitless replies, the chill seized Riklin's heart. He squirmed in his sorrow as he faced Abramowitz—he must trust him, he must trust—and from his drawer he pulled out letters from grateful women, notes from happy fathers, pictures of babies grown up.

Abramowitz glared at him.

"But you must have faith," Dr. Riklin said desperately. "You must have faith." He suggested that other doctors might be able to help. He showed him replies to letters. Then with a tempestuous soul—the desperation, the contempt, the insult—he urged Abramowitz to recognize that his methods were the finest in the universe, that all his notations were accurate, that even the doctors overseas, had they been here, would have despaired, and yet he was not despairing, he still believed with all his heart that a child would be born if they only had faith, for the methods were good, it only took time and faith, and see—his examinations were extremely diligent, he did not waste any time, as soon as he encountered failure he embarked on a new method. Everything was precise and purposeful and diligent and faultless. And surely it was apparent that there was not only a fertility doctor at the root of his soul, but also an excellent secretary, a house manager, a personal assistant. If Abramowitz was not convinced of his skills as a physician, perhaps he would take him on as his assistant. He needed only to say the word and he, Riklin, would abandon his flourishing clinic, dismiss all his patients and devote himself to Rivka. And if Abramowitz did not believe he could help Rivka, he would agree to be simply a secretary, he would leave the clinic, leave it all, emigrate, exile…

"Come then," said Abramowitz.

And so Dr. Meshulam Riklin left his life behind him like a slough.

On April 18, 1955, Dr. Riklin arrived at the Abramowitz Estate. A disorderly array of agents were already in service, Günter's replacements. Each had his own realm of power, and none of them intended to move aside in honor of the failed doctor trailing behind Abramowitz.

Dr. Riklin had to fight, and not in any refined way. He completely abandoned his verbose and flowery style. He buried his old way of thinking. Only rigid efficiency would befit his service of Abramowitz. He assailed the powers of the various agents and fought mercilessly. He cut down their authorities, severed their initiatives, and ultimately bundled their status up into a pathetic little sack that could be tossed aside at any moment.

A new Riklin was born, one who made the lives of his adversaries miserable. He ruthlessly pursued those who sought to take time away from Abramowitz or who were indolent in their work for him. Cold hard law was applied to the lives of workers, assistants and guests. He determined strict rules for every affair on the estate, and if any law was loosened, if a crack emerged, he was unrelenting until it was sealed. In private he would still say, "I am Dr. Meshulam Riklin, widower of Naomi. You will be proud of me yet, Naomi, and you will forgive me." But in the open there was nothing about him that was not the head foreman and personal physician to Chaim Abramowitz.

Rivka mocked the failed doctor's rules. When Dr. Riklin was within earshot she would ask Abramowitz, "Will I not bear a child for you, Chaim?"

"I beg your forgiveness, Naomi," Riklin would say alone in his room. "There is no other way."

His old life quivered and faded and lost its veracity. Only once did an echo arrive to disturb the new Riklin's peace. One day a woman came to the estate asking to see him on an urgent matter. When the doctor refused to make time, she yelled through the gate,

"Just a question, Dr. Riklin! Just a question!" Seeing him turn his back and walk away, she shouted, "You gave me a child, you helped me, Dr. Riklin. But the child is sick, he is not healthy. Please just tell me, Dr. Riklin, just tell me if such things can come from sins…"

As Riklin walked away, the woman—and all of his prior life—simply vanished.

Chapter sixteen

A Little Flame that Creeps Up from the Stovetop Like a Claw 1973

"In my past there are no interesting deeds, no endearing facts, no horrible tragedies, no manslaughter or lovers' quarrels, not even fortunes won or unexpected inheritances; there are shadow-people."
(Yosef Chaim Brenner)

Shmuel earned his medal of courage on the first night of the war. He sat for hours in the tank, his senses dulled, enveloped in a strange, impermeable calm. Ruthless battles raged outside. The battalion was defeated and broken, but Shmuel was oblivious to what was going on, witnessing not a single skirmish. Only at night, after the forces retreated in a panic, did he emerge through the turret and join the troops stumbling to the evacuation area. He sat among the beaten down soldiers with their ashen faces. He looked at Bentzi Tirosh and Shimon Alfasi, at Ronen Avidan the kibbutznik and

Eliezer Akra the religious guy. All his tormenters were now wretched, wounded and exhausted.

The commander scurried around trying to impose arbitrary discipline and collated lists of evacuated casualties, fallen soldiers, and present soldiers. He made more and more lists, running back and forth as if he were of great benefit, occasionally calling out a name and waiting for order to emerge. It slowly became apparent that Reuven Elkabetz was missing. Not dead or wounded or present. Missing.

A few people began to think back dimly. They had seen Ronen take a hit. He was on Edri's squad. Someone remembered the squad had been shelled. Edri was dead. Someone said his tank was stuck near the frontline. Another soldier corroborated that version. Reuven must be in the tank. Then a soldier claimed he had dragged Elkabetz out of the tank and over to the next one—he couldn't make it any further—and he held up his bandaged hands as evidence. Elkabetz had been identified in his new location, but they had thought he was dead. Why hadn't anyone told them he was still alive when he was lying there?

It gradually became apparent that the battalion had all the necessary details: where Elkabetz was positioned, what his condition was, and what surrounded him. They started drawing a map on which they marked the tanks and Elkabetz's estimated location. They consulted and added more details. The usefulness of the map was never questioned. Shmuel, who had seen nothing, watched as his fellow soldiers contributed what they could. It occurred to him that the emerging map did not show the Egyptian soldiers still swarming the area, or the brave man who would use it to save Elkabetz.

Shmuel felt a sleepiness coming over him, and he was embarrassed. But he was tired and miserable and he couldn't see what good the pathetic map would do. Besides, what did he have to do with this war, these people? He looked at Bentzi Tirosh and Shimon Alfasi, at Ronen Avidan and Eliezer Akra. Reuven Elkabetz had never bothered him. And what good were these people to Elkabetz now, as he lay out there somewhere? Poor guy.

Bentzi Tirosh made a correction on the map and Ronen Avidan the kibbutznik slapped his shoulders and said, "You're right, I swear…you're right." Bentzi Tirosh grinned contentedly.

Shmuel watched them and grew angry. He got up and emitted a muffled sound. Because what, in fact, could he say? Realizing that the guys were looking at him, he felt embarrassed again and was overcome with rage. He yelled something, but he couldn't make himself understood. Their contempt—who were they? Nothing—just a bunch of guys drawing maps.

He charged into the middle of the circle and grabbed the map. He yelled again, but he wasn't even sure what he was saying. He was tired. He hated them. It was too bad they weren't the ones lying there wounded, waiting, waiting…

He stood in the middle of the circle holding the map and they looked at him silently—Bentzi Tirosh, Shimon Alfasi, Ronen Avidan, Eliezer Akra. He shouted something else and stormed off, mumbling, "I'll get him." All the guys bowed their heads.

What he wanted to say was, This is why you lost to the Egyptians, you cowards! But he didn't say that. Judging by the communications he had heard over the radio, the whole army was losing, not just his battalion. And besides, if he said anything else it would not take long for them to snap out of it and start harassing him, and meanwhile Reuven Elkabetz waited. At this moment he still had the courage, right now. He would bring back Reuven Elkabetz.

Shmuel marked a large 'x' where Reuven Elkabetz was supposed to be located, dropped his rifle and set off.

It was hard to make his way in the dark, and discrepancies soon arose between the map and the field. The 'x' was finally located beyond the edge of a cliff, in a place that had not even been a battlefield. Shmuel stood helplessly in the dark trying to estimate the distance.

He could smell smoke from far away, and gun oil, and a nauseating stench of gunpowder. He walked in the direction of the smell and his silhouette slowly approached an encampment where a group of Egyptian soldiers sat calmly among the remnants of the battle they had won. Shmuel shrank back and began to slowly crawl, carefully avoiding the beams of light and his enemies' eyes. The Egyptian soldiers ate, and Shmuel's nostrils picked up a comforting whiff of *ful*. He heard Arabic chatter coming over the radios, and engines crudely running their different tire-marks over the roads.

He began to feel afraid. How had he thought he could just find Reuven Elkabetz on his own like this? He advanced to the edge of the encampment, his fear condensed into a crumb in his throat, and he perked up his senses hoping to find something that would lead to Reuven. Eventually he heard a feeble moan, almost like a kitten's, as Reuven Elkabetz strained what was left of his vocal cords. He lay in his overalls between two smoldering vehicles. Shmuel had to be brave, not to think, to dismiss the possibility that it might be a trap. He carefully made his way to the warm groaning body and hushed him with a whisper—"Shhhh…it's me, Shmuel, I've come to get you."

Reuven Elkabetz moaned.

"Please…be quiet," Shmuel begged.

But Reuven's large, desperate body rose up in a newfound hope that he might live, and his fear awakened too. He wept silently. "Thank you, Kagen," he whispered, hazily confusing his savior with Shmuel Kagen, who sat sipping hot coffee with the rest of the guys far away.

"It's Klein," Shmuel said insistently, but Reuven Elkabetz had lost consciousness.

A great silence lay over the desert around them. Shmuel wanted Elkabetz to know who was rescuing him. Now, not later, when he recovered in the hospital. Now. Where did he get the idea that it was Kagen? The Egyptians began to rustle nearby, and a flock of birds screeched past like some otherworldly creatures.

Shmuel gave up.

Moving softly, like a beetle rolling a ball, he crawled until dawn—four arduous hours—to save Reuven Elkabetz. He arrived at the camp and deposited Elkabetz—with severe injuries and third-degree burns, but alive—in the medic's hands. Then he tried to walk away nonchalantly, as if he had just come back from gathering firewood. But the whole battalion danced around him in celebration. The worried probes into who-let-one-unarmed-soldier-go-rescue-a-missing-comrade were replaced with astonishment, rejoicing, and morale uplifted from the abyss of despair. Shmuel Kagen tried to put his arm around Shmuel but pulled back when he saw the flash of hatred in Shmuel's eyes. "Get out of here!" Shmuel screamed, and Kagen stepped back. The soldiers fell silent for a moment, then they started hugging him again, singing his praises, slapping him on the shoulder. Shmuel was taken to the battalion commander, then to the brigade commander. Somewhere in the distance, the regimental commander's voice came over the radio. Shmuel was glorified, praised and exalted.

The award ceremony was postponed twice. By the time it was held, Yehezkel Klein had died, and Shmuel defiantly announced that he did not want a ceremony at all—all he wanted was a leave of absence, or maybe a discharge. He served another two years in a technical unit that—Shmuel wasn't sure what it did, actually. Day in and day out all he did was repair the same device over and over again, an ancient sort of communication radio that broke every time the switch was flipped on. He repaired it and repaired it and repaired it, and instruments were brought into the workshop and taken out of the workshop, until he was discharged.

*

On the day the Yom Kippur War broke out, with Shmuel on the frontline, his father stood on his balcony watching the silent street as usual. He thought it odd when he saw people carrying transistor radios in flagrant violation of the holiest of days. But when a voice carried over from the radio next door, Yehezkel listened carefully.

"Genia, the Arabs! They're coming again!" he called to his wife and looked down at the street.

When Shmuel came back from war he found the guest room littered with Six-Day War victory albums taken down from the top shelves. Albums lay open on the table, the armchairs, the rug. Photographs of battles. Maps of the victory route. Arrows indicating the progression of forces in the 1967 battles. The old victories, which did not belong to the new war, were stained with teacup rings and sunflower seed husks and a banana peel smear. The pages had been turned so insistently that they showed the desperation of the aging hand.

Soon after Yehezkel died, Shmuel's mother finished washing all the dishes in the sink and took her last breath herself. Shmuel was left alone in the world.

He remembered that his mother had a brother who was very ill. He had once gone to visit the uncle in a sanatorium near Jerusalem with his father, but he wasn't sure exactly where it was. There was a large chest in his room, full of model soldiers and toys that his uncle used to stage battles on the rug. When the uncle stopped coming one day, the games stopped too, and Shmuel was glad. He had never liked the soldiers and the battles and the frightening questions his uncle used to ask, like, "What did the hero say before he died?" And the way he called out, "Attack!" "Shoulder arms!" "To the battle!" But he did like to dig through the chest and lift up the fake bottom he had found one day, which concealed all sorts of forms and certificates and lists that the uncle had hidden.

The chest was still in Shmuel's room, and he rummaged through it once or twice. On the yellowing documents he saw the names "Pinhas Lavon" and "Shmuel Azar," a bundle of handwritten notes, and some printed pages with most of the lines blacked out with ink. He thought of putting his medal of courage there, but in the end he kept it in the sewing basket, where he encountered it every time he lost a shirt button.

When he was on his way home to tell Ricki about his medal that evening, he pictured himself getting everything ready, taking the medal out of the basket and putting it down near her. What choice would he have then? He would have to tell her.

But Ricki was gone. She was not coming back.

He paced around the empty apartment. He took two pieces of cake out of the refrigerator and gulped them down with a cup of coffee. He lit the gas rings for no reason, and let four little circles of fire appear. He inspected the flames, swayed with them. He was miserable. Miserable. What if he never saw Ricki again? He held his fingers close to the flames and let the heat tickle him.

She was just a cheap girl. There was no reason to be upset. But he thought about her in the white towel, snuggled in the armchair with her legs folded under her body. She was the most beautiful woman he had ever seen.

He turned the dials back and forth and the flames grew larger and smaller. His mother had forbidden him to go near the flames, but his mother was dead now.

"The boy is a little *meshugge* with fire," she used to sigh to her friends.

Where was Ricki? Where?

Shmuel liked fire. The bigger, the better. The passing wails of fire engines were like adventure stories to his ears. Once he was fortunate enough to see an apartment burn down not far from home, and another time he witnessed a brush fire like a red-black wall, mocking the streams of water they sprayed on it. His mother would not let him go to campfires or Lag B'Omer bonfires, but once she gave in and they went together. They took sandwiches wrapped in white paper and well-washed fruit, and his mother stood with him at a distance, unlike all the fathers helping their kids build the fire. Shmuel looked silently at the flames and felt his soul alight and land, rise and fall. His heart filled with a bliss he had never known before. The flames flickered wildly, then pretended to doze off, then suddenly, without reason, spread their arms and sprouted manes and sparkles, then dozed off again, quietly, softly, emitting only a gentle crackling purr. At any moment a cluster of sparks could fly up into the air and there would be nothing lovelier in the world. Shmuel was even happier when the children carried puppets of Eichmann and Hitler to the fire and tossed them in, cheering at the flying sparks. The Eichmann puppet fell apart as soon as it was thrown in, consumed by the fire as though it were merely a collection of planks. But the Hitler puppet stood tall on its post, almost smiling, its rags burning and smoldering, only the painted moustache still glimmering on the indifferent face. Suddenly one of the fathers ran up and kicked the puppet into the fire and yelled and cursed and beat his fists against the people who tried to pull him away. Shmuel couldn't see anything after that—but he could hear the sobs—because Genia covered his eyes and dragged him far into the dark with her steely hand. They moved away from the fire into the silence of the little streets, back to their dirty gray apartment building.

"Who is Hitler?" Shmuel asked his mother, and for the only time in his life, she slapped him.

Shmuel knew who Eichmann was.

When Eichmann's trial was held they learned about it in school, and the teacher gave them a test on the prosecutor Gideon Hausner's speech. But the only thing Shmuel now remembered from those days was one encounter with Mrs. Midovski in the stairwell. She had never spoken to him before, but when he came home from school one day she stood three steps up and said, "Our only son, Alex Midovski, was killed in the War of Independence. Defending the city of Holon. Why did God save us from Eichmann? He could have saved parents whose son would not be killed." Mrs. Midovski walked down the steps and brushed against Shmuel's backpack as she passed him.

Whenever he heard about the Eichmann trial, Shmuel thought about Mrs. Midovski. She died a few years later, and her husband moved away.

Two days after the Lag B'Omer bonfire, Shmuel went to a field far away from home, and with a fearful heart gathered some branches. He took out a little bottle of flammable fluid from his pocket, one of the forbidden materials that his mother kept under the sink and used to scrub the floor tiles, the walls and the furniture, and he poured the contents of the bottle onto the branches. Then he took a deep breath and lit a match. The flame engulfed the branches and fire leapt up.

When the joyous blaze soared, Shmuel saw ants erupting frantically from a large nest that was now in the middle of the fire. They rushed out of their hole waving their antennae, then folded in on themselves and turned to tiny black dots as they baked. Fascinated,

Shmuel watched the ants die. He was afraid, but he could not take his eyes off the scene.

Ever since that day, he found different excuses to leave the house. He would take a library book, *The Adventures of Captain Juno on Mars*, which was never exchanged, and go off to the fields. His mother sometimes asked why the library smelled like kerosene. Shmuel secretly collected money and bought matches, rags, even a container of bug-spray. On his roamings he would find ant nests to terrorize. The ants suffered greatly under Shmuel's regime. He patiently wet their long, endless columns and lit a quick whip of fire that gathered them up in its path. He poured alcoholic fluids into the openings of ant nests and lit them on fire, waiting for the tormented, frightened ants to rush out. They never had a chance.

One day, because of a thorny bush, the entire field caught on fire and the firefighters worked for a whole day to put it out. When he came home blackened and stinking of smoke, a multitude of colossal punishments flying through his mind, he found his mother sitting by a row of memorial candles. Shmuel managed to slip into the bathroom and scrub his body with soap, dry off and change his clothes without his mother budging from the candles.

In the neighborhood there was talk about the fire. Shmuel expected his mother to realize who was responsible—she always knew everything, and she especially knew about everything he did and even things he only meant to do. He walked around for several days in a state of tense expectation, waiting. He was not convinced he had gotten away with it even when she failed to confront him. To the day she died, many years later, Shmuel's world was a world of anticipation—when would she say something? When a week had passed since the terrible fire, he knew he was only worsening his crime and enlarging his punishment, but he could not resist it.

Again and again he slipped into the yard, trembling, with a couple of matches and a small piece torn from the matchbox in his pocket. At the foot of a concrete wall near the trashcans, sheltered by the thick branches of a lopsided tree, he would gather a few twigs, strike a match and hold up a handful of straw to the flame. He placed

the straw quickly on the ground and held a twig in the cradle of straw.
The flame felt its way around the twig, enveloping and examining it,
until the twig itself emitted its own flame. Shmuel watched the twig
as the fire violated it for a long time. The twig would soon flip over
on its back as if the flame had turned it with invisible arms, and still
the fire would not relent, swallowing and sucking and fondling the
twig. All that time Shmuel would throw nervous glances up through
the canopy of branches, beyond the edge of the concrete wall, to
make sure his mother wasn't watching from upstairs.

He spent many days of his childhood lighting fires, always
looking anxiously through the branches. What would happen if she
caught him? What would happen? But since the day Alma Almagor's
bra fell and covered his eyes with its delicate black fabric, his frightened glances were not on account of his mother. His fear migrated
to Alma, and his breath lit up in a panic—what if she saw him with
the fire?

When the fire died down he would look tensely and breathlessly at the black stain, not thinking and not feeling and not afraid
of anything. But as soon as he got up and left his hiding place the
fear would start to peck at him. His mother would know what he
had done...She always knew.

Shmuel could never understand how she knew everything,
how his acts hurried ahead to snitch on him even before they had
happened. His intentions, his desires, his hopes—everything was
transparent to his mother, like miserable fish in an aquarium. There
was only one incident that left her puzzled by Shmuel's intentions.
And even then, it was not intentional.

On the dresser in his mother's bedroom, next to the alarm clock,
were a few little bottles of perfume. There was one that smelled like
a room full of uncles and aunts, and another that smelled heavy and
cherry-like, and the third smelled like soap. Shmuel liked the scents
that wafted to him from places where there was no Formica furniture
or creaking window blinds or yellowing floor tiles. One day he took
all the little bottles and sat inside his mother's wardrobe. He opened
one cautiously and dabbed a little perfume on his hands. He looked

at the open bottle and held it up to his lips, enchanted. The perfume tasted bitter. Shmuel tasted it again and coughed and sneezed, then started generously pouring the liquid over his arms and neck and head. He emptied out the next bottle too, and the third and the fourth, and waited for something to happen. Perhaps he would reach a distant place. But the only place he reached was the local clinic, where his mother dragged him in a panic as soon as she found him.

She refused to believe the doctor when he said no damage had been done. "Doctor," she demanded, "give the boy something." At home she interrogated Shmuel, shouting, "Why did you do that?" None of his stammerings satisfied her, and she firmly questioned him over and over. "What did you do that for?" There was fear in her voice, as if Shmuel knew something and she had to know his secret. "Why, Shmuel? What did you want?" Over and over and over again.

Once, shortly after the incident, Shmuel's father said, "Mother gets sad sometimes," and tousled his hair.

Shmuel's mother was a woman of troubles: a bandaged foot, a friend in the hospital, errands to run three buses away. On the rare occasions when they had guests, even before they had arrived she would bitterly calculate when the Kleins would have to repay the visit. When they were invited to a wedding she would sigh and concede, "I suppose we have to go." She never disclosed what might bring joy to her life. Every morning she got up with an iron will to do her duties. She cleaned the house, cooked the meals, tidied the closets and swept out the corners. She rarely left the house and almost never looked out of the windows. When she emerged on the kitchen balcony next to Yehezkel's workshop, she would stand for a moment like a leader about to give a speech, but then she would lean over to take something off the laundry line.

What did she like? There was no telling. Shmuel once heard her say, "I like watermelon. It keeps you regular." But on every other day there were only complaints. The back. The head. The feet. She was not like Shmuel, who enjoyed the little bruises on his knees and the cuts on his fingers and on his lips. Little things that allowed him to feel his body.

Shmuel walked around his apartment without Ricki. He thought about his mother, about himself. He did not want to live in this apartment alone anymore. He did not want to be like his parents, like all the neighbors, people going crazy with wallpapered walls and scalding hot tea. He wanted to travel far away. Anywhere. Once his mother had told him about her childhood in Szebnice. The houses nestled among the mountains. The forests. The little animals and the mushrooms they ate. Rain all year round. A river that swallowed up little children. He wanted to go to Szebnice, to the rain. Not wallpaper. Not scalding hot tea.

At first he hoped it might have been a mistake. Perhaps he had misunderstood, and the tattooed giant would come back, and Ricki would come back. But sorrow spread through him and he knew—why would she come back? The giant was gone, Ricki had no reason to be here. His life would go back to being only about Alma Almagor and Fishman the neighbor and Tami the neighbor.

He drifted around the neighborhood restlessly for a few days. He wanted all this to stop. To stop. But the sorrow did not stop.

In the mornings he took a shortcut to work, then he would take the shortcut home. Quickly. Not dawdling, not thinking. Only after dinner would he go off to wander the streets, the sidewalks, looking up at the crumbling balconies. He thought Mrs. Zeller seemed peculiar. So did Esther the secretary. In the middle of the day Mrs. Zeller would take out a glass tumbler and pour herself some brandy. She sat drinking and smiling to herself. Then she would take another drink and almost cry.

He longed to know where Ricki was. He thought about curly-haired Hezi, who owed him a big favor and had now disappeared. Shmuel knew what he would ask for. That was easy.

After two weeks of walking the streets, he got sick of it. One evening he tried to play with his uncle's toy soldiers. He staged a battle between the Eskimos and the Turks. Then between green soldiers and a little bespectacled figure whom his uncle had called "Aharon Aharonson, hero of the Nili underground." He clutched Aharon Aharonson and looked at him closely, after his defeat of the green soldiers. Who was Aharon Aharonson?

He dropped the underground hero to the floor and curled up in the armchair where Ricki had sat.

Who was Aharon Aharonson?

Shmuel had always done all his homework diligently, writing neatly and keeping everything organized. And yet—amazingly—barely a single fact stuck in his memory despite his hard work. He got an A for his "Herzl and Zionism" paper, and the teacher sung his praises in front of the whole class, but very soon after writing the paper he had barely any idea who Herzl was. He worked carefully on "The Leader David Ben-Gurion" and got the highest grade in the class, but had he been asked, he would not have been able to recall even the tiniest detail about him. Who was David Ben-Gurion?

At home, because of his father's vow and his anger at the state, they did not discuss historical figures or movements or undergrounds. Perhaps just a little. Hardly at all. Newspapers were not brought into the house, and the radio played no Hebrew news. When friends from "the former party" came to visit his father, Shmuel was sent to his room so he wouldn't hear the shouting.

In the sixth grade he was asked to write an essay on "My Family." He asked his father if they had any family.

"What's the assignment about?" Yehezkel asked.

"My Zionist family," replied Shmuel. He had his pencil and notebook, and a mechanical, indifferent desire to do his homework as his teacher had asked.

Yehezkel said, "I'll tell you about my family." Then he added, "Don't ask Mother about her family!"

He told Shmuel about his Zionist father, Shmuel's grandfather, who had fought for Palestine and lost, and about his mother, who had also been defeated. There were tears in his eyes.

"How do you spell defeated?"

Yehezkel wiped his eyes. "D-e-f-e-a-t-e-d. Us boys, three brothers, we came to *Eretz Yisrael* and we were Zionists. Yulek, my oldest brother, was a great Zionist even back in our village, and he went to hear speeches at the congress and gave us all this love for *Eretz Yisrael*. But when we came here he was disappointed because there was no culture here, and he went to America. He did well there, he's a tailor.

My little brother Moishe…a great tragedy. We came on the same boat, after Yulek came, but he didn't get along here. He wasn't suited for this life at all. In the end he hurt himself and died. Don't ask. What went through his heart, believe me, it went through my heart too. The whole time I was in the Diaspora, I thought there would be this kind of moment, perhaps when I saw the shores of Israel from the ship, and I thought that at that moment I would feel that this was it, that the new life was beginning. But on the boat there was nothing but trouble with Moishe. He kept throwing up. And besides, we came at night and I couldn't see a thing. Never mind, I thought: the moment will come. Maybe when I set foot on the holy ground, or maybe when I find a job and get my first salary. And it didn't work out. They lowered us off the ship quickly into little boats, and we really couldn't figure out when we were on holy ground. Poor Moishe, it was hard for him, afterwards too. *Oy*, my Shmuel. All I wanted was just one moment, to give me strength for a whole lifetime, so I could say the new dream had begun, that everything I believed in, the Zionism, was starting. But the troubles wouldn't allow it, and then the thing happened with Moishe. A tragedy. I had to be strong, so I wouldn't run away from this place like Yulek. Well, but all this, everything I told you, has nothing to do with your homework. In a minute I'll tell you about our Zionism, but Shmuel, believe me, even after that, all those years, it wasn't easy. But luckily, I had a great medicine in my life, and that was my love for Ze'ev Jabotinsky."

"Didn't study him," Shmuel said awkwardly.

"No, how would you?!" Yehezkel said angrily. "Ben-Gurion you studied, Berl Katznelson you studied, even Tabenkin. But Jabotinsky? No! But that doesn't matter now." He touched his throat as if he felt a moment of suffocation.

"And when were you a hero in the underground?"

"That was later, later."

After the Six-Day War, Shmuel was almost at *bar-mitzvah* age, and his father forgot about his anger with the state in his excitement. He bought all the victory albums, and the victory books, and the victory postcards, and the victory emblems. He also bought the volumes of the *Encyclopedia Hebraica* and placed them on the middle shelf in the living room so that if any guests came they would see the books. He spent a lot of money on the subscription, and each new volume was mailed to him when it was published, like a gift. Almost every evening, with an aching back, Yehezkel Klein would take down a volume off the shelf and read through it until bedtime.

Shortly before 1971, Yehezkel said to Shmuel excitedly, "Soon the volume with Katznelson will come out. Then you'll see what they write about Yosef Katznelson, 'The Black Prince.' Just wait. They'll have to admit that he was a great leader, almost like Jabotinsky, and that if he hadn't died he would be our leader now."

When the note arrived from the post office, Yehezkel rushed to pick up the parcel. Shmuel was home from boarding school, and he stood by his father as Yehezkel paged through the book all the way to Katznelson, Berl. He ran his finger down Kazakhstan, Kelp, and stopped. He paged back. Kazakhstan. Katznelson, Berl. He held the page in his hand and froze. Not there. No Katznelson, Yosef. "But he was a leader..." Yehezkel was stunned. "Better a dead lion than a living dog..."

Every time Shmuel came home for the holidays he looked at Yehezkel and saw a broken man. He felt an urge to put his hand on his father's shoulder and say something. "It's all right," perhaps. Or, "They'll fix it in the next edition." He never said anything.

Chapter seventeen

The Botheration
of Smiling   1949

F rom the day Günter's son, Hans, came to the Abramowitz Estate, his life was driven by political dictates. "We must unionize," he told his fellow Yemenites. But he refused to join the existing unions, dreaming instead of starting his own, a real union with regulations and officers, just like Mapai.

At first Günter gave Hans a trifling job in the estate registry office, but when he demonstrated acumen, diligence, and a clear desire to excel, Günter showered him with public praise and promoted him up the ranks until he became first deputy to the head foreman—to Günter himself. Every evening, Günter invited Hans to his room to review the day's events. As they sat working, Günter extolled his son's merits, and both men held a glimmer in their eyes. "Well done, my son, well done."

But Hans longed for a different life. The worlds outside the estate captured his imagination, and as he looked around at his fellow workers he could not understand why they were so happy with their lot. How could they not long, as he did, to leave the estate? How could they not seek to carve out their own place in the world? He worked hard to come up with excuses for him to be sent outside the walls of the estate, and when he did, he wandered the cities and villages, and sat talking with people in cafés and on street corners. Seeing his country flourish, the land where he himself would one day be lord and master, his excitement was marred by the sight of his suffering Yemenite brothers. Between the walls of the estate his father was revered as a great leader, the sole friend of the master of the estate. Yet throughout the country Hans saw the deprivation and contempt suffered by his brethren, the unkindness with which the other ethnicities treated them. The austerity regime imposed strict rations on all citizens, but the Yemenites were robbed even of the little they deserved. Leaking tents and shacks were the lot of every immigrant living in transit camps, but his brothers were given the worst of the worst. Warm clothes ran out before they could get any, medications were withheld from their children.

"I must save you," he would whisper into his shirt collar as he passed by his brothers living in wretched conditions. "I must save you." But how?

As he was out walking one day, sullenly contemplating his people's hardships, he came across a man who mumbled something and pulled him into the corner of a house, where he secretly offered him a portion of eggs that exceeded the rations and was not at the regulated price. Hans fled, but the man would not leave his thoughts. Something about his darting eyes and nervous speech demanded Hans's attention. He dwelled on the matter for a few days, and one morning, in a miraculous fashion reserved for true leaders, he awoke to find within himself an entire socioeconomic philosophy—a complete and flawless doctrine: We Yemenites will control the black market! We will control it and gain power!

Hans arose as a leader. First he established modest smuggling routes to ship farm eggs to the cities. He slowly expanded the routes, delivering more and more goods, a colorful and fascinating array of merchandise. Because of his obligations at the estate, he never considered owning any of the traded property himself, but drop by drop he grew into a virtual trading post, the natural intersection for every good piece of business. His transactions were protected by miracles of evasion from state inspectors, and luck shone on his business. Traders sent messengers looking for a good price for their black market wares. From deep and dark hiding places, cautious offers emerged. A variety of goods came his way, in the hopes that he would find them a good match.

Hans began to feel happy, a simple sensation that he carried with every breath. He told his father of all the compliments he received, and together they analyzed each one and concluded that it was well deserved. Hans had found his place in life. But in the evenings, in his little room on the estate, his mind filled with thoughts that felt like tears—he had to leave, had to live his life in the city. There he would make close friends, who might even invite him into their homes. He considered asking Abramowitz to let him go, but each time he managed to formulate a suitable speech and pluck up the courage to ask his father to arrange a meeting, the words died in his throat and a great silence descended to the bottom of his gut.

From time to time Hans's business conflicted with his duties at the estate. The duties were endless, and business—if Hans did not approach it, it came to him. In the middle of work someone would come to tell him that a man was asking for him at the gates, unwilling to speak with anyone else. Hans would sigh and gently discard a happy thought—after all, only Günter and Abramowitz usually had the honor of such visits, the will-not-speak-with-anyone-else kind of visits—and he would walk to the gates to see who it was.

Günter was proud of his son. "You know, there was a lady here once...Sarah Abramowitz. She would have liked you." But when Hans described his business plans to his father, Günter silenced him. "My son, perhaps you should use your powers of intellect to study, to get an education...perhaps..."

Wishing to please his father, Hans assiduously read books from his library and made keen observations on his readings, until Günter took to contentedly observing, "The apple does not fall far from the tree." He even came close to believing that they might have the familial relations that an apple and a tree shared. "If only I had been with his mother more…"

Günter often wondered who Hans's real father might be, the one whose seed had warmed itself in his wife's womb. "You might be Tan'ami's," he thought, "he was a good tradesman too, and he did not like to sit in one place."

Hans very quickly lost interest in Günter's books. What good would books be? What would they do for the suffering people? Outside the estate he collaborated with Polish money traders in Tel Aviv, top swindlers from the Sephardic community in Jerusalem, law-circumventing Hungarians, rule-bending *yekke* attorneys, and ship-robbing Saloniki dockworkers in Haifa. Hans knew they respected and trusted him, and he was proud of himself, but he was also aware that they referred to him as "the Yemenite," and he therefore hated them deeply.

"There will be no resurrection of the Yemenite people without unionization!" he would cry out loud, waking himself up, and peek with frightened eyes around his dark room—another of his nightmares.

On busy market days he walked among the Yemenite neighborhoods and stopped to give speeches, urging his esteemed listeners to abandon the promises showered on them by Mapainiks, and banish from their hearts the natural affection toward Yemenite politicians, who were nothing but twittering chicks and whose power amounted to a single representative in the Knesset.

"The time has come for a great power—ours!" he shouted to the shoppers as they carefully picked out fruits and vegetables from the dregs. With tired faces, they looked up and asked, "Is it election time again?"

Hans did not have the patience to explain what seemed to him so simple, so right—that leaders should address their constituents not only before an election; that a true leader had no need for elections; that democracy was best left to Mapai, because what the Yemenites needed was the son of a king, a Lion of Judah! Yet these gatherings produced only insipid questions—"Who sent you?" "When are we getting our ration stamps this month?" "Why only 250 grams of chicken?" "How can that be enough?"

Sometimes he was thrown out of the market, and once he was even beaten. Hans accused Zecharia Gluska's henchmen, and they beat him again as punishment for slandering an innocent man. But even in his desperate state he knew—"I am the leader!"

Hans found his brethren's souls a difficult riddle to decipher. He tried to recruit a following from among the young generation. Bnei Shalom, the Yemenite youth movement, declared war on him, and a delegation of young men came down from Jerusalem to beat him. He turned to the elderly and, oddly, the Bnei Shalom group came to beat him again.

"Perhaps you could be a famous benefactor?" Günter suggested. "Or you could give in secret."

"In secret? Then how will they know?"

"Give, my son. If you give, they will know."

Hans began giving out goods to his people. A widow received a sack of sugar, a young mother got a baby carriage. Two chickens caught up in a rope on the estate were donated to a cantor in Jerusalem. A crate of citrus fruit was left on the doorstep of a needy family in Holon. An elderly rabbi who had great influence on both young and old in Netanya received a weekly delivery of fresh eggs to strengthen his gums. Jackhammers went missing from Solel Boneh's construction site and were given free of charge to a contractor from the community.

"You might be Sabri's," Günter guessed. "He too, his whole life, he did business instead of studying. He was wise, but all he wanted was to get rich."

"I don't want to get rich," Hans protested.

He wanted to lead his people. Once he saw an illustration of Moses and the People of Israel in the Passover *haggada*, and he daydreamed. *And I shall seat my father Günter on the throne of honor…*

He was enchanted by Rivka's kites, and being slightly afraid of her, he looked straight at the kites as they called out to him, "Break free! Break free and set your people free!" He liked to watch as they surged up into the sky. But at night he dreamed that his eyes slipped from the kites and plunged down to the bottom, to Rivka. On the mornings after such nights he was hunched over with fear lest Chaim Abramowitz stab him with a knowing look.

One night, when he awoke from a nightmare, he went out to walk around the estate. Through the window he saw Günter studying. The moonlight bathed his father's face and cleansed his tiredness, anointing him with infinite beauty. Hans was moved. What do we lack? he wondered. True scholars! Not mumblers of Psalms, but people like Father, who understand the ideas of Albert Einstein. He made up his mind that he would be the first. He would lead the way, like Nachshon.

Hans began to spend all the money he made on the black market obtaining academic degrees. Every day he found a truck or a car to take him to Haifa, Tel Aviv or Jerusalem. He traveled the roads from morning to night, poring over his books as he sat among crates of poultry and barrels of fish. At the Technion in Haifa he signed up for electrical engineering, "So no one will say a Yemenite can't be an engineer." At the Hebrew University of Jerusalem he signed up for physics, "So no one will say a Yemenite can't be a scientist." In Tel Aviv he descended upon the Biological-Pedagogical Institute, where he studied botany with Dr. Yaakov Galil, "So no one will say a Yemenite can't be an agronomist," and zoology with Dr. Heinrich Mendelssohn, "So no one will say a Yemenite can't be a zoologist." He found the post-graduate school of law and economics and somehow got into four parallel courses of study: law, "So no one will say a Yemenite can't be a lawyer"; economics, "So no one will say a Yemenite can't be an economist"; political science, "So no one will say a Yemenite can't understand policy"; and business administration and accountancy, "So I can cheat on my taxes."

The Knesset had imposed an income tax on all citizens in September of 1949, precisely the date Hans stepped off a plane onto the soil of *Eretz Yisrael*, knelt down to kiss it, and looked up at the fair-skinned masses around him. Since the day he first read the tax laws, he began to feel a wild battle call throbbing within him, and the powerful tax collector who invaded the people's pockets became his personal rival.

"The black market I do for our Yemenite brothers," he explained to Günter. "But fighting income tax—the biting snake—is David against Goliath!"

He memorized every letter and every symbol in the law, and monitored its ever-expanding clauses and sub-clauses and the infinite complications that the tax collectors developed to locate cheaters and evaders. He learned to predict every decree and find a solution for every trick and deceit. Feeling that his adversaries in the Ministry of Finance were not putting up a good fight and that the impediments he was finding in the law were too apparent, he began sending amendment proposals and pointing out loopholes, so that the battle could be a little tougher, new taxes could arise, and he could fight them all and win.

As he stood on roadsides and at dark intersections waiting for rides, he memorized his lessons, considered the tax laws and invented his inventions. He also took advantage of his exhausting trips around the country to mail his suggestions in letters signed by a series of false names—Elhanan Klemstein, Moshe Grubstein and Avraham Klepter were his favorites. Once in a while he sent a particularly brilliant suggestion under a Yemenite name like Tan'ami, Tzan'ani or Nahari, and his sorrowful suspicions were confirmed: no one paid attention to a Yemenite's suggestions.

One day he slipped up. He conceived a superb amendment for the income tax ordinance, an idea so clever that not even the greatest tax evaders or the most cunning of tricksters could get around it. "King Solomon wouldn't have found a solution! King Solomon would have had to pay taxes!" he told his father proudly. Trembling slightly, he sent a letter to the Ministry of Finance from Rehovot, signed, "Certified Accountant Lolek Abramowitz."

One month later, a hesitant official came to the estate and cautiously asked to show Chaim Abramowitz the letter. When he left, Abramowitz convened the staff. He looked them over until his eyes rested on Hans. "You," he said.

Hans confessed. He whimpered, fell to his knees and held his hands out to beg for his life. Abramowitz swung his boot and stepped on Hans's outstretched hands as if bringing the sky down upon them. All ten of Hans's fingers broke with loud cracks. Abramowitz walked away and Hans was taken to the clinic.

"I wanted them to pay attention to my proposal," Hans sobbed. "It was the best amendment I ever had. And they would have named it after him…after him…"

Günter nodded sympathetically. He felt sorry for his son. "You might be Atari's, he was also very clever, but one day he started talking nonsense and cursing God, and by winter he was dead."

Hans lay in bed for three weeks, his fingers splinted and bandaged. For many long hours he looked at his hands and felt a passing desire to learn how to play an instrument, "So no one will say a Yemenite can't be a pianist."

Günter took time off from work to nurse Hans back to health. He cared for him like a baby, spoiled him and consoled him, but he was soon pushed aside in favor of Rivka Abramowitz. The lady of the estate herself asked to care for the patient, and as if she were the last of the slaves, she spoon-fed him, shaved him, trimmed his fingernails, and bathed him where he would allow her. Morning and night she leaned over him to rearrange his pillows and straighten his blankets, and the space between his body and hers was not large enough even for a tongue of fire.

Hans seethed with insult. It was clear to him that she was not trying to win him over with her feminine ways—she was not seducing him and she did not need him. She had only one man, a man who broke the fingers of sinners, and rightly so. Although her body almost kissed his own, Rivka was focused solely on her nursing duties, on the pillow, on the blankets, the bedpan. As far as she was concerned, this was not a man with pulsating limbs sprawled beneath her as her downy garments caressed his flesh, but a needy patient, a miserable man graced by her favors.

When Hans recuperated, his desire to leave the estate was even greater. Each time he awoke, even before his morning erection had subsided, he began to formulate his request, and the words swelled into sentences, and by evening time they became a speech, a rushing Nile of pleas and promises. But when he had the opportunity to speak with Abramowitz and began to search for the thread of his speech, he lost heart.

"You might be Sa'adi's," Günter said, rubbing his forehead. "He used to think a lot too, and in the end he couldn't say anything."

Hans reluctantly returned to the battlefield. Straining to meet the demand of both his black market business and his duties at the estate, he also kept up with his studies. As soon as he finished one degree, he signed up for another. He completed his history studies, "So no one will say a Yemenite can't be a historian," and went back to the Technion as one of the first students of aeronautics, "So no one will say a Yemenite can't build rockets."

The only thing he found difficult to complete was his driving course, although he longed for a license, "So no one will say a Yemenite can't drive." He grew angry every time he took the driving test, sometimes failing due to excessive confidence, other times for lack of it. Eventually Abramowitz took pity on him and passed a note to an old friend in the right place. Hans got his license, and set off for his first drive in a car from the estate fleet. Let no one say a Yemenite can't drive!

Just after exiting the gates, even before all four wheels were on the road, he had an ugly collision with a poultry delivery truck. Both drivers escaped unharmed and stood at the intersection cursing each other in their native tongue—Yemenite.

Hans went back to the estate with tears in his eyes that annoyingly subsided and resurfaced. Over the next few days he could not rid himself of the memory of his accident. His body had sustained no harm, and the broken headlights were soon fixed, but a great pain took hold of him. A great pain.

Insult. Shame. Sorrow.

Deep inside him the finger of God rose up and pointed at the estate. It was better to stay inside. Here, behind the walls, he could attain the fame and respect he so longed for. The greatness and the glory. And strength. And brilliance. And exaltedness. Everything that gave a man his purpose in life. And what was his?

As the days went by and his pain healed, his yearning to lead his people was renewed. "I think I can help the Yemenite people, Father," he explained to Günter.

"My son, you must help yourself. Rest, don't try too hard. A wife, do you have?"

But Hans found out about upcoming local elections in Rehovot, and he registered as an independent candidate. He went to the local market and tried to garner support. A few people began to gather, and he felt the first buds of optimism, but when he gently tugged on the sleeve of an elderly Yemenite lady as she hurried by, about to miss his speech, she stopped in front of him, opened her mouth wide, and said scoldingly, "Shaul, I'm your grandmother, you fool! How can I vote for you?" She walked away, brandishing her cane.

Hans stood frozen for several minutes, a silent puppet on its strings. With a pale face, his legs slowly lifted and carried him to the council house to withdraw his candidacy. He found a truck driver who agreed to take him home, and by evening he was standing at the gates of the estate. His political career was over.

"You might be thin Tzanani's," said Günter. "He also craved respect and had no luck."

Hans roamed the estate with a heavy heart. He flitted from duty to duty, task to task. Sometimes he stopped to stare into space or watch Rivka's kites. He gazed at the strings that stretched all the way from the body of the kite to Rivka's hands, and a taste of coal crawled up his throat. What was his purpose in life?

People tried to introduce him to smiling young Yemenite women, but Hans found them all too thin or too sad. Occasionally he would pursue one and be forced to subdue his disappointment—he knew that when he achieved greatness, this pain, too, would be sweetly healed.

Günter was making his final steps from secular life to full *teshuva*, shutting himself off in the synagogue Abramowitz had built for him, waiting to spread his wings to Safed as soon as Abramowitz gave his permission. Hans aspired to replace his father, to be as respected as he was, the head foreman to Abramowitz, and he wanted Abramowitz to look kindly upon him. That is how he dreamed it would be. Chaim Abramowitz, the master of the estate, would finally recognize Hans's wisdom and talents.

When Hans's dream finally came true and Günter appointed him as his replacement, it turned out that he had received only half the authority. The other half was given to Lerer the Roman, and the two men fought bitterly.

Lerer complained to everyone: "And if I had a son, and I brought him over on an airplane, would he also become an officer here?" The voices inside Lerer's head were even harsher. Flames sparked deep inside his soul, embers of memory, a fluttering sense that once, in another time, when his soul was different, he might have taken care of Hans with his own two hands, with a shoelace around his neck. But now he could not do it, the pleasures of vengeance were forbidden.

When Günter came back to visit, Hans boasted of his victories over Lerer and a vague look of terror came over the father's eyes— "My son, do not anger Lerer. Lerer is not one to anger."

Hans lowered his head obediently. But what could he do? His struggle to lead the people of Yemen had failed and was now abandoned. The income tax campaign had languished and no longer awakened any warring spirit within him. Since the end of the austerity regime, the black market bored him too. And Rivka…right in front of Hans's eyes she lived on in the estate, another man's wife, and his desire was forbidden. And all the ways in which she came into his view…Sometimes when he talked with Abramowitz he could see the remnants of her meal littering the table, as if she had no hands but tore at the food with her teeth, like fangs, and with her lips and her tongue. Shreds of squeezed-out lemons and hunks of bread dipped in olive oil and spices. And his rousing thoughts—an utter sin.

Only the fight against Lerer gave him joy.

Little by little people began coming to him for instructions, and even Abramowitz would call him to convey his orders, ignoring Lerer. Almost ignoring—he still took Lerer as his bodyguard on his travels. But if he needed advice he quickly telephoned Hans, and Hans's heart would flutter—Victory! Victory!

Yet something murky inside him diminished his joy. Usually it moved far away from his immediate thoughts, but sometimes, in moments of sadness, it lit up and ignited his shame—what was his purpose in life?

Near the end of 1953 Hans first met Bonhoeffer, a religious Jew who used to appear at the gates and try to convince the estate to take in a man or two who needed help. "Room and board for work, that's all. Just a temporary solution, until something else can be found," Bonhoeffer would explain, "Just a couple of days." Then he would quickly fill Hans's ears with sayings of wisdom and quotes, bits of juicy gossip from the district and lessons gleaned from his life experience, which seemed to Hans to come from distant worlds, very distant.

If not for his position as head foreman to Chaim Abramowitz, Hans would have succumbed to the chatter, which was as light and pleasant as a summer breeze. But he was obliged to be suspicious of Bonhoeffer's motives and mitigate any damages he might cause. He conducted an angry account with Bonhoeffer over each of the needy men who were left on the estate for a couple of days and ended up staying several months. He threatened him and warned him. He could have used his status at any moment to simply instruct that Bonhoeffer be banned from entering the estate, but instead he chose to take a personal interest in his affairs and accompany him every step of the way.

Sometimes, from within the torrent of chatter pouring out of Bonhoeffer's mouth, something emerged that touched Hans's heart and made him prick up his ears. He wanted to ask, "And the purpose of life…how does a man find his purpose in life?" But he did not. He grudgingly allowed Bonhoeffer to leave his needy men on the estate. During one of their arguments, Bonhoeffer opined: "Sometimes a man finds his purpose in life in the opposite direction from where he was looking." Hans perked up. "What do you mean?" he asked intently. But all of Bonhoeffer's explanations were more complex than that first sentence, which continued to nag at Hans, demanding his attention even more than the "temporary solution" who was now standing beside him waiting, despairing, asking, "Is there a bathroom I can use here?"

Hans devoted himself to that sentence. *Sometimes a man finds his purpose in life in the opposite direction from where he was looking.* What did this mean? And how did it relate to him?

One day two men from the estate came to Hans. They wanted him to ask Günter to approach Abramowitz on their behalf and ask for permission to leave the estate for a while, so that they could carry out an important act of revenge.

"Revenge on the Nazis," they explained. They meant to become Nazi hunters, to join forces with the people who traversed all corners of the world exposing Nazi criminals in hiding, sentencing them to the Jewish people's verdict. One of the two, Berger, had a blue number tattooed on his forearm. The other, Yitzhak Yeshurun, walked around the estate disrupting its tranquility with stories about his five children who had died in Poland.

Hans felt that he had reached a crossroads. His fate was swaying, soon to be decided.

He asked Yitzhak Yeshurun to talk—not about his five children, for he could no longer hear about them—but about the hunt.

Yitzhak Yeshurun looked at him gravely. "We don't talk. We do."

"Do what?"

"Liquidate."

"Who?"

"Every one of them."

"Why?"

"It's the only way!"

"When do you leave?"

"When Abramowitz says we can."

"When will he say?"

"When your father Günter comes back from Safed he will speak for us. We're afraid."

Hans did not wait for his father. Blinded by a light, he faced his master Abramowitz. "I want to be a Nazi hunter."

Abramowitz looked at him.

"I know I'm a Yemenite...I know..." Hans offered fearfully.

Abramowitz kept searching him with his eyes.

"I'm asking you...please, Sir..."

Abramowitz let him go.

"For a trial period!" Hans promised joyously.

He ran to Rivka and found her flying a kite—it was orange, blue, red and white. Trembling, Hans told her, "I'm leaving to become a Nazi hunter."

"What will you do?"

"Liquidate."

"Where?"

"Wherever it is needed."

"You sound like Yitzhak Yeshurun. Where is your mission?"

Hans dragged his feet over to Yitzhak Yeshurun and Berger, his new partners. He studied the details of the plan, offered improvements, and scanned the photograph of a Nazi criminal named Blich in Switzerland.

Günter came from Safed and helped Yitzhak Yeshurun and Berger get their release from the estate, but the plan was delayed repeatedly because of Hans's suggestions. His partners grew bitter and threatened him, they were losing their minds. Twice the plan was close to being cancelled, and another time Berger pulled out for a week to find new partners. When Hans was finally satisfied and the three men gathered to coordinate the final details, he suggested one more little change. "I will do the killing."

"What?" His partners were astonished.

"I'll shoot him."

"We're avenging our families, not yours..." Berger hissed.

"My five children," Yitzhak Yeshurun whispered.

"Why can't a Yemenite be a Nazi hunter?" Hans asked angrily. Then he fell to his knees and begged, "Look at me—what Nazi would suspect me?"

His partners lowered their heads.

The avengers disappeared from the estate for six weeks. When they returned, they looked satisfied.

"No Blich."

"Gone."

"No more."

Hans went to Rivka and silently handed her a kite. He had bought it in Switzerland; it was designed to fly in the winds of the Alps. Throughout the entire operation, in hotels, on trains, in cafés and in stake-out apartments, Hans had carried the kite for Rivka. He had held the gun for thirty minutes and carried out his job like a skilled hunter.

"Now Ramsen," Berger said.

"My children..." said Yitzhak Yeshurun.

"Ours..."

Abramowitz let them go again, and when the gang returned three months later, Hans gave Rivka a Brazilian kite with a red line down the center. A kite from the jungle. Each side was adorned with seven scarlet fins illustrated with native Indian motifs.

Hans fell at Abramowitz's feet and asked for permanent release. He wanted to be a full-time Nazi hunter, the best hunter of them all. Abramowitz let him go.

The day before he left the estate, Hans came to Rivka, rolled up his sleeve and showed her his forearm. A blue number was tattooed on his flesh.

"Maddar from Rehovot did this for me."

"What have you done?" Rivka looked at him.

"Revenge. Our blood will not be worthless! You'll see. A thousand Nazis I will bring to justice. A thousand!"

"What have you done..." Rivka repeated. She held his arm warmly and caressed him, enchanted, running her finger over the scarred flesh. "What have you done..."

Hans disappeared for several years. From time to time a courier came to the estate with a kite for Rivka, handmade in some foreign country.

A sky-blue kite from Germany. Untersturmführer Hakman.

A Siamese kite from France. Sturmbanführer Mirth.

A silk and rattan kite from Belgium. Scharführer Lakfe.

A bee-shaped kite in orange and gold, made of sparkling fabric and supple wood. Holland. Doctor Ulman.

In 1963, after spending his entire fortune, Hans came home destitute. By then the head foreman was Meshulam Riklin, and he did not like Hans at all. Rivka, whose room was filled with forty-five kites from Hans, took him under her patronage and kept Riklin away from him. She introduced Hans to her new personal foreman, handsome Lev Gutkin. "This is Lev Gutkin, my wonderful aide. For seven years he planned to assassinate the tyrant Josef Stalin, and then Stalin died on him…" She told Gutkin to protect Hans from Dr. Riklin's harassments.

But he was no longer the old Hans. This was Hans the Nazi hunter, the terror of war criminals in hiding. Hans the level-headed, who took no mercy on his victims. He could have risen up and become the leader of the Yemenites, could have attained the dignity a man like him deserved, but instead he rambled silently around the estate, his feet dragging him from one spot to the next, with nothing to do. Sometimes a large grin spread over his face, and sometimes he was expressionless. His walks took him to the walls at the edges of the territory. For long hours he would stand in one place, staring not at Rivka's kites but at their strings as they fluttered desperately in the wind.

Hans withdrew into himself. It seemed he had performed his final act and could do no more. But in June of 1967, the Six Day War broke out, sweeping the nation under its wings, far from the corrosive fear of conquest, annihilation, slaughter. On the fourth day of fighting, Hans turned up in a unit of paratroopers about to seize Jerusalem. They threw him out—what was a civilian doing in the midst of a bloody battlefield? But Hans would not give up. He stuck with the troops until someone finally suggested getting rid of him by holding him as a POW.

"I'm with you all the way to the Temple Mount!" Hans screamed.

Several minutes later he stood as a barrier between the paratroopers and a Jordanian sniper and became a casualty of war.

Günter buried his son near the walls of the estate. He knelt by Hans's grave. "My son, Shaul, my son, Hans, perhaps you were mine after all. I too had everything, yet I was never happy for even one day in my life."

Chapter eighteen

Albert

1937

To: The Very Honorable Mr. Albert Einstein
Princeton University
New Jersey
United States of America

From: Günter Tarhomi
Abramowitz Estate
Palestine *Eretz Yisrael*

May 4, 1937

Greetings to your honor, Mr. Albert Einstein, king of the thinking Jews.

I received your most recent letter and was expecting to relive the delight of reading your scientific thoughts, but I soon experienced a great shock. Is it truly possible that your honor believes I could have sent such a letter as your honor described? Heaven forbid. No such thing. Impossible! Fortunately, the offender herself has confessed to me, with great mirth and peals of laughter. Indeed, in order to explain the entire catastrophe, I must enlighten your honor with an introduction to Rivka Abramowitz, the mistress of the estate.

She is the daughter of Sarah Abramowitz, and being of a tender age, her mother asked me to teach the little girl some penmanship. Teach her I did, and rather well, but it transpires that the child learned to mimic my own handwriting, with the very same form of letters. Our handwriting, thus, is absolutely identical. Should an expert graphologist examine Rivka's handwriting, it is my personality that he would detect, not hers. Indeed, a most worthy little girl, although perhaps it would be best at times for her own personality to be concealed. For she is a mischievous thing, a nuisance to every living creature, frolicking and hurrying about. I sometimes swear she is a she-devil, but one made of honey. Immediately upon receiving your letter, my suspicions were aroused. When I confronted the girl she confessed to the crime and laughed to the heavens. And that is the meaning of the letter—all the awkward words, the questions regarding your honor's outward appearance, they are all her inventions. Ever since I showed her a picture of you, she decided, in her childish innocence, that she had to find the answers to the questions in her heart. Allow me to clarify that I have nothing but admiration for your honor's hairstyle and facial composition, and that I have no observations at all regarding your expression when you smile. My lord is nothing but handsome and noble, and if his face is briefly visited by an expression of grief, it too is beautiful, never ugly. She is a little girl, not much older than seven, and cannot be blamed.

But let this be a warning to your honor, king of the thinking Jews, to watch out for Rivka's tricks in the future. Each letter that I send to you, I first copy two or three times, sometimes even five, and send all the copies at the same time, for here in Palestine letters have wings of lead. Correspondence arriving from overseas, such as your honor's letters, also encounter difficulties. The British pick through every missive as if we were hiding illegal immigrants in envelopes. This is why you may sometimes receive five identical letters, and sometimes but two or three. The theory of probability reduces the chance of one single letter arriving, and if this occurs—suspect it, for the hand of Rivka may be at work.

When I received your letter and opened the envelope with a trembling hand, I believed, to my delight, that our correspondence regarding quantum theory would continue. Your honor has such remarkable patience. But then I read of your insult. I even sensed your anger, albeit beneath a cloak of politeness. Indeed, any person, even the grandest of thinkers, would be offended by such impudent questions, particularly if he believed they were coming from a worthless Jew in Palestine who offers meaningless scientific ponderings. Yet despite Rivka's mischief, you did not omit from your letter a lengthy response to the impudence of my thoughts, as if the angel inside you overcame the human.

I truly and utterly accept all your invalidations. Indeed, if nature acts according to my hypothesis, a troublesome question of energy arises, and it follows that all my calculations collapse, as they should, for their father is nothing but a stubborn Yemenite who troubles great minds. I merely offered your honor a modest scientific suggestion, the fruit of theoretical computations on which I have labored for the past six months, but your honor rejected my thoughts, and I trample them under my heel until their last ember is extinguished. There is no value to my ideas if you pronounce them nothing at all.

What a shame that your honor annuls my discoveries, though, for I worked so hard and made sure the calculations were free of errors or amateurism. Believe me, I have no adequate working conditions in this remote land, even a simple piece of uranium cannot be come by. Without uranium and without the instrument for counting radiation particles, named after Geiger, I cannot conduct a proper nuclear laboratory. In my sorry state I spend much time on theoretical mathematics, and so the theories fill my head and I find myself taking up your honor's time. But now you have given your verdict, you have annulled me as dirt, and I hereby cease to disturb you. Sad, but that is how it must be.

Perhaps I will only convey to your honor that these six months of calculations have not been easy, for here in *Eretz Yisrael* the Arabs have begun carrying out murderous attacks, and although their national conflict is with the British, they are killing us all. I beseech your honor to imagine the atmosphere in which I labor to read difficult articles from all branches of science. Jews murdered on the roads, in the dead of night, in their homes, in their orchards, in their shops, in their beds. Terror and fear grip the settlements and there is no knowing what will happen if the Arabs continue their criminal acts against us. Whenever the Jews are caught in a moment of weakness or at a numerical disadvantage, they are murdered, and their bodies abused. There is great fear among the population. Those who belong to the Abramowitz Estate fear the rioters less, since Chaim Abramowitz's power is on our side, and the rioters themselves respect and fear him. He is a simple man, and does not pretend to be fearless or immortal, but the others treat him as if he were so. They tell stories of his heroic adventures, insist that he has no fear, and seek out his company. Without his protection it is very hard here, very hard.

You should know, your honor, that Chaim Abramowitz often takes an interest in my teachings, and I have tried to explain to him the theory of relativity. Although he leads a life of action, he is a wise man with keen instincts, and I hope I may be allowed to observe to your honor that in the opinion of Chaim Abramowitz there is not much use in the entire business of radioactivity. From his perspective, it is better to engage with explosives and fertilizers, for they are the future. I accept Abramowitz's opinion, as I know how right he is on any matter of utility. I myself, however, look not to utility but to the shivering sensation we both know, the fine grating at the back of one's neck upon the sudden comprehension of an aspect of electron behavior.

But why do I burden your honor with nonsense? If you so desire, you may read the final part of this letter, and if not—please disregard it.

Sincerely, and with a thousand apologies—again, a thousand apologies,

Your servant,
Günter (Yeshaya) Tarhomi

P.S. What is your opinion, generally speaking, of the works of Chadwick?

To: The Very Honorable Mr. Albert Einstein
Knollwood Resort
New York
United States of America

From: Günter Tarhomi
Abramowitz Estate
Palestine *Eretz Yisrael*

July 4, 1941

Greetings to your honor, Mr. Albert Einstein, king of the thinking Jews.

As usual, I write at your explicit request, to disturb your precious time with my trivialities. Again you ask about Rivka, the wondrously lovely girl; perhaps you are unable to forget this girl who wrote to your honor regarding your eyebrows, ears and nose hair. In my previous letter I alluded to her with two words, and wrote of her lust for lemons as an allegory—merely an allegory for the theory I propose regarding bosonic particles. However, rather than address my scientific notions, your honor has latched on to the allusion to Rivka. Indeed, perhaps in your excessive politeness you are insinuating that I should cease my scientific suggestions and instead delve into the matter of Rivka and her lemons. Well then, at your honor's request, I shall explain.

If you were to come to our estate one day, you would find Rivka holding a cluster of seven or eight golden lemons. She will choose her first one, cleave open its body with ravenous fingers and plunge into its flesh with her tongue or teeth, and brush the fruit against the hem of her dress if a bothersome seed should emerge, and lick it again. So devoted is her love of lemons, as if there were no other deserving fruit in the world, that fights erupt between herself and her mother, Mrs. Sarah Abramowitz. Rivka has always cultivated peculiar tastes, and in fact she does not show any interest in food, all her palate cares for are spices and honey and strong flavors. She is indifferent to bread, but loves to dip it in salt and pepper and sugar and oil and turmeric and cumin. She does not like to eat milk and eggs or rice and potatoes, and does not desire all the things that our people long to eat and lick their lips over in their dreams. She is not afraid of sour, salty or spicy foods, even craving the Yemenite *skhug*, a spicy sort of condiment that gets its flavor from garlic, peppers and hunger. Rivka of course has many other attributes, both physical and mental, for she is growing up here, amidst the cruel reality of our lives.

I have told you about the events, the riots led by Arabs against the Jews as part of their fight against the British. Politics is a truly complicated affair here, for we Jews agree that the British are corrupt, and they are inclined to support the Arabs, yet the Arabs fight them. In fact you cannot find a single person who is not fighting someone here in the holy land. At the age of seven, Rivka was already exposed to the cruelty of life. Wounded and dying men were brought to Abramowitz's estate, survivors of a convoy attacked on the road. With uncommon naturalness she went to the men and began to bandage their limbs, clean their wounds, ease their pain. The doctors did not stop her, for they sensed a trusty, confident touch. Imagine a little girl who did not recoil from the revolting wounds and the dying men's groans. She knelt down on her knees to disinfect, bandage, and dress. Can your honor picture it? A nightmarish scene, people screaming, their flesh torn, and in the heart of it all a tiny girl, light as a doe, hovering among the wounded to aid them.

I shall be very regretful, your honor, to know that your thoughts have filled with these terrible images that will not leave you for days and will perturb you as you try to enjoy your scientific pursuits. But this is how it is with us, and those who wish to engage in science in *Eretz Yisrael* must face this trouble too. As you reside now in the holiday resort of Knollwood, I am sorry to litter your pleasant thoughts with scenes that are, for me, a daily reality. But now I shall gladly clear your mind of bad thoughts by inviting you to imagine Rivka standing in the midst of the estate, and this time she is flying her kites. Her little hands tug firmly at the strings, with a grave expression on her face, alert, as if the temperament hidden beneath this child's countenance is also soaring. She is a great expert in kite-flying, ever since a British captain introduced her to the pursuit. It is a lovely sight to behold, and it removes the worries from one's heart. Perhaps it is thanks to this peaceful sight that even in the midst of anxieties and excessive work, I am able to devote a little thought to matters of science, and that is how I reached the hypothesis that you invalidated completely, although I very much hoped that this time you would find some merit in my words.

Your invalidation of my hypothesis is my command to relinquish. But just so that I can bid farewell to my beloved idea, I will write it for you again, in summary, and every letter that I write shall be peeled away from my memory until the idea has no trace, and I shall throw it away as you command.

In fact, why should I trouble you? For as you read my worthless words you could be spending your time on your monumental work, which for some reason lingers while the whole world eagerly waits. Why should you add to your troubles the nonsensical stuff that I send you from across the ocean? Better for your honor to engage solely in your own work, for we are all awaiting the next scientific miracle. What I find extremely interesting is that, had you taken from my worthless idea the merest morsel, for example the futile contemplation of a possible additional particle, an unknown one, perhaps then your work would progress. For even your honor must agree that if one assumes for a moment such a theoretical particle, whose Yemenite originator has surprisingly and foolishly decided to define in such a way that its wave equation is hopelessly tied up with a complex probability function, meaning that the sampling space for this probability is sampled along complex domains, then one achieves balanced equations, and if only for this reason it is inadvisable to completely invalidate my idea—but invalidate it you have, and what is left for me to say?

Instead of distracting you with worthless pleas, I shall tell your honor what he wants to hear—moments from our simple life on the estate in *Eretz Yisrael*. Here is an incident that happened to me. I looked through my window at the gardens one day and saw all of the dedicated workers scattered around the yard doing their work. Suddenly Chaim Abramowitz appeared and the whole yard tensed and everyone gathered around him. The appearance of the master of the estate altered the uniform dispersion, and I was inspired to comprehend that this simple scene might somehow depict the secret of the universe. Imagine, if you will, a particle that imparts all its surrounding particles with mass, namely affecting the way they resist change in their motion. I suddenly understood that if such a boson particle were discovered, it would certainly explain some hitherto unsolvable problems in the monumental work that your honor, along with other genius physicists, presents. But you have told me to relinquish, and relinquish I shall. Finally.

I am your servant,
Günter (Yeshaya) Tarhomi

P.S. What is your opinion, generally speaking, of the works of Hans Molisch?

To: The Very Honorable Mr. Albert Einstein
Princeton University
New Jersey
United States of America

From: Günter Tarhomi
Abramowitz Estate
State of Israel

October 10, 1948

Greetings to your honor, Mr. Albert Einstein, king of the thinking Jews.

Here I am writing to you again from the Jewish state, our state, Israel. The Abramowitz Estate is currently in the eye of a great storm, as you know. Chaim Abramowitz is engaged in a desperate search for his only brother, Lolek, who has gone missing. He invested great efforts to protect his brother's safety and prevent him from joining our state in war, but all signs indicate that the young man disobeyed him and was among those who arrived on our shores and went straight to the bloody frontlines. At this time we are all busy with the search, and I myself am assisting Sarah Abramowitz while her husband travels.

This is no time for idle scientific talk, even if it engages the very foundations of existence, but since your honor wrote a few words in his letter regarding my ideas on solving the Schrödinger equation, I cannot be so impolite as to write to your honor solely about the battles and the despair and the hope and, yes, the joy in our hearts.

You do not believe there is merit to my new idea, and you write that you are unfamiliar with its theoretical basis. I was somewhat surprised, as I did send your honor the bibliography for all the referenced articles. Then again, I have been surprised in the past by your honor's choices. You surely recall my astonishment when you wrote that you had no knowledge of the scientist Hans Molisch, the man who studied the chemical interactions between plants and coined the term *allelopathy.* As you will recall, upon studying his works my thoughts shifted to nuclear physics, which are immeasurably complicated, and I suddenly understood the answers to some unsolvable questions: it was the theory of allelopathy that I had to thank. I appraised you of my research and raised a few hypotheses, but you denied them and claimed you yourself had investigated the very same direction and found it to be futile. What is the point, therefore, in insisting? How could I dare limp over the traces of your footsteps and hope to find something that you yourself did not? I abandoned the thought without delay, like a bolt of lightning, like a thrust of the sword.

Yet I wish to clarify, for one last time, this direction of thought, this seed of an idea, that perhaps there is another article, an ungodly creature, which exists and yet does not exist, hidden from the eye but amounting to a mass, much like Jonathan and Ahimaaz hiding in the well (I refer your honor to Samuel ii, Chapter 17), and it, the particle, neatly explains the inequality that causes such discomfort to your honor.

I abandoned this idea, as per your request, but still I look back with one last glance, because my mind is determined to think that there is pure truth in my tiny idea, and how can I leave it to die in the desert? Much as in the not-so-distant past people did not understand the ways of electrons, which operate by trespassing upon their neighboring atoms and not letting go, kneading their flesh until the adjacent atomic structure reorganizes itself into a new pattern, resulting in a balance of energies, whereas today every lowly person discusses this truism as if he had seen the atoms with his very own eyes—thus there may yet be discovered another secret, my particle.

You have invalidated my work in general, but you have not revealed to me where I went wrong, and I must assume that your honor is blessed with a rare instinct and has no need to delve into every single equation. For this reason my heart very well might have broken if not for the fact that on that very same day when you discredited me, which happened to be my birthday, Chaim Abramowitz gave me the gift of a real Geiger counter, the likes of which even our universities do not have. Imagine to yourself: Chaim Abramowitz's days are rent with emotional torments, his spirit dangling between hope and despair as he searches for his lost brother, and yet he found a sliver of time to acquire a gift for me. I truly have tears in my eyes. As you can see, there are those who treat everyone magnanimously.

I should add that my lord Abramowitz has changed his mind about nuclear physics, and now wishes to know what a person would require in order to build an atomic bomb. I believe he asks in jest, although I have learned to know my lord Abramowitz well, and his demeanor never contains jest. It has been five months since the declaration of our state, and still our war for independence rages and our finest young men continue to pay with their lives. Perhaps one day we will require nuclear weapons, and I shall be happy if from time to time your honor would send me a few of the prescriptions, for I am certain you have unlimited authority to peruse the wonderful project of our nation's son, the esteemed Jew, Robert Oppenheimer. For the time being we have no real need for this weapon, and besides, our estate gets along nicely. Concern for Lolek's welfare is the only thing that tears the skies above us and darkens our faces and disturbs the calm.

This is all I wanted to write to you, your honor, but I now recall that on the margins of your last letter you added a question regarding the Hebrew Bible, which caused me such great confusion that I almost forgot to reply. Indeed, I did not know that your honor took an interest in Jewish wisdom, and I wonder whence this sudden question on the Bible arose? I can certainly enlighten you on the sins of Sodom, as I am very familiar with that episode, and I am happy to be able to add to your honor's wisdom, though it is all-encompassing. But I must caution you that I have some astringent opinions on certain things, and this is one of them. In my youth I was married against my will to a woman who was with child, and recently I was married again, to a woman named Ruth, née Mintz, and now you ask me about Sodom but you forget that Sodom was not brought down alone, for they were a pair—Sodom and Gomorrah. Surely your honor will understand that the biblical story could have sufficed with one city to illustrate the episode of the sinners and their punishment. But not for nothing were two cities chosen, one of which, Gomorrah, has an extremely feminine name, in contrast to the masculine nature of Sodom. The moral iniquities were committed by both cities together, the feminine Gomorra and the masculine Sodom, and to this day all immorality and ugliness involves both males and females, jointly, interlocked in the bitter and evil fate that awaits them after their hopeful encounter.

I do not know what flaw the Creator placed in me, and for which of His sacred purposes, but I have never seen the reason for women. I have heard that even among the greatest Torah scholars, men who are weakened from continual studies, a perusal of the laws regarding women causes their flesh to seize their minds and bring down their towers of pure intellect. And myself? I am free of this desire. Even the most wonderful of women, Sarah Abramowitz, who redeemed me from a miserable life, did not awaken this yearning within me. For four-thousand seven-hundred and six days she has rewarded me with the sight of her beauty, but has not aroused within me the tempests that afflict other men. And if not Sarah, which daughter of Eve could do so?

Perhaps it is better if your honor, king of the thinking Jews, should pose his question to another person, one better than me, for I find that a bitter air has suddenly taken hold of my spirit, so much so that I intend to crumple this page and discard it.

To: The Very Honorable Mr. Albert Einstein
Princeton University
New Jersey
United States of America

From: Günter Tarhomi
Abramowitz Estate
State of Israel

October 10, 1948
Afternoon

Greetings to your honor, Mr. Albert Einstein, king of the thinking Jews.

I shall tell your honor a strange tale, one that is ultimately related to sweet Rivka, who seems to interest and delight your honor very much, for in each of your letters you enquire as to her wellbeing. This peculiar story does not begin with our lovely Rivka, but with a Jewish fellow from Italy by the name of Stefano Lerer, who recently came to the estate in a condition of uproar and lightning and thunder. Chaim Abramowitz quelled the tempest in the man's body by imposing a regime of hard work, and restored him to peace and tranquility. But it was then that he took the man on as his personal bodyguard.

Is your honor asking himself why he did so? There is a secret in the soul of this Lerer, which to you, your honor, I shall reveal. A great violence lies dormant within him, and he himself does not know what sort of wild beast is hidden inside him, curled up sleeping for as long as it is not needed. I shall tell you a story. One day, Chaim Abramowitz took Lerer and myself on a business trip, and since Rivka accompanied us, and since in recent years she has grown afraid of horses, we traveled on foot, an exhausting journey. In the middle of a field, a group of rioters attacked us. I cannot testify first-hand, as Abramowitz instructed Rivka and me to hide behind a rock. All I could see was a terrible Lerer erupting from within Lerer, and then a roar cut through the air. I heard a brief struggle, two shots and several groans. When Abramowitz called us out, I saw four bodies laying before us, and they were not a handsome sight, certainly not for a girl as young as Rivka. But she, as if barely noticing the dismemberment and the puddles of blood, walked casually up to Lerer, who had a bullet in his stomach, and began to dress his wounds. They still had to rush him to the doctor and operate on him, but the doctors swore Rivka's light hands had saved Lerer! A wonderful young girl, you might say. But observe the nature of this she-devil. She keenly observed the violence within Lerer during that incident, and what did she do with that terrifying knowledge? She began to take Lerer into the fields so that he could sap honey from the wild beehives for her. And if at first the bees treated him as they are wont to do and attacked him furiously, they quickly learned their lesson and now permit him to take freely from their honey, so long as Lerer does not erupt from Lerer.

That is Rivka. A lovely girl. You never know which side of her soul she will show you. I still remember the day when an estate worker came to me sobbing. We call this man "Psalms," although the name his mother gave him is Giora Sabri. Every evening he recites a chapter of Psalms to Abramowitz, which makes the master happy, and together we interpret the intricacies of the text and it brings joy to our hearts. But this is not Psalms's great expertise, the talent that brings him worldwide fame and reaps profits for Abramowitz. With the finest hair of a paintbrush, Psalms can inscribe the entire Book of Psalms on an eggshell, or the blessing of Jacob to his sons, in its entirety, on a grain of rice. Imagine to yourself, you who contemplate atoms and electrons. Place a magnifying glass over the grain and all the letters appear flawlessly. Of course, if your honor should desire, we should be happy to offer you a gift of the entire theory of relativity adorning an egg or a handful of beans—you need only to ask. But I was meaning to tell you about Rivka and Psalms. Well, one day this little she-devil demanded that Psalms post a real mezuzah on her dollhouse. She angrily insisted even after Psalms consulted a rabbi and was told that it must not be done. Rivka is most unpleasant when she is stubborn, and before Psalms came to me he dared to go to Sarah, Rivka's mother, and to Chaim Abramowitz himself, the lord of the estate. But Rivka made a mockery of their interference on behalf of Psalms. She lowered her head obediently, but as soon as she left she caught hold of Psalms and made all sorts of threats that a girl should not even know of and a man should never hear from a woman—threats best left to your honor's imagination. But the Lord was kind to me: when Psalms came to me in tears, I went to Rivka and explained the prohibition, and the little one kissed me and went to ask for Psalms's forgiveness. That was the end of that. Imagine, your honor, such stubbornness over a mezuzah for a dollhouse.

Chaim and Rivka seem so different from one another, but fundamentally, as it turns out, they are extremely similar. It is odd, but sometimes a stepfather and daughter can develop similar qualities and appearances, as if they were blood relations. As if it is never too late to turn a stranger into the fruit of your loins, your own flesh and blood.

Perhaps your honor will be so kind as not to abandon my letter at this point, though I wish to trouble you with a new scientific idea. This idea was born not two hours ago. I should have comprehended the subtle hint emerging from your honor's choice of words in your previous letter, but at the very moment that my mind accepted the disappointment, it collided with a newly emerged thought, and I saw a way of solving all my computations and offering your honor one more look at them.

I truly would not bother your honor by dancing around you once again with a two-hour old hypothesis, unless I sensed that this time I have come across a steadfast notion. Even at a time when all my thoughts are devoted to the search for Lolek and to helping Sarah, still this idea gnaws at my heart, demanding that I offer it to you, and so I have no choice, for the idea consumes me.

I shall present it concisely: Perhaps the whole model representing the material of the universe as if it were made of particles is fundamentally flawed. Perhaps, for instance, our world is like an extremely crowded spiderweb, and there are no particles but rather multidimensional expanses of webs. Of course I am presenting my hypothesis in this way to endear it to you, and the webs are nothing but an allegory, and if your honor wishes, I shall send you a dozen mathematical pages explaining the entire idea.

And perhaps this whole notion is nothing but nonsense. Your honor shall decide, and I am,

Your servant,
Günter (Yeshaya) Tarhomi

P.S. I have not forgotten your request, and in my next letter I shall reply to you on the matter of the sins of Sodom. For now, perhaps I might ask again, what is your opinion, generally speaking, of the works of Savitch and Curie?

To: The Very Honorable Mr. Albert Einstein
Princeton University
New Jersey
United States of America

From: Günter Tarhomi
Abramowitz Estate
State of Israel

May 10, 1952

Greetings to your honor, Mr. Albert Einstein, king of the thinking Jews.

You did not reply this time either about my extremely complex work, but again you began your letter with a question from the Bible, and it seems you prefer your new interest in the traditions of your people to a scientific dialogue. I can recommend to your honor that you seek a learned rabbi who can answer all your questions, for I am an utter ignoramus, and truly I know only half the interpretations to every problem raised in the Bible and the Gemara. To the matter at hand, you have indeed understood all the similes used by the poet of Song of Songs to describe the form of a woman, and have not been mistaken at all in comprehending the translation. Your honor is wise.

Indeed these verses are supremely beautiful, and you wondered in your letter whence such deep inspiration comes to the world. In response to which I can only say that he who has witnessed the full beauty of a woman just once in his lifetime would not pose the question you pose. If only you had seen Sarah Abramowitz when she was alive...

But you were impressed by one particular image, more enigmatic than the others, that pomegranate to which the poet likens the temples of a woman: "As a piece of a pomegranate are thy temples within thy locks." Your honor should understand that every word in the Bible has a body and wings and a shadow on the ground and a halo above its head, and even groundwater beneath its feet. A real Jew who reads these verses finds that the simple words are constantly accompanied by their wings and shadows and halos and groundwater. A Jew who reads this beautiful verse from Song of Songs instinctively recalls the Book of Judges, which tells of the sinner Abimelech, King of Shechem, who attacked the tower of Thebez, and from the tower a woman threw upon him a piece of millstone and shattered his temples. Before he died, Abimelech pleaded with his boy to kill him, so that it would not be said that a woman had done so. For even at the moment of death, man's greatest fear is the shame of dying at the hands of a woman.

Your honor must read again the verses of Song of Songs, and he will see that even if he himself is not proficient at all in the interpretations, as he reads he is accompanied by depths and heights, and then perhaps the fear of faith shall penetrate him.

I have already told you that my master Abramowitz has not yet released me from my position, and I await his signal allowing me to retire to Safed, to study the Holy Book night and day. I have already found a nook in a tiny courtyard, not far from the synagogue of the Holy Rabbi Yitzhak Luria, and the good family has agreed to rent it to me. Meanwhile, I manage the estate, and with me my son, Hans, and while we may not be father and son like tree and apple, still I love him and am proud of him and he is a source of comfort to me in these difficult days. In the blink of an eye he reads through my physics books and offers keen observations, as if he has spent many years in the laboratories with Max Planck. So clever is my son Hans, certainly his wisdom is greater than mine, but he is not studious, and he seeks a life of statesmanship.

Our estate has completely severed itself from the State of Israel because of the state's iniquities, and Abramowitz truly despises it, though he once fought so tirelessly for its independence. Still, he wisely turned a blind eye when the estate was connected to the power and water grids, and does not even fume when he is billed for these services, but he will not maintain any relationship with those who wronged him. His new wife, none other than our Rivka, whom we have been discussing in our letters these many years, is, conversely, interested in the goings-on outside the walls, and she is as stubborn as Chaim himself, if not more so. Sometimes she bows to his wishes, other times she turns one of her ruses on the world. What does she find there outside? An austerity regime and rationing and plagues of locusts and corruption and a polio epidemic. Is this what the Zionists built their country for? Sinners, all sinners, and I too must cleanse my sins. My soul longs for Safed, where I will find the roots of my spirit and remove myself from the defilement. I am no longer angry at your honor for extinguishing every last ember of my ideas on the basic physics of our world. I will confess that I was angry. But no longer. In truth a man cannot sit in a desolate land, laboring to man-age a great estate from morning to night, and still dare to believe that the ideas emerging in his head have any scientific value. No longer. I shall go to Safed, where the holy men are buried, and I shall find the purpose of the world.

Rivka begs me to stay, and her pleas are sweet, but I can stay no longer. I must remove myself to Safed with my loneliness and face the righteous men, that is all I can do. Your honor, king of the thinking Jews, should know that Rivka's soul is more dear to me than any in the world, just as my own Hans is. Days as plentiful as the waters of a river have passed since I led her to the swing I built myself, based on the lovely instructions of Sir Isaac Newton. Since that day I have taught her as much wisdom as I could, and carried her on my back when she ordered. All that remains now is our identical handwrit-ing, and her nature, which is well hidden, not only from grapholo-gists. On her wedding night, when I saw the door close behind her in Abramowitz's room, what can I say? A fist grabbed hold of my gut. For this was Rivka...True, she was a woman, but as long as she had not been taken as a woman, she was nothing but a tender child. I was afraid. But I shall be so bold as to write to you, your honor, that from the distant spot I took myself to, through the many walls of the estate, I could hear the shouts of joy—perhaps you are famil-iar with voices of pleasure such as these, the hoarse merriment of a woman in bliss. And that is Rivka for you.

During those moments I felt a flicker of weakness, and for one instant—and this I confess only to you—a thought erupted within my mind. For it was in that very same bed that Sarah had lain before her, and for a moment, before I could vanquish the thought, an image of Sarah on the bed appeared before my eyes. I shall yet fast for many days because of this image, and I shall cleanse my body of the thoughts. My soul cries out—to Safed! I can live no other way. Think, your honor, if you were forced to be something other than what your soul desired—if, for instance, you were prevented from engaging in science—what would your life be?

I have finished a whole letter and have not included even one scientific line, see! And this despite several pages I wrote to myself on the physical notion of "time's arrow," namely the direction and purpose of time. But since the entire world awaits your profound pronouncements on this matter, I shall add no more.

I am your servant,
Günter (Yeshaya) Tarhomi

P.S. What is your opinion, generally speaking, on the works of Martin Deutsch regarding positrons and electrons?

To: The Very Honorable Mr. Albert Einstein
Princeton University
New Jersey
United States of America

From: Günter Tarhomi
Holy Community of Safed
Beit-Yosef Lane
C/O The Adlers, in the courtyard
State of Israel

Cheshvan 5714
Weekly *Parsha*: The Life of Sarah

Greetings to your honor, Mr. Albert Einstein, king of the thinking Jews.

    Cold and dark reign supreme here in Safed, and their bodily
impact purifies one's thoughts, rendering one's mind free of excess.
The more I absorb myself in studying the Torah and the Gemara and
the writings of our sages, the more I find myself incidentally entertaining scientific ideas, including some in your realm of interest, the
physics of the universe. For example, you surely recall that I once
asked you to contemplate one single particle that is responsible for
attributing mass to all the different particles of matter. You utterly
invalidated my idea, but now my mind has become generous and it
offers me sophisticated notions for which I have no need or interest.
Perhaps you would like to peruse them? Again, I offer you a complex
wave equation that solves many problems of unbalanced computations, but this time I allow a single unique particle, which, when it
comes to the particle—as the bull comes to the beast, if you'll forgive
me for saying so—given a certain probability, changes its sign from
positive to negative, or vice versa, just like Balaam, who was brought
to curse and ended up blessing. This is merely a hypothesis, the tip
of a hypothesis, a crumb of a hypothesis, but if the calculations I
have drawn up alone are correct, it will neatly complete the picture

of creation. This is a theoretical particle, the product of a mathematical study that you will surely negate, as is your custom, and there is no knowing whether the particle actually exists in the world. But if your honor likes the idea, and if you do not trample it beneath your feet, there is a chance that such a particle shall one day be discovered, leading to the explanation of certain problems. If this should ever occur, I will propose that it be named Balaamium, and we shall no longer require Hellenized names for the atomic particles, names that bring me sorrow when I whisper them.

Deep inside, in my inner thoughts, my soul still longs to hear your opinion on the old matter I once brought before you, my theory that spiderwebs represent the shape of our world better than do the particles among which scientists have been wandering for centuries, including your honor. I truly believe that the world is better explained by this theory than by the misdeeds of the electrons, cursed be they, and the rest of the particles, the drudges, whose every reaction now appears to me like one of the pogroms carried out against our ancestors.

In truth, though, it is no matter whether the universe is interpreted this way or that. Obsessions that gripped me for many long years have been shed, and I now thirst only for the holy Torah. And what of those theories of mine which you trampled upon? They do not matter. No longer. But you should know that there is truth in them. The wise man Galileo Galilei proclaimed, *Eppur si muove*, and did not concern himself with the cursed Inquisition—so too, I no longer find your agreement essential, your honor, my king, king of the thinking Jews.

Here in the little town of Safed, the alleyways burst with synagogues and yeshivas and other institutions, and poverty rolls from one stomach to the next, and the wind whistles at night to comb one's flesh with its iron teeth, and I myself have fallen ill with pneumonia, of a strain that greatly impressed the physician. With the generous funds of Chaim Abramowitz I give charity, and I am contributing towards a new neighborhood for young people on the hillside, and I purchase Torah scrolls for the community in memory of the late Sarah

Abramowitz, and find husbands for orphan girls, and do other sorts of good deeds in secret. The fruits of Chaim Abramowitz's riches allow for the flourishing of a good life of Torah, but I myself am forbidden any earthly pleasures. My flesh has sufficed with its sins heretofore. Since restricting my needs to a morsel of bread, a floor of stone, and well water to bathe in, my spirit has found only goodness, and I do not wish to plunge it back into the depths. You will recall, king of the thinking Jews, that for three whole years after Sarah Abramowitz's death I did not write to your honor, and gave no sign of life, and in fact I cannot say where my life was. I walked and worked and talked with people, but where was my spirit?

Here, in my new life, my spirit has been renewed, and I do not wish my body to bring another disaster upon it. Caution is my duty. At times I find myself in good spirits, my eyes skipping over a chapter of Gemara, when suddenly they fall on a simple word, or even a secular word spoken outside my window, such as when, last night, a man shouted out asking if anyone knew where he could find a tow truck, as his vehicle had given out while ascending Mount Canaan. A simple thing, yet upon hearing this word, "tow truck," my entire soul was swept up in pain. Is there any explanation for this phenomenon in your honor's theory of electrons?

I find other weaknesses and infringements in your honor's secular world too, but I shall not dwell on them, and besides, I do not wish to uproot you from your world completely. I still hope that one great day you will publish something new and brilliant on "the arrow of time." Based on the calculations that sometimes fly around my head, I am lost and confused by the thought that it might be possible for time to go backwards, to retreat. That perhaps life can go back and turn around and emerge anew, all with scientific and physical proof. We await your pronouncements, sir. Why intrude upon your great theories with my trivialities?

I cannot conclude without a brief response to your two questions. Regarding the measurements, I have enquired and learned that it is the width, not the length, of the Holy Temple, may it be built speedily in our day, Amen. As to the second matter, my favorite verse

Chapter nineteen

The Man With a Limp
1977

One Friday, almost three weeks after Ricki had disappeared, Mrs. Zeller placed her soft hand on Shmuel's shoulder and breathed into his ear. "Shmuel, honey, my bedroom radio is broken and I can't live without it. I like to lie in bed every evening and listen to the music it plays for me. Oh, Shmuel, what sweet days…when I was young…" Then she burst into tears.

Shmuel was taken aback. Mrs. Zeller's breath was sweet with brandy as she handed him a pink radio and still maintained her grasp on it. She gently pushed it against his stomach and said, "Fix it, Shmuel. Fix it." Then she flipped her stole over her shoulder.

Shmuel looked at the radio. His hands had already sought out the problem. A simple matter. One or two minutes. "I'll need two days," he said. "I'll take it home and bring it back on Sunday."

"My poor thing," Mrs. Zeller wailed. "Who will take care of me? Who will let me sleep without my mind full of thoughts?"

Shmuel shook his head like a mule. He wanted the pink radio, just for Shabbat, so he wouldn't be completely alone.

"Don't ever leave me, Shmuel," Mrs. Zeller wept. She grasped his shoulders and held her face close to his. "You know, Shmuel, my husband's brother is doing everything he can to steal the business from me. Yesterday, Shmuel, yesterday…he proposed to me. Marriage! And with my husband still alive! His own brother. What do you say to that? The bastard wants Mrs. Zeller's money…wants Mrs. Zeller's body…what a madman…marry me?! Such an idiot…I'd sooner marry Hitler…"

Shmuel could discern the wrinkles around her eyes. Her tears were indenting soft ridges in her makeup. He wanted to cry for himself, for Ricki, but only a sigh came from his chest.

"Fix my radio. For it to break now of all times! Who will remove the evil thoughts from my sleep? Who will caress my body beneath the covers? You know, I even thought I might give in and marry the bastard—what do I care? Everything is lost…let him enjoy it, the bastard, I'm dead anyway."

Shmuel stared at the Sony radio and plunged his fingers into it, trying to evade Mrs. Zeller's brandy odor and ruined makeup and the look in her eyes. He took the pink machine and rushed home, where he spoiled himself with a big meal, turned on all four gas rings to watch the fire, then went into the bathroom with two apples and the image of Mrs. Zeller, her lips dipped in brandy, her eyes teary. He was gripped by a passion he had not felt since Ricki. In the bathtub he floated on a tempest of thoughts. He soaped himself thoroughly and washed his hair, and tried to imagine Mrs. Zeller whispering in his arms. But his fantasy languished, and the water had turned cold. He got out and sat in Ricki's armchair wrapped in a towel.

All morning on Saturday, Shmuel's passion for Mrs. Zeller burgeoned into an increasingly heavy weight that urged him to go to bed for a solitary encounter. But he denied himself this pleasure, knowing victory was imminent, and decided to set himself a condition: he would not pleasure himself until he had fixed the pink radio. He got up immediately and worked on the repair. When the radio came on Shmuel was flooded with the noisy sounds of a soccer game.

"A Kafkaesque goal!" shouted an excited voice with an Arabic accent. Shmuel switched it off. Fixed.

Mrs. Zeller began taking her clothes off. Seduced. She crawled towards Shmuel's growing strength with womanly surrender. He left the workshop and collapsed on his bed, smiling, allowing Mrs. Zeller to continue leading him among the valleys and through the depths, in the blue waters of the necklace around her neck.

But he wanted Ricki. Only her.

In the evening he felt just as he had when Ricki left. Sorrow. Sorrow. He went for a walk but found no peace. As he wandered past Doctor Rassin's clock shop, he noticed a palm tree burning. It shot arms of fire up into the sky, its force increasing from one moment to the next. The tree trunk stood in the belly of the fire, surrounded by smoldering rings as blood-orange jets burst forth like trumpet blasts.

Shmuel looked at the fire. He was riveted.

He wanted to be someone else.

To have a heritage.

Or a wife.

He wanted the sorrow to stop.

Something good to happen.

Ricki to come back, everything to be as it was.

Not to go on the same way.

Not to go on the same way.

Not to go on the same way…

As he leaned against a stop sign he noticed a short religious man standing on the street in a heavy winter coat. He was dark-skinned and his eyes glimmered. The man smiled at Shmuel and waited for him to smile back.

A grin emerged on Shmuel's lips. Of its own accord.

The man limped over to Shmuel. "First I shall ask—do you like fire?"

"Yes," Shmuel answered, hypnotized.

The palm tree suddenly roiled as if it were about to take off, and Shmuel was only barely able to listen to the little man who glowed in an auburn tone, his image reflected in each of the clocks in the storefront, their hands turning on him.

"Your names, if I may ask, what are they?"

"I'm Shmuel."

"I have a few questions for you, Shmuel. May I?"

"Yes." Shmuel was curious. The flames behind the man had subsided somewhat.

"First I will ask what your profession is, Shmuel."

"In the beginning, after the army, I got a job at the Museum of Prehistoric Man. But that didn't work out, and now I repair electrical appliances."

"Wonderful, Shmuel, wonderful. And how old are you, Shmuel?"

"I was born on the eighteenth of April nineteen fifty-five."

Shmuel's reply seemed to make a great impression on the man with a limp, and his coat fluttered excitedly. "The day of Albert Einstein's death, Shmuel! The day the king of the thinking Jews died!"

Shmuel lowered his head humbly.

"Look here, Shmuel. There is a wealthy and strong man who might be interested in your services. Would you like to find out more?"

Shmuel felt heat emanating from the man with a limp. Soulful heat. It was calming, beneficial. "All right."

A strong breeze picked up and the palm tree reignited. Rings of shadows descended onto the street and over Doctor Rassin's shop window, but Shmuel looked only at the man, as if he were forbidden to remove his gaze.

"All right, yes," he repeated, practically crying, "yes…"

Shmuel did not speak much longer with the man, who called himself Günter. He agreed immediately to go and work for someone named Abramowitz in a place called the Abramowitz Estate. All he dared to ask was, "What about a salary?"

The man with a limp laughed. "Salary? Name a figure and that will be your pay. Do not fear. You will be given clothing and food and a nice apartment and no taxes. But the bulk of your reward will be a life lived beside Chaim Abramowitz, may he be blessed, a man who came to this country at fourteen, was orphaned, and in the cruel desert of his orphanhood he would not bow down, but rather fate bowed down before him, and with his own two hands he built his home and his estate and his business, and he has not a single connection to the state that surrounds him. You should know that for us the state does not exist. Not at all."

"My father too…" Shmuel began to say, but he stopped. He was afraid. He did not want the opportunity to disappear. He was afraid the limping man would suddenly vanish behind the flames and Shmuel would be left alone with his life again, without a heritage, without Ricki, without anything.

The man with a limp smiled. "Your father…" He shook Shmuel's hand and began walking away. "Don't worry, Shmuel, don't worry. Soon, God willing, we will call for you. A man named David Bonhoeffer will bring you to us."

"Bonhoeffer?"

"Bonhoeffer. He is the one who delivers new workers. Things are going to change in your life, Shmuel. For the better."

Shmuel stood motionless. His eyes were fixed upon the burning palm tree. When he looked away for a second, he found that limping Günter was gone.

Still trapped in his old routine, Shmuel began to prepare for his new life, but there were endless delays. The only sign that anything was about to change was the telephone, which usually sat silent but was now a hub of activity. At all hours of the day calls came from the Abramowitz Estate "on behalf of Dr. Riklin," or "on behalf of Stefano Lerer," or "on behalf of Shaul Atulov." The phone chirped and quivered and cawed. Constant spurts of ringing demanded Shmuel's attention. Extremely polite people conveyed very long messages that often completely contradicted the previous ones. There were questions, instructions, and fluent recitations of all sorts of things that sounded to Shmuel like the history of a faraway place or a great personage. Here and there among the polite callers were also a few ungodly characters, filthy people who used different voices at varying times of the day, introduced themselves as having something to do with the Abramowitz Estate, chattered, clicked their tongues, and even snorted into his ear.

The other minor change was that Shmuel inexplicably began to read through his father's encyclopedia set. He took the first volume off the shelf and read it devotedly, every evening, until he fell asleep on Ricki's armchair. Day after day, volume after volume. His father's subscription had remained active after his death, and over the years an occasional note had summoned Yehezkel to the post office for a new installment. Shmuel did not know how to cancel the subscription, nor did he have any idea who was still paying for it. So he collected each new volume and placed it on the shelf.

When he was reading the encyclopedia, and only then, Shmuel felt protected against sorrow. If he looked up from the page for a moment he experienced wrenching pain: Ricki was gone and would not come back. He would quickly look down again.

One night there was an important call. A sharp voice interrogated him over the phone. Was he ready?

He had been for ages. Why hadn't they come for him?

His matter was being looked into.

Looked into? Shmuel panicked.

Not everyone was worthy of being counted among Chaim Abramowitz's workers. His crew was resplendent.

Then the voice lost its eloquence and proceeded to hoarsely whisper a long complaint about newly hired workers who had ended up being such disappointments, and there was no way to get rid of them, and they kept moving up the ranks, competing with people more worthy than they, it was such an injustice, and so caution was essential, and Shmuel must understand that there was never a single wasted moment on the Abramowitz Estate. Every night, Mr.

Abramowitz himself examined the day's events, and if he found even one unutilized minute, it was bad—very, very bad.

Shmuel was no longer certain he wanted to be part of this resplendency, to be swallowed up on this Abramowitz estate—what was so bad about his life now? But the voice on the other end of the line seemed to read his mind and began talking about Chaim Abramowitz, the master of the estate, a pioneer of pre-state settlement. He exhausted Shmuel with historical details, so much so that he almost did not hear when the voice announced that tomorrow, Monday, there would be a call at exactly eight o'clock and Shmuel would be given the date of his summons to the estate.

On a winter day with low clouds, a dusty van drove through the puddles across the Abramowitz Estate. A call came from one of the buildings: "Bonhoeffer's here, Bonhoeffer's here!" Whether in celebration or in warning, it was hard to tell.

The van slowed to a stop and a rotund figure burst out of the driver's seat. Bonhoeffer. Next to him sat an anonymous figure trying to shrink back into his seat.

A stern man with an unpleasant complexion asked angrily, "Why have you come this time, Bonhoeffer?"

"Now, Riklin, you know that Bonhoeffer only comes when he is needed. And this is Shmuel!" He gestured at the figure now hesitantly exiting the vehicle.

Shmuel's presence was a great mystery. No one would admit to having known of his arrival, or that he was invited, or what purpose he could possibly serve on the estate.

Why have you come here? Shmuel was asked. He could not say.

Chapter twenty

The Widow's House   1953

*"As long as there is life in you, there are sublime
deeds and there are exalted moments"
(Yosef Chaim Brenner)*

When Lev Gutkin was three years old, his father was taken away by four men sent by Stalin, and he and his mother had to leave their apartment overlooking the river. For the rest of his life, whenever Lev Gutkin tried to remember his father, all he could see was a distant seaside resort and a toothache that had cut the holiday short.

They lived in a series of miserable apartments, blackened basements and enclosed balconies partitioned into rooms by a curtain. From time to time Gutkin's mother had to put on the finest of her worn out clothes, apply her last remaining makeup, and entreat this or the other official—the very same men who once, in the good old days, had worked with her husband. When she came back late at night, drenched in an odor of alcohol and sweat, she would pick up Gutkin from a neighbor. "Pigs, they're all pigs," she would mumble into the night air and hold him close. In the middle of the day sometimes, gazing out the window or standing by the filthy gas-ring in the shared kitchen, she hissed, "Pigs, they're all pigs." Her efforts kept her and her son alive, but it became increasingly difficult to find a "pig" who would agree to grant her favors. She had to burst into offices and shed tears, tug at the sleeves of indisposed officials. She was finally obliged to accept a favor of sorts, entailing residence near a distant train station on the outskirts of Siberia. Two months after she moved with her son to this miserable region of dark winds and knotted trees, the Second World War broke out.

Gutkin, by then a young man, could hardly wait to see the armor and infantry troops filing by as they marched to their deaths with a song on their lips. But all he caught was one glimpse of a far-away trio of planes passing silently like wild geese. The war did not reach the remote district, where instead of fire and conquests they had only hunger and poverty. To their west, the front pushed closer and closer to Moscow, but Gutkin's mother still longed for the city, and worked hard to obtain a reentry permit. Every time she went to plead her case before the local official, Gutkin remained under the care of a smiling widow who lived next door. At first their conversations were rigid, but the tension eased once the widow revealed her breasts to Gutkin and let him touch her wherever he wished. Eventually, she showed him what a man is supposed to do with a woman.

The widow made Gutkin work before he could have his fill of her body. Every day she sent him into the forest to chop wood for her stove. As she stood watching, he hacked the logs into splinters with a steel axe. She showed him how to gather mushrooms and break into the village storehouse. All morning she worked him and watched him, occasionally pulling her dress open in front of him, to remind him of their impending merriment. Gutkin's muscles grew taut and his tendons strained and his thoughts filled with violence and impatience. In the afternoons, exhausted from working and waiting, he would eat at the widow's table and then be free to pounce on her.

Young Gutkin's time glowed with pleasure, each new day crowned king as it pushed the other aside and celebrated its reign, hour after hour. It was good to be Lev Gutkin. Only when his mother returned from her travels, mumbling about pigs, was his bliss diluted with distaste. He looked at her unkempt hair, which did not regain its shine even after she scrubbed herself in the bathtub for hours, and he looked at her clothes, which could no longer withstand the grueling travel, and his happiness was marred. Every day his troubles were erased, only to return in the evening. He put out of his mind the all-consuming war raging through the world, the newspapers reporting of heroism on the fronts, and the fact that he had once had a life in Moscow and had found pleasure in mere child's play. Sometimes he stopped to marvel at the villagers walking hunched over like his mother. He could not understand how these grown adults, who had already discovered the secret of bedroom pleasures, were not rejoicing in this bliss every single day from morning to night.

Sometimes his mother was late coming home, and Gutkin remained happily in the widow's house. He would rest his head on her lap as she darned her clothes and sang softly. Once in a while she ran her kind hand through his hair and Gutkin smiled with his eyes closed. He would ask the widow sleepy questions, and she would shake her head and answer heavily, "Men are this way, women are that way."

One day he found the courage to ask, "How did your husband die?" He did not know that the question would change his life forever and would one day find him standing on the roadside near an Israeli town named Tiberias with a gun in his hand, waiting for Prime Minister David Ben-Gurion.

The widow sat up straight. "My husband was killed because of informants. Stalin's men, *tfu*." She started to weep and she held Gutkin to her and told a complicated story of hatred, and asked him to do to her what he had already done twice that day. As she held him and moved him inside her, she whispered, "You are like Arkady. You are the only one like him, the only one…" Gutkin felt tears in his eyes, and with them he felt his love for her, and for her late husband, who was once the village leader but was taken to Stalin's camps. When he felt his ecstasy bursting out he whispered, "Pigs, they're all pigs," and he flowed and flowed, and did not know that this pleasure with the widow would be like a mother tongue for him, that every delight with all other women ever after was destined to be as stammering and clumsy as a sentence spoken in a foreign language. He only knew that the widow was lying in his arms, that he was Lev Gutkin, that he was happy, and that this was how it would always be.

From that day on the widow insisted on retelling the story of why and how she had been widowed, a tale involving informants and beet crops. After she gave herself to him she always wept, "You are still young, perhaps you will take revenge on Stalin. But me, *tfu*, this is my life."

His mother showed him the papers she had obtained and talked about a permit that was sure to come, a favor owed to her by a certain official. She looked old, her eyes sunken. She was a stranger who insisted on spoiling his happiness with her incomprehensible mumblings.

One day a trace of the war arrived. A redheaded young captain who had been thrown off the front for reasons that remained murky was appointed as the village's wartime leader. The villagers were not told the reasons for the appointment, but the new head soon introduced some organizational changes in the village administration— namely, the former head and two of his deputies were sent to an unknown location. Two days later Gutkin saw the captain coming out of the widow's house. The widow said to Gutkin, "Do not come anymore. One has to live…"

Gutkin obeyed. He turned and left.

"Go," she called after him. "*Tfu*, it's all Stalin."

Gutkin walked for many days. Through the village, through the forest, along the railroad tracks, then back to the widow's house. A dim lump of thoughts burned inside him, and once in a while a clearly intelligible notion shone out: what he had done with the widow was possible with any woman, yet he wanted only the widow. This was difficult to understand. Being in bed with a woman was blissful, wonderful, better than anything else. And there was no other woman he wanted. Only the widow. He wanted her to caress his hair and whisper, *Men are this way, women are that way.*

The icy Siberian winter skies enveloped the village and tortured its dwellers while Gutkin roamed. He did not know that he had forever lost that simplicity with which a woman would shed her dress for him and sprawl on her back with open legs. He did not know that in Leningrad the Germans had despaired of their siege and that on the Stalingrad front they had begun the final retreat of February 1943. He was Gutkin, and he wanted the widow. He hated the red captain, and Stalin's army. He hated Stalin.

Dark trains raced through the station once in a while, cracking the strips of ice on the tracks and exhaling their soot. The trains tormented Gutkin more than anything. He could see shadows in the windows of the widow's house. The red captain. The widow. He crouched by the house in the freezing cold, stoking the fire of his thoughts.

The days came and went. Every so often a lucid comprehension would sting Gutkin—never again, there would never again be anything.

Things did happen to him. The stockkeeper's wife pushed him against the dairy wall one day and whispered in his ear, "My handsome one," and then some rude words. He thought about doing something with Tasha, the village idiot girl, like everyone else did, but when she stood naked before him he only touched her hair and ran away.

The war continued through spring, though the armies already knew who would win, but the Germans still had two years of retreat left before their defeat, and during those years Gutkin and his mother lived despondently in their hut. She had stopped making her journeys. She sat huddled in layers of clothing by the stove, rocking back and forth.

One day Gutkin went to the woods near the river and saw his adversary, the red captain, standing by a cluster of trees. He was completely naked, and he wobbled as he stood with his back to Gutkin, as if he were drunk. His clothes hung from a tree, and so did his gun in its holster.

Gutkin knew what he had to do. He moved with dwarfish heaviness, his mind a jewel of envy. He was determined. His fingers reached out to the holster and grasped the frozen metal. *Men are this way.* Some die, others love. He raised the gun and aimed at the captain's pale back. It occurred to him that the gun might be locked.

Where was the catch? Did he only need to pull the trigger, or were there any other steps he must take? He was determined, but as soon as he moved his finger the captain jumped up and disappeared in a flash behind a bush. Gutkin shivered. Pain. Jealousy. He thought about pulling the trigger—he had to shoot, even into the air. But the bullet was captured in the chamber. His heart begged him to shoot—shoot now!

Still holding the gun, he ran all the way home. A train stood not far from the house, unloading sacks of damp sugar and loading up with pigs. Gutkin jumped on the train with the gun beneath his coat and made his way back to Moscow to join the famished masses, the lax supervision, the end of the war, the great victory.

When the war was over he registered under a fictitious name for a high school completion course. A short while later, when his mother died, he received a permit to bury her in Moscow and was surprised to discover that he must bury her in a Jewish cemetery. That they were Jewish. He watched with revulsion as the *yids* took his mother's coffin away and lowered her into the earth, mumbling.

He spat on the ground. *Tfu.* And walked away.

Gutkin could not find his place among the students. He kept his distance from them, and from girls. His body burned with desire to sleep with a woman, but failure followed failure. Women wanted him and tried to drag him into their rooms in vain. He hated them and focused on his studies, which he also hated. On the streets, everywhere he went, hungry women reached out to him. He bought sex from them, sometimes beating them instead of paying. In his room he took the red captain's gun with its single bullet out of its hiding place, and placed it beside him while he ate or drank or gazed out the window at the large chimneys across the street. He could feel the loathing emanating from him, blossoming and growing.

He did not think about his mother very often. About the widow—all the time. Every time she came to his thoughts he was struck by pain, yet he persisted in thinking. Thinking. He could see her sprawled on her bed, laughing, crying. In his mind's eye she would change her mind and smile invitingly. Like her, he would mumble to himself, "Stalin, *tfu*, Stalin," and keep his guard against listeners, informants, the various characters that swarmed the streets of Moscow, agents and traitors and people who made a living sending their fellow humans to hell.

His thoughts must have slipped out here and there, because one day he was invited to an underground poetry circle. He had no intention of going—what did he care about poetry? But he happened to find himself in the area. He discovered that what had been billed as underground poetry—which he took to mean that the lines might include the occasional "down with all rulers" or "long live freedom"—was in fact the sort of underground that declared quite openly, "Death to the leader!" and included bold recitals against Stalin, his regime, his moustache, and the memory of his mother and father. Gutkin was horrified by the candor, the audacity, the danger, but he could not find the strength to leave the circle, and he became a loyal adherent, coming to every meeting to listen to the verses, never offering his own opinion, only caressing the women with his gaze. The regular crowd included a huge, curious-looking man who declared with every toast, "If there is an informant here, let him inform! I don't care—to hell with life!" He drank, and devoured, and took from the girls, and beat his poetry out as if driving nails into a wall. "Inform, if you wish. May filthy Stalin take my life. To us, my love!"

Gutkin was drawn to the giant, to his power, and his attraction did not subside even when it turned out that it was the giant who was informing the secret police. Due to a bad case of stomach cramps, Gutkin did not come to the meeting when the agents turned up and arrested everyone, sending them away to—who knew where. He met the giant on the street some time afterwards, and felt no grudge or fear. They shook hands and the giant invited Gutkin for a drink. They sat down as two friends. With a shudder and a certain nostalgia, Gutkin recalled the days when the giant would stand in the little room, his shadow cast on the walls, roaring, "All poems are rubbish. There is only one poem to me, and that will be when someone comes to tell me, 'They've slaughtered Stalin—freedom to all!'"

Gutkin looked at the giant's undiminished height and felt a pang in his heart—why hadn't the giant informed on him too? After all, it was only by chance that Gutkin had not shown up at that meeting. If they ever found the gun in his room...After a few drinks the giant got up and said, "There's work to be done." He clapped his hands together and left.

Gutkin sat for a while longer. His head filled with pictures of his mother and recollections of the widow. The memories hung over him and darkened his mind. Something of his father also emerged—the memory of a strip of beach and a boat in the background. A decision erupted within Gutkin: he would assassinate Stalin.

When he got back to his room he took a cardboard file out and wrote on it boldly, "Josef Stalin." Then he began to think. Why had so many assassination attempts failed thus far? He had to know. It was certainly not the tyrant's bodyguards who had thwarted the attempts. The enemy was haste, eagerness. He had to be cautious, had to plan carefully. Only then would he succeed. Stalin would die!

Gutkin spent seven years refining his plan to kill Josef Stalin. He studied the roads around all the government buildings and memorized the style and alertness of each and every policeman, soldier and agent in the guard. He measured distances, calculated angles, times, lines of vision, the effects of mist, frost, snow, sun, humidity. In his notebook he recorded how long it took him to run various distances, both in the dead of winter and in springtime. He studied all the publicly available information about the thwarted assassination attempt masterminded by Lyushkov in 1939. He investigated and exhausted every rumor about the airborne assassination attempt that may or may not have occurred at some point in the thirties. He listened to gossip, opinions, jokes, estimates, guesses and secrets.

At May Day parades he squeezed through the crowds to catch sight of his target. It was not yet time. Not yet. He would run home to think of more options, examine more obstacles that must be considered, and all the while the gun sat beside him on his desk.

When he finished his studies he was sent to a post-graduate technical institute to train as a forest engineer. He met a nice woman named Tania, whose laugh he did not despise, and they cooked together in the common kitchen. Tania was married, but she was probably a widow: her husband had been taken hostage by the Germans during the war, contrary to Stalin's orders. When he returned to his homeland he had been tried and sent to the camps. Tania did not speak of him, only wrote letters that were never answered. Gutkin wanted to show her his gun, his diagrams, the assassination plan to which he added another minor detail every day. He wanted to talk to Tania about Stalin, he wanted to trust her, for her to be the one soul to whom he could give his life. But he saw fear in her darting black eyes, and knew he must not talk.

Tania asked Gutkin to come and live with her in the village where she was born, far away in the south. Together they would get a transit permit. But Moscow was important to Gutkin: he had to measure distances over sidewalks and intersections, calculate viewing angles, lines of fire, times and dates in the government buildings. And so Tania found another man and disappeared with him.

Gutkin concentrated on his plan, gathered more information, improved maneuvers, added ideas for back-up and response. Sometimes he would stand in his apartment and wave the gun out the window. If anyone saw, so be it. If anyone informed, so be it. The bastards.

Every evening he walked through the neighborhood thinking only of his plan, of the five minutes he was preparing for. Five complicated minutes. March. Run. Sneak. Evade. And one shot. He sometimes passed by the synagogue at the end of his street. *I am a Jew*, the words would flash blindly through his mind. *I am a Jew and I will kill Stalin.*

When he finished his studies he was almost sent to oversee forestation in the Ukraine, but he was saved by finding a poorly paid job at the archives of the Ministry of Forestry, where he maintained lists and wrote report briefs on index cards. Every day after work he devoted himself to the assassination, endlessly refining and polishing the plan. As he lay on his bed, he sometimes thought of Tania in between the images of Stalin, and his heart filled with courage.

Bravery. A desire to find her. To tell her that he loved her. An age-old pain would rise up from the ashes.

It was easy for Gutkin to think about Stalin. But alongside his planning there were always more thoughts, shadowy creatures that wanted to take shape but never did. They always included the widow, and Tania, and his mother, and a long-forgotten evil woman whom he had once tried to interest in love. Fragmentary contemplations, raw ideas, embryos, drops, shards. *I will never be able to love* was there, hovering like a cloud, never materializing into a full thought. *I neglected my mother* also seared his consciousness, fluttering undeciphered. Sometimes, like a trickle of blood, there was *No matter what I do I will never be happy*, a contemplation that pained and gnawed but never became apparent.

Seven years had passed since Gutkin took upon himself the burden of assassinating Josef Stalin. And then, in 1953, Stalin died.

Gutkin took the news quietly. A small darkness took over his thoughts.

I am a Jew, he inexplicably thought.

Three weeks later he fled to Poland, and from there to Croatia, and on to Italy. In Italy he boarded a ship about to set sail for Palestine.

Chapter twenty-one

In Praise of the
Temporary Solution   1953

Y ou would not have wanted to be Adonai the God of Israel when David Bonhoeffer stepped out of his van on the side of the road and cried out to the heavens in prayer.

It was not every hour or even every day that Bonhoeffer turned to his creator to resolve their differences, but when he could no longer tolerate the ways of the world he lost no time in initiating an inquiry. First he would rub his hands together like a boxer, reminding his God that he had already prayed the standard Jewish prayers that day, so that it would be quite clear that this conversation was not part of the ordinary prayer service. Then he would look up and ask two questions: *Why is this the way of the world? How long will things go on this way?* Not being a patient listener, he would start to shout before waiting for an answer, great roars erupting from his body as he raised his fist at his God and barraged him with more questions, and yelled and roiled and begged until concerned drivers began to slow down and ask if he needed help.

These episodes did not take much time out of Bonhoeffer's busy schedule, because his charity work was still always calling. He dismissed the drivers kindly, not before making a halfhearted attempt to find out if any of them might wish to perform a *mitzvah* by adopting a needy man or employing someone in between jobs, and with renewed energies he would climb back into his cargo van, where he would beat his fist on the panel between the driver's cabin and the back, and announce to his charge: "Off we go!"

Bonhoeffer was never seen alone. He was always shadowed by some anonymous character, a distraught creature who needed refuge just for a while, "a temporary solution." Almost every day Bonhoeffer's van materialized before the eyes of some person of means, a farmer or factory owner, someone who might agree to host a needy man willing to work. "Give him somewhere to stay, just a couple of days," Bonhoeffer would ask with a desperate look in his eyes.

Bonhoeffer's art was to fold two-year stretches into a mere series of two or three days. On his travels among agricultural communities and factory yards he sometimes found a temporary solution he had left there ten or twenty years earlier, and he would pat him—and himself—on the back. "See, God willing, everything works out in the end."

People believed they could remember Bonhoeffer driving around forever, lending a helping hand to anyone who needed it, assisting all who crossed his path. He had been there even before the state, traveling the country, saving, helping. He had appeared among the Palmach fighters in the fields of Latrun one day, as if having sprung right out of the battlefield. After shedding his gun he enlisted in his new mission: anywhere help or welfare were needed, there was Bonhoeffer. When the state was founded and the labyrinthine Ministry of Welfare surfaced, still Bonhoeffer found work to do. "I handle the ones Welfare doesn't want anymore," he explained, thoughtfully drawing a line between himself and the Ministry.

Bonhoeffer looked like someone who had just finished dragging a cart through the mud. His beard was always damp and his forehead glistened with sweat. He wore the overcoat of an orthodox man, which would have improved his appearance if not for its unraveling hems and the protrusion of his solid potbelly.

He was generally considered a righteous man, but even he was tainted by rumors. They said he was a yeshiva student who had lost his faith; that he was an adulterous rabbi who had fled his congregation in Belgium; that he was a Christian minister; that he was a Nazi, a young S.S. officer who had sworn to convert to Judaism in the death camps. Bonhoeffer scoffed at the rumors, but they did anger him. "You Jews, you're always worried about what happened in the past." He viewed all gossip as a waste of time, unless it was part of the idle chitchat designed to soften people's hearts long enough for them to agree to take in a needy person.

"Look at him, such an excellent work horse. If you'd like, he can show you how he hauls sacks. In Moscow he was a porter, he has muscles like the Cedars of Lebanon. Since coming here his life has clouded over, he lost his home. But he hasn't forgotten how to carry sacks."

People believed that over the years they had acquired an immunity to Bonhoeffer's powerful arguments. But they were wrong. If Bonhoeffer made up his mind to convince someone, he worked at it single-mindedly. At first the person would resolve not to waver. After a few words he would begin to feel a thread of weakness. Then came a stream of doubts, and finally a fleet of guilt sailed painfully out of his heart. Bonhoeffer knew exactly when to rest his case. He sensed the moment and hurried to reel in the miracle, retreating to his van like a panther, waving his hand dismissively as if refusing to accept some unspoken fee, and before anyone could move he drove away, leaving the new host behind with his temporary solution.

While Bonhoeffer handled one temporary solution, the next was already waiting in his van—Dmitri or Hezi or Conrad or Moshe—and as soon as he reached his destination, Bonhoeffer would try to give the new one away. Sometimes, if the heavens smiled upon him, he might even be able to deposit two at a time and they would step out of the van just as if it were Noah's Ark. After all, they required so little, and it was just a couple of days.

Bonhoeffer routinely found himself in hopeless situations where persuasion was impossible. And yet he had to try, and tensions rose, threatening to erupt. His goods were people with flawed providence, and in return he could promise only the shadow of a *mitzvah*, a feeling of goodness that would glimmer in one's soul. He also offered the estimation that damage, generally speaking, would not occur. But after all, these were not people who were entirely right. If they were, they would not have needed charity. And so Bonhoeffer was sometimes obliged not only to persuade, but to excuse. Here a bed frame was broken, there some bills disappeared. Here a few friends of the temporary solution came over for a drunken squabble, there a temporary solution tried to force premature adulthood on the youngest of the family daughters. The temporary solutions had a wonderful ability to shower their damages upon the most generous hosts, and at times Bonhoeffer had to face their wrath and listen to them with a forgiving look.

"Of course we need more workers, Bonhoeffer. And guess why?! To fix the damages left by the last character you brought us! Bonhoeffer, are you listening?!"

"Where is our car, Bonhoeffer? When that Moshe of yours came here he was limping with both legs. 'Let him rest and work sitting down in the kitchen,' you said. But when he saw an unlocked car, he ran to it!"

"Bonhoeffer, this time we're going to the police. Do you understand what this means—a disturbed man like that, running around with my gun?"

Bonhoeffer was always the first to admit his mistakes. He would hasten to commend the angry family and complement them for being so concerned for public safety—there was an unstable man in possession of a gun—even while their own checkbook had been stolen.

A mere twenty minutes later he would be apologizing to yet another family. Just before Rosh Hashanah he had brought them one temporary solution, and delivered another to the Goldbergs, and now there was a gun missing over there and a warehouse on fire over here.

"*Nu*, I forgot to mention that the poor man, God have mercy on his soul, his mind is sick with a love of fire. I can see that you have already been introduced to this love. I beg your forgiveness. And you see, the other poor man, the one at the Goldbergs—such a nice family—well, I gave them your warning—the warnings got switched—and for two whole days they wouldn't let him get near a match. And that one, without cigarettes he could lose his mind—and indeed, as you see, he did! No one knows where he is, and the worst of it is, he took a gun. How did he find it? The devil only knows. He took it from a drawer. But this one of yours is entirely different. He abstains from smoking—every person has one admirable quality—but he really does like to light fire every chance he gets, and I could see even from afar that he got his chance. The devil! But smoking? No, he doesn't smoke. He's a good man, all in all."

And so Bonhoeffer stood there rattling on, praising the temporary solution while behind him the warehouse went up in flames, consuming two tractors—one insured, the other not.

In return for all of Bonhoeffer's deeds, his God rewarded him with tremendous and decisive faith, which he grasped like a machete and used to hack his way through life. His right-hand-man, alongside his faith, was a bottle of Rémy Martin that was always with him. The bulbous belly of the bottle shone in his hand, or beside him on the passenger seat. The cognac was smuggled in for him by some sailors, an illegal transaction that seemed to provide a small glimpse into his mind, an avenue to investigate its recesses. Bonhoeffer was often asked how he could justify such a crime. In response he would close his eyes, as if to imply that there was a *halakhic* loophole that permitted the consumption of smuggled Rémy Martin, but that he was not at liberty to explain it. And even if he were, who among the questioners could understand the minutiæ of the world of Gemara?

Bonhoeffer himself was half a rabbi, or perhaps a third. He had begun his rabbinical studies but had never finished. "Too many words there, and a man's heart wants action," he explained with a sigh, followed by a stern warning: "Rabbis are the finest of men!" Then he would look to see if any of his listeners indicated hostility toward rabbis.

Bonhoeffer liked to pray alone. In synagogue, reading in public, he found it difficult to concentrate. Thoughts trickled into his mind about assistance and charity and finding homes for temporary solutions, distracting him from the prayers with the impatience of a spoiled child tugging at his sleeve. He would try with all his might to focus his thoughts, to tie them down to the words in the prayer book, the heartfelt intention, the tunes, the supplications, but from somewhere out there one simple word would jump out of its line and lift him up to the skies, to other worlds. After a while he would return and scan the prayer book awkwardly, as confused as someone who wakes up to find himself hanging from a parachute. Where were they? Which page were they on?

The study of the daily Talmud page also caused him anguish. Bonhoeffer was averse to long-winded debates, and the pages of Talmud made him particularly uncomfortable: he had the vague sense that the most important things were being said behind his back. He adhered to the words of the Bible like a gecko to the wall. All he needed were the three books: Torah, *Nevi'im*, *Ketuvim*. In fact, just the Torah was best, because afterwards the text got a little complicated and stopped providing any comfort to one's soul. The Torah was a breath of fresh air. And if he came across any kind of Judaism other than the simplest and most ordinary strain, he lost all measure of charity.

"Reform Jews? May their name be erased! Burn all their synagogues!"

"Burn?"

"Burn!"

"And the Torah scrolls inside?"

At that point Bonhoeffer panicked and saw himself running into a burning synagogue to rescue the holy books, making his way through the flames into the chamber, looking around and thinking, 'I should not have burned it, I could have convinced the *gabbai* to take a couple of men in, but it's too late now.' The windows shattered from the heat, tongues of fire lapped up all the pews, and any chance of housing a needy man here was lost. But perhaps they would take in a few temporary solutions to help clean up the mess and resurrect the ruins? Bonhoeffer took a hesitant step and watched as jobs for the needy went up in flames.

"*Nu*, you mustn't burn synagogues, even if they are Reform," he finally acceded. He allowed himself to hate the Reform Jews without burning their synagogues. And if he came across such a Reform Jew in trouble, he would immediately take him under his wing.

Bonhoeffer was sometimes caught trying to slip out before the evening prayer. As soon as he heard someone needed his help, he would push his way to the exit while people murmured, "Wait a minute, Bonhoeffer, you haven't prayed *arvit* yet."

Bonhoeffer would stop and say bitterly, "*Nu*, all right, all right," and finish his prayer with a sour face at the edge of the room before hurrying out to his van, mumbling, "*Nu*, well, they pray and they pray...*Nu*, Jews..."

Instead of praying silently in his heart, Bonhoeffer preferred sermonizing. The sermons erupted of their own accord and did not subside until he had scanned all the chambers of his mind and found them emptied of outrage. First he would find a partner for a dialogue about important matters. Soon another curious person would interfere, and before long anyone who had an opinion had joined the circle. Bonhoeffer would listen and answer every question, and the partners slowly turned into an audience, and then Bonhoeffer would find a bench to stand on and begin his sermon with simple, practical advice, such as, "Drink a lot in the summer time, it's good for the kidneys." Rivers of Torah soon overflowed, verses mined from the Holy Book, to which Bonhoeffer added his own touches. He revived forgotten verses and dug deep into the backrooms of the 613 Commandments, occasionally enlightening his listeners with his own invented verses.

The seasons affected his imagery. In the fall there were more clouds and pomegranates, in summer blue skies and the Garden of Eden. A steady generator ran in his heart, inventing and using as needed—honey, fire, Torah, pearls and eagles. He always made use of his surroundings. If he was standing with Meshulam Riklin and they were both looking out at Rivka's kites, the sight immediately prompted a pointed allegory: "My people, Riklin, are also wild kites. Sometimes you can find such a kite in the form of a human being, very handsome but with one torn string. Offer just some small assistance, and it will take off. For example, in my van over there, just by chance, pure coincidence, is precisely such a man-kite. He needs a home for a couple of days. He will earn his keep and do no harm. Let's go and get him now, before he changes his mind. Look at those beautiful wings!"

From the van emerged a fellow who looked nothing like a kite but had a pair of darting eyes beneath bushy eyebrows, a moustache and a beard. He behaved politely and had a slight limp, which gave cause to wonder how he would work. Bonhoeffer quickly dismissed all doubts, praising the wonderful traits that might be hiding inside the man. He pulled on people's charitable strings until he felt them begin to unravel. He squeezed out an agreement and quickly vanished.

To Bonhoeffer, there was no one who could not be praised. No one who was entirely sinful.

Someone had once started painting the Ten Commandments on the side of Bonhoeffer's van. Broad strokes in a brandy-brown color covered up the attempt, but the tablets were still visible, along with a bold beginning of "I am Your Lord."

Bonhoeffer was a permanent fixture in people's memory. No one ever asked where he lived or how he made a living. His biography was a riddle. Bonhoeffer himself peppered conversations with pieces of his life as examples and lessons, but the fragments did not form a coherent narrative, providing only shards and gaps.

"No, I never married," he said, "which is a bad thing, not good. A sailor doesn't always find a good mate. A man seeks a woman like the very foundation of his soul, and if the Creator does not see fit to provide, that is the end of it."

"Once I tried to be a painter," he told some people. "I was accepted to the academy, but then the war, *nu...*"

There had been a war in Bonhoeffer's life. But which one? No one knew. A terrible war, it seemed. One that had decided many fates and taken its toll on Bonhoeffer as well. He sometimes referred to it as an explanation for some facet of his life.

His sources of income were even more obscure than his past. A quick glance into the back of his van revealed an ever-replenished variety of goods. One day there was a box containing ten red transistor radios. The next day the box was gone, replaced by sixty copies of *Logic*, by M. Blum. The books disappeared within a day, and instead came a crate of apples beneath a dozen toilet brushes bundled in twine. Night fell, morning rose, and in the very same place sat a chicken in a basket, contemplating its death. Off the van went, back it came, and now there was a heap of bagged fertilizer at a bargain price, topped off with a rusty pair of shears.

The goods in the van came and went like objects responding to a tidal rhythm. A heap of raincoats and copies of school textbooks. Little bags of buttons and a sack full of nurses' caps. A few very crushed balls of wool and a huge bottle of oil. Pictures of a bride tied together with string and a lump of orange-grey wax. A bottomless pit of products that no one wanted. All the clothes in the store that no one ever takes off the hanger. All the bruised tomatoes at the stall that shoppers turn away from in disgust. All the books that fill the shelves as nothing but bookends for the ones that sell. These were gathered up by Bonhoeffer into his van, the younger siblings of the people for whom he found solutions.

The inside of the van was decorated with photographs of rehabilitated temporary solutions embracing wives and children, smiling happily at the new temporary solutions as they rattled in the back of the van. The faces in the photographs projected a promise: salvation will come. Among the photographs, inexplicably, were also pictures of Judy Garland with a plunging neck-line. Some of the solutions couldn't help but wonder if the famous actress had been one of the portables transferred in the van. And sometimes their loins burned as they looked at her picture, desire erupting from their bodies like a dagger—Woman, lie here before us, woman.

Donations, charity and contributions were Bonhoeffer's life-blood, and because of his faith he never rejected a gift. Once he drove into a lot with six needy cases in tow, all dressed in old Beitar Jerusalem soccer uniforms. The iconic yellow *menorahs* on the shirts drew cheers. Beitar fans were scattered throughout the country, in every reserve duty battalion, every office and every *moshav*, like bold pioneers straying far from mother Jerusalem to conquer little pieces of wilderness for her. They came out to the van like Robinson Crusoe greeting his rescuer, and generously agreed to host a needy man for a couple of days, just a temporary solution. On one *moshav* the men were forced to play a match against the local team. They gave away six goals and were booed off the field, but one man was allowed to stay, just for a couple of days.

Comprehending the potential of the uniform and the surprising new markets it might open up, Bonhoeffer had his men appear in Beitar shirts again, and also experimented with Bnei Yehuda's orange shirts, Hapoel Haifa's red ones, and Hakoach Ramat Gan's purple ones. He even acquired some knowledge in the nuances of the soccer league, so that he could discuss the burning issues of the day with all the potential hosts.

Bonhoeffer also started a few fashion trends. His wallet was a white birthday goodie bag, perhaps a souvenir from a party. One day he noticed someone watching as he pulled the bag out of his pocket, loosened its white string and took out a few bills. "It's the most convenient thing," he explained in defense, and when no mockery followed, he plucked up the courage to promote the idea. "See, when you want to open it you just pull here a little, and there you go. And to close it you just go like this, no problem, and it's all in the bag. A bag for coins and a bag for bills, and a bag for your ID, which tells you that even an old man like me has a place in the State of Israel."

With its halo of Israel's independence, the idea began to seem simple and appealing. A few days later, a truck-driver walked into a kiosk and pulled out his new wallet, a birthday bag illustrated with three balloons.

When did Bonhoeffer bring the first temporary solution to the Abramowitz Estate? Opinions differed. Some remembered two solutions arriving shortly before 1948, and a lone testimony claimed that as early as 1933, not long after the estate was founded, Bonhoeffer had first turned up at the gates. But Bonhoeffer himself denied this version—he hadn't even been in the country then, he said. He refused to answer subsequent questions, saying only that back then he was in the war. He agreed with the official estate records—the ones in Günter's memory—which showed 1953 as the year of the first official temporary solution, whose name was Avraham-Union-Avraham-United.

Bonhoeffer had proudly introduced both parts of Avraham to Günter as if unveiling the new model of a sought-after product. "This man had a political mishap. And let me tell you, he was a fine young man, a person of great stature, one of the first kibbutz founders to set up his home among the Jewish people. And then, a political mishap. You know about the rift in the kibbutz movement, of course. One side said Josef Stalin was the "Sun of the Nations," the other said Josef Stalin was Satan. *Nu.* One day a charming kibbutz, common property, common ideas, and the next day—bang! A rift. This one calls itself "Union" and the other, "United." They draw a borderline, and every member has to decide which side he's on. A savage battle. A scar drawn right down the middle, dividing lands, dividing homes and families and hearts. And our Avraham, as you know, was a fine young fellow. He watched the other members, watched his world split into two, torn into shreds of Union and United, and he had to choose. The line tears through families, unravels stitches, and it gets closer and closer to him. Our Avraham—what does he care about Josef Stalin? All he can do is watch his old friends, the only family he ever had. He was being asked to decide—abandon these ones or abandon the other ones. His friends dug into his soul from both sides, and since he was unable to choose, his soul split in two, and now he is Avraham-Union on this side and Avraham-United on the other. But this mishap—what is it to us? The main thing is that he is a dedicated worker. He left his kibbutz, and if his unity is undermined in any way, it is barely noticeable."

Avraham-Union-Avraham-United joined the estate and never

once, in all his years of service, even when his divided soul threatened to dismantle his very being from within, did his rift harm anyone else.

After bringing Avraham-Union-Avraham-United, Bonhoeffer found a way to drive through the gates of the estate every week. His keen instincts told him to slip past Abramowitz and make his case to the estate foremen, simpler fellows like Hans or Lerer or Harkin. He also recognized the depths of compassion in Günter, but he was wary of him. He kept his distance from Rivka Abramowitz, too. If he detected that she was in good spirits, he would go straight to her for a decision. But if he sensed from a distance that there was something else in her, something more dangerous, he would retreat and flee, for Rivka was not a simple person at all. Often, as he spoke to her about the temporary solution in the back of his van, just a matter of a couple of days, he felt a strange desire to forget about the temporary solution and put Rivka herself in the van and drive away. But why? Why would someone like Rivka need a place for a couple of days? Rebuking himself, Bonhoeffer would subdue his own instincts with the help of some Rémy Martin and slip away to try his luck with Hans or Lerer or Harkin, simple fellows, undoubtedly more simple.

It was Bonhoeffer, more than anyone else, who felt the mood change on the estate when Dr. Meshulam Riklin arrived. Tiny cracks in the procedures were quickly sealed up by the doctor, and the tortuous paths on which Bonhoeffer worked his magic were closed off, leaving him no way to embed his solutions among the estate workers. Meshulam Riklin enforced a monolithic regime that was angry and strict.

Bonhoeffer, a tireless servant of the Lord, was forced to improve his methods. And then his God sent him handsome Lev Gutkin.

Chapter twenty-two
The Wandering Jew   1955

> *"He writes of love in polemic language,*
> *at times even with hostility and the obduracy of*
> *an old man…and even with cruelty…"*
> *(Meir Yaari on A.D. Gordon)*

Every day at four in the morning, Dr. Meshulam Riklin got out of bed, slowly put on his socks and some comfortable clothing, stepped into his shoes and placed his notebook under his arm. A new day was rising on the Abramowitz Estate, and Dr. Riklin welcomed it, proficient in his duties and prepared for any surprise. He would close his eyes for a moment and imbue his soul with Abramowitz's hatred of the country—the Zionist state, murderers of the innocent and executers without trial—and walk out of his room, up the dark path to the center of the estate.

The first thing he would see were the rows of little houses now covering the old orchards, then a network of paths between the warehouses and workshops and the barns, coops, stables and pens. A few lights flickered here and there, evidence of the night shifts still at work. The path beneath his feet dipped into little valleys, then rose again, passing clusters of houses and small gardens and intersecting with yet more paths. In the offices that had proliferated along the gradual slope leading down from Abramowitz's house, Riklin would begin his first morning round and not rest until night.

When he felt tired during the course of the day, he spurred himself on and overcame his weariness. Sometimes he mixed up a medicinal concoction to give himself a burst of energy. He observed a vegan diet, eating only small amounts of fruit and grains, and in winter he drank water out of the little stream that ran through the estate, hunched down at the water's edge like a dog to lap up liters of water with his eyes open. He guarded his health fanatically. "I am a healthy man," he would conclude, sneering as he observed the other residents, on whose bodies he could always see the punishment of the meat and flour they ate, the sugar and oil they gobbled.

From the day he came to the estate, trailing behind Abramowitz, Riklin imposed a routine of work and obedience, with rules ever more extreme and laws constantly sharpened. He looked down with pity upon at least half of the workers, perhaps two thirds, and in moments of fury he wished he could fire them all and replace them with proper laborers, ones like there used to be. But Abramowitz forbade Riklin from firing anyone, promising a livelihood for every worker who stayed with him "even through hard times." Riklin complained and grumbled and collected reasons to fire specific workers. "Geitzev, for example. Take, for example, Geitzev," he would mutter. But he could not persuade Abramowitz.

It was beyond his comprehension how such a wonderful estate had managed to acquire such a useless collection of despicable, downtrodden people, who covered the hillside and filled the houses with their insipid and unvanishing lives. They trickled slowly into all realms of the estate, one by one, disrupting all of Riklin's laws like weeds covering a mountain, until the enterprise sagged under their weight. Every night, before he closed his eyes, Riklin would reflect on one of the miserable characters who deserved to be thrown out. He would study him well and fill his mind with wrath and hatred, then try to drag the poor man into his dreams, where everything was permissible, where there were laws and there was a judge.

An unbalanced sort of equilibrium existed on the estate. Riklin refrained from firing any of the workers, but he could turn them against one another, encircle them with his weighty rules, and enforce hard labor upon even the most indolent. Rumor had it that lazy Reuven Geitzev had been kicked out of the Jewish labor brigades by Trumpeldor himself, but Riklin managed to force him into the dairy barn, where he had to record each cow's productivity and identify any shirkers. Eisman, the dairy manager, lorded over Geitzev to win favor with Riklin and negate the effects of the informants who reported his every act. Even a little pail of milk he had taken to his room to make cheese "like in the olden days" was docked from his pay "in lieu of wages." Eisman turned a wide and suspicious eye on each of his assistants in the dairy, but had he been asked to speculate who the rat might be, he would have picked Levi Tzelnik, who insisted on working in the dairy despite severe hay fever that caused his arms to break out in a rash, and who shook his head nervously whenever he was offered a break. Another possibility was Avraham Brenner, who claimed to be related to the great author Yosef Chaim Brenner. He lectured about the author's doctrines to anyone who would listen, but few did, because wherever Brenner went he was shadowed by a story from back in the Palmach era, whereby a mistake he had made in the heat of a battle had brought about the deaths of half his division.

Fate had a sense of humor, and a casualty from that very same battle, the artist Benyamin Simil, joined the estate. Riklin sent Simil to work in the dairy office, right next door to Avraham Brenner, so that he could burrow into Brenner's conscience from morning to evening as he watched him out of his good eye, leaning his one remaining arm on the table. In his youth, Benyamin Simil had been a founding member of Kibbutz Alimim. He gave up his art for the common good and went to work in the fields, but the lonely evening hours, when he gazed achingly at the horizon through a window draped with mosquito netting, gave rise to a wonderful new craft, mastered by no one before or since: artistically illustrated mosquito nets. And not mere crude brushstrokes, but subtle caresses with the finest of bristles, gossamer after gossamer, square after square, producing masterpieces with titles such as, "Berl Katznelson Holding a Sheaf of Grain," "The Wind Caressing Chaim Weizmann's Hair," or "Workers Listening to a Historic Speech." A huge demand arose for his work, but what good was demand when he was thrown off the kibbutz because of attempting "inappropriate intimacy" with a fellow member? He joined the Palmach, distinguished himself on the battlefield, and one day fate introduced him to Avraham Brenner.

Just as he attached Benyamin Simil and Avraham Brenner to one another, Riklin engaged in other matchmaking, attempting to group all the members of the estate into knots of resentment and vengeance. He wove them into nerve-wracking twosomes and threesomes and dreamed of banishing them all. Every evening he looked through his notebook and studied the crop of leaked information, suspicions, and incriminations. He decreed punishments, switched workers, reinforced supervision in suspect areas, formulated laws, and finally called in Mendel Chen and Amram Bukai, the estate criers, to disseminate the new orders throughout the estate. Mendel Chen and Amram Bukai, who hated each other, shook up the peaceful estate to deliver Riklin's news to every last nook, knocking on every door and rapping on every window except in the silent island far from Riklin's reign of terror, the hilltop home that housed the master of the estate.

Riklin was always prepared to be summoned to the house, anticipating the encounters with both fear and longing. His eyes were drawn to the house from wherever he was, and he always measured his distance from it. But only when the order came did he hurry up the path, trembling with fear. When Abramowitz asked him a question, Riklin answered tersely, afraid to bother his master with trivialities. If Abramowitz took an interest in something, Riklin did not rest until he had thoroughly explained every detail. "I'm a chatterbox," he would say apologetically. But he wished their conversations could go on forever, and after his meetings with Abramowitz he was filled with a desire to go back to his childhood, to his parents' bedroom, to climb into their bed and fall asleep.

Sleep was not easy for Dr. Riklin. In his dreams Naomi came to him. Spirits raged within him, tearing windows through his soul and charging out in the dark. Only when he awoke and the morning slowly rose over the estate, did he begin to feel any comfort—first just a strip of horizon, and by noon a full embrace. His spirit knew that all his hard work was for the man who sat in his home, intent on his business, while the entire estate thrived on his power. Riklin would look up at the hilltop and feel no pain or deprivation. No sorrow. Only purpose.

In the distance, beyond the shadowy mountains, the country went about its business. The Bank of Israel Act, 5714—1954; Penal Law (Amendment of Revocation of Capital Punishment for Murder), 5714—1954; Military Justice Act, 5715—1955. But Riklin looked to the sky, the earth and the sun, seeing nothing but the world of the estate. Sometimes within this world of goodness, Rivka Abramowitz would suddenly appear to trap him in conversation as if he were not a busy foreman. Her words always intimated at her odd delight in reminding him of his original role: his failure to give her a child.

The more Riklin tried to evade Rivka and escape her look, the more determined she was to hold him and talk at length about this or that, invariably alluding to Naomi. What did she want of him? Those eyes, not black and not blue. The long neck. The hips. How had she not borne him a child? And although he told her everything she wanted to know about Naomi and their two-year marriage, Rivka always found new questions, and her probing light threatened to expose even those bad moments, the ones that would never have occurred had he known how short his life with Naomi would be.

He would have forgiven Rivka for everything if she had not allowed her innocence to be exploited by that dubious man of piety, Bonhoeffer, who took advantage of her to infiltrate the estate with new tenants, characters of the worst sort who suddenly appeared before Riklin in the dairy, in the garden, more mouths to feed, bodies to clothe, reckless hands to watch. Riklin thought he could persuade Abramowitz to prohibit any new residents, even ones approved by Rivka. He had already formulated a law in his notebook: new tenants only when authorized by Riklin. But he was never able to see the idea through.

"What is Rivka's role here? What is her role and what is mine?" he wondered angrily. Sometimes he walked right up to Abramowitz's doorstep, stood with his back to the house and inspected the expanses of the estate—his expanses, his domain. He felt his power swelling and his might rushed down the hill like an endless flood, pouring over the houses, the land, the workers and the yards, swallowing up every other force and shredding it to bits. But then, all at once, he would weaken, ashamed of his former, frailer nature, the biblical verses he used to quote, the poetry he had tried to write. Once, encouraged by Naomi, he had even sent a poem to Avraham Shlonsky, but it was rejected. What purpose had all those joyless words served?

Dr. Riklin would take a deep breath and slowly exhale. Strength again—now he was afraid of no one, and his powers returned. Then, carefully, before Rivka could spot him, he would walk down the path and continue his work. Sometimes he wondered what things would be like if Rivka was not there. He pictured an entirely flawless kingdom, where Chaim Abramowitz lived alone on the estate.

He tried to enlist his new persona whenever he faced Rivka, but he failed, feeling weak again, and ludicrous, as he had in his early days when he was a young doctor, poor but talented. What did Rivka want? Hadn't he suffered enough? And his love of Naomi—why did Rivka yearn to know about that? He had told her everything. Everything. How he had met Naomi when she was his patient. A young sick girl from the powerful Mussadof family, a pillar of the Bukharan community in Jerusalem. How they had brought her to him because he was an unknown doctor, in the hopes that rumors of her illness would not spread through Jerusalem and diminish the value of her sisters too. Three times she came before he understood that this was the woman he was desperately seeking. She had been placed in his hands and there would never be another. What did Rivka want of him?

One day Riklin found out from his informants that Rivka sometimes went to the cemetery near Ness Ziona where Naomi was buried. He was overcome with nausea, an internal filth that did not leave him even in sleep. He ate nothing for three days, fearfully sipped water and could not suppress his nausea until he was willing to replace it with fear, deep cold fear that poured into his bones and stayed there without him knowing why. He felt his old nature, the pathetic one, rearing its head. What did Rivka's visits to the cemetery mean? What should he be afraid of? Would Naomi rise from her grave and tell Rivka things that Riklin did not want told? Let's see you! Take my beautiful wife out of the hands of death!

Finally Riklin went to Berger the driver and demanded that he take him to Ness Ziona.

"Where to?"

"Where you take her."

"Who?"

"Her." Riklin glared at Berger.

Berger felt a shiver run up his spine and a lump in his throat. "Okay, okay…"

When Riklin visited his wife, the first time and every time thereafter, he found subtle signs of Rivka's presence around the grave: a candle or flowers or a dropped bracelet. What did she want of his life?

Naomi's grave was adjacent to the fence, in a shady corner. Only one other grave was nearby, and it had a tearful inscription lamenting a decent man who had been persecuted until he took himself to his grave. "An innocent man. He thought he had come home. But he had come—unto death." Riklin never saw anyone at that grave, but it was surrounded with plants and flowers that were faithfully tended to. Someone made sure they were always watered and pruned.

Riklin did not want to decorate Naomi's grave. What good were flowers? Naomi of the Mussadofs. How he had fought for the proud Bukharans' permission to marry her. They would not give her sisters to anyone outside the community, but her, the sick one, his Naomi, they allowed to be taken by a stranger, and after the marriage they abandoned her. Naomi's frightened eyes had shown that she knew her own end, as if she was always looking through binoculars at her future. And how encouraging she was to him, giving him strength and asking for nothing. From the first, he loved her so much that he never took the time to find out whether she loved him back. Her paleness…she had never left the Bukharan neighborhood in her youth. He wanted to fortify her with his love, to strengthen her body. He took her on tours of the country so that she could soak up the healthy sun. He encouraged her to walk, almost forced her, scolding when she lagged behind. Together they climbed archæological barrows, fresh excavations only just discovered, the slowly emerging prehistory of the land. But his explanations did not excite her, she could see no grace or glory in the soil. She faltered ahead with a tearful face. He loved her, he loved her so much, but the illness of her flesh joined forces with the sorrow in her soul. What could he do?

She had to grow stronger. He devised a strict diet. He did not enforce his veganism on her, but removed all fatty, spicy and salty foods from her diet. As soon as he realized that she went to her friends to eat the forbidden foods she missed, he forbade her to visit them. It was for her, all for her. Her family caused her such pain. From the day they married her off to a poor stranger, it was as if she had been sold. They never invited her to their homes or their celebrations. One day he would take revenge, he would hurt them. Those cunning merchants, so wealthy—they must have known how she would end up. But what was she to them now, married to a poor doctor? Poor? He would get rich! He would show them! The whole country would be knocking at his door, and then they would come to him and beg. But Naomi, she was the most important thing. His love for her was so great. He prayed for her love, and with the voracious tenderness and the terrible softness, came also the cruelty.

One day Dr. Riklin came to Naomi's grave and found all the greenery around the neighboring grave ripped out of the ground. Someone had beheaded the plants and torn them up, a few were even tossed onto the dry earth around Naomi's grave. On his next visit the plants were dry and dead, as if the anonymous visitor had stopped coming, or perhaps that was the person who had destroyed the plot. One single plant was still alive, a Wandering Jew that had been thrown down next to Naomi's grave and had managed to send one little shoot into the earth and take root. From deep in the soil it was drawing moisture to survive.

Riklin leaned down, pulled up the root and flung the plant away. But on his next visit he found the Wandering Jew had clung to the earth again, sending out roots. Its grayish-green leaves, like sharpened ears, tumbled and crawled beside the grave. Riklin pinched the stem off from its roots and placed it on the cement frame of the grave. Without the meticulous greenery the other grave was completely naked—Naomi's only neighbor, the suicide, now looked strange, unlikable, even menacing. Riklin sat next to Naomi's grave and stared at the other one, unable to escape its loud letters. *He thought he had come home. But he had come—unto death.* Riklin had only been married to Naomi for two years, and he never knew whether she had joined him out of love, or because she knew that beneath her beautiful whiteness she was sick and lost, undeserving of anyone who was not handicapped, a widower, lame, or worse.

On his next visit he found the Wandering Jew where he had left it, arid and grey, but the following time he found that someone had moved the dry stalk and the plant had attacked the earth again, sending out roots to draw moisture from the depths. Riklin was impressed. He felt a new sense of affection for the exhausted stalk. He divided it into several parts and placed them on the ground. "If you survive this time, I will protect you forever."

The stalks were alive and embedded in the earth the next time he came. He gathered them up and took them back to the estate. He gave them no water or sunlight. Those who survived he placed on harsh rocky terrain with no soil. When it rained he covered them with sheets to prevent the drops from quenching their thirst. Every plant that failed was pulled up and removed. *If you survive this time, I will protect you forever.*

Riklin followed his Wandering Jews for months, scornfully examining their deaths. And then one piece of stalk got away and slid through the rocks. After Riklin left, it found a path to water, light and earth. It secretly developed into a robust specimen that grew quickly to evade Riklin's eyes. It sprouted new leaves on its head and sacrificed old ones on its tail, almost as if it had feet to carry it forth. A hardy, stubborn Wandering Jew, asking for no favors, neither water nor soil. If it was only left alone, it would find a way to survive.

One day the new specimen surfaced before Riklin, and Riklin cupped the plant in his hands, his affection escaping. "Dear one," he giggled, "dear one." He fingered the plant's leaves and felt a little drunk. He thought about Naomi. Guilty? Why would he feel guilty?

But if he could be given the chance to love her again, he would do it better, he would love her better.

He kneeled down by the plant. So strong, such determination to live. "Dear one!" he called and pulled the plant up by its roots and threw it up in the air, giving it the chance to save itself one more time, if it could. Then he walked unsteadily to the nearest office. He fined two workers and shuffled over to the dairy. He forced a confession out of Eisman, threatened Geitzev, and proceeded to the pen, where he caught Burkman trying to distill alcohol out of a withered eggplant. He fined Edri the supervisor for not keeping the straw clean. Then he ran down to the stream, buried his face in the thick growth and wept.

The next morning Riklin found his Wandering Jew wrapped calmly around a rock, its roots clutching the earth. He leaned down and ran a comforting finger over the plant's ribs and spines.

*

Bonhoeffer was the first to perceive the cracks in Riklin's wall. He brought a new candidate one day and introduced him to Dr. Riklin, hoping he would take him in as a temporary solution, just for a couple of days, five at the most. While he was there, Bonhoeffer suggested, perhaps the young man could herd Riklin's Wandering Jew.

"Herd it?"

"Yes, you know, take it to spots where there's fresh water and sunlight. He is a fine young fellow, this man of mine. If you ask him to take it, he'll take it. Ask him to keep watch, he'll keep watch. A good fellow, all in all, and anything the police might tell you is a drop in the ocean compared to the truth."

Chapter twenty-three

The Elders of Hashomer
1958

W *"The world is conflict-ridden, but it is also*
diverse, and sometimes beautiful"
(Yosef Chaim Brenner)

hen Rivka Abramowitz was two, she suffered from nocturnal fits of anger that hurled her body back and forth against the bars of her crib and brought Sarah rushing in. "Daddy, Daddy!" Rivka would cry from within her stupor of rage. She would scream out and her arms and legs would flail in rejection of Sarah's touch, responding only to Chaim Abramowitz's hand. He knew it was not him she was calling for, but her dead father, although at his touch she would soften, acquiesce, and retreat into a sweet slumber. The next night she would wake up shouting again, demanding, refusing to relinquish her father.

At seventeen, only once, Rivka asked her mother if she could visit her father's grave. She laid a wreath of flowers on the grave and never went back.

Seven years after her marriage to Chaim Abramowitz, Rivka asked Harkin to talk to his friends who were veterans of Hashomer, and bring her those who had known about her father. Shortly thereafter, elderly men with brawny physiques and stony glares began to visit the estate. They sat with Rivka and recounted about her father and his heroism, then about their own heroic deeds at the turn of the century, and the struggles, and about their current troubles now that they were forgotten. "Not everyone did well for themselves in this country," they complained.

Some wanted to join the estate and live out the rest of their lives there, and Rivka instructed Riklin to accept them unquestioningly. As if Riklin did not have enough trouble with the mental cases who trickled into the estate thanks to Bonhoeffer, and the various types who took refuge after serving Abramowitz within the Zionist state, now he had to contend with these dinosaurs, who stepped right into estate politics, reinforcing Harkin's faction and worshipping Stefano Lerer, rather than splitting up into manageable individuals.

Dr. Riklin was aghast at the elderly men's refusal to recognize his status. They interpreted "head foreman" as someone who was responsible for providing them with clean socks, and "doctor" as a man before whom they could open their mouths wide and ask about infections and heartburn. Immune to any harm, they roamed the estate making their excessive demands, announcing "Rivka gave permission" and "Rivka approved," waddling along behind Riklin while he worked, showering him with requests, pressing notes with detailed demands into his hands. It seemed to Riklin that every single day signified a holiday or a custom or a ceremony or something they had to observe—

Torches and Bibles for a memorial ceremony.

Dried fruit for Tu B'Shvat.

A notebook for songwriting.

A halter for a horse.

A medical prescription.

Sixty bullets for an old Mauser pistol.

And more and more. It was a circus.

Egberg came to Riklin one day and announced, "I never eat corn, because my experience has taught me that its consumption leads to more urgent bowel movements than I can withstand," as though the head foreman had to file this important fact away as a cornerstone of menu planning. Another time, Eskin came to complain about, "*Nu*, you know…a little loneliness." Riklin would have happily offered Eskin the company of jackals or dragged him into a wasp nest out in the fields. But only this morning Eskin had given Rivka some tiny shred of information about her father—that he had liked to eat lemons more than anything—and Rivka had gone off to commune with her kites in a state of excitement. Dr. Riklin's only option was to call Geitzev from the dairy barn and sit him down to listen to the lonely old man.

One day a group of three veterans announced they had been invited to the unveiling of a monument in memory of something or other, and they could not turn up empty-handed. Something was needed—perhaps a roasted chicken, a bottle of wine, and some guns. A dairy goat would be nice. "Rivka gave permission." Another time the old men invited a member of the Second Aliyah to lecture about the draining of the swamps and the planting of eucalyptus trees. They needed three axes for a couple of hours: "Rivka approved." Two of the old men somehow found religion during their stay on the estate, and for Sukkot they needed the ceremonial four species, or at the very least an *etrog*. If not for Bonhoeffer, who had once again purchased a crate of invalid *etrogs*, it was doubtful that Dr. Riklin would have found a solution. In return, he had only to turn a blind eye to Chaim Pagin, a young man Bonhoeffer left on the estate temporarily, just until he could find another solution. After hopping off Bonhoeffer's van and helping to carry the *etrogs*, Pagin was annexed to the estate with his feeble mind and his cargo of memories, which he scattered everywhere he went.

The elders led a sparse and meager life. Whenever they remembered something about Rivka's late father, they were to go and tell her. When Rivka asked one of them to come and answer her questions, he had to acquiesce. But other than this limited obligation, they dedicated their daily routines to their own health and well-being, ignoring the bustle of work on the estate and refusing to read Riklin's regulations. The only regulations they had ever recognized were the founding rules of Hashomer—and they had never actually read those either.

Riklin made some enquiries and discovered that of all the veterans scattered around the estate, only a tiny minority had ever been connected to Hashomer itself. He realized that he was surrounded with "former candidates," "temporary associates," admirers and stragglers. Any real Hashomer guardsmen who had survived would not have needed the estate as a sanctuary. But these men were not at all apologetic. They were protected by their stock of memories about Rivka's father, which was far more important than actual membership in Hashomer.

One rainy evening in November 1958, Dr. Riklin retired to his room earlier than usual. He did not check on his friend the Wandering Jew, as he normally did, only tossed his shoes and notebook on the floor like heavy bricks and, lying on his bed, confessed, "I am tired. Very tired." He rubbed his eyes and contemplated his existence. "As a matter of fact," he thought, "I am sad." His world had seemed gloomy for some time, full of shadows hovering over a sinister swamp. The only brightness was the figure of Chaim Abramowitz. And his plant, his dear Wandering Jew. "Tomorrow everything will pass," Riklin determined with glassy exhaustion, and went to sleep.

He was awoken by loud banging on his door.

Fire?

Inferno?

Disaster?

Panicked thoughts flew through Riklin's head. He was prepared. But when he opened the door he found only a Hashomer veteran, who marched in as if the estate laws were but a pat of butter in the sun.

"Yes?" Riklin asked.

"I'm a fan of the Hapoel Haifa soccer team," the elder explained.

Riklin stood waiting.

The old man stared at him with astonishment and then looked

back as if expecting to find someone to share in his indignation. Then Riklin saw a cluster of veterans' heads emerging in the dark, crowding around the doorway, clucking their tongues and shaking their heads in disbelief. Riklin looked at this monster with multiple heads the color of pale yokes, each with a bald cap and bloodshot eyes.

"Haven't the tickets been purchased yet?" a question came from the murky crowd.

From the recesses of his memory, Dr. Riklin vaguely recalled a request filed, something to do with the soccer cup final, a special match to celebrate a decade since the establishment of the State of Israel, which had murdered Chaim Abramowitz's brother. How had the request slipped through, evading the organizational procedures?

"The match is in two days," said one of the men, igniting Riklin's anxiety.

"Rivka herself said there would be tickets," another added, illustrating the magnitude of the disaster.

Over the next few days Dr. Riklin achieved an inconceivable feat, one of those accomplishments that remain mysterious years after their success. He consulted with three of his assistants, then set off on an urgent trip that took him from the port of Haifa to the Jerusalem Workers Council and the city bus company. Thirty-two tickets were obtained, wrested at an astronomical price from the hands of fervent fans.

On the eighth of November a party of Hashomer elders were driven to the stadium near Tel Aviv, where they witnessed Hapoel Haifa's victory. They came home late, full of noisy impressions that rattled the silent night of the estate and Riklin's heart.

Dr. Meshulam Riklin sat on his bed and looked at the darkness outside his window. He hated them. Hated. He would not let anyone take away what he had achieved. No one would dare. Lines had been crossed. Crossed! This was war. He had to destroy them before he himself was destroyed.

In the morning he got up for work as usual. As he walked up the path he was joined by Egberg, one of the monster's heads. Walking feebly beside Riklin, Egberg proceeded to explain something at great length, with various outbursts gushing out of his account, a river with no end. When the path intersected they came across the Wandering Jew coiled around a stone, its silvery-purple leaves glistening in the dew. Egberg leaned down swiftly, severed the plant from its roots and trampled it under his heel. "Weed," he said.

Riklin wanted to lunge at the man and strangle him, but the plant scorned Egberg, and even as Riklin restrained himself he saw it begin to heal, the trampled leaves wilting as fresh ones sprouted. The Wandering Jew saved itself and was about to crawl away to a new resting place.

When he saw the expression on Riklin's face, Egberg pulled back, noticing a dark glimmer shining from the depths of the foreman's eyes. "I'm going to have my tea now," he said and quickly walked away.

Riklin looked out to the distance. On the edge of the estate a kite was flying in the air—Rivka was trying to control, to display confidence. She did not sleep at nights, she was weak…they were all weak. He knew there would be a war. His body pulled taut, his muscles stiffened. He watched the kite keenly. These kites Rivka kept receiving from overseas—who was this Hans, Günter's son? What were his hopes? Every time a package arrived, Riklin removed Hans's love letter and gave Rivka the kite on its own; there was enough trouble as it was, without love. What was this Hans thinking, writing love letters to Abramowitz's wife? And what sort of a name was Hans? And Günter, what did that name mean? A part of Riklin wanted to angrily mock these Yemenites who took German names. But he was suddenly carried away by a simple ray of joy. He looked at the estate and felt dizzy. Happy. All his troubles seemed insignificant. Ever since he had been in the presence of Abramowitz he had finally started to live. After so many years of death disguised as life. Now he was completely happy. Happy. He closed his eyes and trembled. He could whisper the name Naomi and a sword would not slice through his body. Happiness.

He knew his chance would come. He would have his chance to get back at the veterans, and at Rivka. He just needed patience.

When he looked down at his Wandering Jew he found it had resprouted and vanished.

*

In late 1958, while eavesdropping on Abramowitz, Dr. Riklin picked up a few outlandish words: oil, diamonds, gold. There were prospects of international trade between the estate and foreign countries, and Abramowitz even met with a few ambassadors, declaring that he had no connection with the Zionist state. Agents from the Israeli security service came to investigate, and left after a conversation in which all attempts at politeness broke down. Abramowitz had his hands in deals the country coveted, and ominous signs began to pop up: a resurgence of call-up letters for the young Lolek-Leon-Arieh Abramowitz, paychecks for Dr. Lolek Abramowitz. They searched tirelessly for the defector, reserve duty sergeant Arieh Abramowitz. The Ministry of Education demanded to know where the child Leon-Arieh Abramowitz was. Why had he not been registered for the first grade? Abramowitz's informants warned him that the state was angry. The system was angry.

One day Abramowitz was arrested by five policemen in uniform, and for two weeks he was subjected to a shapeless accusation, although even the police demonstrated very little proficiency or confidence in its nature. Riklin hired a team of lawyers who easily turned the accusation into a tight-lipped apology, but by the time Abramowitz returned to the estate and the affair was forgotten, Riklin had taken advantage of his master's absence to sense that without Abramowitz at her side, a thin layer of Rivka's self-confidence fell away, revealing something trembling beneath her calm, a certain caution in her movements, in her eyes. Riklin knew this was his chance to defeat the Hashomer elders. He went to war.

Dr. Riklin had long ago acquired some information about Egberg as a gift from one of his informants. This despicable creature had always introduced himself as a Hashomer man, a veteran member with plenty of feats under his belt, but Riklin knew his secret: Egberg had never been in Hashomer, and in fact had been nothing but a straggling admirer. Now he sent for Egberg and sat him down in his office and threw the truth in his face. He accepted neither Egberg's denial nor his rage nor his recollections of heroism. He waited patiently until Egberg's voice cracked and he got down on his knees and begged Riklin not to expose his shame—after all, his friends, the only friends he had ever had, couldn't remember anything now, and who really cared whether or not he had ever been a member?

Egberg whimpered and cowered before Riklin and smiled a terrible smile, and whispered that he would do anything in return for Riklin's silence. Anything. And so Riklin made him expose the transgressions of every single one of the monster's heads. In his notebook he recorded statute violations, former homosexuality, ideological shallowness, forged election results, false testimonies inserted into minutes, thefts from public funds, violence against farmers, mockery of the national anthem, nighttime harassments of Jewish settlers, the theft of a cow, distortion of justice in a trial, poisoning a horse, fraudulent records in the organization papers, collaboration with an Arab thief, looting, guarding while drunk, failure to keep a secret, theft of hay, shooting over the heads of a pair of lovers, setting fire to a hayloft, poisoning a well, setting off false alarms, neglecting guard duty. Everything went into Riklin's notebook while Egberg sniveled and begged him to stop, insisting his memory was empty. Riklin mercilessly forced him to produce more and more stories. When he was completely satisfied, he sent Egberg away and proceeded to inform on him to the rest of the elders.

The old men declared a trial, and their excitement grew as they reminded one another of various clauses from the regulations, and added amendments, and cackled and elbowed each other in the ribs. On the evening of the appointed day, Egberg was summoned to stand before the group. On Riklin's instructions, a feast had been prepared, with huge roasted chickens, potatoes glistening in oil, steaming dishes of vegetables, coarse bread and fine red wine. A prosecutor and judges were named, then with shrieks of glee the roles were switched, and switched back again, until the men could no longer remember who was prosecuting and who was judging, and they all shouted and screamed together and made sounds like the blowing of the *shofar*.

Rivka, enchanted, stood glowing among the prosecutors. Dr. Riklin noticed her childish beauty as she nervously awaited the verdict.

"I wouldn't be surprised if he has a noose around his neck by morning," Eskin whispered in her ear.

"A goose?" asked Grossner.

"A noose!"

Grossner sighed. "My hearing…My memory's gone too. You know, I really was suspicious of Egberg. I didn't remember him, but I kept quiet. Where is the bravery I used to have? *Ach*…Facing three men with one gun, I used to…Now what's left?"

The trial was disorganized, the prosecutors quarreled and wandered back and forth between the judge's seat and the tables of food. Bornstein gave a moving testimony involving a vine bower in the Galilee and grapes the color of a young girl's cheeks. Ferberg's testimony was cut short by hecklers. The crowd demanded that Egberg be allowed to speak, and then they insisted that he be silenced, the traitor! They called out to stop talking and start acting. Someone said the hanging should start immediately, and someone else yelled out that the traitor should be allowed to deliver his final words. Eventually someone took a harmonica out of his pocket and began to play a mournful tune. From somewhere in the distance an accordion responded. The elderly watchmen began to sing, humming and playing, and by the end of the evening Egberg was sitting with them and singing, a glimmer in his eyes.

The songs brought the elders back to their youths, and they began to tell stories about the difficult days when they had protected the early Jewish settlements. Eskin fondly recalled his relationships with the women in the *moshavot*, and Gelzer offered his own story of two virgin sisters from Ein Harod. The veterans raised their glasses to each of the men, and to their host, Chaim Abramowitz, and Eskin brought up a story from the twenties about a married woman who had fallen in love with Abramowitz. Shimoni also remembered one of

Abramowitz's women, but this was a completely different one, from Jaffa. From every corner came competing tales of how women used to invite the young orphan into their homes to eat at their families' tables. How they wanted to give him a warm home and a warm bed. How the men were cautious around him. How his name traveled like a shadow among all the Jewish settlements. The elderly watchmen cheered for the young Abramowitz who had devoured his prey, and their eyes shone.

Harkin silenced the elders and ordered them to put an end to the party. Then he apologized to Rivka.

"It's all right," she said, grinning. "It's interesting actually. It all happened years ago, even before he met Mother."

Harkin walked Rivka home and apologized again. "It's my fault, I was the one who brought them here. These were the only ones I could find. Believe me, the good men from Hashomer are gone now, or else they're planted deep within the state, high up in the party establishments. There's no Israel Giladi or Israel Shochat here. They're nothing, the ones I found. Believe me, I rode with your father, and I guarded with Meir Hazanovitz in Yavnel, and with Berla Schweiger in Mas'ha. Those were real Hashomer watchmen. These men here, they're nothing. Don't be sad."

"Don't worry," Rivka said, smiling.

The next morning Dr. Meshulam Riklin began meeting privately with each of the Hashomer elders. From his notebook he revealed to each of them what he knew, and demanded more information, confessions, admissions. He offered every man a choice: walk away from the estate and leave a good name, be known forever as a watchman who had rode in Hashomer alongside Alexander Zaid and Israel Shochat; or bear the shame of having his iniquities made public. By the time Chaim Abramowitz came home from prison, the estate had been emptied out of most of the elders. Bonhoeffer took them from Riklin and worked to find temporary solutions. He was excited to have the honor of introducing these needy cases as real Hashomer veterans, and gleefully prolonged his conversations with every potential host, taking one step back and another forward until he had half-tearfully discharged each of the old men. He treated each arrangement as if he were bestowing a favor upon the host, and was thus able to demand that they recognize their indebtedness to him in the future, a debt that would be written off immediately if they agreed to take in a temporary solution for a couple of days. Three at most.

Rivka met Chaim in the doorway to their house when he returned. "Hello, Chaim," she said and kissed him.

*

A strange wave of break-ins began to spread throughout the country. In the small hours of the night, windows were shattered in archival institutions, Pioneer Houses, and minor museums. Documents were taken from shelves and display cases, sometimes just rummaged through and left in disarray. The wave lasted for six months, and finally Rivka Abramowitz was caught breaking into a Pioneer House on the *moshav* of Segef. The secretary and the security guard took her home to the estate and let the matter fade away into oblivion.

Chaim sat with Rivka in their room. She was still wearing her burglary clothes: black trousers, a black vest, a dark overcoat. She was barefoot.

"Why?" he asked.

Rivka went to her bureau and took out a tattered notebook from one of the drawers. The diary of a woman named Fania Bat Alon. "Someone stole this from the Pioneer House on his kibbutz and sent it to Günter. Someone wanted me to read it." She showed Chaim the page where the book had lain open for many years under a glass case, for the perusal of anyone who wanted to learn about the pioneers' lives:

> *Today we inaugurated the chicken coop, and Benyamin gave a wonderful speech. A hundred mottled hens populate the coop, loud and hardworking, and the members laughed when Benyamin joked that if each hen gives according to her ability, each will receive according to her needs, just like real "members"… These are good days in our meager abode, Hallelujah!*

Abramowitz looked into Rivka's eyes, but she looked away and turned the pages of the diary to an entry that had not been sun-drenched.

Yesterday my "young friend" appeared again, and I could not get rid of Benyamin. Eventually the opportunity did arise, and the rest...I cannot tell. He has not the heart to understand a woman, but his body is so strong. Afterwards, when I lay in bed at night, thoughts came to me, and the flutters of delight returned. I am a sinful woman, but I know—I shall sin again and again. I heard the cry of the jackals and a shiver went through my body. They are as terrible as he is. He has no tenderness and he has no mercy. His body demands and demands, insistent, and I am but a woman...

"It's you," Rivka said. "I know it is."

Abramowitz looked at her.

"Tell me about the women," she said.

"What did the man who sent the diary want?"

"The question is what I wanted. When all this happened I wasn't even born yet, and you were a grown man, with women..."

"After I met your mother there were no others."

"I sought out the stories about you. I wanted to know."

"It's a good thing you were caught on Segef. Those are my people. Don't take a risk like that again. You are my wife."

Rivka stood up and took her coat off. "I was nineteen when we married. I was just thinking...the mad Englishman, Major Manors...I was thinking, how did he manage to kill her? How did you not protect her? Why didn't you protect her?"

"I made a mistake."

"You made a mistake?"

"I made a mistake."

"Don't make any mistakes with me."

She sat in his lap and touched his neck with her hair, and rubbed her bare foot on his thigh, and smiled at him, and giggled. Then she pulled him to her forcefully, inside her body.

Chapter twenty-four

Only the Dead are Dead
1961

I n early 1961, handsome Gutkin completed his final preparations for the assassination of Prime Minister David Ben-Gurion.

Since arriving in Israel seven years earlier, Gutkin had moved from town to town and held a variety of odd jobs. On his third day in the country he had found himself in a brawl with two tradesmen, and a man named Greenhaus had picked him up off the sidewalk, dressed his wounds and taken him to his home. "I'm a Jabotinsky man," Greenhaus said by way of explaining his kindness. Gutkin did not know who Jabotinsky was, and he hated communists, but he kept quiet.

While Gutkin was recuperating in Greenhaus's home, Green-haus tried to interest him in politics. Gutkin did not like to be around people, but he found Greenhaus to be not especially irritating, except that he talked too much, repeatedly informing Gutkin what Jabotinsky would have said on every matter. There was nothing of importance in Greenhaus's ideas, but Gutkin learned from him about the government's iniquities and the terrible wrongs committed by David Ben-Gurion. When Gutkin suggested simply doing away with the man, Greenhaus recoiled. This was a prime minister of the state of Israel, he explained. Gutkin replied that they had everything they needed: a reason, a gun, a volunteer. Greenhaus looked frightened, and adamantly refused. But he agreed with Gutkin that Ben-Gurion himself was courting behavior that, if taken to its extreme, would lead to the political relevance of assassination. Still, he was a Jewish prime minister and could not be murdered.

As soon as he recovered, Gutkin wanted to leave, but his host held him back with insistent pleas. When he finally left, Greenhaus looked at him fearfully. "At least keep me updated on where you are… stay in touch," he implored.

Gutkin proceeded to wander from place to place. He did not need much. He made a living working as a porter, or doing electrical and plumbing repairs. What could this little state offer a certified forest engineer from the vast country of Russia?

Once in a while Greenhaus invited him to dinner in a little restaurant and gave him a small stipend. "Take it, take it. You're young, you need it. My wife and I, we are disciples of Jabotinsky, and we have more than we need."

Their conversations were terse. Gutkin had no interest in talk. What could he talk about? Sometimes he had an angry outburst and made all sorts of accusations against a shocked Greenhaus, who would explain himself and try to appease Gutkin and mend their friendship with promises. But the meetings were mostly devoted to Greenhaus's nostalgia and political heritage.

"I still remember when I was young, in Tel Aviv…1933…I heard David Ben-Gurion calling my teacher and master, Vladimir Ze'ev Jabotinsky, 'Vladimir Hitler'—yes. And then he called our people 'Hitler's deputies.' And all this in 1933, before the enemy of the Jewish people had even come to power. How could I forget? How can I forgive? And my whole family…in the Holocaust…

"And later, the blood libel. The bullets that killed Chaim

Arlozorov. They laid the blame on Ahimeir and his fine men, as if it were not clear that Arabs had shot him. But it was convenient for them. And I knew Avraham Stavski...not guilty...not guilty. David Ben-Gurion snagged all his political advantages in one net, and he would have lost if not for the death of the greatest leader of our generation, the guiding light, Vladimir Ze'ev Jabotinsky. Soon after that, another hero of Israel passed away—Yosef Katznelson, the 'Black Prince.' *Better a dead lion than a living dog.* And yes, Ben-Gurion gloated over the demise of his enemies, but he will yet meet with a bitter end...bitter...the people will avenge..."

Gutkin's blood boiled. His bones felt as if they would shatter his skeleton and run out to seek revenge. Now! Why was David Ben-Gurion still alive? All Gutkin needed was one word and his gun would do the work. But Greenhaus only waxed nostalgic, and stared at Gutkin longingly, begging for something but never articulating his desire.

When his pocket money from Greenhaus ran out and he did not want to hear about Jabotinsky, Gutkin found work. Hauling, plumbing. Once Greenhaus got him a proper job with a locksmith in the south of Tel Aviv. He lasted there a whole year, and learned how to pick locks and put together delicate instruments. But then he got into a fight over money with his employer. He knocked the man down, robbed the cash register and fled.

In the evenings he would sit in cafés and listen to news from the radios that always hung from the walls, and read newspapers left by other customers. "Ben-Gurion Celebrates Birthday." "Ben-Gurion Forms New Government." "Power Struggles Between Moshe Sharett and Ben-Gurion." Women disturbed Gutkin in the cafés. One of them gave him a wristwatch. Others asked questions, took an interest. He hated their perfumes, their makeup, their dresses and high heels. The proximity of women gave him a sharp headache, like the gnaw of a rat. Their smiles made him nauseous. And sad. He did not want them, but they came to him. He discovered that he was handsome. He did not want to be handsome. He wanted to be a redheaded captain and live with his widow. But his desire sometimes raped him until he gave in, and then it would vanish, leaving him lonely and disappointed. Everything—the women, the touch, the end of pleasure—everything was disappointing.

Sometimes, for a few moments, he enjoyed feeling empty and limp. Sometimes he thought of shooting himself. He had the gun. And the courage.

Handsome Gutkin roved about the country living in different neighborhoods, different cities. At nights he had trouble sleeping, and he would get up and add a new drawing to the cardboard file labeled "David Ben-Gurion." He leafed through the "Stalin" file too sometimes, and tears came to his eyes. All the diagrams, the analyses, the specifications of actions and reactions—but there would be no more Stalin ever again.

No matter where he moved, Greenhaus found him. He offered Gutkin odd jobs and tried to make him come to meetings. On holidays he invited him to his home. Gutkin resisted: What was the point? Sometimes he agreed to tag along with Greenhaus to various ideological circles in his friends' homes, in repair workshops and miserable little balconies. He almost never spoke at the meetings—these people's nonsense was meaningless to him. He had the occasional outburst, but they never understood him.

Once Greenhaus paid Gutkin to break into an apartment and salvage some documents of great importance for future generations. Another time he paid Gutkin a generous sum to retrieve an important memoir written by a deceased leader. Gutkin easily picked the lock and broke into the apartment, but he ran into the leader's screaming widow. He hit her over the head with her late husband's memoirs and fled.

He could not stop thinking about his gun. He had to use it. That unused bullet was obstructing the barrel, giving Gutkin no peace. For seven years he monitored Ben-Gurion's every deed, never forgiving anything. He despised Greenhaus's and his friends' forgivingness. They would never dare pull the trigger of a gun. They talked and talked and did nothing. Frothing with anger over Israel's withdrawal after the Sinai Campaign, lambasting the Prime Minister for caving to international pressure, and then—forgiving. After all, they reasoned, Ben-Gurion had held successful negotiations with the Polish government, and now Jews could come to Israel. Let sleeping dogs lie. They were too forgiving.

Anger was a constant presence in handsome Gutkin's life. And headaches. Terrible pains that dug into his soul. He wanted to use the gun for one important shot. A meaningful shot. One day a policeman stopped Gutkin after he jumped a rope outside a cinema. The officer simply told Gutkin to go to the back of the line, but the gun almost leapt into his hand, urging him to shoot. He spat at the officer and ran away. Three policemen joined in the chase and Gutkin ran past houses, through alleyways, courtyards, across all the city's miserable spots. Why had he come to this country? Only dust and stones and miserable people. After he outran the officers, Gutkin sat down on a filthy stoop to catch his breath. The gun was in his waistband. His headache was mounting. Only a shot would ease the pressure, but not just any shot: he wanted to shoot Stalin. But there would be no more Stalin ever again. Gutkin bowed his head and covered his face with his hands. A young woman dressed immodestly came up to him and smiled. He threw a stone at her and ran.

In 1959, Tzipkin had a reliable report that David Ben-Gurion had once again called the leader of Herut, Menachem Begin, a "clown." Begin was not a total adherent to the extreme positions of the group, but they were nonetheless committed to protecting his honor.

"A clown—imagine! Jabotinsky's disciple…"

Rage and fury filled the room, but all the heroism died down when Gutkin asked, "What are you going to do?"

"History will prevail," Greenhaus mumbled.

Moishe Tenkler added his own murmur, "His punishment will come from the annals of history."

Forgivers. Miserable forgiving creatures.

In March 1960, when Ben-Gurion boldly met with Chancellor Adenauer, Greenhaus found Gutkin in his home on the outskirts of Jaffa and cried to him for an hour. Ben-Gurion was desecrating the memory of Jews slaughtered and tortured in the Holocaust, our brethren who were murdered on the soil of Europe!

"What should we do?" Gutkin wanted to know.

"A criminal act, a criminal act…" Greenhaus said, turning red. Then he left.

With a fluttering heart, Gutkin started making plans. His gun was ready, but when he asked the forgivers to review his plan, they announced that the Nazi oppressor Adolf Eichmann had been captured in Argentina thanks to a glorious Israeli operation—the Jewish soul of David Ben-Gurion had been revealed!

Gutkin was furious. Forgivers! So many years, wasted years. Here was the gun, here was the man who deserved punishment, here was Gutkin. A single shot, and the three would be one.

Gutkin turned all his energies to the David Ben-Gurion file, taking out pages, replacing them with others. He sketched and measured and switched and checked. The moment had come, there was no turning back.

In January 1961, Gutkin learned from the papers that the Prime Minister and his wife were on holiday in their usual hotel in Tiberias. He had stalked Ben-Gurion there twice before, and had a detailed sketch of the hotel in his file. Without consulting the forgivers, he decided to go. This time a shot would be fired.

He traveled to Tiberias on a crowded, smoky bus, squeezed in next to a young woman who wore makeup and perfume. Gutkin's head ached. When the woman smiled at him, he almost drew his gun, but he somehow quelled his irritation and transferred his thoughts far away, forcing himself to memorize and repeat all the assassination stages.

In Tiberias he went straight to the hotel. He found the convenient ditch he knew from his previous ambushes, between the gardens and the yard. He noticed that the yellowing bushes had grown taller, slightly diminishing his line of fire, but the escape route was still open. There was the front door, where David Ben-Gurion would soon appear. And there was the path to the gardens, which Gutkin would sneak up after counting to five. And there was a good spot to fire one clear shot. And there was the path that led to the alleyway, and from there on to the streets that would carry Gutkin away.

Silence enveloped the hotel. Gutkin crouched down.

"Excuse me, Sir, if this is about the Prime Minister, I'm afraid he won't be arriving. He resigned this morning. For good, this time."

Gutkin looked up to see a middle-aged man with Yemenite features standing above him with a kind look in his eyes.

The Yemenite said, "Your Ben-Gurion resigned for good this time. He won't be back."

Gutkin shook himself off. Pain was pressing his temples against one another. The world turned black and began to flicker. Then silence.

He woke up in the Beit Mizrach Synagogue in Memory of the Righteous Sarah Abramowitz. The Yemenite man was standing beside him looking worried, dabbing Gutkin's forehead with a damp washcloth. "Sir," he said, "you must not worry. Your consciousness was lost, but it has been recovered. Do not worry. Nor have you lost your gun, which was pressing into your stomach. We have removed it, Sir, to ease the pressure on your diaphragm."

Gutkin took a deep breath. He was thirsty and frightened. But his spirit was profoundly calm.

"Indeed, one can easily pass out from the heat here in Tiberias. Where I live in Safed there is fresh mountain air. You were waiting for Ben-Gurion in vain. He has resigned. I too was waiting, to ask him for an autograph. My son, Hans, who works in Europe, asked me to go. Ben-Gurion sent our forces to capture the Nazi enemy Adolf Eichmann, curse him, and my son Hans, who is in a similar line of business, was extremely impressed."

Gutkin let the Yemenite man chatter on without knowing who he was or what he wanted. But he found it pleasant. The Yemenite left and came back with a glass of cool water. "It's hot today, very hot. Please drink, Sir."

Gutkin sipped the water. He closed his eyes again.

"Now, Sir, tell me where you live."

"Why?" Gutkin asked.

"So that we can tell your relatives that you are fine, and help you get home," said the man reassuringly and placed his hand on Gutkin's forehead.

Pleasant.

Comfortable.

Gutkin took a deep breath.

Suddenly good.

"So, where do you live, Sir?"

*

In early 1961, Lev Gutkin appeared at the gates of the Abramowitz Estate. In his hands, apart from a small bundle of personal belongings, were two cardboard files labeled "Josef Stalin" and "David Ben-Gurion." On his waist, concealed and threatening, was his gun, which he placed under his pillow as soon as he was assigned a room.

"Günter sent me," he announced to anyone who looked at him. He was irritable. He felt the place closing in on him.

After being forced to spend two hours completing forms full of suspicious questions, he was summoned to the estate foreman, Dr. Meshulam Riklin, for an incoming interview.

Riklin glared at him with two hostile eyes. "What can you do?"

"Günter sent me." Gutkin was getting annoyed.

"We take in anyone Mr. Günter recommends. Without him I would not be here myself. But you will have to work, Mr. Gutkin, and work hard."

"What kind of work is there here?"

"We will match you with the right job, unless you are interested in any particular kind of work."

Gutkin rolled his eyes impatiently. The amiable Günter, after letting Gutkin rest in Tiberias and then in Safed until he recovered, had told him about a special place where he could rest and work, and said everything would be arranged to suit him, and he would only have to focus on his health. And now here he was in this place, sitting opposite a man named Riklin who had a pair of eyes that he did not like at all. His journey here had been difficult. Three hours in a rickety van with that man, Bonhoeffer, who had filled his head with tall tales the whole way.

Dr. Riklin silently studied the paperwork. The silence annoyed Gutkin. Why were they asking so many questions? Why were they so concerned about diplomas and drivers' licenses and special needs? Fools, the lot of them. He remembered the failed assassination, and asked Riklin, "Did Ben-Gurion really resign?"

Riklin looked up with his disquieting eyes. "Here, with us, the first rule is we don't discuss what goes on out there, in the state, and we don't take an interest in it. Soon we will teach you the history of the estate master, Mr. Chaim Abramowitz, and then you'll know."

What sort of a place was this?

"I know how to do some electrical work and construction," he told Riklin. "And some locksmithing."

Dr. Riklin sighed and called a secretary in. Gutkin was led to the dairy barn to meet his new supervisor, Eisman.

"We never have any electrical problems here," Eisman grumbled. "Do you know how to milk cows?"

One week after handsome Gutkin arrived on the Abramowitz Estate he saw the religious man, Bonhoeffer, bringing in a new man who looked sort of like a lopsided sack. Gutkin filled with rage—is this what I look like to them? He thought about his gun—I will fire it one day. For now, he hunkered down and did his work quietly. For now, things were good. They let him be, and he could live. But that afternoon, when he was told Abramowitz wanted to see him, Gutkin became worried. He didn't want to leave. Why were they throwing him out?

The master of the estate invited him for a meal, but Gutkin's stomach was churning. He was afraid he might vomit, or have diarrhea.

Riklin spoke first. "We understand that in Russia you were certified as a forest engineer?"

"That was a long time ago…"

"Perhaps you can help," Abramowitz said. He ate slowly. The silence tortured Gutkin. He longed to hold his gun.

Riklin turned to him. "Mr. Abramowitz has spent a lot of money on forest lands. He is being asked to invest in growing trees for industry. We already have two specialists, but perhaps you could also provide an expert opinion?"

Gutkin shook his head. "It's been many years." He was getting more nervous. He reflexively reached to his side, where he usually hid his gun. He stroked the empty spot, tried to look at Abramowitz, and mumbled again, "It's been many years."

A young woman came into the room and kissed Abramowitz.

Pain fluttered inside Gutkin.

Abramowitz introduced the woman. "This is Rivka, my wife."

Dark-haired, tall. Long slender fingers.

"Are you the forest engineer?" she asked.

"I was certified at the technical institute in Moscow," he said, suddenly proud.

"And will you help us?"

Gutkin nodded. "I am a forest engineer."

When he left the room, Abramowitz commented to Riklin that judging by his behavior, Gutkin had a gun hidden somewhere, and it must be found. "But let him rest. And give him Barda's memorandum to read."

After two weeks on the estate, handsome Gutkin was given a stack of reports to read through. Most were summaries of methods he understood little about, but here and there he found a familiar term, and he made the occasional comment. He did not think he had been helpful, but the next day, in the barn, Eisman let him change a lightbulb in the calving area, and he seemed to have earned a new-found respect.

Gutkin was especially surprised by his response to Rivka. He did not mind standing close to her, or when she smiled at him. She was a woman, but she belonged to Abramowitz, and in her presence his old anger did not rise up, or his usual hateful desires. She would come to visit him in the dairy barn, wearing floral dresses, and ask him about his life in Israel, about Siberia, his childhood, his parents. Gutkin did not find it painful. He was impressed by Abramowitz's power and the way he ruled over everyone, including Rivka. Perhaps I'll shoot Abramowitz, he thought.

Handsome Gutkin felt good. A new tranquility had come to

him. He found his work in the barn satisfying. People did not bother him, except one man, Avraham Brenner, who kept trying to excite him by talking about Russian literature. Gutkin wanted Rivka to come and ask questions, even about the bad things. He watched sadly as she socialized with other people on the estate, simple workers like himself, and from time to time he heard her peals of laughter ring out. She took an interest in everyone, not just him. And there was that religious man, Bonhoeffer, who sometimes turned up at the estate and spent long hours with Rivka, monopolizing her attention.

When Rivka came to the barn and stopped to talk with Gutkin, he offered enthusiastic answers to all her questions. She was a drop, he was a river. He talked about Greenhaus, Tzipkin, Yehezkel Klein. He almost told her about his gun, and about David Ben-Gurion, and he unflinchingly confessed to his apartment burglaries. He wanted her to know. When Rivka took a keen interest in his burglaries, Gutkin panicked. He had to make up success stories and boast of events that had never occurred. Her responses led him to entangle himself in a web of lies, but he was not angry at her. Every time she appeared in the barn he stood before her and gladly continued his deceitful tales.

He was not surprised when she said to him one day, "I need your help." She wanted him to help her break into an archive. He would have to climb up three floors on a thin drainpipe. That was it.

Gutkin was excited, and almost shouted: One man, one gun, one bullet, awaiting your order! But Rivka did not want any shooting. Only his help. She wanted him to do what Chaim had forbidden her from doing.

Still, when she called him one night, he took his gun out of its hiding place and shoved it in his waistband. She explained where he should go, what to take, and what to say if he was caught. Gutkin smiled crookedly to himself—a man with a gun would not get caught.

Berger drove him to the site, and Gutkin was thankful that he kept quiet the whole way, as if there were no one else in his car. He waited for Gutkin while he broke into the building, ignoring him when he got out of the car and ignoring him when he got back in with a book under his arm. The break-in was a success. When they got back to the estate before dawn, Rivka was waiting for Gutkin in his room wearing only a thin nightgown, her body radiating from the warmth of sleep. In the dark she slowly leafed through the pages, ripped one out, then told him to break in to the same place again and put the book back. "You've done wonderful work," she whispered, brushing aside his doubts.

Several more times she slipped into his room and woke him with a touch to his forehead. "I need you..." Berger would be waiting outside.

When Rivka asked Gutkin to keep a little box in his room with the papers he had stolen for her, he happily agreed. On his free nights he tossed and turned in bed, unable to fall asleep, and then he took the box out of its hiding place and replaced the pages with his gun until he finished studying Rivka's secrets. Her scent was on the pages, and it reminded him of the widow. And it pained him. And attracted him. Chaim Abramowitz was mentioned in all the papers, but Gutkin found no interest in the writings. He was intrigued only by one long-ago episode about a banker with the same name as Gutkin's father, who had insisted that he should not pay to support his wife's children, because they were not his own but the product of her adulterous relations with two British officers, Brady and Frey, and with a young boy named Chaim Abramowitz, who was only sixteen at the time of their affair. A single page with rust marks from a paperclip noted the wife's utter refusal to confirm adultery with the British men, and her vigorous denial of an affair with the boy Abramowitz. In her defense, she pleaded that despite her loneliness and her husband's coldhearted indifference to her needs, and his apathy to her distress as a young woman, she had never once allowed the boy Abramowitz to defile her honor.

Handsome Gutkin could not understand it. Why did Rivka need these cheap words? But he felt heat pulsing through his body. At night he tried to dream about her, but in the morning he woke up without knowing what he had dreamed. He squabbled with Eisman in the barn, and struck him on his head. Riklin threatened to throw him off the estate, but Rivka intervened and he was transferred to the locksmith's workshop.

The gun in his room troubled him. Once or twice he thought about shooting Abramowitz, but he was wary. He started looking in mirrors. "You are handsome," he said, consoling himself.

Rivka would wake him at night, surprising him with her breath on his ear, "Get up, Gutkin, get up."

He broke into the Emek Hefer documentary center. The Zionist archives. The Hashomer Hatzair archives. The Jabotinsky archives. He collected minutes from the chamber of commerce in Haifa, from the craft and industry department in the Jerusalem municipality. Three times he broke into the Sirkin library until he found what she wanted. In the courthouse in Rehovot he had to exert himself four times. One night he almost got caught. The night watchman in a small party branch encountered Gutkin on his way out and shone a flashlight in his face. Gutkin kicked the watchman and fled. He roamed the streets until morning with the gun stashed in his clothes trying to find Berger. At noon he managed to get back to the estate on his own, and Riklin fined him for tardiness and absence, and said there would be an inquiry to determine the severity of his punishment. For one breath Gutkin thought of pulling out his gun, but then he calmed down. Because he was happy, he had peace and quiet, and the ever-approaching shot was almost there, he could feel its heat— soon he would shoot someone deserving, someone he respected, like Abramowitz.

When Rivka came to his room he excitedly explained his failure and trembled slightly when she ran her fingers through his hair and said, "You are a brave man, Lev Gutkin."

His gun was on him, his body was tense, and the shot was close. So close. I am handsome Lev Gutkin…

When Rivka came home, Abramowitz gave her a long look. "I was out walking," she said, smiling. She bowed her head. Then she looked up. She smiled again.

He leaned down to kiss her, but she turned away and laughingly bit his chin and did not let go. She clutched him with her white, hard teeth, shaking his chin until he grasped her shoulders roughly. He let go and pulled her to him by the back of her neck, forcing her to give in and kiss him, to wrap her hands around his neck, to hang from his body, to climb up his body and touch his stomach with her hunched knees.

"Now fall," she said. They dropped to the ground, and she, embraced by his body, tried to roll onto him, then surrendered and let him mount her.

*

Dr. Meshulam Riklin's informants reported that Rivka had begun studying accounting, office management, and contracts. She visited all corners of the estate, sat with the workers and asked questions. She spent time in the barns, the chicken coops, the crop fields. She went from one office to the next and observed how it was managed. She opened all the estate ledgers and submitted queries to a variety of administrators.

"What else? What else?" Riklin asked, and mercilessly interrogated his informants, convinced they knew more than they were telling him. They were lying! Rivka was taking the estate away from him! But he would win. Win! No one would come between him and Abramowitz. He had defeated better people, and he would defeat her too. No one would come between him and Abramowitz.

He found the remains of Rivka's discarded lemons everywhere, and their vapid looks gave him no peace. Even worse than the lemons were her kites. When he met with Abramowitz to discuss matters of the utmost importance in the private recesses of the house, Rivka would suddenly emerge from one of the rooms, looking cheerful and lighthearted on the outside, but her eyes would glare at Riklin as if to say, At any moment, if I want to, I will look deeper inside you and I will ask questions, and you will unravel with fear.

Her professed age was thirty-one. Her youth was behind her, but she was still an attractive woman. Why did she always make

Riklin think of Naomi? Especially when she held one of her wayward kites up in the sunlight, the muscles of her shoulders and forearms bronzed and sculpted. Why? He could not understand it. They were so different, yet he was drawn to look at her. Perhaps something about the lines of her body was still childish, needing supervision and care. But she did not want his supervision at all.

Her eyes could capture him at any moment, but Dr. Riklin found himself staring at her with his gaze locked. Naomi, the daughter of a Bukharan family, her skin bronzed yet somehow pale at the same time. She was so different from Rivka, yet so alike. Their bodies had the same determination not to bear children. He had known from the first that Naomi would not give him a child. Not only because of her illness and her weakness. There were women who were simply that way, they did not have children, there was no hope. And not only had she given him no children, but she had orphaned him of herself. Was he to blame? Not at all. But if it could only be mended…

After her death, Riklin had kept searching for Naomi. He took an interest in the occult, in faiths that crossed the bridge between the land of the living and the land of the dead. He wished she could return, so they could fix things. Although he soon abandoned these ideas as ridiculous magical thinking, his feverish dealings with the occult taught him how easy women were to fix. His name traveled among barren women, his reputation grew throughout the country and beyond. He had a mad idea, which he himself half-mocked, that rather than returning from the land of the dead, Naomi would be reborn from one of the women. This was why he had been given this clarity, this healing skill. The idea troubled him, threatening to win him over, and although he belittled it, he found it somewhat comforting and believed it might hold a grain of truth. He soon began to tire of it all. If all this success served no purpose, what good was it? But then Abramowitz arrived and he was saved.

Rivka's figure permeated the estate and gave him no rest. She tried so hard to sabotage him. As soon as Abramowitz invited him over she dropped all her engagements and came home to be there when Riklin arrived. He would reach the house and find that Rivka had dragged Abramowitz into the private amusements of a couple. Having no orders to leave, Riklin had to wait and listen through the walls to the muffled sounds, which made him extremely uncomfortable. Once in a while, Rivka's voice would come through sharp and clear, and she sounded like an exhausted woman in the pains of her first labor.

Riklin's informants began to speak of nights when Rivka waited for Berger and Gutkin to return from some sort of trip that was not recorded in the ledgers. They were unable to find out what exactly the three were engaged in, but Riklin believed he could get Rivka into trouble by confronting Abramowitz with her deeds. He planned to wait and find out more, biding his time until the moment was right. He told his informants to pay special attention to any nocturnal activity involving Berger, Gutkin and Rivka.

But Dr. Riklin missed his chance. Before he could make his move, something happened.

*

"I met a man," Bonhoeffer told Rivka one day. "Not a very nice young man. An orphan. He has some diaries that his mother wrote, and your Chaim is mentioned there. He said he would sell them to you. Should I arrange a meeting?"

Rivka's eyes lit up and then narrowed questioningly. "How did you know I was looking for that sort of thing?"

"Chaim said that if I met anyone who had old documents related to him, that I should tell you, because you were looking."

Then Bonhoeffer stopped to think. He looked at Rivka awkwardly and said, "Oops, I think I accidentally let out a secret..."

Still, the meeting went ahead. Rivka set off to a dimly lit apartment in Rehovot, where a gaunt man handed her some papers written by his mother. "I just found them hidden in the wall, after she died, and your husband's in there, everything about him. She hid this for forty years, the old whore. I was looking for her gold in the wall, I need money. I've already sold all her land, and this apartment doesn't belong to me anymore either. I'm going to use the money to buy all of Habass's orchards, and Altschuler's, and I'll burn them! You'll see.

Just pay me for the old whore's diaries she hid from me, from everyone, and you'll see. You just pay me and I'll buy up all the orchards."

The woman's writing was refined, her words longed to be poetry. Of Chaim she wrote, *An orphan, an orphan like my heart.* She begged, *Let him to do with me as a harvester does with his crops, a vinedresser with his clusters of grapes.* Then she wrote of various acts between a man and a woman, and described a two-day trip she took with him, far away from her unloving husband. *His body is as strong as my desire,* and, *my despair is steel, as is his back.*

"So, how much?" asked the gaunt fellow.

Rivka waved her hand to quiet him.

He is sad, and only I know his sorrow. We are both orphans—he from his father, I from hope. Our end is in death and turmoil.

He is not an orphan, but an amputee—his father and his mother have been severed from him. My hand reaches out to caress his head, he is a fledgling thrown from his nest, yet my hand meets a voracious lion in his lair.

I am afraid of him, and I want only him. If he leaves, I will die. If he comes, also. I am miserable, so miserable. I am awaited by the empty wells, the dark sea, the bottle of poison. And until my death—I will grasp him, I will ask him for life.

"I'll burn all the orchards!" cried the son.

Rivka bought the diary for a modest sum, and the son insisted on kissing her hand.

"Tell me, why are you searching for this?" Bonhoeffer ventured on their way home. In the back of the van sat a hardened young man who had already been rejected in three different places. Bonhoeffer, somewhat apprehensively, was hoping the momentum of his trip with Rivka would lead Riklin to be lenient and give the man a try for a couple of days—how bad could he be? He didn't look so bad. The way they had cursed him on the last *moshav*, no one could be that deficient, they must have missed his core of goodness.

Rivka did not answer him.

Why are you searching for this?

She leaned her head back. Strange thoughts came to her mind.

Chaim...he knows everything. He knows I'm still looking without his permission. And he knew the Major was mad. He knew everything... including about their meetings. He controlled everything...

"Bad thoughts?" asked Bonhoeffer, and offered the Rémy Martin.

"No thanks. Chaim objects to alcohol."

"And I don't? I also object to alcohol."

Rivka laughed. "Oh, Bonhoeffer, I don't like saints, but you... you're different."

"Ha..." Bonhoeffer said, blushing. "A saint...The people look for sins, the sins find the people."

"But I really do like you."

"Oh, women...woman." Bonhoeffer laughed and stretched his thumb up to uncork the bottle. He focused, staring at the cork, and two cars honked their horns behind him, one as it veered to the left in a panic, the other as it swerved to the right. Bonhoeffer took a long swig and built up his courage for the next attempt. "Since you like me so much, I have here in the back of the van a man of a certain kind. You might call him a thief, and some might agree. You might also call him a cheat, a sloth, a liar, even mentally ill. But still, a couple of days is all I need. A place for him to sleep, eat and work. And he won't kill any chickens while he's there. Definitely will not kill any chickens, I promise!"

"Chickens? Why would he kill chickens?"

"They said he killed some...they got it wrong. Twenty chickens? Why would a man need twenty? Does he have twenty stomachs? No! One!"

Rivka giggled. "Let's see what Riklin says. I'll put in a good word. But remember, only a couple of days."

"Of course, just until I set something up. In the north, up in the Galilee, there's a *moshav* that wants him. There might even be three. I'll have to choose. It'll take me a couple of days to decide, you can't rush these things. And don't worry. He will work!"

"All right, Bonhoeffer, all right."

"Just, maybe, put him far away from the coops...just in case..."

He took a victory sip of Rémy Martin. They were nearing the estate now, and he had a temporary solution. But he still had the other problem—why on earth would a man steal another family's photo album? And why would he make off with five pairs of pruning shears?

Rivka returned to her thoughts—Major Manors, the mad Englishman. He had defected from the Mandate, and might have tried to join the estate. But they had turned him away. They had an order to turn him away. He killed Mother, and left me...

She closed her eyes and tried to stop thinking ahead, but her thoughts were stronger than her. I was nineteen then, now I'm thirty-one. Nineteen...thirty-one...

Bonhoeffer's van reached the gates. The sentries were about to stop him to search the van, but when they saw Rivka, who nodded to them to step back, they let him in.

Bonhoeffer was thrilled. "Maybe I'll look for some more of those documents for you, hey? I have connections!"

Rivka opened her eyes.

I was nineteen...now thirty-one...

"Goodbye, Bonhoeffer," she said. She strained to smile and jumped down from the van.

When Rivka got home she called for Gutkin. "I'm releasing you from our business. We might continue another time. We might do something else one day."

Handsome Gutkin stood looking frightened. She went up to him, tussled his hair, and looked fondly into his eyes. "Go now."

Gutkin was shaken. He left her room. Outside the house he trembled and felt anger bursting out. He started to run. But where could he go? In his room he sat panting. What did they think? What did they think?! That he couldn't do it? That he wouldn't shoot? He would! His mind was racing. He took the gun out of its hiding place and pushed it into his waistband, still shaking. Seven years Stalin, seven years Ben-Gurion. And his life? A waste. Nothing. Bastards! He wanted to wave his gun around, to shoot someone.

He blindly ran to the stable, took a rope and a horse. Then

he broke out of the estate. Bastards! He did not know how to ride, but he ran alongside the galloping horse. What did they think? That he couldn't? He would!

He stopped in the woods and climbed up onto the horse and sat under a large tree. Bastards…With trembling hands he looped the rope around his neck and tried to tie it into a noose, but he could not do it. When he finally managed to tie the rope to a branch, he stroked his old gun a little, peered into the barrel—perhaps he would see the bullet waiting—and trembled and rejoiced. Hurrah! Glorious death! His hands searched for the trigger. He found it—Cavaliers, onward! He pressed with the fingers of both hands, ready to fire a shot into the back of his neck, his fingers squeezing one another. It might have been the right hand or the left hand that jumped first, or perhaps it was both together, and Gutkin fired one shot into his body. The startled horse broke away in a gallop and left Gutkin hanging on the rope.

When handsome Gutkin appeared at the gates of the estate one month later, he walked unsteadily and seemed slow, as if his body were weighted down with earth.

Riklin fell on him with questions. "Where were you?" he roared. "Where's the horse?"

"Where's Arrow?" sobbed Zvi from the stables.

Gutkin could not remember a thing. He remained cool and calm. He listened patiently to all the questions. He blinked dreamily. He nodded. He said nothing.

Riklin suggested killing him right there and then. He had stolen a horse, and a rope! No one seemed to need him anymore. Although he wasn't serious at first, Riklin sensed consensus around him—perhaps he really should kill Gutkin?

Then Rivka was called. She had been searching for Gutkin all month. She had dispatched men. Persuaded Chaim to do something. North. South. She had begged for them to find Gutkin and bring him back to her.

"Here you are," she said. She pulled Gutkin out of the circle and held him to her. "Here you are."

The doctors treated Gutkin and told Rivka he was in good health, but there was a defect of sorts in his soul, something hiding.

"Hiding?"

"His personality is...empty. Erased. There's really nothing do be done with him."

But Rivka demanded that Abramowitz give her Gutkin. If no one wanted him anyway, she would take him.

"As what?" Riklin wondered.

"As a personal secretary," Rivka replied. "If Abramowitz can choose a failed doctor to be his head foreman, I can choose Gutkin."

Gutkin had lost a lot of himself. At first he wandered around completely devoid of personality. The residents of the estate avoided him. They claimed that at nights he looked through people's windows and pierced their skin like a mosquito to suck out their characteristics. They awoke bitten and confused in the morning, in a state of irritation. People swore they had been bitten, that they did not feel themselves, that Gutkin was reconstructing a soul and a personality for himself. The estate was in turmoil. People demanded that Gutkin declare whether he was dead or alive—had he committed suicide, or had he failed at that, too?

But Rivka protected Gutkin, and he, full of patience toward himself, improved day by day. He seemed to be measuring the qualities he gathered, shortening and expanding and repairing as needed, until eventually he patched together an entire soul and walked around with it cautiously, as if deep inside him the rehabilitation was still ongoing, his qualities still feeling their way, reaching out gently to one another.

Gutkin seemed to have been built primarily from Dr. Riklin. He had somehow found Riklin's forgotten parts, the ones he had sworn to throw away on the day he followed Abramowitz to the estate. And now Gutkin naturally rolled out words of flattery to his benefactress, Rivka. He easily recited biblical verses and ancient sayings, and they sounded very much like the words the young Meshulam Riklin used to whisper to his wife Naomi.

To justify his existence and fulfill the role of personal secretary, Gutkin performed simple jobs for Rivka. Delivering something to someone. Making sure her papers were in her case. Remembering the name or address of some person. People looked at him and whispered among themselves. They were afraid. What made them particularly uncomfortable was his slowness. But the facets of his personality gradually came together, and everyone began to accept him. His handsomeness also returned, and Rivka would look at him in delight and say, "You are so handsome!"

Gutkin had retained only a few echoes of his former character: women made him sad, the name Ben-Gurion made him furious, and whenever a train went by his heart sank.

One day Gutkin heard there were elections in the State of Israel. And then Ben-Gurion became prime minister again. He went to Rivka in a state of confusion. Someone had once told him that Ben-Gurion had resigned for good. So how could this be? He remembered a shot. Someone had shot Ben-Gurion. Or perhaps they hadn't? His memory was hazy. It had happened before the first day, before *Let there be light.* But for several nights he could not sleep—hadn't Ben-Gurion resigned before?

His life was focused on the little things Rivka asked of him. He felt useful. He recorded all her needs. He kept her calendar. Her meetings. Her trips. But in 1962 he heard that David Ben-Gurion had agreed to extradite the Jewish Soviet spy, Robert Soblen, to the United States. Gutkin was angry. Greenhaus and Tzipkin would not have forgiven. But who were Greenhaus and Tzipkin? Deep black holes swirled beneath his tranquility. He was scared of falling...falling down into the chasm.

In 1963 they announced once again that Prime Minister David Ben-Gurion had resigned. For good, this time. Gutkin was furious. Someone was playing a joke on him. But he calmed himself down, knowing that a frightening black world lay waiting beneath. He must not grow angry. No matter what David Ben-Gurion did.

In November he heard talk of a distant event. The American President, John F. Kennedy, had been murdered by an assassin.

Gutkin felt somehow close to the affair, and was alarmed by his slippery feelings. He had to concentrate on work. On Rivka. Not let his thoughts wander.

In 1965, when he heard Ben-Gurion had left his party, Gutkin waited for himself for a long moment, but nothing inside him shifted or moved. The black world was gone. It had stopped swirling underneath.

And it was good to be Lev Gutkin. Good and simple and easy.

Part Three

Chapter twenty-five

I was a Soldier in the Testament Army   1964

> *"The situation is grave and nearly hopeless,*
> *we may fall into our enemies' hands and lose our state...*
> *But the Jewish people will not be lost because of this.*
> *They have a capacity to endure—five million in*
> *the United States, three million in Russia, and*
> *another million in Europe..."*
> *(Shlomo Goren, Chief Rabbi of the IDF,*
> *a few days before the Six Day War)*

The winter of 1964 was wet and cold on the estate. The wind slammed into trees, rooftops and tin boards. Aged structures collapsed, and one night of hail destroyed all the crops. Puddles welled up on the ground, and the stream carried an ugly froth.

Abramowitz and Riklin sat in a room deep in the recesses of Chaim and Rivka's private wing of the house. Riklin looked around for Rivka. She must have left the estate again without telling anyone. She had promised...and Abramowitz did not reprimand her when she disappeared for hours, days. What did she do out there? Then again, why should Riklin care? The main thing was that she was gone, while Abramowitz was right here with him. But on the dining table he could see the remnants of their meals, empty dishes, hunks of bread and fruit, lemons with their flesh sucked out. On the floor lay a sheet carelessly pulled off a bed.

"This country is going to be eradicated, Riklin," said Abramowitz. He spoke harshly, cruelly, about a great war. Soon. Within a year or two. He spoke about Nasser. About a union among all the Arabs. About the little people here in Israel who busied themselves with their little matters. There had been an Arab summit in January, and there would be another one soon. More decisions. "The estate has to be prepared if we want to survive. We need money, power, and alliances."

Riklin struggled to listen to Abramowitz, but his thoughts were still snagged on the first words he had uttered. *This country is going to be eradicated.*

Eradicated.

In the past Riklin might have allowed that word to play with him for a while. Naomi had been eradicated, while he…To be eradicated as a single being, as one, as a solitary person—in his youth the thought had curdled his blood. To die by the knife, by the axe. When he used to hear about people he knew, murdered one fine day, it scared him, and he would wonder when they would hear the same news about him. They would torture his body, cut off his ears, his penis. But to be eradicated as a people, as one of many, that had seemed less frightening then. That was a destruction he could tolerate. But not anymore. Not now. Now he wanted to exist. To be. With all of life's troubles, and the tiredness. Still, to exist.

He closed his eyes. He wanted to curl up inside Abramowitz's palm and rest there forever.

"I have a plan," Abramowitz continued, pulling Riklin out of his daze. Riklin's jaw dropped as he listened. Nasser…Hussein… Abramowitz wanted to find a way to reach them. He was well aware that the state would try to stop him, even declare him a spy, but eventually they would beg him to use his connections for them, as he had done in 1948. "I know them, and we don't have time for arrests," he explained. "This country is going to be eradicated, and we have to survive."

Riklin's face stiffened with anger. The damn state—murdering innocent people, executing without trials. But Abramowitz reached out his calming hand.

"I have a plan. For six months now I've been cultivating a certain person with great potential. He says he can reach Levi Eshkol, Pinhas Sapir, Yigal Allon. Now it's time to find out."

Riklin wondered why Abramowitz needed the government ministers of a country that was about to be eradicated, but he did not ask. He was excited by this talk. There would be something momentous to do, risks to take, following Abramowitz fearlessly with no regard for the dangers.

"I intend to invite this man here. His name is Romek Paz, formerly Pozowski. He's a small man, gets excited over big business. I've already tested him a few times, and there is no amount of money he is not capable of wasting. A huge talent. He'll help me move ahead with my plan without putting myself at risk. He'll report what they know about me, what they're planning to do to me. That's important. I don't have time for their interrogations. I have to sell a lot of assets, transfer money into accounts in Europe. My people there have already made the contacts. Everything's marked. People in the Jewish community, in the Arab consulates. We need a lot of money, and we will survive. They'll destroy the state, but they will respect our independence. And afterwards? Afterwards there'll be another struggle. Wars never end. My father once told me, 'War is history's vitamin.'"

Riklin felt tension in his throat. Great things. Glorious days. The Arabs would invade Israel, drunk on their triumphs. In their frenzy of celebration they would destroy everything, murder, loot. When they reached the Abramowitz Estate they would need to be reminded of the pact. There might be a battle. Riklin imagined flames and screams, people dying. In the end the invaders would retreat and their leaders would respect the pact.

He felt blood dripping from his nose, but when he held his hand up, his face was dry.

"My plan is complicated, but it will work. It's only a fraction of what I'm contemplating. One day I want to set up a small army."

"To fight off anyone who tries to invade?" Riklin once again saw the Arabs, their eyes ablaze, ignoring the pact. A war of desperation on the estate, shoulder to shoulder, Rivka fleeing. Only the most loyal keep fighting.

Abramowitz broke into his thoughts. "I want to set up my testament army."

"Testament army...?"

"If I have to die, I will die my way, with everything after my death exactly the way I want it. I need guards, people who will be prepared to make sure everything happens, my death, my wishes."

"A testament army..."

"My father chose that name. We used to discuss it."

Romek Paz was invited to the estate later that week, and the three men sat in Abramowitz's garden. While Romek looked out indifferently at the verdant expanse full of lemon and apple trees, Riklin silently examined this first soldier in the testament army: he used a cigarette holder and blew smoke rings in between describing in great detail his ties with every member of the party establishment, the government, the Knesset.

Abramowitz explained Romek's part in the plan. Romek smiled. "I understand that if the Arabs win, I'll come out on the right side, and if we win I'm also on the right side. That seems fair."

Abramowitz smiled too. "A lot of people will be on the right side and still die."

Romek held back another smoke ring. His eyes flickered for a moment. "Which reminds me. If the Arabs invade, I'm bringing my sister Genia and her family to the estate. A husband and a kid. I would leave the husband behind, but one must have pity..."

Abramowitz did not answer. Rivka walked over to the garden sucking on a lemon. Romek looked at her glistening lips.

"This is my wife," Abramowitz said.

"And the lady's name?" asked Romek, half-standing up in a bow.

"Rivka," replied Abramowitz. Rivka smiled and looked straight at Romek. Then she walked up to the house in slow motion, turned back to Romek for a moment, and smiled at him again. The sunlight sketched the outline of her body beneath her frock.

Romek Paz stared. He lit a cigarette and put a great deal of effort into his next smoke ring. "I like living. What can I say? Life is beautiful, it shouldn't be wasted."

Dr. Riklin began to despise him.

"The lovely wife reminds me a little of my sister," Romek chattered on. "When she was young, I mean. She was beautiful. And of all the men in the world she had to choose that idiot. Tell me, Mr. Abramowitz, inspire me—what would you do if your only sister married a complete idiot?"

"I never had a sister," Abramowitz answered dryly.

"Yes, I know, you had a brother, and he's still missing. I've done all I can about that. Really, no one knows what happened there. And I took his name off the books in the Ministry of the Interior for you. Twice."

Abramowitz looked at Romek and his eyes lacked color or expression.

Romek lit another cigarette, threw a bored glance up at the sky, and distractedly stroked his chin.

Riklin was annoyed. How could he speak to Abramowitz like this? He did not seem to understand who Abramowitz was. How dare he?

Romek continued his ponderings. "Mr. Abramowitz, the first stage will be easy. Who would want to get on your bad side? But getting hold of all the information, everything they're planning to do with you, that'll be difficult. You're talking about atomic secrets, crazy stuff. Who's going to talk to me about atomic secrets? About people the security services are looking for? That's difficult…I'm not sure if I can do it."

"People who can't do it are a dime a dozen. From you I want success. Only success."

"And if I can't…?"

"What do you think?!" Riklin interrupted, but Abramowitz silenced him.

Romek kept slowly stroking his chin as he looked at Abramowitz. He sat comfortably in his chair, unperturbed. He had seen Abramowitz's type before and could easily act unimpressed. "*Nu, nu*," he said, "there's no need for threats. I mean, this is for the benefit of us all." But something in Abramowitz troubled him deeply. Perhaps he was getting drawn in for no good reason? He was being asked to do things that had a very small chance of success, but on the other hand, the sums of money that had been mentioned were like music to his ears. He turned to Dr. Riklin as if to a friend. "I always say, life should be enjoyed. And I will ask that this ideology be respected!" Then he blew a few smoke rings and turned back to Abramowitz. "Let's say I leave here now and begin working. After a week we talk, we see where things stand, yes?"

"No," said Abramowitz. Then he dismissed Riklin. "Come on," he said to Romek, "I'll walk you to your car."

They walked together. Abramowitz spoke and Romek listened. When Romek got into his car his face had turned white and he was shaking his head absentmindedly.

After Romek left the estate he drove straight to the hotel where he had been living for the past six months, a necessity of his position on a review committee he had set up. He was planning to spend the evening with a woman he had had two affairs with, one before her marriage and the other afterwards, but now he felt he did not want her. Perhaps he would just sit in his room alone this evening. But that seemed impossible too. He needed fresh air.

He went out for a walk. The meeting with Abramowitz was still churning inside him. Strange. A troublesome feeling. Burdensome. He was hungry but did not feel like eating. All the restaurants looked repulsive, menacing. He left the main streets and walked through the residential neighborhoods. He was about to walk into a corner store, but he felt nauseous. What was happening to him? He thought he would go back to his room and sit on his bed with a cigarette until he felt better. Then he would go and see the woman. Yes. He would salvage something out of this evening. She was an exciting woman. Devoted. The type that refused to let go afterwards, but still.

His feet led him further and further away from the hotel. He was alarmed at the sight of the balconies that seemed to have grown beards of wet laundry hanging from lines. And the houses, long ugly rows with no end. He was cold, and when he noticed a ground-floor apartment with the door open and a sign that said, "Synagogue," he did not hesitate. Amused at his own impulse—after all, what was God to him?—he went inside. He spoke to the surprised *gabbai*, who helped him pray for the souls of his father and mother and four brothers and two sisters, Gitl and Bronke. They had been such beautiful and mischievous girls. Gitl was ten and Bronke was twelve. Just as lovely as Genia. But she alone had gotten out in time—stubborn— she had gone to Palestine.

After they prayed, the *gabbai* invited Romek to share a meal with him; no one else would be coming to the synagogue for another hour. He served Romek a bowl of thin broth with dumplings, and together they dunked pieces of bread in the soup and slurped noisily. Before he left, Romek scribbled the man's name and address on his cigarette pack. He decided to cancel his meeting with the woman. On his way to the hotel he would send a few telegrams from the post office, including one to Abramowitz—not because he had to or because of any urgency, but because…because…he would send the telegram and feel a weight lifted from his heart.

When he finished his business at the post office, Romek decided to have a proper meal. He went into a fine restaurant and ate dinner, which he charged to the party account with a flourished signature. He strolled back to the hotel and pointed an imaginary wand at various items in the shop windows he passed—I'll buy that one, and that one, and this, and two of those.

The next day Romek insistently pursued a woman he met, and was rewarded with complete success. When he went back to his room he felt much better, and gave no more thought to the weakness that had taken hold of him the day before, a sort of tired sadness. He lay in bed smoking and thought about Abramowitz's wife, whose name he could not remember, but he found it exciting to think about her long fingers. He lay fully dressed, looking up at the ceiling, and decided he could probably seduce the wife. But business came first. Abramowitz was offering him huge sums of money and control over budgets, and in case of war and defeat he was also offering him life. It was a challenge.

Romek Paz worked hard for a whole week gathering information. He probed around and examined how to initiate the conversations Abramowitz wanted him to have. At the end of the week a driver came to take him to the estate.

Abramowitz listened quietly as Romek spoke. "I'm going to Europe tomorrow," he said finally. "What you have here is nothing. You've done no work. Now look, I'm giving you names, people whose job in the security service is to follow me. You'll try the things we talked about with them. I don't want any mistakes. Riklin will give you all the details of my itinerary. Who I'm meeting, when. You have to find out what my status is in the security service. Understand?"

Romek felt scolded. He had done the best he could. But he did not complain. He spoke with Abramowitz for a while longer, and was then driven back to the hotel, a new one where he'd been staying for two days. It was better than the other one, nicer. Abramowitz's money was starting to bear fruit. Romek showered, changed his clothes, and looked out at the street from his window. He wanted to keep working for Abramowitz. Definitely. And not because of the war stories—he found Abramowitz's prophecies of war and alliances meaningless; he had listened to the best of the analysts, and there wasn't going to be a war. Nasser was making threats to solidify his rule in Egypt, and after the war of 1956 he had learned that he could not employ a brutal foreign policy. But Romek was enchanted by Abramowitz. What he had heard about him frightened him a little, but fear was not a bad thing for a man.

He called room service and ordered a light meal. He wished he could attend to his personal affairs—a woman he had met in town—but he had to visit the party office for some business, completely unglamorous matters which nonetheless had to be done. If he did not handle them himself, someone else would look through the reports, and that would not be a good thing at all.

He liked overcoming his adversaries, taking control of committees, of resources. He hated the prolongment of work. Routine was what killed a person's inner man. All those cursed positions that one was forced to stay in for three, four, sometimes five years after obtaining them. How? How did people stick with one job their whole lives?

Abramowitz. He was the key to Romek's happiness. It had been a week now since Romek had begun to feel that Abramowitz was the one who would rescue him from a small life. What they were doing now was only the beginning. There wasn't going to be any war, but there would certainly be big business with Abramowitz. He just had to make sure Abramowitz realized how valuable he was.

He lit another cigarette, the last one in the pack. He would have to go out for more, and his brand was not easy to find, not even in this fine hotel, which was looking grander by the minute. He would have something to eat, then go out. He did not feel like staying in his room. He would walk a little, stretch his legs. Then the office, that would not be too bad, and then, finally, the little brunette—*oy*, that brunette…to taste her forbidden fruits. And then listen to her whining a little—her husband, her life, so hard, so bad. *Nu*, every pleasure had its price. Tomorrow he might go and visit Genia. He could play with the boy for a while. Little Shmuel. And Genia would make her *latkes*. He needed to feel at home. And he would tell her how he had prayed in memory of Gitl and Bronke. Or perhaps he wouldn't.

He looked impatiently at the walls and at the window. He would be back here later tonight with the brunette. Lust spread through his body. The anticipation began to hurt. He had a thought—the fault was in the room. It was fancy but boring. Perhaps he would ask for a different one tomorrow. No, he would move to a different hotel. He might even consider renting an apartment. He had already bought his own apartment twice. He had comfortable mortgages, very comfortable, both times, but the moment the movers had put down a couch and two armchairs in the living room, he had realized he did not want an apartment after all, that he couldn't stay there even another minute.

He soon pulled himself together and reminded himself that his business traversed the entire country—how could he settle down in one place? Why fight his nature? He was destined for guest suites and hotel rooms. Romek put the thought out of his mind and went out to buy his cigarettes.

*

During 1964 Romek was happy. Abramowitz was pleased with him. Leaks from the security service were successfully extracted, and Abramowitz often nodded with satisfaction. Not bad, not bad, these connections of yours.

If Abramowitz had only known how difficult it was for Romek to get every single word, every detail out of the bastards. And what they asked of him. Greedy. The lot of them. All the promises he had to make, the arrangements, the funds. They blackmailed him. And he blackmailed them too. But they could snitch on him, they could report that young Romek Paz was taking an interest in investigations. That he might be a traitor, a spy. The twists and turns, the revenge on anyone who asked for too much. But he could also be forgiving, knowing how not to pull the line too taut. Caution was critical.

Romek was proud of his country's security service agents. They exposed every scientist Abramowitz located, every embittered young doctoral student in Europe. They knew he traveled to meet people and rewarded them for their expertise in nuclear physics. They followed him without missing even one trip, one conversation, one little agreement. All the technicians, the craftsmen, they knew about everything. And Romek Paz had to navigate it all, leaking things out, leaking other things back in. Explaining that Chaim Abramowitz was not a traitor. Sometimes he felt suffocated, exhausted, but he disregarded it. This was his road to the big life. He was a double agent. Maybe even triple. But wait—he was no spy! He had betrayed no one. This was all nonsense. The whole thing was nonsense. Even the things he read in the reports, which he scanned before passing along. Quotes from talks Abramowitz held with Riklin and Günter, in private, which somehow reached the ears of the security service. "The only thing that will tempt the Arab leaders is nuclear capability. After they conquer Israel they'll fall at each other's throats. But they'll listen to promises about a bomb…"

Romek could not understand Abramowitz—was he trying to get an atomic bomb?—but he did his work and Abramowitz was pleased. Finally here was the man Romek had longed for. All this time, everything he had done for the party, for all his political patrons, they had all disappointed him, even the ones who had seemed as giant and aloof as gods. How hard he had tried to be worthy of their presence, the things he had done, and not done. But from the moment they took him under their wing he had discovered how gray they were. Insisting on petty arguments and conflicts, promoting their own agendas. And when, at moments of rest and camaraderie, one of them would take the time to speak with Romek, all he would talk about was some little intrigue. A trap he had set in preparation for the next meeting. A speech that would ridicule his opponents. A committee he would take over. Romek listened and listened, and the cigarette butts piled up in the ashtrays. His were elegant, rolled with Turkish tobacco, and theirs—anything they could get their hands on. It was no wonder he skipped from one patron to the next. And all the while behind his back they called him disloyal. Turned their noses up at his fine clothes, his manners, his ways with women. Boring men.

Abramowitz, though, gave him everything. And asked for everything in return. It was a little stifling. And frightening. But Abramowitz gave him power. He did not teach him methods, or tell him what to do, but suddenly Romek had the power to do anything, to suck dry every public fund and toss out its empty shell. Big business! Big courage! No limits!

Romek watched Abramowitz work tirelessly, as if he could sense the war approaching, though still invisible. But things were quiet. In June 1964, the National Water Carrier was inaugurated. The Syrians tried to divert the sources of the Jordan. A few gunfire incidents. A couple of threats. Nothing more. In May 1965, the spy Eli Cohen was caught and hanged in Damascus. David Ben-Gurion left Mapai. Diplomatic relations with Germany. The Israel Museum opened. A new port in Ashdod. A new Knesset building. Quiet.

Whenever Abramowitz invited him to the estate, Romek was excited. He felt small and diminished, yet at the same time great and powerful. It was all so confusing. The wife, Rivka. And Abramowitz himself. The accomplishments Abramowitz demanded of him, always wanting more. And his voice when he shared his thoughts with Romek.

In 1966 Romek Paz began to think Abramowitz no longer needed him. He called on him less and less frequently, demanding fewer and fewer results. Romek looked through the reports but they clarified nothing. Had Abramowitz finished his preparations? Had he given up on his plan? In fact, he realized, he no longer cared. Because he loved Abramowitz now. Yes, loved him—what a man! A giant! Standing above history. Outside history. Huge! Whatever his plans may be.

Sometimes Romek came to the estate and was not allowed to get close to Abramowitz. He would walk as far as he could and watch Abramowitz from a distance, just outside the border of the estate. Sometimes he stood beside Rivka, beneath her kites. Stood silently. Looked out to the distance. As if he felt his gaze was joining with Abramowitz's. The trees scattered on the hilltops. How empty... how different from his childhood landscapes.

By the middle of 1967 war was in the air. The war Abramowitz had predicted. He had been right about everything. Romek was scared. War. In May the war went from inconceivable to inevitable. Romek bought the newspapers every day. The articles were so long, it was hard to concentrate. But the black headlines were clear: Nasser Implements Threats With Other Arab States and Soviet Encouragement. Foreign Countries Express Displeasure with Nasser, but Set No Demands. Despite Prior Statements, un Withdraws from Sinai and Gaza. Egyptian Armored Forces Openly Enter Sinai. Forces Deployed in Syrian Region. Movements on Jordanian Front.

"Will there be a war?" Romek asked Abramowitz.

"Yes."

Romek shuddered. But he was not afraid. Why should he be? This time, he had found a safe-haven, and not just for himself. Genia would come, and the boy Shmuel. That was as it should be. This time they would not be able to say he hadn't saved his family.

A young secretary lay in Romek's arms in the hotel, sobbing,

"I survived Auschwitz. Auschwitz, I survived…" Her eyes searched Romek's for reassurance; perhaps from his position high up in the party, he knew about plans for salvation and victory.

The papers announced: President de Gaulle Cautions Israel: Do Not Open Fire. Nasser Closes Straits of Tiran. Americans Insist Israel Should Not Act Alone.

Romek examined the people around him. The fear.

Abramowitz summoned Romek to come and see him. He spoke briefly and released Romek from all his obligations until further notice.

"But I want to be with you," Romek mumbled. He looked at Rivka Abramowitz sitting nearby, indifferent to the conversation, paging through a glossy magazine, her slender fingers idly stroking her lips.

"When the war breaks out, you and your family will come here," Abramowitz reassured him.

But Romek wanted more. He did not want to leave yet.

"Are you scared?" Abramowitz asked.

"No."

"People are scared. You can feel it on the streets. The smell of fear, Jewish cologne…"

"Yes…"

Romek looked back at Rivka, hoping she would look up, intervene, invite him to stay on the estate. But she only smiled at him dreamily and reached out slowly to the fruit basket.

Romek drove to his hotel and went up to his room. He was not afraid. Why would he be? He was just tired. Lately Abramowitz had been draining him. And rightly so, now that everything was ready. But the exhaustion…And the state was making demands on him too. Officially he was posted in the civilian defense corps, and somewhere there was a note for him with an address and all sorts of code words. But what did he have to do with this war? He was a soldier for Abramowitz. He had operated in a civilian framework in the War of Independence too, so his talents wouldn't be wasted in some military outpost. And even before that, during WWII, he was sent to Istanbul to try and rescue Jews from the Nazi terror. And what? Had they honestly thought he could save people? That anyone could? Madmen. Even if he could have, wouldn't he have at least saved his own family? Madmen. What did they send him there for? What was the delegation for? Bastards!

He lit a cigarette and stubbed it out.

Bastards!

Later that evening his anguish died down. He had finally broken through a certain woman's modest façade. She was the wife of a party member; not young, but tempestuous. He had dinner with her in a good restaurant and sat staring into her eyes. Would she be eradicated too? He took her to his room and had a wonderful time. After they were finished he stood by the window and looked at the woman sprawled on his bed. Blessed be the life that enabled him to have such women. He might have felt a lucky man if he weren't so tired.

June 5, 1967 found Romek Paz in a lovely guest house in Safed, a plan made long ago that he saw no reason to change. He sat on the veranda with his legs stretched out and surveyed the scenic Hula valley. The first reports came over the radio. The Voice of Cairo related dizzying Egyptian feats. Romek should have shown up for duty at his civilian defense branch, where he was to manage homefront security in one of the residential neighborhoods. But they would find a replacement. Not to worry. It was best to sit here and wait until some components of Abramowitz's plan came into effect.

Abramowitz had promised that the Arabs would win and the country would be destroyed. Perhaps it would be better for Romek to leave the guest house immediately and fetch Genia and the boy. What would happen if he was too late? He had to hurry, save them while he still could. But his body was leaden and his heart was pounding. He lit a cigarette. He had to hurry, to save them…

Chills ran up his spine. He felt as if his feet had frozen. It was so cold. Perhaps he would ask the proprietress to bring him a blanket.

Chapter twenty-six

We Are Here to Afforest the Expanse　　　1967

> *"In 1939, Mordechai Gumpel made aliyah…*
> *He wrote to his parents in Germany that he had been assigned*
> *to work as a forester. After a few weeks a letter came*
> *from his mother. 'I am filled with joy as I imagine you*
> *in the fresh air of the forest in Palestine,' she wrote.*
> *And he replied: 'When I bend over, I can reach*
> *the canopy of the forest we are planting these very*
> *days in the rocky terrain of the valley.'"*
> *(Ha'aretz)*

Five months had passed since the end of the Six Day War, and Abramowitz asked the forester Meir Glop to build a garden on the estate. Glop was found by two of Abramowitz's men in a shack near Maoz Zion, and was brought to the estate hunched over and chuckling the whole way. A massive mane of hair topped his head and cascaded over his ears and down to his shoulders in two gray waves. Tufts of hair stuck straight out and curled back like fishing rod hooks. His face, hidden behind tresses, was wrinkled and shriveled, and he constantly emitted a peculiar snicker.

"I am ready," he told Abramowitz.

"Ready?"

"The garden requested by Mrs. Sarah Abramowitz. All the plans are drawn up. The materials are stored in barrels. Mrs. Sarah will have her garden!"

"Mrs. Sarah is gone," Dr. Riklin hissed. He despised Glop already, and found his obsequious voice chilling.

Glop grinned nervously and exposed his teeth. His eyes darted around.

"Mrs. Sarah Abramowitz passed away almost twenty years ago," Riklin continued, "and this garden will be in her memory."

"Oh...so there will be a garden." Glop seemed relieved. He shuffled closer to Abramowitz, and Riklin had an urge to pounce on him and break his neck, crush the man, trample him into the dust.

Abramowitz looked at Meir Glop. "I understand you can grow any tree?"

"Even firs in the Negev desert. The secret of life and death is in the hands of Meir Glop!"

"Good," said Abramowitz. He instructed Meir Glop to plant a European garden. A garden with trees like the ones in the parks he had played in as a child.

"And where will I live?" asked Meir Glop.

Riklin had to find him comfortable rooms and provide for all his needs and demands. Glop also required a place for "scientific preparations," and he was taken to Günter's old experiment sheds.

Over the next few days Meir Glop dragged wooden and tin barrels into the sheds and filled them with water and various substances he poured out of little bags. He vigorously mixed the liquids in the barrels, tasted them, stirred and cackled. He pulled out sticks, sieves and neatly folded fabrics from his bags. Always stooped over, he scurried among the barrels and discharged grunts of satisfaction and the occasional flare of protest.

Dr. Riklin looked on with disgust. He dragged Geitzev out of the dairy barn and sat him down to oversee matters and record all of Glop's requests.

A defenseless shipment of seedlings and shoots arrived from Europe, which Meir Glop promptly swathed in his treatments.

He wrapped the seedlings in a variety of fabrics, including leather drenched in cold liquids, then pierced their flesh with tiny toothpicks dipped in a substance whose smell sent shock waves through the estate.

"The secret of life and death is in the hands of Meir Glop," he chuckled, "and those fools at the Jewish National Fund threw me out!" The notes he pinned to the plants hinted at his secrets: "Two hits of cold," "Frozen at first," "Cold cold cold."

Every day Abramowitz came to see the nascent garden and examine the emerging growth, mere intimations of bushes, saplings peeking out of bundles.

"I am cheating the trees, and they think they're in Europe," Meir Glop giggled.

"You can cheat trees?"

"You can cheat people, so why not trees?" Glop cackled wildly and shook his head uncontrollably. Suddenly he hunched down by a tender shrub, held one long finger out to its stalk, touched it and mumbled something. He looked up at Abramowitz with large, shining eyes. "And from the Jewish National Fund they threw me out! What do you say to that?" He snorted again and slithered away among the seedlings like an eel.

Meir Glop's saplings grew and blossomed, reaching out with the beginnings of strong trunks and sturdy roots, without succumbing to the foreign climate. An engineer named Luria was invited to design a network of paths among Meir Glop's trees, near the hilltop of Abramowitz's house. Tractors and excavators began driving at the rocks beneath the ground, breaking through and defining the borders of the garden. Luria built a complex structure of intersecting paths that twisted and turned every which way, an enjoyable and always solvable maze designed to hide within the thicket of Meir Glop's greenery. He built little pavilions, gazebos and sheltered decks. A tower went up on the high point of the garden, and an expert from Italy named Pietro Molinaro was brought over to cast a large bronze bell. When the foundation work was complete and they began the finishing touches—fine gravel on the paths and benches along the sides—Meir Glop started to transfer the fruits of his labor into the garden.

He assembled a miraculous garden of European trees that flourished in the soil of Israel, utterly indifferent to the heat and aridity. He planted Abramowitz a thicket of raspberry, lilac and crabapple bushes watched over by an assortment of trees: maple, ash, elm, and several varieties of northern oak. Around the paths and benches he created flourishes of hazelnut shrubs, black elder and viburnum. They were healthy and vigorous, impudently resisting the onslaughts of *hamsin* and the pressures of arid air. Poplar and styrax trees—whose leaves usually rustle in the ghostly winds of the far northern forests—were planted in groups and clusters like soldiers securing their posts. Walnut and chestnut trees, heavy and aged from the moment of their birth, were placed at some distance from one another, so that their branches could grow and intertwine and shelter the bushes with deep shade. Lastly, Glop planted a few samples of fir, beech and birch trees that were destined to be enormous.

Every day, when Abramowitz walked down the path from his house to the garden, Meir Glop would emerge from the thicket and skip from plant to plant, his body hunched over. "Trees are fledglings. At first they are in danger, and you have to care for them. Afterwards, when the tree grows big and strong, it will survive even in a wholly unsuitable environment." He grinned, baring his gums. "Believe me, you can force anyone to be anywhere. And if they don't want to? Let them die. No one is forced to live."

Abramowitz smiled crookedly.

Glop came closer. "I had a brother, and I convinced him to come to *Eretz Yisrael*. And in the Galilee, he fell. The War of Independence. In the Galilee, they don't know where. Missing, they said. What do you say to that?" But he did not let Abramowitz answer. "No one is forced to live!" he roared. "No one is forced to live!" Then he vanished from Abramowitz's sight.

Due to a rumor that Günter had fallen ill with another severe case of pneumonia, Rivka insisted that he be brought to the estate. But Günter, who appeared gaunt and pale, refused to lie in bed; instead

he was drawn to walk through Glop's young garden. "Unbelievable…
unbelievable," he murmured, holding his nose right up to a fir, *Abies
pinsapo*. He fingered the black elder, *Sambucus nigra*, and the ash,
Fraxinus, and the birch, *Betula*. "The wonders of the Creator…the
wonders of the Creator…I have never seen scientific proof of such
botanical acts, and I know everything, from the blessed works of
Professor Shlomo Ravikowitz to the excellent writings of Professor
Zohari on adventitious plants. Once I might have felt a scientific
inclination to settle down here and examine Mr. Glop's work with
seventy eyes, but alas, I cannot…"

Günter had his doubts about Meir Glop himself. He was horrified as he watched the little man slither around the bushes, lick his
lips, snort and cheer, taste the leaves, bite into branches, then choose
which materials to add, what to inject into the plants' flesh and how
to fertilize their soil.

"I believe he is mad, Sir," Günter decreed with dry erudition
to Abramowitz.

After the death of his son Hans, Günter had found he was
unable to live in Safed any longer. But he also could not live on
the estate, nor anywhere else. He could not. To keep him busy,
Abramowitz asked Günter to traverse the country and recruit soldiers
for the testament army. Apart from a salary, Abramowitz also gave
him a car and a driver, but Günter preferred to travel by bus, sleep
on benches in Torah study houses, and dine in soup kitchens. He
gave most of his pay to the needy, and used the rest to set up synagogues named after Sarah Abramowitz in remote neighborhoods, and
equip them with Torah scrolls named in memory of Hans. Occasionally one of the estate people would find him and insist that he eat a
nourishing meal, sleep in a comfortable bed for a few nights, and see
a doctor. Afterwards Günter would be sent on his way to continue
looking for soldiers.

Abramowitz was immersed in plans for his testament army. From
time to time he ordered the sale of an asset. At first drop by drop,
then in a great torrent. He shed factories, hotels, polishing plants,
workshops, farms, lands. He gradually diminished his domain. He

also gave up some of his most loyal devotees. The victories of the Six-Day War, which eliminated the fear of destruction, led many of his employees to join the Israeli state. They wanted a part of it—of the victory, of the nation, of the life. They were afraid to stand up against Abramowitz and tell him what they wanted, preferring to slip out of the estate under cover of night. They spent weeks and months living in fear of emissaries who would come to force them back. But no one came.

Every morning Dr. Meshulam Riklin made a list of the people who were missing, possibly missing, or suspected as missing. His notes were full of question marks, enquiry orders, calls for action. But Abramowitz told him to crumple up the lists and throw them away. Let people be. Do not bring them back. Do not look for them.

Riklin was horrified. When Abramowitz left he would take the lists out of the trash, straighten them out, and study them with a crooked face—they had to search for these people. They had to! It seemed to him that since Israel's great victory in the Six Day War something in Abramowitz's soul had slammed shut. His silences had grown longer. He had always been a man of few words, but now he would invite Riklin over and then sit without saying a word. Together they would sit in the garden Meir Glop had built, among the sprouting trees and bushes, in silence. Riklin would look at Abramowitz, fearful for a moment, wondering if he might be losing his mind. And what would become of Riklin if that happened? But he put his fears aside. After all, people still folded like cards if Abramowitz wanted them to. His capabilities were boundless, everything was as it had been, fear was only for the weak. Abramowitz was still a success in all his endeavors, and his health was impeccable.

Impeccable. Apart from that one bothersome pain in his knee, like the prick of a needle. Dr. Riklin tried to treat the pain, but Abramowitz resisted—what for, he asked? Riklin did not give up. He brought in specialists, wrote thorough descriptions of the problem to physicians in the U.S., in France, in Italy. He described the nature of the pain both orally and in writing, focused all his attention on it, talked about it, dwelled on it, until one morning he got out of bed and felt the prick of a needle in his own knee, a twin to Abramowitz's pain. Dr. Riklin could not conceal his satisfaction. There was a covenant of the body between him and Abramowitz.

After a while another weak spot emerged in Abramowitz's health. He suffered from a mild but troubling case of rheumatism, and three months later Riklin diagnosed the same illness in himself. Like Abramowitz, he felt the pain mainly in his wrists. Abramowitz rejected Riklin's treatments, and even on days of intense pain he ignored the suffering and conducted his business as usual. Riklin, committed to his all-encompassing job, was less immune to the pain, and on such days, which they both experienced concomitantly, he took frequent breaks to rest. He force-fed himself tranquilizers and herbal remedies, to no avail, and was practically in tears from the pain and the helplessness. When the throbbing subsided he would stand up tall and repress the memory of the pain and growl with satisfaction: he was unflinchingly loyal to Abramowitz, and in these days not everyone was.

Riklin viewed Rivka with new contempt. Shortly after the war, she began spending time with new friends: generals, politicians, intellectuals, and various characters whose occupations were vague and who were referred to by some as "colorful." She seemed to have shed the passing years, her childish beauty now a thousand times more glowing. But Riklin found no value in beauty without loyalty. He fantasized that fate would put Rivka and him to a great test. A King Solomon's trial. One would pass, the other would fail. He strained his imagination trying to picture the minute details, but his scenarios always remained too pale for his taste. "A great test," he murmured, "a great test."

His heart pounded with fear when Rivka came to Abramowitz one day with her neck damp from sweat and her hair clinging to her temples; she had been out flying her kites for a long time before coming to betray the master of the estate. She said to him simply: "That's it. Enough with your boycott. I want us to be part of the state."

*

Dr. Riklin overheard tail ends of conversations, accusations, tempers raging. They were arguing: the rift was opening.

"Chaim, open your eyes. We lost. We wanted it, but we lost. And meanwhile everything is happening around us, happening all the time. They're building and planting and laying ground work. Look at the communities, the forests, everything so beautiful—"

"They killed my brother."

"Stop. Enough. You're done with your war."

"You can stop if you want to."

"Look at this state that you hate so much. What was it when you came here? And look at it now."

Riklin waited. Exulted. It was happening. Conversations erupted, voices rose. All he had to do was wait. But over and over again he watched with panic as, at the height of an argument more bitter than death, Rivka's look would suddenly soften. "Come here, Chaim," she would say, and take Abramowitz's hand and lead him to their room, the sweat still glistening on her skin, her eyes narrowing. She would smile, as though she had not just uttered the most terrible words, and she would retreat into the depths of their home, to their private rooms, where she worked her malicious ways. Chaim would follow her, and they would get further away, and she would giggle, and their voices echoed in Riklin's ears.

What is the value of a beautiful face and a blossoming body without total loyalty?

Riklin comforted himself. Nothing was over yet. And there was the pain, the needle in his knee, Abramowitz's pain, which lately had been appearing in his temples too. A sharp headache. He had to ask Abramowitz if he had pain in his head too. Why hadn't he mentioned it?

Riklin did not lose hope. He followed the frequent arguments, and the silences that remained like puddles when the fights died down. He monitored Rivka's trips. She would leave for a few days, come back, leave again. Her eyes disclosed turbulence. You are not so wonderful, he thought; You are not so strong. He could feel her doubts. Her suffering. Perhaps one day she would finally get up and leave the estate.

He noticed that when she came back from her travels she did

not argue for a day or two, as if out there, in the distance, she had made a decision to keep silent. She always resumed her quarrels with Abramowitz by mentioning how she wanted to get an identity card. As if this, a mere piece of paper, was the essence of the matter, the thing that would make her happy. Then she talked about friends, about living a simple life, about quiet and tranquility. How laughable. Her boldness increased in Riklin's presence—it was not by chance that she always showed up when he and Abramowitz were talking. First she would speak about this and that, and then—the state, the identity card, the friends, the quiet.

"Coward," Riklin would whisper.

And he somehow knew, when it finally occurred, that this was what the picture would look like: just as they were busy reviewing the estate affairs, Rivka chose to disturb them with her final notice.

"I've made up my mind. It's enough. I'm joining the state. I want a country, I want to pay taxes, to carry an identity card. That is what Jews dreamed of—not of an estate without anything. And that is what Mother dreamed of, too."

Riklin stared at her beautiful eyes, her body, her treachery. He turned to look at Abramowitz, who studied Rivka silently as though he had been waiting a long time for this moment, for the betrayal, so that he could look at her this way, at her flushed, daring face, her defiantly pursed lips.

Rivka stood closer to Abramowitz, trying to rouse him. "I'm joining the state, Chaim. Do you understand? If you tell me to leave this place, I will."

Abramowitz tensed. "And if I don't?"

"Then the estate will be divided."

"Divided?" Abramowitz gazed at Rivka.

Riklin wanted him to hit her. Now, hit her. Damned women...

Abramowitz rolled the new idea on his tongue. "Two estates?"

Rivka kneeled down, took his hand in hers and held it to her forehead. "Please, Chaim, come with me. Let's forgive the state."

"There will be two estates," Chaim said. He looked at Dr. Riklin. "There will be two estates," he repeated, with a look of wonder on his face.

Rivka demanded her own house, to be built on the edge of the estate, where her peace would not be disturbed. Handsome Gutkin began hiring architects, draftsmen, builders, contractors. All were clumsy peasants like him, who made mistakes and corrected them, squabbled and made up. The work was overseen by an engineer named Hirsh, who was said to have committed suicide on a small agricultural commune in 1912, but here he was on the estate, measuring beams and rafters down to the millimeter.

When the house stood they began planting lawns, and a grove of lemon trees, and flower beds. They dragged archæological artifacts into the garden from territories liberated in the war—statues of lions, stone archways, carved rocks.

No official division was declared between Rivka's people and Abramowitz's people, but everyone thronged to the area under Rivka's control. Abramowitz stopped no one, and he himself came to see her with Stefano Lerer at his side. "Since you're alone," he said, "take Lerer with, to protect you."

Rivka smiled. "All right," she said. "Come and see." She took Abramowitz by the elbow and showed him her house, the garden, the trees. From afar Riklin could see him enter the new house. He watched Rivka, her body, her steps, and Abramowitz drawn after her. He knew the detestable giggles that would soon come from her room.

Riklin could sense Abramowitz observing Rivka grow more and more distant, and he vowed to make up for her betrayal by increasing his own loyalty. So that Abramowitz would not lose his strength. So that he would be as great and strong as always. Justice would win.

Riklin's one and only friend, his Wandering Jew, also preferred to spend its time in Rivka's domain, as close as possible to the new mistress. Sometimes, when his work took him to Rivka's house, Riklin found his plant sprawled across the floor tiles, dozing coiled around a candlestick on the dresser or under a potted plant, consoled by the knowledge that this house was always open, and that although it would never be considered man's best friend like a dog, it had come as close as possible. If the Wandering Jew appeared in Abramowitz's domain, it was only to enjoy the wonderful European garden. From time to time it emerged there, examined the possibilities, checked out this or the other thicket, admired Glop's work: three years after the first seedling was planted, the garden was a modest glory, albeit a juvenile one, of shrubs and trees and grasses that strove with full force towards their ideal forms.

Abramowitz walked through the garden in astonishment and stiffly caressed the tree trunks, the bushes, the ferns. Meir Glop crawled out of a nearby bush on all four, his back hunched, and stood up to face Abramowitz as he contemplated a fir. "Wait and see what a magnificent tree this will be one hundred years from now," he assured Abramowitz. Then he licked his lips and leapt back into the bushes, only to emerge from a gap in another bed of plants. "And here, mushrooms! They don't know either. Forest mushrooms, but there is no forest here—it's all deceit!"

The garden had yet to take on the tranquil form of a European park. The tallest trees were less than ten feet high, and the hesitant ones, particularly the firs, were not much more than three feet tall. The surrounding fauna invaded the garden cautiously. They dug burrows and populated shafts and hovels. By the time the shrubbery began to intertwine, the soil darken, and the birds land indifferently on trees they should not have been accustomed to, Abramowitz was spending most of his days in the garden. Early in the morning he would sit down on a bench and spend his time thinking until evening.

When guests came, they sat on low benches, surrounded by crabapples and lilac, beneath an ash tree. On a wooden table they spread out documents, maps, contracts, photographs, notes. On their way to see Abramowitz, the less proficient visitors lost their way navigating the complex paths, but not for long. At all times one's soul remained calm, secure in the knowledge that the labyrinthine paths would soon open up. The wandering seemed temporary, and it was. The guests soon appeared before Abramowitz with a slight smile of relief. Even Riklin, who walked the engineer Luria's routes every single day, was not familiar with all the paths, and several times he was angrily defeated by the engineer's cunning and grew impatient at the wasted time. His peace was particularly disturbed by the presence of Meir Glop, who wandered among his creations, popped out of the thicket, jumped when his head brushed against the foliage. Meir Glop felt an inexplicable closeness to the Air Force planes that appeared in the sky over the estate, sometimes far away like a pair of contemplative lines in the heavens, at other times deafeningly close. Glop would stop his work and look up with a giggle, then wave and cheer at the pilots. Only Pietro Molinaro's bell, which rang at regular intervals, sent him rushing back into the greenery in a fright.

When dusk fell, the difference between the two sections of the estate was more pronounced. Rivka's lands were flooded with light and her houses emitted signs of life. On Abramowitz's side, apart from the necessities of work, the homes were quiet and dark. Quietest of all was the house on the hilltop cloaked in its owner's silence.

When Rivka began hosting grandiose parties, and the lawns around her house filled with generals, politicians, cultural figures, and theater luminaries, the invisible line between the two halves of the estate emerged in full force. Darkness and quiet on one side, and on the other peals of laughter, boastful voices, joy and happiness and intrigues and slight intoxication. Here and there some perfumed guests would mistakenly wander over the line and find themselves on a dark and windy piece of land. A devilish chill would run down their backs like a knife as they wondered, *Who lives here?*

In 1972, Rivka's side of the estate watched the Munich Olympic Games on ten Silora televisions. People crowded around the little screens that flickered in black and white, their hearts drawn especially to the Jewish swimmer, Mark Spitz, who won seven gold medals and aroused a great sense of Jewish nationalism in Günter. He had always been able to recite every world record in swimming, in all the different strokes, but now, for the first time, thanks to the television screen, he saw a competition in a real swimming pool with his own eyes, and his soul swam alongside Mark Spitz, onward and upward, all the way to the champions' podium.

Only to Bonhoeffer did Günter confide a tiny doubt that had

crept into his heart like a spy in Jericho. "I find it a little odd that the swimmers race like whales to the wall, as if that is the wondrous shore, only to turn around as soon as they get there."

The two men looked longingly at the pool as it became a Jewish body of water under Mark Spitz's wings, and quietly allowed one another to sit idly, instead of studying Torah. They watched the track and field events, which featured two extremely hardworking Israeli athletes, Chana Shezifi and Aviva Balas. They were all swept up in Esther Shahamorov's dash from heat to heat on her way to the medal podium, but then came the terrorists' slaughter of the Israeli competitors, and the Silora televisions brought scenes to one's heart that one's eyes could not fathom. Neither Günter nor Esther Shahamorov would stand on the medal podium. The sport was over, the televisions were turned off. And the rest of the world went on competing.

Rivka's parties stopped for a while, but picked up again soon after. Some of her guests spoke softly about orders they had given to liquidate the terrorists wherever they were, at any time, under any circumstances.

Dr. Riklin watched the parties. Rather than suffice with his spies, he stood in the shadows himself to observe the revelers from the darkness of Abramowitz's side. He recognized many of the generals and the senior politicians; they used to come to Abramowitz to seek his advice and money, and now they had betrayed him, drawn to the ageless Rivka, to her glamour, to the magic of her body, that damned miracle, the attention she drew from every man, even the most improbable, like Riklin himself. But she was not young, and her body was not all that handsome anymore, and her hips were widening, and long wrinkles ran down her neck, and crows' feet circled her eyes. But all this had become part of her spell, arousing passion, and Riklin knew that the traitoress did not deny herself to his master, Abramowitz. He could hear her cries of joy from Abramowitz's room, and this acquiescence of hers was a double betrayal. How could a woman be so disloyal to a man?

Dr. Riklin despised the unfaithfulness. Rivka, the Wandering Jew, the people who had deserted. He glared at Rivka with narrowed eyes as if trying to decipher this woman who had allowed him to meet Abramowitz and be saved from a life of misery yet still be a failure. Forces deep inside compelled him to spy on her. To look, just to look. To examine her, not as a man, not with any passion for this traitoress, but as a former gynecologist, to whom so many women had given up the secrets of their bodies. He watched her from the shadows when she came to talk with Abramowitz or to make love with him. He observed her among people, and alone, and through the window of her room. He would get close to her and disappear before she could notice him. He stared at her when the three of them sat together, in circumstances that were becoming rarer and rarer. At night, in bed, he would unload the cargo of his thoughts and whisper his ideas—

I, Dr. Meshulam Riklin, was a women's doctor. I gave fertility to the most barren of women, and I developed my methods alone. I knew women, all the lines and the circles that tie a woman's organs together, the things men do not see and women do not know of. If you want to decipher a woman's fertility, step back from her womb and from her ovaries. Investigate the roots of her eyelashes, the sockets of her eyes, the curves of her shoulder blades, the backs of her knees, the second smallest toe…

One day he spied on Rivka as she climbed a lemon tree near the border of her territory. He saw her come down from the tree, her arms laden with lemons, staring into space without seeing him. He felt like a hunter. She was unaware of him, and he could stab her with his discerning eyes, invade and understand her; she would not slip away. But by the time he had focused his gaze, she was out of her trance and standing right before him, watching him. Her figure looked like that of the young girl she used to be—dark, clutching lemons. But she was not a girl. She was over forty. For one moment, before he saw her cruel eyes stab him, he noticed a soft pleasure that lingered dreamily on her face. The fragment of a moment was quickly lost beneath a dangerous visage, as the beast rejoiced at its prey.

Riklin fled with a pain in his chest. He was short of breath. He felt that he had been caught in a sin. But from that day on, he understood. How had he never recognized Rivka's infertility before?

It was such a decisive infertility, almost as though she were a boy. And that active force that trapped men in its charms, his master too. The unrealized youth. As a very young girl, when she had only just begun to be courted by men and to respond with modest acquiescence, she had been taken by Abramowitz, her youth sealed up.

Dr. Riklin recognized beyond a doubt the force that beat inside her, urgently demanding redemption. She was no longer a young girl, and the force had no way out, so it asserted itself in other ways. But Rivka, who ruled over her side of the estate, should have no illusions—she could not hide a thing from Dr. Meshulam Riklin, not even that which she hid from her own self. In the past they had said of him that even a log of wood had a chance of fertility with his help. He was not to blame that in this woman some other force had dived deep inside, distorting and blurring. All the signs he had always read in every woman had been hidden in Rivka, but today he knew: Rivka did not want a child. All her powers had united to prevent Abramowitz from defeating her. But Riklin knew everything now, and one day he would tame her.

Meanwhile, he had to sort out the problems in the dairy barn.

*

The last party of the fall season was meant to be held on a Sunday, during Sukkoth, but on Yom Kippur a great war took everyone by surprise. At midday it burst out to confront soldiers like Shmuel Klein, in the basalt heat of the Golan Heights and the scorching Sinai desert. It came to the lowliest of soldiers, stuck on guard duty in the worst positions at the most undesirable times. And these wet-winged fledglings became its emissaries, summoning the others from their beds, their tents, their synagogues, their sweet holidays. It was October 6, 1973. The Yom Kippur War had begun.

Chapter twenty-seven

Life is Like Pulling a Cart
1974

> *"A nightmarish image with no human form*
> *whatsoever is what Brenner has made*
> *out of the People of Israel…from his inner sin*
> *of self-deprecation before European culture"*
> *(A.D. Gordon)*

The Yom Kippur War was over. A junior soldier named Shmuel Klein was promised a medal of courage. No one on the Abramowitz Estate had heard of Shmuel Klein yet. They did not know that despite his heroism, he was sent to do electrical repairs in a technical unit, just like he had done before the war. They did not know about his quiet desperation, which slid quite easily into an acceptance of his fate, marred only when the award ceremony was twice postponed and not rescheduled before his father passed away. Who would Shmuel Klein show his decoration to now?

In another part of the country, in February of 1974, a young reserve duty captain named Motti Ashkenazi sat down in front of the Prime Minister's office and began a protest. He had been the commander of one of the only outposts not taken by the Egyptians on the Suez Canal front. He called for the dismissal of Defense Minister

Moshe Dayan and an investigation into the disastrous complacency that had preceded the war.

The war had passed over the Abramowitz Estate much like the migrating birds did every fall. Emotions had run high, but for different reasons: a conflict had erupted over a new allocation of resources among Rivka's and Abramowitz's people. The parties convened and branched out into committees to discuss the various issues, but by the time Israeli forces broke though to the Canal, not even half the arguments on Rivka's side had been elucidated. When the army was within twenty miles of Damascus, there was still no end in sight to the barn crisis.

But the great rift that divided the post-war State of Israel in a wave of protest, despair, and bereavement, penetrated the estate and drove it into its own mode of discord. Berger the driver asserted a new demand: he wanted to join Captain Motti Ashkenazi's protest—after all, he was also "against Moshe Dayan." Abramowitz gave his permission. Berger took Yitzhak Yeshurun with him, and they were among the first to join Ashkenazi's one-man protest, which soon grew to be thousands-strong, ultimately forcing Golda Meir to resign. Yitzhak Rabin became the new prime minister.

Berger was not the only one with new demands. People wanted to leave, to switch jobs, to change the rules. Everything. They protested and grumbled and complained, until life eventually sent them back to the beaten track with a heavy heart. Hot and dry despair descended upon the estate, as on the entire country, gathered up from the hopelessness of the reservists, now home from the war and loathe to return to their routines. People felt that it was impossible, that they could not turn a blind eye, that an outburst must come, that something must change. Must. The flow of emigration from Israel did not spare the estate either. Many residents moved to foreign countries. Even Harkin, the elderly Hashomer watchman, went to Canada at the age of ninety, where he lived on a farm with his two nephews, who had fought on the Golan Heights in the Armored Corps. He worked just as hard as he always had, riding on horseback and protecting the herds with his rifle. Berger, who found no peace even when the protest succeeded, left the country, and Yitzhak

Yeshurun went with him. One of their suitcases apparently contained Riklin's Wandering Jew, so that it too slipped away and emigrated. Both estate and country continued about their ways.

"Life is like pulling a cart. And at the end? Who wants to think about the end…" Bonhoeffer explained, a flower from his bouquet of ideas.

In the years of crisis after the war, Chaim Abramowitz accelerated the sale of his assets and virtually ceased to engage with the outside world. He spent most of his days sitting in Meir Glop's garden and taking slow walks through the paths. Once a day, at sundown, Pietro Molinaro's bronze bell chimed and startled the surroundings with its nostalgia. Abramowitz watched the bell as it swayed, pleased with Molinaro's craft. The Italian had been killed in a car crash soon after finishing his work.

Sometimes Abramowitz heard the echo of a thought—*I have tired of it all*—like a migrating bird from a faraway land. From time to time he went out driving, usually alone, but sometimes with Dr. Riklin. On those occasions, he would break his silence with statements such as, "There was no road here when I came to Israel," or "There were no trees here, nothing." And "There were no houses here." They drove to the cities, where Abramowitz went straight to one cinema, and then to another. In between movies he enquired about lightning rods, which he continued to install throughout the estate. He had instruments that used German methods and American methods and British methods. Günter's old devices were still intact, but they now had younger, more sophisticated siblings, promising massive layers of protection. A crisis erupted after Rivka agreed to Abramowitz's request that lightning rods be installed in her part of the estate, but then changed her mind. Disagreements also broke out between Gutkin's men and Riklin's men over the distribution of crops, the paving of a new road in the estate, demilitarization of prayers in Günter's old synagogue, and various other matters. The more Riklin and Gutkin and their advisors tried to settle their differences, the more they grew entangled in bitterness and hatred.

Atolov, a former Mapai man, left a strong mark on the estate when he employed his rare talent to bring in several new telephone lines just as easily as though he were picking wild flowers in the fields. Other citizens waited for up to a decade for a single line, but Atolov pulled his strings and fattened the estate with dozens of lines. The estate residents fell upon the telephones, placing urgent calls and trivial calls and calls to one another, and the bills—no one knew where they were sent. As he walked through the estate, people cheered for Atolov as if he were a triumphant warrior. When Dr. Riklin caught him staring unflinchingly at Rivka one day, buoyed by his newfound pride, he observed in an ostensibly disinterested manner, "I once knew a man who openly courted Rivka, and he's been in a sanatorium for years now, with a broken soul. Men should be careful of Abramowitz." Although Atolov made no response, Riklin took note of his trepidation and planned to exploit it. But then he saw Bonhoeffer's van parked in the middle of the estate, though no one had informed him of his arrival. Ever since Rivka's men had built two gates into the wall on her side of the estate, there had been an increase in undesirable and unnecessary events, culminating in the characters Bonhoeffer brought in right under Riklin's nose.

"How are you?" Bonhoeffer waved at Riklin when he realized he had been seen. As Riklin approached, Bonhoeffer asked quickly, "And how is Mr. Abramowitz?" Perhaps this would prevent the difficult questions that were sure to follow.

"Abramowitz feels fine, thank you," Dr. Riklin replied dryly.

"Strange…to me he looks a little sad," said Bonhoeffer.

"He is not sad!" A menacing wave of anxiety and vague embarrassment washed over Riklin. Where did this Bonhoeffer get the audacity to talk about Abramowitz like that? He hardened his spirit. This saint would have to be taught a lesson. He craned his neck out to peer into Bonhoeffer's van. "Are you alone?"

Bonhoeffer sighed. "Alone, always alone. As they say, foxes have holes, and birds of the air have nests, but the son of man hath not where to lay his head."

"By alone I mean alone, in the simplest sense. What do you have in your van, that's what I want to know."

Bonhoeffer threw up his hands to summon the heavens and the trees to testify on his behalf, but said only, "How's the leg?"

Meshulam Riklin sighed. The leg bothered him. The needle pain in his knee had crawled up to his thigh, and no matter how much he questioned his master he could unearth no similar phenomenon. It seemed Riklin's pain had stopped sufficing with an imitation of Abramowitz's more senior one, and was paving its own roads, a pioneering spirit that Riklin found most troubling. He came to his senses. "Bonhoeffer, let's not mince words. If you have someone in the van, get lost, the two of you."

"Actually I don't have anyone today," Bonhoeffer replied. "Today, in fact, I was invited here. Rivka asked me to come, and how could I refuse?" He walked past Riklin on his way to Rivka's office and thought to himself, I'll have to see about the two guys in the van later.

When Bonhoeffer walked into Rivka's office he took advantage of the occasion to ask about a few things on his mind. "What exactly is the nature of the relationship between you and Mr. Abramowitz at the moment? I'm confused."

Rivka laughed. Her eyes bespoke distress.

"Oh. I see. You're also confused…Ahhhh." He put a silencing finger to his lips. He was pleased with his success. It often happened that people's affairs skipped in front of his eyes like kid goats without him noticing them, but this time he had been insightful enough to pick up on something important. "It's no wonder there's all sorts of gossip," he said quietly, "no one can understand it even if they try."

"I really don't know," Rivka confessed.

"I understand. You were the one who left him, but you're not convinced that you wanted to leave?"

Again he had managed to comprehend a matter that was not at all straightforward, and he was happy. This was the intuition that people spoke of sometimes, a talent ascribed to great rabbis, the heart-sensing heart. Now that he had apparently developed the skill, it would be extremely useful if it grew to allow him to intuit the mindset of farmers and factory owners. "When will you decide?" he asked.

"Bonhoeffer, this is not something you decide. It's complicated. And anyway, my relationship with Chaim is a private matter."

"Private?" Bonhoeffer said loudly. "Private?! Ever since you broke up everyone has been suffering. I bring someone here, I'm told I can leave him for a couple of days, and then some other guy pops up and says it wasn't coordinated with him and he didn't give his approval, and the whole thing is cancelled! You have to make up your mind. And I must tell you that Judaism sides with one estate, not two!" Fearing he might have raised his voice a little too much, Bonhoeffer leaned over to Rivka and whispered, "Perhaps what you need is some mandrake fruit. I happen to have a crate-full of mandrake liqueur in my van. It's slightly expired, if you take an extreme view of things, but on the whole it's excellent stuff."

"I don't drink, Bonhoeffer. Thank you."

"I've heard they also make fresh mandrake juice."

"Well, Bonhoeffer, I called you here on a certain matter, something that could provide jobs and living quarters for a hundred of your men. But let's start somewhere else. If you want to help me decide about my relationship with Chaim—"

"A hundred men?"

"Later. Now, you remember you got hold of some material about Chaim for me, things people wrote about him?"

"*Nu*, yes. Things from long ago, when he was young."

"How long have you known him?"

Bonhoeffer's look turned dark. He had to be careful now, consider every word. "Wait a minute, let's see...I came here after the war...that's for sure...only after the war. So I've known him for maybe twenty years, maybe more, not much more."

"And what do you think of him?"

"Only good things."

"Have you heard that he killed people? Ruthlessly?"

"Killed?" Bonhoeffer fingered his shirt collar. "Ruthlessly?"

"I'm asking."

"No. Maybe just in the regular way. Like everyone here...There was a war of independence, and if Bonhoeffer had known how to aim a rifle, he would have killed too."

"Perhaps you heard about things he did? Bad things? Very bad?"

"Wise men have said, Worse than doing bad is being bad..."

"And Chaim, is he bad?"

"Bad? In what way? So many *mitzvahs*…Look around you, on the estate. And besides, I always thought, from the first day I saw him, to this day, I thought he looked like a bit of an orphan…needing…needing warmth."

Rivka looked at Bonhoeffer. She was clutching a stack of papers. There was a pleading look in her eyes. "Help me, Bonhoeffer. I was a little girl here on the estate. I was born here…and I'm married to him, and I know him. A woman knows her husband, doesn't she?"

"A woman? Her husband? Yes, yes."

Rivka put her hands together and held them to her mouth. "Bonhoeffer, I read things about him in the archives…people were afraid of him…"

Bonhoeffer looked at her. He stretched his neck out and announced, "I, David Bonhoeffer, declare that Chaim Abramowitz is not a bad person."

Rivka leaned back. "Did you know my mother?"

"Oh! Mrs. Sarah Abramowitz." Bonhoeffer's heart soared. Suddenly he narrowed his eyes. "I've heard about her…I've only heard…I wasn't here. I only came to Israel after the war."

"Why doesn't he ever speak of Mother? Why is Günter the only one who mourns her?"

"As it is written, 'Follow me, and let the dead bury their dead.'"

"I don't understand."

"Well, it's theology. But Chaim is not the only one whose behavior is incomprehensible to others. For example, some people gossip about you…I mean, you married your mother's husband…and they say things about you."

Rivka perked up and Bonhoeffer panicked. He coughed and blinked and looked at his watchless wrist. "I'm late. I have important business in Givatayim. I made a mistake. I bought all the taxi-roof lights from Carmel Taxis when they changed over to new ones. I thought I could easily sell them at a profit, but I'm taking terrible losses, such a mess. They say 'Taxi' just like they should, and the bulbs are fine, but nobody's buying. Such a problem! Perhaps you'd like some? Sixty lights, all in working order. But I have to run now. And what do you say? I have two-hundred meters of faulty copper wire with me. It used to be quality stuff. What do you think? Should I sell, or wait for faulty copper prices to go up? Well, I mustn't be late…"

"Bonhoeffer, you're staying here."

Bonhoeffer dammed his flow of talk.

"I was nineteen when I married Chaim Abramowitz."

"A blessed occasion indeed. *Kol sasson ve-kol simcha.*" Bonhoeffer tried to recover.

"Only nineteen."

"Hmmm?"

"But now I think…"

"What do you think?"

"I was nineteen."

"Yes…as you said. But as for me, if you don't mind…the taxi lights…I mustn't be late…" Bonhoeffer stuttered and skipped backwards, threw out a "see you later" and was on his way.

Rivka sat still for a long time. On the desk in front of her were papers full of columns of numbers and other administrative documents. She reached out to one of the desk drawers, took out a bright yellow lemon and a knife, and started cutting the fruit into segments.

*

Bonhoeffer restrained himself for four days, then snuck into the estate from Dr. Riklin's side. When Riklin caught him, Bonhoeffer carefully enquired whether he happened to know if Rivka was looking for him, and if so, what for.

After his van was examined and they found nothing in it apart from ten sacks of coriander seeds that had started to sprout, Riklin agreed to talk with Bonhoeffer. Calmly.

"Rivka has been traveling for the past three days. Something secret. She took only Lerer with her. Gutkin is here, if you feel inclined to talk with that sort of person."

"What, there's something wrong with Gutkin? A nice guy."

"*Nu*, he held a gun to his own neck and missed."

"Success is not always the most important thing," Bonhoeffer said defensively. "In the Olympic Games the main thing is participation."

"What do you want from Rivka?"

"From Rivka? I think she had a proposal, a place for a hundred needy men, food and work. Have you heard anything?"

"There's no place here," Dr. Riklin declared.

"I know, I know. But you don't know what she meant?"

"Why don't you ask her? It seems you are welcomed with open arms over there."

"Yes…I will when I have a chance." Bonhoeffer looked around. "Maybe you need a beggar? I have one, he sits at the Herzl-Jabotinsky junction. Perhaps he could sit here instead?"

"Bonhoeffer, finish your business and be on your way. I'm going to work." Riklin started to walk away, then stopped. "Bonhoeffer, we have a lot of old buckets in the barn that you can have."

"Thank you! May God bless you, Riklin!" He turned eagerly to the barn with a sack at the ready in his hands. He knew about the buckets, and had Riklin not caught him he would have already been loading the treasure into his sacks. But now he wouldn't have to elude Riklin's watchful eye. Buckets! Bonhoeffer already had three potential buyers in mind, including a nice one at Jahami's, in the Ramle market, but it was best to wait for a good price with this sort of merchandise.

In the barn he went to see Avraham-Union-Avraham-United, the first of his temporary solutions on the estate. Avraham had been working in the barn for decades, and every time Bonhoeffer came to visit he looked at him longingly—when are we going home? Bonhoeffer would sit with him and count the days, the years, the hours. He consoled the ancient employee with talk of endless possibilities, doors into a world where the kibbutz had never split and there was no Union and no United, just everyone together, and Avraham would go home, his own rift healed.

Back in his van, Bonhoeffer found a jug of the Mahajna family's precious olive oil. "It's a gift from Riklin. He's in a good mood today," a worker explained.

Dr. Riklin was walking through Meir Glop's European garden at the time. He thought about the serious business with Atolov that he would have to contend with, and about that no-good Gutkin, who was shaking things up and diminishing some of Riklin's own accomplishments. But on these kinds of days, at the end of spring, he sometimes experienced an inexplicable blossoming of generosity. There was a wisp of joy in his soul, and even a desire to whistle. His hardworking heart, full of disappointments and fear of the future, was suddenly tender, with feelings that did not burst out but filled up his soul. He was happy. Everything was good. He strolled through the garden, inhaling the subtle mint of the European leaves, and felt the breeze breaking through the walls of shrubbery, warm and flat, tickling him with its tongue, and he almost felt like falling in love.

Dr. Riklin chuckled. Love—at his age! What he would really prefer was a different sort of pleasure. The broken neck of Gutkin, for example, or a secret that Abramowitz would tell only to him, only to him, only to him…

He took another enjoyable breath and felt the end drawing near, the latter part of the sweetness that had come to his soul for no apparent reason. It would soon depart and leave him as Riklin, only Riklin. He slightly regretted the jug of oil he had given Bonhoeffer, and the old buckets. A waste.

By that time Bonhoeffer was well on his way to the Ramle market, where he would pour the oil into bottles at Marji's, so that he could derive the largest possible profit from this miraculous gift. And he still had the buckets, pure profit, and in the background there was the matter Rivka had alluded to, a hundred jobs for needy men…a hundred! Had the Creator intended to finally award Bonhoeffer an entire hour of enjoyment, he could have sufficed with all this. But he took a gamble—perhaps more than was necessary—because at Tigra junction Bonhoeffer picked up a young hitchhiker with a scant blond goatee. In a spirit of goodwill, he tried to get to know the young man, and talked with him about the confusion in his life—a severe case of being enamored with Buddhism. Bonhoeffer thought the Creator had given him this young man so that he could restore his faith by the time they reached Ramle, but even after he recited his finest saying—"If you're on the wrong train, you won't fix anything even if you run backwards"—the young man still did not seem impressed.

"You must be careful with this Buddhism," Bonhoeffer admonished the awkward young man.

But instead of abandoning his enthusiasm, he began to explain himself in a slow, deliberate tone, as if Bonhoeffer were expected to take notes. Bonhoeffer responded good-naturedly to the youthful, sparkling nonsense, full of longing for total faith but choosing the wrong vessel. But again the young man had an answer for him, and another, and his wall of answers began to seem strong, and all of a sudden Bonhoeffer realized with alarm that it was the young man who was trying to convert Bonhoeffer—that he did not perceive himself as a candidate for conversion at all.

"You're not willing to open your eyes and see, really see," said the man, his voice professional and polished, like a salesman, and hardened, as if he never lost his prey, and this time, chillingly, Bonhoeffer was the prey.

Bonhoeffer arched the back of his faith, stood its hairs on end, exposed its teeth, and tried to prove the superiority of Judaism.

Unimpressed, the young man only asked calmly, "Did you used to be a minister by any chance? I've heard a few ministers speak in American churches. You remind me of them, with your persuasion methods."

Bonhoeffer's back hardened. He felt somewhat embarrassed. Who was this person? He tried to search for another opening into the heart of the lost young man, who was trying to lead others astray. He asked what he was doing in Israel.

The man waved his hand weakly as if to indicate that this story was too complicated and too long for him to tell right now. He looked out the window. His face was still turned away from Bonhoeffer when he said, "The landscape here is mad."

"Why?" Bonhoeffer asked, still sensing his previous fright, that this young man was not a devoured lamb but a devouring lion.

"I don't know. In America, where my family is, instead of going to high school I spent two years backpacking around the country. You see everything there, landscapes, people. Here, Israel, it's a tiny speck. But the landscape here…I don't know…" His voice was soft for a moment, confused. This was his call for help, and Bonhoeffer was there for him.

"You're from America? Your Hebrew is so good. No accent. Usually American Jews, although good people, they speak Hebrew as if a dentist left a bandage in their mouth."

The young man did not smile. Bonhoeffer knew his jokes were falling flat, as were his persuasions. But the Creator would give him strength, and this young man would see the light.

"I came to Israel right after the Six Day War. I wanted to join the army, go to a yeshiva, and live in Hebron, my grandfather's city. But when I got here I found that no one was ready for my dreams yet. I was barely seventeen, even after faking my age, and they didn't want me in the army. Then I discovered that Jews couldn't live in Hebron yet. The only thing I could find was a yeshiva, but it was boring so I left."

"Boring? A yeshiva?" Bonhoeffer was hurt, and felt his voice crack. A little drink might help, but that would be awkward before this young man who needed a role model. He decided to let the yeshiva comment go—it was possible, conceivable, just for a very short moment, to be bored with the tractates, those long ones, the ones that dwelled on affairs far from one's heart…perhaps…

"In the end I wandered around a few yeshivas. I enlisted in the paratroopers. I was tempted to do an officers' course, and then the Yom Kippur War broke out. I survived, I stayed alive, but the soul… At first I thought the war had extinguished my soul, darkened it, but today I understand that it was the light, the illumination."

Günter might have been useful here, Bonhoeffer thought.

"Finally I was enlightened about the ills of the society I live in, ills I hadn't wanted to see before. A boastful society, with no direction, Jewish but not Jewish, and I had come here after one or two generations of assimilation to be Jewish, even orthodox, but I suddenly felt…this was not what I had been looking for."

"People have grown a little distant from God, they haven't put their confidence in Him," Bonhoeffer concurred.

Then the young man launched into a polite but venomous speech about his views on the world of yeshivas, and Judaism, and nationalism. Eventually he told Bonhoeffer how, quite by chance, he had found himself in a student debate on transcendental meditation, which had ultimately led him to discover Buddhism, the truth he had been seeking.

Attempting to contend with the man's excitement and decisiveness, Bonhoeffer tried to probe his roots. He asked about previous generations, before assimilation, and the hitchhiker responded effortlessly, fully able to cover and hide, reveal and glorify, with expert fluency. Bonhoeffer experienced a dull terror, afraid he might end this trip with Buddhism flowing through each and every one of his limbs.

"My grandfather," the young man said, "was a Hebronite Jew named Mordechai Barkha, seventh generation of Hebron dwellers. On a premonition, he fled before the 1929 massacre, and immigrated to the United States with his wife."

"The *kadosh baruch hu* led him there…"

"The *kadosh baruch hu?*"

"Of course. A man does not just leave *Eretz Yisrael* and go to America for no reason."

"I see. You know, my grandfather became a great Zionist in America, but he was a smart man, according to my grandmother, and he used to tell anyone who would listen that even during the Second Aliyah, the apex of Zionism, almost two million Jews emigrated from Russia and Eastern Europe, but only twenty thousand, maybe a little more, chose *Eretz Yisrael*. The rest chose America."

Bonhoeffer sighed.

"My grandfather became a Zionist in America, but he observed his Jewishness. He did big business on the stock exchange and got rich very quickly. They told me stories about all his assets, and the people he kept company with, including, according to the stories, all sorts of beautiful women, not Jewish, whom my grandmother didn't know about. But fate is fate, and not long after he emigrated to escape the Hebron massacre, the great financial crisis struck New York in 1929. When the stock market collapsed, my grandfather lost all his money, and just like that he went from being a wealthy man to a pauper with huge debts, including money owed to some major New York and Chicago criminals. And then he simply disappeared."

"Ran away?"

"Maybe. Look, big criminals chased him, and all sorts of FBI agents, because it turned out he was doing business with all the *goyim* indiscriminately, and they all turned up at my grandmother's house, and she had to leave too, with the baby they had in America, my father. They hid from the police and the thugs and a few officials from the Jewish communities. But from somewhere out there she got regular payments in the mail, and when she died the money kept coming to my father, to pay for his *bar mitzvah*, and his education, and then his business, until one day my father decided to take off his yarmulke and stop being Jewish, and then the money stopped, bang, just like that. Dad told me he tried wearing the yarmulke again, but that was it, the money never appeared again."

"You don't say…" Bonhoeffer murmured. The young man spoke in simple language, like many young people who had sat here in his van before. But Bonhoeffer feels things. Bonhoeffer can't be cheated: this was a great and awesome test.

"I asked Dad whether he wanted to see his father. He said that at home they were forbidden to talk about him, in case something terrible happened. Because, you see, they kept pursuing my grandmother, even ten years after Grandfather disappeared. Millions were lost because of him. And so my dad got used to that. I did too, you could say. I had to. Dad was always at work, almost as absent as Grandfather. He worked shifts on Christian holidays, because he was Jewish, and he worked on Jewish holidays too, because he didn't celebrate them. And he worked weekends. He was happier at work than at home. That's the way it was. I grew up almost without a father and completely without a grandfather, even though I'm named after him, Mordechai-Matthew. But my last name is Berk, because no one could pronounce my grandfather's name in America. Unlike my dad, I searched for my roots a lot. Like I told you, I dropped out of high school to get to know America, and I came here to be a Jew, to settle Hebron, but here my light came, my peace, and there is only one faith, Buddhism."

Bonhoeffer sailed away with Mordechai-Matthew's story. That grandfather, that Elijah the Prophet, he was enchanting. What else was known about him?

Mordechai turned to Bonhoeffer. "Look, we don't have to convince each other. You agree that the main thing is the desire to be a good person, to believe that there is a purpose in life, and to want redemption. That's enough. The rest is method. Judaism, Buddhism—what difference does it make to you?"

Bonhoeffer smiled. The young man spoke truthfully. And so pleasantly. Why proselytize?

"The problem is that sometimes you feel stuck. You work and work and feel that you're not getting any closer to your destination. And then, maybe, the problem is in the method. And if the intent remains the same, what does the supreme power care what you call him? Or which prayers you pray to him? What difference does it make? Why not try a different method with the same intent?"

Bonhoeffer tensed up again. Another assault. The responses started rising within him, answers as good as sweets. But the young man sniped first.

"Tell me, are you sure we haven't passed Ramle?"

Bonhoeffer looked at the road signs and realized they had. "Ummm...," he said awkwardly, "I have a shortcut. It's just up here, right, then right again, another right, and then we'll be there."

"Okay," said Mordechai-Matthew, and they drove quietly along Bonhoeffer's shortcut.

Creator of the World, Bonhoeffer thought, in your kindness you have given me another twenty minutes to bring this lost son back to Judaism, and I thank you. It's a good thing I missed the turnoff to Ramle, although in terms of the market hours...Give me the strength to see the sign at the next turnoff, so we don't go through that red light like we did back there, when I got a ticket in Hadera.

Mordechai-Matthew began again, offering pointed definitions of Judaism and its beauty, and the truth that reinforced it. Then he held up Buddhism beside it, and drew the connections, and did not try to show that Buddhism was better than Judaism, only carved out perfect slices of Judaism and pointed to gaps, faults, contradictions, difficulties, slight leaps of logic.

His words were sharp, critical. Lies, it was all lies. But Bonhoeffer grasped the wheel strongly with both hands and his mind filled with all sorts of thoughts, ideas he had entertained in the past, heresy, semi-heresy…thoughts that came from tiredness, from disappointment, lies that took hold of one's soul. He always got rid of the thoughts easily, turned them away like mutinous sailors walked down the plank…to the sharks.

Mordechai-Matthew did not give up. His words were so fluent, so light, effortless. His face was young and showed no fervor, it did not have the exertion of a missionary. But the superior force of a merchant was in his bones, and Bonhoeffer was frightened, powerless. Perhaps he should peruse this Mordechai-Matthew's theories a little? Perhaps it was not all just an abomination? Mordechai-Matthew was staring at him, and his heart jumped, and he started to wonder, Where, where was the force of God?

Bonhoeffer paged through the Torah in his heart, but salvation did not come. He uncharacteristically sought beyond the five books of the Torah, wading into the Book of Judges like someone leaving his apartment wearing nothing but a towel. But there, on the pages where he usually felt so uncomfortable, came the whisper he needed, the whispered prayer of Samson, the blind hero, as he stood between the pillars of the Philistines' temple.

Bonhoeffer shut his eyes and whispered, "Oh Lord God, remember me, I pray thee, and strengthen me, I pray thee, only this once." With his eyes still closed, he took a vow and promised his God a *mitzvah*, a special act of kindness, not the ordinary kind, something he had never yet done, just as long as He gave him strength.

Mordechai-Matthew yelled, "Look out!!!"

Bonhoeffer, with his eyes closed, had run another red light, just as three cars crossed the intersection.

Bonhoeffer opened his eyes. Everything was fine, except that Mordechai-Matthew beside him was as white as a ghost, his eyes frozen, all his smooth talk crumbled into a chaotic mess.

Bonhoeffer cleared his throat and said calmly, "Ahhh...I trusted my God. And you?"

Mordechai-Matthew crumpled back into his seat. "Tell me," he whimpered, "is Ramle still a long way to go?"

Bonhoeffer rattled the wheel a little, to confirm Mordechai-Matthew's faith. "Just another two lights to Ramle." He smiled kindly at Mordechai-Matthew, waited for the next light and said sweetly, "Now, Matthew, let's have an experiment. We'll go through a red light, and you put your confidence in the Creator of your world, your God. When you see the cars coming at us like the Philistines attacking, call out the name of the one you truly believe in, the one and only, the King of kings."

They approached the intersection and the van careened through a sea of honking horns. With terror on his face, just as they passed under the red traffic light, Mordechai-Matthew screamed, "*Shema Yisrael!*"

His face was pale—he had looked right into the eyes of the driver in the car to their right. "*Oy...Shema Yisrael...,*" he groaned.

Bonhoeffer gently slid onto the shoulder of the road. "Here we are, this is where you wanted to go."

Mordechai-Matthew flopped out of the van with a forced smile on his face. "Thanks," he mumbled.

"A pleasure to meet you. God willing we will meet again."

"Thanks." The young man had trouble shutting the door. Bonhoeffer pulled it shut and drove on to the market, still trembling inside. He had come very close to being devoured...very close...but he was saved.

He took a deep breath and clutched the wheel with both hands. He felt a hint of redemption in his fingers.

Chapter twenty-eight

Rivka   1974

Rivka believed her decision was lucid, her resolve deter-mined, but she approached Abramowitz in his garden three times and did not have the courage to speak. Three times she slipped away, and on the fourth time she collided with Meir Glop and fell to the ground as he fled squawking.

She sat on the earth and looked around at the garden, then slowly got up. A row of maple trees remained between her and Abramowitz. There he was, sitting with his head bowed as if he were dozing, but his eyes were open and bright. Drawn to him, she looked into his eyes, got to her feet, walked over to his chair beneath the shadow of the ash trees and hazelnut bushes, and told him she had made up her mind that she wanted to separate. They would no longer be husband and wife. She could say nothing more than what she had already explained, but she wanted to be liberated, and she might wish to marry again, although she knew that at forty-five this was almost a joke. In any case, instead of a divorce and other such nonsense, he could simply allot her a portion of his property. Her business up to now had been nothing but an amusement, child's play with the toys he gave her, and she had never been subject to the threat of impoverishment. She wanted her own part, she did not care if it was tiny, but from now on she would act as a free woman. As to the residence, she was willing to accept anything he decided, she was not tied down to any particular piece of land, especially not to the estate.

Abramowitz turned away. "Anything she wants is hers. She has only to let Riklin know."

"Isn't there anything you insist on?"

"The garden. It's mine."

"That's it?"

"No. One more thing. Lerer must continue to protect you."

Rivka softened, but Abramowitz closed himself off and dismissed her with a wave of his hand. She felt banished, and for a moment she wanted to run to him like a child, but she stopped herself—from now on she was free—and walked slowly to the other side of the estate, her side.

From now on she was free.

When she reached the wooden door installed by Gutkin in her house, she was seized by anger. She convened all her people, intending to announce her new independence, their independence, and to set laws, and promise that everything would still be fine without Abramowitz, that they did not need him, that their side of the estate would blossom and gain strength. But when she stood facing them her words withered and shriveled, and after a long silence she informed them that from now on the two parts of the estate would be severed.

No more moving from one side to the other.

No traffic.

On the other side, Riklin also declared a severance. But Rivka ignored him. She waited for the real announcement. She waited for Abramowitz. What would Abramowitz say? What did he think?

No response ever came from Abramowitz.

At first the two sides had to grit their teeth and allow Günter to serve as a go-between on every affair concerning their common limbs. Riklin continued to appear on Rivka's section to handle daily matters that arose from the embargo, his face expressing indifferent serenity. Sometimes Bonhoeffer had to cross back and forth, and as he did so he asked people to recommend a "special *mitzvah*," which he had sworn to perform for his God in return for the Mordechai-Matthew miracle. Perhaps someone could think of an appropriate *mitzvah*? Bonhoeffer also took upon himself to loudly compare the conditions of the workers on both sides of the estate and float gossip from one side to the other.

"Whose side are you on?" he was sometimes asked.

"Whoever I am, I will always belong to God!"

"That's not an answer," they said disappointedly. As compensation, Bonhoeffer would offer a piece of juicy gossip about some occurrence on the other side.

The distance between the two sides swelled. Rivka's side embraced the State of Israel. She enthusiastically paid her taxes, made donations and purchased government bonds. She built diamond polishing factories, for export, invested in desert agronomy, for Ben-Gurion's vision, and purchased crumbling businesses, for resuscitation. She even instituted a custom of inviting groups of schoolchildren to the estate before Independence Day so that they could learn about how things used to be. They dragged scythes, sickles and plows out of the warehouses—relics from the past. And they stashed Avraham-Union-Avraham-United and a few other temporary solutions in the warehouses—relics from the present.

Group after group, the children wandered among stations on the Abramowitz Estate and learned how scythes were swung and plows were pulled. The highlight of the visit came when they gathered in Rivka's house to learn how things used to be "from an old pioneer."

"Children, I was a brave pioneer," Bonhoeffer would begin, sliding into his role. "Things were very dangerous all over the Land of Israel. Exactly where your city stands today, a lot of Arabs used to live…"

From the other side of the estate, Riklin would watch and run to report his findings to Abramowitz in the garden. His reports featured all the news his spies had collected, and every evening he deposited stories of Rivka's hardships and failing businesses at

Abramowitz's feet. He gave his reports eagerly, joyfully, fearfully. Each account added another story to the tower of Rivka's troubles, every detail made its own contribution. But whenever Riklin crossed an invisible line, Abramowitz would simply say, "Help her," and the tower would come tumbling down.

Riklin told Abramowitz about Independence Day on Rivka's side. About the schoolchildren. About Bonhoeffer. He wanted to tell him about Rivka's diamond polishing factories, a business that turned out to be less than glimmering, but Abramowitz closed his eyes, indicating that Riklin should stop talking.

Riklin waited. The minutes ticked by. A branch creaked in the wind. Abramowitz opened his eyes.

Riklin boldly asked about Abramowitz's nights—was he sleeping well? Had he felt the need to sleep more than usual lately? Was he ever overcome by sudden drowsiness?

Abramowitz cut him off. "I don't sleep. I think."

"Yes. But still, perhaps some vitamins…a slight change in nutrition…"

"The thoughts are not mine."

"They're not?"

"Have I ever told you about Mordechai Barkha?"

"Mordechai Barkha?" Riklin was concerned, but he soon recouped. "Don't worry, you are not weakening!"

"Weakening? Of course not. I am happy."

Riklin stood beside Abramowitz and listened to his story, caressed his rheumatic wrists, and felt that he too was happy.

Abramowitz finished liquidating his businesses. He sold, abandoned, and scattered them to the wind. Most of Rivka's time was devoted to her own businesses—cement and stone, plastic and nylon factories. If she needed a favor, she used her connections, both old and new. After the Yom Kippur War, many of the friends who used to fill her parties had lost their powers, but even as the war was still fatally raging, she had found herself a new class of people who could influence laws and regulations: Doctors. During the war she volunteered in hospitals, treating the wounded with an expertise that surprised even veteran physicians. Since she moved from shift to shift, from hospital to hospital, and did not abandon her work even long after the war, when all the "kindly aunts" and "angelic souls" had disappeared from the wards, the doctors got to know her well. When she augmented her volunteer work with lavish donations to benefit this or the other doctor's longed-for new wing or department or research institute, Rivka was secretly permitted to witness surgical procedures and real operations, and sometimes she was even allowed to reach out and touch a patient's flesh and blood.

"Maybe you should just study medicine?" they suggested.

But Rivka preferred her line of work, and was adept at recruiting new friends. She quickly learned that no one in the country, however powerful, was immune to the influence of a senior specialist or hospital director.

"The land supervisor? I hold him by the balls twice a year," one of her new friends joked.

If she got into any trouble that required a little pinch on the cheeks of the law, she knew how to solve it.

Those who watched Rivka from the sidelines were astonished by her new persona. She conducted all her business with acerbic resolve, and when she consulted people, particularly men, they seemed distracted, strained, as if intent on resisting bothersome contemplations, fears, and deep discomfort.

"You need to rest," Günter told Rivka.

Rivka did not subscribe to one of Chaim Abramowitz's fundamental rules: he would never dismiss even the most useless estate resident. Without batting an eyelid, she fired anyone who made even one mistake and withheld pay from those who faltered. From beyond the fence she was watched by a jealous Riklin.

Only handsome Gutkin, who made constant errors, was kept on as Rivka's head foreman. Treating him like a priceless treasure, she did not replace him even when she received job applications from former bureau heads, senior secretaries and military commanders—a swarm of people ousted from their jobs following the Yom Kippur War investigations.

Rivka asked Günter, "How is it that of all the people I'm surrounded by, Gutkin is the only one I'm comfortable with? I don't like being with people, I wish they would leave, resign, disappear forever. I only feel comfortable with Gutkin."

Günter cleared his throat. "There are some things I understand. For example, why you stopped flying kites the day my son Hans was killed defending Israel. That is an honorable act. But this soulful attachment to Gutkin...Here there is deep psychology at work, and I am no expert in women's minds."

Bonhoeffer told Rivka, "Gutkin is no honey...he is no Torah scroll...but he is what you were looking for. That is an important understanding, which you reached through your heart, and I admire you. We should not look for people who are perfect, but for people who admit that they sin, and who need kindness, and who want to grow."

"I don't understand..."

"The main thing is that your heart understands, and I drink to it," he said, and emptied a little glass of Rémy Martin down his throat.

Rivka asked Gutkin repeatedly: Was he happy in his role? Would he like a different job?

From the first, Gutkin did not feel talented enough to serve Rivka. Many things he should have known or remembered or paid attention to slipped between the cracks of his patchwork soul, and every time there was a conflict he felt defeated, dragging behind him the constant shadow of failure and discomfort. Arguments between Atolov and Riklin seemed glorious to him, and if he tried to interject his own words, they were quickly dismissed. Still, his new nature prevented him from feeling bitterness or despair, and when Rivka said she was pleased with him and had no interest in replacing him, he trusted her.

Rivka spread a safety net of expert advisors beneath all of Gutkin's stumbling steps. Most of his time was spent entertaining her on her travels. She always asked him for stories about his past. The shot he had fired into his own neck had removed any shame or embarrassment, and to Rivka he recited the minute details of his life, always in a uniform tone of voice, never raised or lowered. He told her how much he hated women, especially when he experienced moments of lust, and how he used to beat women, and might have even killed one. He told her about a man he had killed back in Russia, in a fight, and that there might have been someone here too, at night on the beach in Haifa. He told her about his robberies, his lies, and the hatred of good people that often erupted in him. He told her about Stalin. He also talked about Ben-Gurion, and the redheaded captain, and the widow, and Greenhaus, and his mother…yes, his mother.

On each trip, as if she were pulling a note out of a hat, Rivka chose a topic, which became the subject of Gutkin's detailed descriptions. No holds barred. No hesitation. From faraway. Gutkin felt no sense of belonging to these recollections, and he led Rivka through them like an eager guide in a nature reserve. Together they dwelled in Gutkin's world, touring its remote corners, happy to revisit familiar places and marvel at new ones. The world around them, near and far, ceased to exist, and even Lerer's shadow faded into the distance.

Together they dove into stories of hatred and loneliness and long travels and abandoned homes. Violent nights, conspiracies, and the scent of Gutkin's gun. A skirmish with noisy neighbors on the other side of his apartment wall, and the things he liked about the body of a blind young woman he had met, and how he would often contemplate the glory of his sexual organ, hating it, and how once he threatened it with a straight razor.

At this point Lerer decided that a broader interpretation of his role as bodyguard was in order. "Why do you have to listen to all this?" he asked Rivka.

Rivka was furious. "Mr. Stefano Lerer, you do not understand women, and I have never seen you with a woman. Don't interfere."

Lerer sat back silently and resumed whittling a piece of wood with his penknife, using slow, deliberate movements.

In the evening Rivka found Lerer sitting in his room gazing at an old photograph.

"I came to apologize," she said softly.

Lerer looked up uncomprehendingly.

"The things I said…I didn't mean it." Her voice was thin and strained.

Lerer smiled as if to exonerate her, and Rivka walked into the room. Lerer put the photograph down on his lap, picked up his pen-knife and went back to whittling.

"I like listening to Gutkin, to his stories, that's all."

Lerer nodded. His knife whittled.

"Does that seem strange to you?"

Lerer said nothing. Rivka examined him, this man who long ago, in her childhood, had attacked two Arabs who had ambushed her and her father, and despite being stabbed in the stomach with a knife, had broken their necks and not stopped digging his fingers into their skulls even when they made splintering sounds, and had swung their bodies wildly in his hands. Rivka also remembered one echoing shot, and Lerer not letting go, his blood spurting on theirs.

Lerer kept whittling the wood. Patiently. His round face was calm. Someone had once called him the Italian Bar Kochba, she had heard. She had never noticed before how empty his room was, how bare—a bed, a bench, a cabinet and a table. His status on the estate entitled him to a spacious home, and his salary would enable him to furnish it lavishly.

He was mad. Completely mad. This silence. What interested him? He could lurch at her at any moment, just like that, and afterwards he would not even know that he had murdered someone.

Rivka breathed heavily.

"I like to listen to Gutkin. To anyone, really. Anyone who has something interesting to tell me. Do you understand?"

"Yes." Lerer held out the photograph. "Father, Mother, Uncle Davideh, Cousin Laura," he said.

"Yes." She looked at the photograph. A dark girl. Her eyes black, penetrating.

Rivka apologized feebly and left the room.

One day Gutkin told Rivka that Greenhaus, the man who had once eaten the Mapai party flag in an omelet, had died. According to his lawyer, for some reason he had left Gutkin all his property, which included a number of houses and an enormous amount of savings, all for Gutkin.

"I'll have a lot of money," Gutkin said.

"And will you want to leave your job here?" Rivka asked.

"The money could last me for the rest of my life. Twice over."

"What will you do?"

Handsome Gutkin shrugged his shoulders.

"Then stay with me, Gutkin."

"Now I'll be wealthy. I can live in a big house, somewhere quiet. I'll have everything."

"Gutkin, I don't want you to leave, but you will always have my blessing. Think about it alone, and make your decision."

Gutkin could not sleep that night. The scent of the pine trees drew him out of bed and he walked all the way to the end of Rivka's side. The fir trees swayed in the breeze in Abramowitz's garden, and he could smell the swamp sedges. Chaim Abramowitz sat in his chair, giant and still, almost entirely hidden by the thicket. Gutkin knew that Rivka stood here sometimes. Looking. Watching. Then slipping away.

Gutkin stood frozen, hunched over.

Men are this way. Some die, others love.

He stood facing the firs and a forest wind blew through his heart. An old wind, from distant times. Frost and sorrow.

Should he leave the estate? Should he stay?

His feet led him back to his room. To bed.

Gutkin went to deliberate in his sleep, and never got up. He died with his doubts, in the forty-ninth year of his life.

*

A replacement for Gutkin was sought but not found. Rivka grieved, she missed his reminiscences. Gutkin's job on the estate, after all, was performed by others even when he was alive, but no one else could tell her Gutkin's stories, no one could sail away to his past for her, leaving no tracks, free of shame.

"No one will ever be like Gutkin."

But eventually Rivka found herself conversing with Lerer, drawing acts he half-recalled out of his memory. She pulled out recollections from the days on the estate, from the War of Independence, battles, fragments of terror, and memories from long ago, in Italy,

Rome, piazzas and wine and the Tevere river, and a beloved cousin, Laura, who was killed in Bergen-Belsen.

Abramowitz labored over every detail in his army. His people's living quarters were restricted to the houses near his European garden, and any burst pipes or broken windows or split beams beyond that area were no longer fixed. At night the light shone from only a few houses, and by summer time they too were covered with branches from Glop's garden, which crawled across the estate swallowing up walls and roofs, drowning the houses in a shadowy screen of hazelnut, maple, ash, elm and oak. The paths going down to the crop fields and the stables and the workshops were consumed by weeds, all but reclaimed by nature. Only the path leading to the front gates was still clear, trampled by car tires and human feet.

At the end of that year Abramowitz and Riklin went to Tel Aviv with Abramowitz's new driver, Har-Zion. As they walked down Allenby Street, Abramowitz suddenly stopped and tilted his whole body to the left. He grimaced, and sweat poured down his face. Riklin rushed to support him, but Abramowitz swung his massive right hand and knocked him down.

Dr. Riklin lay on the ground for several seconds while Abramowitz tried to straighten himself. Har-Zion stared at the two men.

"To the car," Abramowitz ordered.

He walked slowly, his shirt stained with circles of sweat and his twisted face turning white. His tongue hung out slightly. He could barely control his own legs, but he moved forward while Riklin danced around him, reaching out to support him but not daring to touch.

Har-Zion held the car door open. Abramowitz got in.

"Home," he said.

In the car, Riklin tried to examine Abramowitz.

"You've had a stroke," he moaned. He gently touched Abramowitz's face, examined his eye sockets, his palms. Abramowitz began to slowly regain his form. His mouth loosened, the paralysis in his body was almost gone.

"Don't tell her," he said when they reached the estate. He took a few deep breaths, got out of the car on his own, and walked to the house. Riklin followed fearfully, three steps behind.

At the door Abramowitz turned to him. "Go and oversee the work. I'll be all right."

"But if it was a stroke…"

"I'm all right."

"I'll come in the evening," Riklin said pleadingly.

"In the evening," Abramowitz said. He walked into his room and slammed the door.

Chapter twenty-nine

Days of Love   1977

Bonhoeffer was beaten up. One day near the end of 1977, he was brought to the estate with casts on both arms and both legs. He had lain unidentified in Ha'Emek Hospital, near Afula, for a week, mumbling, "Abramowitz...Abramowitz...," until someone figured out where to take him.

Bonhoeffer had trouble explaining what had happened. He thought some laborers had come to ask for his help, men brought over from Turkey to do construction work. A contractor refused to pay them, and Bonhoeffer went to see the man and sort things out. As far as he remembered, the contractor had lost his temper, but he wasn't sure, since the beating had affected his memory.

Bonhoeffer spoke to Rivka with tears in his eyes. "What's going to happen? There are a lot of places where I left people, I promised it was only for a couple of days. How can I leave them even one more day?"

Rivka looked at him with her round, innocent eyes. "We'll take care of it."

He lay in bed, slowly recuperating under Rivka's personal care. After a while he was able to move fairly well on his feet, limping even less noticeably than Günter did. He went back to work, but something in him was extinguished. After his recovery, he would often arrive at the estate without even a single temporary solution, just for no reason, filled with memories of a distant youth—

"In my town even the butcher was a saint. He used to wear his *tallis* when he slaughtered the animals."

There was a new sadness in his eyes.

At first he would take restorative walks with Abramowitz, who was secretly recovering from his stroke. But when Bonhoeffer tried to interest Abramowitz in his thoughts, his stories, his memories, Abramowitz's face turned grey and Riklin would quickly whisk him away. Eventually Bonhoeffer found a more welcoming audience in the form of Günter, who, while traveling the country looking for the exceptional few who could meet Abramowitz's exacting demands and join the Testament Army, found time for the occasional break to spend with Bonhoeffer.

Günter found that it was only in Bonhoeffer's company that he experienced a slight dampening of the great yearning that tortured his soul and forced him to move, to walk, to travel, to roam. Günter had a sincere desire to care for the injured man, but his attachment to Bonhoeffer was also a source of comfort for himself. With Bonhoeffer, he could talk about Hans. Just a little. Ten years had passed, but what were ten years? Nothing but days. How great was the pain folded into every thought, and how, he wondered, was it possible to utter even one real word? To speak of how Hans had not been his son, but had become his son.

Günter walked alongside Bonhoeffer, supporting him from time to time. When he asked, "How does Mr. Bonhoeffer comprehend the ways of the Creator, blessed be His name?" Bonhoeffer waved his arms and Günter continued to walk with him. Bonhoeffer issued contemplations of heresy and sorrow, and there was a power in him—a power of sorts.

Günter would look at Bonhoeffer in amazement and realize that this was what the cryptic sages meant when they spoke of the innocent, righteous man. There was not a single strand in Bonhoeffer that did not belong to a core of righteousness. How did one attain such unblemished virtue?

When their walks led them to the barrier between the two parts of the estate, they would look each other in the eye.

"Difficult times," Bonhoeffer lamented.

"In the beginning it was different," Günter sighed. "And Sarah Abramowitz was here…"

"I didn't know her…didn't know her…" Bonhoeffer insisted, absolving himself of any presence on the estate prior to the nineteen fifties. He turned to Günter. "If your honor wishes, you may tell me about Sarah. Perhaps it is easier to speak of her than of your son, may God avenge his blood. Speak and I will listen."

Günter would conjure up the image of Sarah, and his nostrils would fill with the scent of the terrible Dnieper river in faraway Russia, and his heart would find solace as he spoke of her, and somehow he also began to feel comfort over Hans. Without even talking about him, speaking only of Sarah, yet still…

Up the path he would limp, with Bonhoeffer at his side like a breath of fresh air.

Although Bonhoeffer's body finally felt better, his mind rejected this turn of events. For he knew that the Creator had intended something by causing him pain. And that even the evil contractor, the rogue, was a messenger of God. It did not take him long to arrive at a reckoning of the soul: I promised the Creator a special *mitzvah*, something unique, and I tarried. Couldn't find it? I did not look hard enough! I did not open my eyes. I did not open them like a Jew, to really see.

Chaim Abramowitz himself had enlisted in the efforts to rehabilitate Bonhoeffer, paying him generously to run errands. And that very day, at the end of 1977, right at the edge of the year, Bonhoeffer was asked to bring a new recruit for the Testament Army, a man Günter had found by the name of Shmuel Klein. An expert in electronics and fire.

Bonhoeffer arrived at the address written on his note, and it occurred to him that he had seen this building before. But as soon as he saw Shmuel Klein nervously approaching the van, his thoughts ceased and he felt a tempest of excitement in his soul: this man was connected to the special *mitzvah*, the final one.

"Hello, Shmuel Klein!" he called out.

"Hello to you, too," said Shmuel. "Are you Mr. Chaim Abramowitz?"

Chapter thirty

Blondes, They're Distracting 1978

*"My darling, the closer one gets to reality,
the less frightening things become."
(Alexander Levy, designer of the
"Pagoda House" in Tel Aviv, from
his final postcard to his wife
on the way from Paris to Auschwitz,
August 25, 1942)*

Blondes, they're distracting," declared Bonhoeffer.

Shmuel nodded. He had yet to grasp exactly what Bonhoeffer's role on the estate was, and he phrased his responses cautiously.

Three months had passed since Shmuel was driven through the gates of the estate, and a surprising number of people had been introduced to him as important figures in his new life. They tried to enlist him in battles whose nature he did not understand and was afraid to ascertain. They came to him with friendly faces and asked for his opinions on the various controversies of the day: a newly vacant position, a recently issued instruction. But Shmuel, who had not had time to form an opinion on these issues, attempted to avert any hostility or· damages by mumbling and grinning. He was sorry that his diligent reading of the *Encyclopedia Hebraica* had not made any significant contribution to his new life. True, he could demonstrate expert knowledge on Theodor Herzl, Israel Zangwill, Titus, and even Pinsker from the Ps, but in the domain of the estate these were considered trivial when compared with "the Geitzev business," "the future of polishing workshops in Netanya," or "Lerer acting strangely."

Shmuel liked his life on the estate. The instruments he installed were successful, and even the frightening overlord, Dr. Meshulam Riklin, had stopped harassing him. Bonhoeffer was his constant friend, and apart from his persistent efforts to interest him in marriage, Shmuel found him flawless. Bonhoeffer was a good man, who liked Shmuel and demanded nothing of him. Except for the marriage business.

But at nights, alone in his room, Bonhoeffer's words lingered with Shmuel and soon altered their direction—Ricki. Where was she? Shmuel's heart ached.

Still, life was good on the estate. Shmuel even saw Mr. Chaim Abramowitz once.

A few days after he arrived, Dr. Riklin told Shmuel that Abramowitz wanted to see him. Early that evening, he was led to the master's home. There were no lights on inside, and the darkness was punctured only by the halo of a full moon. Riklin walked Shmuel through a number of rooms, deep into the house. There, in the dark core, he found himself in a large room where Abramowitz was seated on a chair.

Shmuel trembled.

"Mr. Abramowitz would like to speak with you eyeball to eyeball," Riklin said to Shmuel.

"But what about your eyeball...?" Shmuel asked cautiously.

"I'll be the one watching. You'll just be listening," Dr. Riklin instructed.

"Just listening?"

"Listen. That's all."

Abramowitz started talking. He began with things that frightened Shmuel, speaking in short, truncated sentences about an army and a testament, eventually progressing to more comfortable topics like electronics and fire. Shmuel realized he was being asked to build some sort of machinery system.

"Like the one that didn't work in the Yom Kippur War, but this one won't involve a canal, and this one will work," Riklin explained.

Shmuel did not know what they were referring to, but he remained obediently silent.

Over the next few days, one of Riklin's assistants, a former engineer named Gershon Pell, offered some clarification. "They want you to design a system that can light a fire remotely, with the push of a button. If you do it, they'll carry on with you."

"That's pretty easy," Shmuel murmured.

"We'll see about that."

A few days later Shmuel showed Riklin and Gershon Pell a modest system with a switch that would remotely spark a fire using a small engine and an ignition device. "But for what you want, for a big system, I'll need a control box…large-scale experiments," Shmuel stammered. He had built dozens of similar devices before, for his own pleasure, but he had never had to make a system designed to set fire to an entire estate at an appointed time.

Later, privately, a tight-lipped Gershon Pell explained that he himself would design and build the system and the control boxes, and that Shmuel had only to make the ignition device. Nothing else. He stood very close to Shmuel and added that if he had his way, he would build that part too, but Riklin was forcing him to use Shmuel's device.

"Why?" Shmuel probed.

"You have a real passion for fire," Gershon Pell whispered forlornly, "that's the only reason they chose you."

Shmuel nodded very slightly.

"They choose the best in every area, and that's why you're here. But if you fail, I'll show everyone what engineer Gershon Pell can do, even without being a pyromaniac."

Shmuel almost wanted to fail, to make Gershon Pell happy, but he knew he would succeed. He had built several installations before, and had lit them from near and far, with slow flames that suddenly leap up, or blinding fire that lasts only half a second, or a series of intermittent sparks, or a jet of fire that bursts out under pressure. He tried to understand what type of system Gershon Pell was building, but Gershon Pell spat out—

"You just build an ignition device! Only an ignition device! The rest will be built by me! Me! Me! Me!" He trapped Shmuel in the corner of the room and stood with his huge, tortured face close to Shmuel's. "No one apart from me knows the big picture! No one!"

Then he walked to the other corner and huddled on a chair. He seemed defeated. He mumbled, "Abramowitz knows the big picture, too. So does Dr. Riklin. But other than them, I'm the only one." After a short silence he added, "And Atolov too…he knows it…"

He hung his head.

"For three years running I was an outstanding member of the Society of Engineers," he said finally. Then he stood up abruptly and walked out of the room.

The next day Shmuel presented Pell with six alternatives and a list of materials, as well as a few small electrical devices. Gershon Pell read the list and started yelling as if Shmuel were asking for stones from the Wailing Wall. But he calmed down after a minute, studied the list again and, wrinkling his nose, said he would write up the requests in formal engineering language, with a cost calculation, and present it to the authorizing parties.

"The authorizing parties?" Shmuel asked nervously.

"Dr. Riklin."

All the items on Shmuel's list soon arrived at the estate, accompanied by state-of-the-art tools, and three days later he presented Gershon Pell with a metal egg of sorts that contained his entire construction: a heart of flammable material surrounded by a mechanical optronic system that would ignite when set off.

"Activate it," Gershon Pell said.

Shmuel turned a switch and a huge flame flexed its muscles from within the egg. Its shadows briefly took flight on the walls, then shrank back into a compact, brawny, vertical flame.

Gershon Pell chuckled bitterly. "Yes…This, any child with

a matchbox and some magnesium can do. But what about a safety threshold? Neutralizing false alarms? An adaptive regulation mechanism? Hah? For that you need an engineer with diplomas!"

"I suppose it could be improved," Shmuel concurred.

"Your device needs fundamental revision."

"Okay," Shmuel said, and proceeded to summarize what he had understood. "It has to let you set the magnitude of the fire in advance?"

"Yes."

"And it shouldn't be able to just start a fire accidentally?"

"Right."

"And you should be able to turn it off immediately if it goes off by mistake?"

"Yes."

"Okay." Shmuel had never tried to curtail a fire before. Why would he? Why shouldn't it be as vast as possible? What could be more magnificent than a fire raging in several stages, with colors, and shards of metal, and pieces of ignition material? Why try to control it if by chance, just by accident, it was already lit?

Still, what Gershon Pell was asking for seemed easy. Shmuel had already composed the entire mechanism in his mind, and he presented another organized list of components he would need, and more materials, and of course, all the same things he had requested before—after all, Gershon Pell had seen them all burnt to a cinder with his own eyes.

Gershon Pell muttered threateningly and announced that he would once again present a formal list with cost calculations to the authorizing parties.

Two days went by, and when Shmuel invited Gershon Pell to see his new device, the former engineer was taken aback. He looked at the tiny device, then peered at the control windows and the row of switches lined up on a board. They were designed to enable a range of adjustable safety and preliminary settings.

"What's that?" he asked sharply.

Shmuel explained the function of each part.

"Activate it," Gershon Pell growled.

This time Shmuel drew out another device, identical to the first one, so that something would still be left of his work after the activation. He instructed Gershon Pell to flip the switches in different configurations and demonstrated how his machine could withstand all of Gershon Pell's demands. Then he allowed Pell to shake the device, kick it, throw it into a fire and wildly press all its buttons.

"All right, so far it's pretty good," Pell admitted.

"Now we'll make some fire," Shmuel said happily. He asked Gershon Pell to turn the switches to the open position. "Turn it on," he said, and an enormous flame spat out again, slowly maturing and stabilizing.

"Not bad," said Gershon Pell.

Shmuel nodded gratefully, recognizing that Gershon Pell was behaving graciously, even though he had hoped Shmuel would fail. He cleared his throat and said, "I'm sorry about what happened to you with your wife."

Gershon Pell lit up in a peculiar light. "What did you say?" He lumbered over to Shmuel like an injured bear.

"I heard she left you and your heart was broken," Shmuel mumbled. Only yesterday Bonhoeffer had told him that Gershon Pell was a genius, the most talented engineer anywhere, and a kind-hearted man, and that Shmuel should not be afraid of him, that he was short-tempered because of the tragedies that had befallen him, first the thing with his wife, then a disaster in a commercial building that had led to Gershon Pell's name being erased from the Registry of Engineers.

Gershon Pell began to hiss like a snake, then roar and wave his hands, and before he could carry out any of the threats he was screaming about, a few men arrived to extricate Shmuel and quiet Gershon Pell. They called Riklin, who came running to see what was going on with the team that was supposed to, when the time came, ignite the entire estate.

The two opponents were removed to opposite corners of the arena. Dr. Meshulam Riklin scanned the metal egg.

"Is it ready?" he asked.

"Ready," said Shmuel.

"Not ready," said Gershon Pell, resurfacing in the world, just a split second late, from the depths of his bleak conversation with his ex-wife. "It needs more tests, in my opinion."

But Riklin ordered a demonstration. Shmuel looked at him fearfully. He narrowed his eyes, set the switches on the egg, and like a magician on stage, allowed Riklin to transmit the electrical signals through the control box. "It's not igniting because the switches are set to prevent ignition," Shmuel informed his audience. "But now..." he said, and changed the position of the switches. Riklin turned the signal switch on, and up leapt a beautiful flame like a diver leaving the board. Then it settled into a vibrant, bright fire.

"Now you can pour water on it, sand, anything...the flame will keep burning," Shmuel said cheerfully. "But to burn an entire estate you have to build something really strong. This is just a sample."

Shmuel was trespassing in enemy territory, but the people in the room were listening, and his confidence grew. He felt like he had in the war that day. He was the one who would rescue Reuven Elkabetz.

"It was Gershon here who taught me that you need reliability and safety," Shmuel continued. "Without him I would have just created fire. Now, in my device, the ignition occurs when a metal pin drops to the bottom. If there is any external source of heat, or something that could cause an unintended ignition, the first thing that bends and gets destroyed is the pin, and then the ignition is essentially neutralized. Look, try and activate it without sending a signal into the photoelectric eye. Do whatever you want. Hit it with a hammer, pour acid on it, throw it into a fire. It will only work with the photoelectric eye."

"Very nice," said Dr. Riklin, examining the flame closely.

Shmuel's nerves subsided. He silently thanked Kalman from the electronics store, who had sold him kits for building instruments when he was young and placed tiny electronic components in the palm of his hand, and when he got to know Shmuel very well, and their conversations teetered into under-the-table topics, such as their common love of fire, he had taken Shmuel to the back room and had shown him how to install all sorts of pyrophoric substances, leaping embers, lumps that grew hot, engorged and glowing chemical compounds, sparks of every type, gases thirsty for a match, materials that ignited with the blow of a hammer. "Better than a woman," Kalman used to giggle as his huge eyes glowed.

Now the application of Kalman's theory sat burning and vibrant in Shmuel's hands, and Riklin liked it. If only he could bring Kalman here, Shmuel though, with all his imported materials…utterly illegal substances…military…he could achieve three times as much!

"What do you say, Pell?" Riklin asked.

"Take a trial period, my love, a break from me, come back when you make up your mind," Gershon Pell mumbled.

"What?"

"Everything's fine," Gershon Pell shook himself out of it.

And the work continued.

First they completed a single installation that was capable of lighting a huge fire. This was the first stage in implementing the system Chaim Abramowitz wanted. Shmuel was driven with his device to a location carefully selected by Riklin's men, in the heart of the Jewish National Fund forests. They installed the system secretly, and once the lookout men confirmed that the forest watchman would not be a problem, they activated it.

Meir Glop was allowed to come along in a separate vehicle with his own driver. "They planted pine trees…resin…turpentine," he cackled upon seeing yet another of the Fund's creations maliciously destroyed. "They threw me out, and what…resin…turpentine!" he roared and cheered as the gang fled the blazing forest.

The Firefighters' Commissioner investigated a series of arsons that year. Entire forests went up in flames as helpless little fire trucks rushed to terminate the spreading catastrophe. Scorched earth was exposed where pine trees had once blossomed. Sometimes, in the midst of the bleak scenes, the sunlight revealed pieces of stone walls, old stopped-up wells, smoldering remains of prickly-pear hedges.

The investigators nervously tracked the criminals who were decimating forests and getting away with it. "It's a political statement," one of them surmised. "They're choosing forests planted on abandoned villages." The Security Service started to look for politically conscious arsonists.

Shmuel, meanwhile, was analyzing his experiments, which consisted of listening to Gershon Pell roar until he finally pursed his lips and authorized Shmuel to develop the next stage, at the cost of another pine forest. Shmuel was sad that they always had to leave as soon as the forest was lit. They had chosen him for the job because of his passion for fire, so why should he be ashamed? He would have liked to watch, even from a distance. The fires winked at him and hummed. Deep inside, where his machine remained, the blazes shot out lashes of fire, its flames proliferating. And what a shame that he, Shmuel, was on the outside, just like when his mother had grabbed him with her iron hand and dragged him away from the bonfire.

Shmuel tried to befriend Gershon Pell, but to no avail. Pell was a tyrant, and he was always angry at Shmuel, as if he blamed him not only for his ex-wife falling in love with his army commander, but also for his dismissal from the Registry of Engineers. Gershon Pell tried to diminish Shmuel's role in the project as much as he could, and expressed joy only when Shmuel made even the tiniest mistake.

Shmuel spent far more comfortable hours in the company of Bonhoeffer, who happily presented him with a plan.

"You need a wife, Shmuel. Like oil into your bones. A wife. You'll see. A wife for a man is a like a seven-branched *menorah*. Highly recommended."

When he was alone, Bonhoeffer gloomily pondered, "Perhaps this is the special *mitzvah*, the one final *mitzvah* that keeps Bonhoeffer in this world. Perhaps I should hurry."

Since Shmuel's first days on the estate, when he had wandered around, lost and confused, Bonhoeffer had been his pillar. Shmuel went to him with various dilemmas, as well as practical problems, such as what to do about a missing button.

Bonhoeffer examined Shmuel's coat. "A bride and a sanctified wedding, that's what you need. A woman to sew your buttons on." But for the time being, he took Shmuel to Petrov the tailor.

Bonhoeffer declared a multistaged training program. First, he would study and memorize Shmuel's personality in order to create the mold of his perfect woman, one who would match "the roots of his soul." After that, he would locate potential candidates. And finally, Shmuel would meet with the suitable women and a happy ending was sure to follow.

It was not only the special *mitzvah* that drew Bonhoeffer to spend time with Shmuel, but Shmuel himself. He found qualities in the young man that even Shmuel was unaware of—he had a kindness, a fundamental, innocent kindness, which had never had the opportunity to manifest itself. Bonhoeffer rubbed his hands together like a boxer and imagined the woman who would win Shmuel, and he was seized by a joy he had not known since the hateful contractor had crushed his bones. He inflamed and goaded Shmuel—

"A wife is a good thing, Shmuel. You have to get one. Your whole body needs a wife. Don't give up. It has to be done. A wife to say blessings at the table with, and to see the light with. A stone in your priestly breastplate. Don't give up. Warmth for your body, light for your soul, the greatest blessing of all." Bonhoeffer himself was almost tempted to get a wife.

Meanwhile, as he worked alongside Gershon Pell, the wrinkles on Shmuel's brow increased. The system he had designed was progressing nicely. In one forest, they had already buried six barrels that shot out torches of fire at the flip of a switch, a mountain of flames that instantly devoured a whole forest as Shmuel stole one breathless glance before fleeing. But the closer his system got to being declared worthy of integration within Gershon Pell's "big picture," the stricter the demands became. One day he was referred to Chaim Abramowitz's certified scientist, the final adjudicator, for a review. He was excited to discover that this was none other than Günter, the dark-skinned, limping man who had found him on the street by the burning palm tree and recruited him to the estate. But now, in the little room, Günter's eyes were cold and critical.

Günter scanned the system, listened to Shmuel's explanations, and lingered over every single component. Shmuel looked at the pictures hanging on the wall in the dimly lit room. He did not recognize Rabbi Kook, but was happy to find Albert Einstein. He remembered looking with his father at this very same picture. He recalled their exchange.

That's Albert Einstein, Shmuel. A wise man. He invented a bomb that killed hundreds of thousands of people.

May God avenge his name...?

Oh no, on the contrary. He's Jewish, one of us. When the state was established they asked him to be president, but he turned it down. Just like that, turned it down. But no matter, one day we'll bring his remains to Israel.

Günter looked at the picture too. "Now I will ask some questions," he said, "and I will not stop until we both know that your system is adequate for Chaim Abramowitz's needs. But don't worry, Shmuel, you are a skilled man. As we both recall, you were born on the day Albert Einstein died."

Shmuel pricked up his ears and waited, but Günter was still looking at the picture.

"When my son Hans died on me, I used to look at this picture of the king of the thinking Jews, and find the strength to get through another hour...another single minute..."

"Yes," Shmuel murmured.

"And when Mrs. Sarah Abramowitz died on me, and there was no one for me to turn to with my grief, and around me I found no one else grieving as I was, and it seemed I was all alone in a world that had forgotten Sarah, I turned my tearful eyes to his picture..."

"Yes."

"And I did not accuse anyone. I did not bear grudges. It would have been easy to think: I am grieving, the one and only person grieving—why? But I did not bear grudges."

Shmuel's face remained expressionless.

Günter waved his hand. "And now we shall also gather strength from him, from the king of the thinking Jews, because for Chaim Abramowitz's sake I must question, and probe, and keep at you until any shred of doubt is removed."

Günter finally looked away from the picture. He studied Shmuel at length, as if trying to recall what he was doing there, then suddenly his face became alert. "Well then," he said, and showered Shmuel with questions. He gravely described various scenarios and mishaps, difficult environmental conditions, unexpected twists, and demanded that Shmuel explain how the system would behave in each and every case and utterly convince him of his arguments. Just when Shmuel thought the difficult test was about to end and his unique system would be declared triumphant, Günter pondered—

"What about a direct lightning hit? How will the triggers sustain the neutralization and prevent the system from going off, heaven forbid? Mr. Abramowitz is extremely concerned about lightning, and he requires absolute protection against it. How will we test your system? It's hard to test against a direct lightning hit. How will we summon an experimental bolt of lightning to strike the system precisely on the trigger?"

Shmuel was perplexed. He realized he was not sure whether the cut-off switches could sustain the direct tension from a bolt of lightning. Then he grew annoyed: Where was this question coming from? He loved his system. He had built it and enhanced it and adapted it to fulfill each of Gershon Pell's obsessions. Now he would hand it over for Chaim Abramowitz to use, but it was still his. His! And what did he care about lightning? What more could they want?

"Tell me yourself, Shmuel. I will trust your studied answer." He stared at Shmuel with his sad, intelligent eyes. "What will happen if lightning strikes the system?"

Shmuel wasn't sure how to answer the question. He wondered what more they could want of his wonderful device. He felt his heart changing shapes—hexagon, rhombus—and then he made up his mind—

"The system won't be set off by lightning."

"It will not?"

"I'm positive." He shrank back in his chair and looked at the toes of his shoes.

Günter twisted his face, tormented with doubts. There would have to be a rigorous scientific investigation. He looked at Albert Einstein out of the corner of his eye, then turned back to Shmuel. He sighed deeply and sent him away.

The next day, Dr. Meshulam Riklin informed Shmuel that Günter had approved his system.

Throughout the estate, workers began digging long trenches and pouring terraced cement surfaces. Although Gershon Pell withheld all information, there was no doubt in Shmuel's heart that this flurry of preparations was connected to his ignition system. He also vaguely knew that Gershon Pell was demarcating "zero day" in his diagrams—the day the ignition system would be installed—but what this date was, or what the precise nature of the system was, he could not tell. How could they expect him to answer all their questions accurately? To know what the system could or could not do? Shmuel was burdened with more and more worries.

Bonhoeffer stepped up his search for Shmuel's wife. He began to seek out candidates, sometimes inviting Shmuel to join him on a preliminary observation. He took Shmuel with him on a few "temporary solution" drives to show him the eligible brides, and if Shmuel nodded his approval, he worked his clumsy charms and organized a meeting.

Miraculously, Shmuel was not tense or nervous before his meetings with these women. His days of fire had imbued him with bravery, and he even felt that he had something he could converse about with women. He was not allowed to discuss the experiments and the system and the Testament Army, but he talked about himself, and about general topics, according to the flow of the conversation. On two occasions he brought up Jabotinsky, and once he mentioned Pinsker from the Ps, the point where he had stopped reading the *Encyclopedia Hebraica*. But his conversational efforts never amounted to anything.

The women were friendly, even pliable, and Shmuel's heart raced at the thought that they might offer some immediate physical acquiescence. But his soul decreed: No. Something was missing in these women.

"Maybe, deep in your heart, you want a blonde," Bonhoeffer said in an accusatory tone.

Shmuel furrowed his brow.

"Blondes are far from God," Bonhoeffer decreed, and went back to his goading. Because he knew that his *mitzvah* must be performed. "If you had a wife, Shmuel, do you know how happy you would be? How much blessing would be in your every act? A wife is good, good…" He chewed on his lip.

"We have to keep trying," Shmuel sighed.

"I will!" Bonhoeffer promised. And somewhere out there, he could sense a brood of feminine spirits just waiting to win over Shmuel.

But one day things did not go as planned. Trying to reassure Shmuel and relieve his despair, Bonhoeffer said warmly, "Don't worry, Shmuel. You'll get married. You will build a Jewish home, and I will conduct your ceremony!"

"But you're not a rabbi," Shmuel observed quietly.

"*Ach*! And you don't have a wife yet!" Bonhoeffer retorted. He bundled Vladek, Borris and Ezra into the back of his van and drove off in a rage. Somewhere out there his insult cooled off, and he returned a week later.

Shmuel welcomed him with sincere remorse. "I think I know what the problem is. My heart is not free."

"Not free how?"

"There's a woman I want, but you won't like her."

"Blonde?"

"No, she has shiny black hair, and I love her, I think. But there's a problem…"

"What sort of problem?"

"First of all, I don't know where she is or how to find her."

"That is a problem," Bonhoeffer confirmed.

"And another thing…the kind of work she does…it's not good."

Shmuel told Bonhoeffer everything. About Ricki, and the giant, and curly-haired Hezi who never said hello, and Shimi. Bonhoeffer listened with a supportive expression, without interrupting, and only occasionally interjected his insights like a detective starting out on a job.

"Ricki is a prostitute," he concluded gravely from Shmuel's

descriptions. "And Shimi is her pimp. And she left because the guy who was staying at your place left, and he was the customer."

"I want to find her. She's the one I want."

Bonhoeffer stroked the top of his head, shifting around his yarmulke as he did so.

"And if we find her together, and after a while you decide you don't want her, will your heart be available for other offers?"

"Yes," Shmuel said decisively.

"You'll have to tell me everything again from scratch. We have to find a lead."

So Shmuel told him about Ricki again, and as he talked his heart overflowed with longing. He felt ashamed—such a thing! To fall in love with a prostitute simply because she had sat near him wearing a towel, curled up in an armchair with her legs folded under her body, and had put on her glasses and looked so sweet, so strange and sweet and clean.

Bonhoeffer announced that there was no problem.

Shmuel was excited—no problem?

Bonhoeffer proudly spread out the fan of his acquaintances, in particular a few sailors and tradesmen who might know Shimi, or even Ricki.

Shmuel's heart sank. He didn't want them to know Ricki.

"Give me a couple of days."

Shmuel was disappointed, knowing what Bonhoeffer meant by a couple of days, but Bonhoeffer picked up on his look.

"Oh, don't worry. When I say a couple, I mean a real couple. Not the kind of couple I usually mean. Meanwhile, you do your work on the estate, because as they say, idleness is worse than labor."

The fires in the forests had left their mark on Shmuel. He felt stronger and more confident. People had always appreciated his work, but this time it was serious business, not just repairing a fan for Mrs. Zeller. People like Chaim Abramowitz believed in him—a man with a heritage, with a history. A man who had frightened the British, and the Arabs, and the Israelis. Shmuel was still not allowed to see the big picture, but he knew that he was a vital link in this thing called the Testament Army. Besides, he was starting to believe that the small change that was occurring within him—which could yet grow into something big—was not only because of his work on the estate, or even because of Ricki, but a result of the *Encyclopedia Hebraica* that his father had loved so deeply and pinned so many hopes upon—not for his own sake, because not everyone goes down in history, but for Katznelson, his Katznelson, not Berl, the regular one, but Yosef Katznelson, the Black Prince. Yehezkel's heart had been broken not by alienation or by hard work or by the state, but by the encyclopedia's failure to mention the Black Prince. Yet from the day Shmuel had started reading random entries, a solid content seemed to have been added to his body, a new skeleton that gave him the strength to be more of Shmuel. What did Shmuel care about Florence or Lenin or Pinsker from the Ps? And what would happen if he were able to read past the Ps one day? Either way, he felt that he was changing. Changing for the better. That the encyclopedia was working inside him.

That was it.

He felt confident, unworried.

Perhaps just a little worried.

He was worried about the big picture. He was not unaware of the fact that Abramowitz had hired snipers and archers and a former bomb-squad member and an explosives expert and various other types, all working alone or in little groups, all hard at work building systems. Was it possible that alongside his own system, which was meant to ignite a fire, another system was being built that would blow up the whole estate? And what about the man who dealt with toxins? And the dogs that were brought to the estate in the middle of the night? Günter also worried Shmuel with all his questions.

But Shmuel comforted himself. He had built a fantastic system. He was allowed to light massive fires that pleased everyone. Things were good, and he was coming up with inventions that everybody loved, apart from Gershon Pell. And he had a friend in Bonhoeffer, and he might soon see Ricki.

Ricki!

Ricki…

Chapter thirty-one

At Times of Happiness, the Heart Pays a Price
1978

At four o'clock in the morning Dr. Meshulam Riklin got out of bed, put on his socks, dressed in comfortable clothing, slipped a shoe on each foot, picked up his important notebook, garbed his joints with their rheumatism, clad his chest with a weak pulse rate adapted to his master Abramowitz's, reminded his left knee of the piercing pain in Abramowitz's knee, infused his soul with Abramowitz's wrath at the Zionist state, which robbed and executed unjustly, equipped his heel with a painful twist of old age, left his room and plodded up the path in the darkness.

He did not know that at midday his life would change.

It was Zero Day, and starting at five that morning, workers began to install the ignition system throughout the estate, while Gershon Pell paced back and forth in anguish, clutching pages of diagrams that flapped and bent in the wind. Hunched over, he moved among his dispiriting workers with a pounding heart and eyes ablaze, as if he were the one who would be set afire when Abramowitz gave the order.

The workers lowered cords and control boxes into the trenches, and Dr. Riklin threatened each one of them that they too might be lowered into the ground and buried. They placed the activation devices on concrete surfaces and calibrated them, and anyone who did sloppy work earned sky-darkening bellows from Dr. Riklin. He kept a portion of venom for the control room, where only senior employees were allowed, and he cursed Gershon Pell for being "the zero of Zero Day." This made a considerable impact on Pell, who stood gaping with a dim expression, as if the words had penetrated the nucleus of his soul.

When Riklin went back out to the workers, feeling that he had not yet exhausted his emotions and that a little more yelling might be in order, he encountered the perfect opportunity, for coming right toward him was Shmuel Klein.

Throughout the early hours of Zero Day, Shmuel was on the margins of everyone's awareness, and in fact no one noticed that he was missing. Even when he finally appeared they didn't ask him any questions. There was no need for him. But Shmuel was not insulted— on the contrary, he stood patiently, though nervously, rehearsing a variety of speeches that all consisted of a request to be released from service in the Testament Army and from life on the estate. He had already sworn that if they did not let him leave he would escape. But why wouldn't they? They had released Itamar Farkash, the highly respected toxins expert, once he had finished his covert work. What did they need Shmuel for? Nothing at all. Besides, no one but Gershon Pell, who was now darting around yelling at indifferent workers, knew the big picture.

When he saw Dr. Riklin, Shmuel began to pull the words out of his throat, and although he barely stammered through his request, he did not flinch from Riklin's gaze.

Riklin lowered his eyes and replied curtly that Shmuel could leave.

He could simply leave.

They did not need him anymore.

According to Chaim Abramowitz's laws, Shmuel was entitled to live on the estate for the rest of his life, if he so chose, but if he wanted to leave he could do so and would be handsomely rewarded.

For several days before his encounter with Riklin, Shmuel had been consumed by his search for Ricki. At first it seemed that Bonhoeffer's couple-of-days would be true to their traditional form, but then he turned up and apologized, explaining that his fishing net had gotten slightly entangled in the search for Shimi and Ricki—and besides, he had run into a farmer selling a dozen broken beehives, and the negotiations had taken longer than expected.

And Ricki?

Bonhoeffer had spoken with authorities in Ricki's field, but had yielded no results. To add further hopelessness, the experts had told Bonhoeffer that 'Ricki' was probably an assumed name. This was what people meant when they spoke of a dead end.

Shmuel rebuffed the despair. "That's her name. Her real name. I know it." Refusing to accept Bonhoeffer's defeat, he announced that he would look for Ricki himself. He only asked that Bonhoeffer advise him on where to look—where, according to his experts, did one find prostitutes and pimps?

But Bonhoeffer was insulted—Shmuel was his *mitzvah*, he explained. Would Cinderella have been saved without the fairy god-mother?

Shmuel was allowed to join Bonhoeffer on a few trips. Since he had already built the ignition devices, and they had been placed in storage until Zero Day, there was no use for him now anyway. Gershon Pell made it perfectly clear: "Him, I don't need anymore."

Bonhoeffer and Shmuel explored the most impure and miserable streets and neighborhoods. They even tried their luck at a newly available technique, ordering women of Ricki's sort over the phone. Shmuel waited for them nervously in his apartment, dressed in a specially purchased suit. One after the other, he opened the door for these black-haired women who came to service him, but none of them was Ricki. Shmuel sent them away, although sometimes his body tried to resist and circumvent the main target—Ricki—so that it could linger on its own objectives. But Shmuel reminded himself that he was no longer Shmuel of the body, but Shmuel of love, and surprised the women by paying in full for them to leave. He was impressed: here within arm's reach was a woman, and in his pocket was a wallet full of bills that could be handed over to purchase the woman's compliance. The very possibility of such an arrangement caused great excitement in Shmuel, but soon after the excitement came denunciation. After all, he was trying to save Ricki's honor, so how could he desecrate these women?

Shmuel felt particularly proud of these new thoughts, which he had come up with completely by himself. Some of them might have been copied from Bonhoeffer, but only a few. Every day, three times a day, Bonhoeffer and Shmuel put the search on hold and sat down together to eat to their hearts' content. As they ate, they talked, and Shmuel was surprised to discover how many opinions Bonhoeffer had. He was no longer just a strange, kind man, but a righteous man, like the ones Shmuel's father used to tell him about, men who did righteous deeds in secret, and pretended to be beggars, back in his old country. Bonhoeffer understood people, he truly understood them, just as Shmuel understood electronics. During these meals, he analyzed Shmuel's psyche, and Shmuel felt that everything Bonhoeffer said was really happening, the sadness and the fear, and a creeping desire not to meet Ricki, to replace her with a different woman, an easier one, and leave Ricki behind like a bittersweet dream.

Bonhoeffer also talked about international politics, and shared his insights on various historical and national affairs. Shmuel wished he could understand, but he had only read as far as Pinsker in the *Encyclopedia Hebraica*. He had not read about Russia, although he knew about it because of Lenin, Vladimir Ilyich. And Dzhugashvili, Joseph Vissarionovich, better known as Josef Stalin. And Peter the Great. And the First World War.

Either way, what did he care about Lenin, Vladimir Ilyich? It was Ricki he wanted.

One day when they finished their meal in a café, Bonhoeffer stopped to talk with the proprietress about buying an old set of dinnerware, and Shmuel restlessly walked outside. His thoughts were begrudgingly trying to decipher something Bonhoeffer had said: "Acts don't come from thinking, but from being willing to take responsibility." And then a young woman spoke to him.

"Hello, Shmuel."

Shmuel looked at her.

"You don't remember…" She sounded disappointed. Then she made up her mind: "All right, I don't remember either."

Ricki.

The green tips of a bunch of scallions jutted out of her shopping basket.

Ricki.

She looked different, but very beautiful. Shmuel, thrilled, knew he had to say something to stop Ricki from being angry. "I do remember," he managed.

He would have to say something else, a few intermediary words, before he could tell her that he was looking for her, that he wanted only her, that he thought he was in love with her. But what could he say? The words creaked out of him like the groaning turns of an old projector, words about Chaim Abramowitz, his greatness, the estate.

"Buy me a cup of coffee," Ricki said.

Side by side, they walked into the café Shmuel had just left. And in the café, Shmuel labored over two pieces of cake and two cups of coffee, until he was able to divert himself to the next stage in the encounter. He began to tell Ricki the highlights of his recent life, without the forest arson, and without the desperation in his heart. But he did mention explicitly how much he had missed her.

"You missed me?" Ricki smiled. Her clothes were so simple. Shmuel's eyes were drawn to the funny ribbon in her hair. He felt a fluttering of wings inside him, and he was happy, but there was also a tinge of pain. How could he say everything he wanted to?

They talked, and felt that the whole world was trying to listen. They talked and talked.

Ricki said, "Shmuel, you should know that I didn't want to be what I am."

"I didn't want to be what I am either." Shmuel wiped his lips with a napkin.

"No, you're really nice," Ricki protested.

They felt that they were ready. Yes, ready to be together.

Shmuel was embarrassed. He reached out to his cup of coffee and held it up in front of his face. She is so beautiful, he thought. So beautiful.

And then Bonhoeffer was there, balancing a stack of sixty plates, and he looked at Ricki with contentment, but there was also a flicker of indifference. He chattered about the plates and asked for Ricki's opinion: "These sort of cracks, do you think they ruin the beauty of the plates?"

But Shmuel brought the conversation back to the spirit of the operation—

"Bonhoeffer, Ricki here would like to leave. She needs an hour to get her things in order, pick up some stuff, and then we'll meet at my apartment. From now on, the address is secret."

"If Shimi catches anyone..." Ricki said, and ran her finger across her neck.

"So both the rooms in your apartment will be occupied now?" Bonhoeffer enquired.

"Yes, and remember, the address is secret."

"Don't mess with Shimi!" Ricki said, looking frightened. Her face froze in fear as she thought of him.

"Of course not," Shmuel said. "I'll wait for you here."

"Much happiness to you both," Bonhoeffer said, ready to step on the ceremonial glass. "But me, I'm an old man with business to do. I'll go and look at some lamps I can get for free, and tomorrow I'll come back to make sure the nest is warm." He giggled awkwardly and left.

Ricki touched Shmuel's cheek with two fingers and walked out. After she left, Shmuel ordered another cup of coffee and another piece of cake. His nerves were a little jumpy from the coffee, but somewhat sedated from the cake. And more coffee. And more cake.

One hour. Two. Three.

No Ricki.

Four. Six. Nine.

A day. Two, three. On the third day Shmuel had to go to the estate, because that was where he worked and lived, after all. His system was being installed soon, and they might need him. As for Ricki…he didn't want to think…he couldn't.

At the estate Shmuel met Bonhoeffer. He didn't want to run into him, but he did. And he had to tell him that Ricki was gone, that she had never come back.

"Maybe she got lost on the way?"

"Lost?"

"Just like Little Red Riding Hood…"

"No, Bonhoeffer. She didn't come. That's it."

"I saw the way she looked at you. Bonhoeffer understands women. She didn't just not come. Something happened."

"Something happened?" Shmuel echoed, and half of him became worried again, but the other half was hopeful—perhaps she had a good reason for not coming.

"We'll find her," Bonhoeffer announced

"How?"

"I don't have an idea yet. But that's good."

"It is?"

"Because my mind is free. An idea will come."

"How?"

"Just like you tie up a goat as bait for a tiger, you have to start with a goat thought, and the tiger thought will come."

"Bonhoeffer, stop." Shmuel began to cry.

He had never cried. Not at home, not at boarding school, not when Benzi Tirosh and Shimon Alfasi and Ronen Avidan the kibbutznik and Eliezer Akra the religious guy teased him, not when his father died without seeing the medal of courage, not when his mother died. Now he cried, and Bonhoeffer stood silently, then put a feeble arm around Shmuel's shoulder.

"Tiger!" Bonhoeffer roared suddenly.

Shmuel jumped.

"We'll ask for Günter's advice! He's on the estate today!"

Lately, Shmuel had been trying to avoid Günter, because he sometimes dreamed about lightning striking his system and destroying it, or about a herd of cows with heavy hoofs, or a train falling from the sky, and Shmuel always had to face Günter and explain why his system had not withstood the attack. But this time he went gladly, goats and tigers prancing in his mind.

Günter listened to the story from beginning to end, without questions or comments, his eyes on Shmuel. Finally he said, "Well, Hezi owes you a favor. He is the only opening in this whole story. Find Hezi."

How? Shmuel wondered.

"How?" Bonhoeffer asked.

Then Shmuel had a brilliant idea. "I'll go and see Mr. Bart, who used to rent his apartment to Hezi."

"Another tiger," Bonhoeffer observed.

They drove quickly to Mr. Bart's apartment and Shmuel knocked on the door. Bonhoeffer, by his side, murmured, "So in fact, apart from your place, there's an empty apartment in this building… how many rooms?"

And there was Mr. Bart.

He looked at Shmuel. He could have made things difficult—after all, he did not have much joy in his life now that he no longer made love to Edith Piaf—but a pair of tiger eyes was upon him, and Mr. Bart quickly brought a piece of paper with curly-haired Hezi's contact information. Half an hour later, Shmuel was standing at Hezi's door.

"I still owe you a big favor," Hezi said as soon as he opened the door. He wasn't sure why tigers popped into his mind when he looked at Shmuel.

Shmuel told him about the mysterious events of the last few days.

"Shmuel, you're a good guy. Don't get mixed up in this. They're tough, these guys. I got mixed up with them and it was a world of trouble."

"Where's Ricki?"

"Shmuel, do yourself a favor, forget about her. Ask me for a big favor, anything you want, just forget her. You want me to get you girls? Money for the two days? What?"

"Where is she?"

"I don't know. But Shimi—they call him Messiah—is probably holding her at his place, and you won't get anything out of him. Trust me. A grain of sand he won't let through his fingers."

Still, he gave Shmuel an address. "He doesn't live there, trust me, but that's where she'll be." A sleepy girl appeared behind Hezi, with wonderful golden hair and a white blouse tied over her short shorts.

Bonhoeffer and Shmuel rushed back to the van to make a plan.

"Did you see the blonde?" Bonhoeffer asked.

But Shmuel was already intent on the plan, which consisted of a very simple proposal: he would go to the address and find Ricki.

"A tiger plan!" Bonhoeffer said approvingly.

"And you'll wait for me on the next block in case we have to run."

"I have a map!" Bonhoeffer said excitedly. He pulled out a crumpled stack of papers from under the seat, and after peeling away a map of Rafiah and a guide to the Shivta antiquities, he found a map of the city. There was the street, more of an alleyway really, surrounded by a spider web of identical alleys forming a dense, menacing thicket.

Shmuel looked at the map. "You wait here in the van." He pointed to something that looked like a main street. "And I'll go here." He indicated Shimi-Messiah's alleyway. He looked at the entanglement of side streets and thought back to his medal of courage and Reuven Elkabetz.

Bonhoeffer dropped Shmuel off near a row of stores and repair-shops, and waved at him warmly as if he were going off to pick wildflowers. Shmuel had to search for his courage again. He had never seen such a place before—lopsided houses in states of disrepair, strewn with laundry lines, buckets, missing pieces of concrete. Was this where she was being held?

With cautious tiger steps, Shmuel made his way through the side streets. His heart jumped when he scared a stray cat, and he had to stop and pull himself together. Here he was again, setting off on a private battle, like when he had earned his medal. But this time it was himself he was rescuing. Himself.

Although he was focused on Ricki, who was trapped somewhere out there, somewhere very close, the surroundings began to instill a nagging doubt in Shmuel. And the doubt became a question—did the new director of the Museum of Prehistoric Man know there were houses like this in Israel? A neighborhood like this? And Shmuel's father, had he known that in his own city there were places that looked like this? And that people had to live in them? Had he known that such streets existed in his country, which he was so proud of at the beginning, and at the end too? And Jabotinsky? Had he known? And Pinsker?

With great sadness Shmuel brooded on his questions, and revived himself, and with his sadness he ducked between two buildings down a lane. Now everything depended on him, alone in enemy territory.

The deeper he went into the neighborhood, the more oddly familiar it seemed. Here was a corner store. There was a mother with her baby. The neglect, the crumbling walls, the building with its balcony collapsing onto the sidewalk leaving a gaping hole. The mother and her baby walked around the balcony pieces and the baby looked at Shmuel for a moment, and Shmuel remembered that he had ended up in a place just like this when he went searching for an abandoned lot to do his fire experiments in as a child. Drawn further and further inside, he had found himself suddenly surrounded by a group of terrifying boys. They were short one soccer player, and forced him to be their goalie. He spent two hours standing in the relentless sun, hugely disappointing his teammates, and he was shunted back and forth between the teams to balance out the odds. When the match was over, they kicked him off the field with jeers instead of thanks, cruelly commenting on every flaw in his body. If he were to meet those boys now, as a tiger, he would pay them back.

Navigating with the map, Shmuel turns right, then right again, left at the intersection, and right. He is getting closer. As he turns a corner, a figure runs out onto the balcony above him: Ricki in a wonderful pale green robe with her black hair tied back.

"Shmuel! Shmuel! Run!"

But the robe amazes Shmuel, so lovely and colorful, and his feet will not move, and he looks up at her and a door slams and heavy footsteps come running down the stairs.

"Run, Shmuel! Shimi's coming down to you!" Ricki yells. Two heads peer out of a neighboring window and quickly retreat back into their own troubles. A guy comes out of Ricki's building and approaches Shmuel menacingly. He grimaces in pain and holds one hand to his lower back.

"Shimi, leave him, he's nothing," Ricki begs.

But Shimi-Messiah glares at Shmuel with carnivorous eyes. Yellow, ridiculing eyes.

"Let her go," Shmuel recites, as if establishing the beginning of a negotiation.

Shimi-Messiah is a man of few words. He looks at Shmuel, sees a nuisance, and gestures at him lazily. "Get out, dumbass."

"He has the keys, I've been here for three days!" Ricki wails, and her abundant hair slips out of the ribbon. Shmuel's heart soars up to her, but Shimi-Messiah cuts down his hope by simply producing a knife. "*Yallah*, get out!"

Shmuel looks at Shimi, then at the knife, and takes a slow step forward, as if in consideration of Shimi-Messiah's backache. Shimi-Messiah holds the knife up threateningly and warns, "*Yallah!*"

"Give me the keys," Shmuel says. On the outside, he looks like a chubby bear, but inside he is a courageous tiger. His tongue is dry, he can barely breathe, knowing he is about to fight.

Shimi follows his senses. "Amos!" he calls out.

"Give me the keys," Shmuel repeats.

"Amos!!"

"Quick, Shmuel, Amos is coming! Quick!" Ricki pleads.

Ricki's call stirs the opponents. Shmuel advances. Shimi holds the knife up. Shmuel manages to grab the knife—not by the handle but by the blade. Shimi tries to pull the knife back and leave a deep gash in Shmuel's fingers, but Shmuel, with all his might, his burning, his panic, grasps the knife and instead of coming away from his hand it travels towards Shimi-Messiah until the handle stops at his gut. Shmuel lets out a roar that sends Bentzi Tirosh and Shimon Alfasi and Ronen Avidan the kibbutznik and Eliezer Akra the religious guy and Sergeant Adika and Bakhtin the medic and all his torturers and haters and troublemakers straight to hell. His body embraces Shimi's with the knife between them and his hands tighten their grip, and they crush, and they pulverize, and the fight goes on breathlessly until Shimi-Messiah rasps, "Amos!!!" There is a breaking sound, and Shimi-Messiah goes limp as Shmuel relentlessly presses, and his pressure compresses Shimi-Messiah, and compresses all of Shmuel's desire to win, and his desire to get the key, and his desire for Ricki, he has to have Ricki, her smile, he wants her to sit in his apartment again, in the armchair, in a white robe, reading the books that belonged to his mother, who did not live to see, and his father, who did not live to see, and everyone, who did not live to see, and Shmuel, may he live to see.

"Shmuel! Shmuel, let him go!"

Ricki's shout descends from other worlds like an eagle, and Shmuel rouses himself, and there is Shimi, wilted and whimpering, and Shmuel lets him drop to the ground and digs into his pocket and pulls out a bunch of keys. Two of Shimi's ribs are cracked or broken, and he squirms, clutching his gut and moaning, but he still tries to grab at Shmuel, who makes several failed attempts to throw the keys to the balcony—they fly up, and back to Shmuel—and Shimi-Messiah, folded over, comes to his sense and screams, "Amos!!!" and Ricki screams, "Quick!!!" and the keys fly up for the fifth time and land on the balcony, and Shimi-Messiah reaches for the knife, but Shmuel, whether by accident or deliberately, history will never know, stomps on Shimi-Messiah's hand, and Shimi cries out again, and there come Ricki's feet hurtling down the steps, and she comes out to Shmuel, and his grin is huge, and there is no way of knowing how she has had time to change her pale green robe into a light blouse with a blue collar and yellow pants, and she calls out, "Run,

Amos is coming!" and who this absent Amos is remains a riddle, but a short-lived one, for a head pokes out of a nearby window and Shimi looks up with a crazed face and yells, "Amos, get them!" and Ricki yells, "Run, Shmuel, it's Amos!" and Amos is huge and menacing, and his figure disappears from the window only to emerge in the lane and chase after the fugitives.

Ricki breaks into a run. "Run!" she screams and drops her sandals. Shmuel hurries after her, his windpipe scorched, but he stops by Ricki's sandals and bends over to pick them up. They have tiny buckles with little orange feathers. He can hear shouts coming closer, and wild footsteps, and he looks up in a panic—could such a large man be possible? He starts to run, fire in his gut, drawing strength from Ricki, who stops to wait for him and says, "Come on," and Shmuel does, with her sandals, and Ricki turns out to be fast and strong, and Shmuel makes sure they're not running off the map, and finally they see the main street, and Bonhoeffer near the van, examining a crate of broken candles that might be for sale, and Shmuel yells, "Bonhoeffer, quick!"

But Amos is quicker than Bonhoeffer, and he emerges out of the alleyway and for some reason rushes at Bonhoeffer and starts choking him, as if he knows who is at the heart of this affair, and Bonhoeffer opens the van door, not to flee for his life but to quickly pull out his bottle of Rémy Martin and whack it against Amos's head, and the mountainous hulk falls.

Three pairs of eyes flutter silently. They quickly climb into the van to save themselves from the now recovering Amos, and from Shimi who limps out onto the street, moaning and yelling something that sounds hostile. Bonhoeffer starts driving, Ricki and Shmuel sit beside him catching their breath, softening, clinging to one another shyly.

Bonhoeffer looks at them contentedly but realistically, with little faith. Because women like Ricki have so many troubles in their souls, and injuries, and scars, and Shmuel does not have the strength to heal her hidden wounds, and it's a shame, because she does have such a sweet face, and maybe there is a core of goodness inside her, for there is a spark of the divine in everyone, even in Amos, who somehow reappears alongside the van, running like a madman, almost catching up, but Bonhoeffer presses down on the accelerator and ignores the red light.

They reach Shmuel's apartment without further mishap. Parked by the entrance to the old building, they ask Bonhoeffer to stay a while. But he refuses: something urgent came up last night, a matter of life and death.

Life and death?

It's not Bonhoeffer's life that is in danger, but last night he learned about a complicated predicament, and tomorrow he must go to the Abramowitz estate to find a temporary solution for a needy man. If Shmuel wants to give notice at the estate that he's leaving, perhaps he could come with Bonhoeffer.

"And Ricki?" Shmuel asks.

"Doable...doable. But I noticed they don't like women there, apart from Rivka," Bonhoeffer mumbles.

"Yes, you go, I'll stay in your apartment," Ricki says, smiling, and her laziness is so lovely to Shmuel, like a cat that has adopted him, and her eyes are already indulging in his look.

"*Nu*, so tomorrow I'll be here," Bonhoeffer sums up. The couple gets out of the van and Bonhoeffer watches them and sighs: It's a nice story for now, and the mercies of Heaven are great, but no... they won't last...maybe a couple of days.

Once he was alone, Bonhoeffer turned his thoughts to his next mission, but his neck rebelled, craning to watch Shmuel and Ricki disappear into the building. A growl escaped his chest. He got out of the van, slammed the door shut, and began rubbing his fists together. It was time for another prayer between prayers.

Bonhoeffer held his head up and began with a heartfelt cry. He pleaded to the Creator of the World for the two young people climbing up the stairs, and demanded that He do with them as best He could. Perhaps He could bless them even before they reach the door and open the gates of His mercy. As he begged and frothed and pleaded, his fists raised at the balconies, blinds, and laundry lines, a bolt of lightning suddenly punctured the sky, filling the cap of the world with white light.

Bonhoeffer quieted down. He dropped his fists and waved his hand warmly, as if this response was even more than he had asked for. Then there was another bolt of lightning, like a bark piercing the whole sky. Bonhoeffer looked up one more time, his soul wishing to accompany the pair as they opened the door and walked into the apartment and looked at one another awkwardly.

"Nice, nice..." he giggled.

He opened the door and got into the van. He had been given his special *mitzvah*. He reached down for a new bottle of Rémy Martin, but instead of turning the cap he simply cradled the bottle in his palm as if protecting and sheltering it. He sat like that for a moment or two, silently, his potbelly pressing against the steering wheel. His breath was short. His heart beat quickly.

"On we go, on we go..." he said, shaking himself. He looked up at the sky, and at the top floor apartment, and tried to make sure the heavens and the earth were securely fastened. He giggled, and did not know that the next day, when he arrived at midday to take Shmuel to the estate, he would find that Shmuel had left that morning, and that when he arrived at the estate he would discover that Shmuel had already been there and had talked with Riklin and had been released and gone back home, and that in fact Shmuel Klein's role in Bonhoeffer's life was over, and Bonhoeffer's role in Shmuel Klein's life was over, but not necessarily done with.

*

In the early afternoon of Zero Day, with the system installed successfully, Bonhoeffer's van drove into the estate and a nervous Bonhoeffer stepped out. He opened the side door and drew back a pale pink curtain he had recently installed. A tall, beautiful woman in a black evening gown stepped out, and Bonhoeffer gave her his arm—rather, he gripped her wrist, and led her to Riklin with the usual request.

The woman did not look like someone who needed Bonhoeffer's help, and the crude way in which he held her arm also seemed peculiar, but the curiosity soon ended.

"Her problem," Bonhoeffer explained, "is that she's a he. I mean, she's a male. God help me. That is the problem." He was extremely embarrassed, and felt out at sea far from anchor.

A closer look revealed a few hints: the Adam's apple, the crude makeup, the broad shoulders. Something about the hips.

"And the worst thing is," Bonhoeffer continued, "that Ali, that's his name, he's not one of us, the poor guy." Recognizing his name in the waterfall of foreign words, Ali smiled cautiously, a smile that contained a degree of shame. Both an Arab and transgender—this required an apology to all creatures of the world.

Meshulam Riklin was seized by excitement. "Poor thing. How can I help, Bonhoeffer?"

"A couple of days, maybe three," Bonhoeffer estimated. And this time it really was a temporary solution, he clarified. Up until two days ago, Ali had lived his life happily and needed nobody. But then two of his cousins came to the club where he danced and his family found out about the whole thing. Now they wanted to kill him, but they would change their minds if he agreed to become engaged immediately to a cousin. Ali needed a place to think, preferably without fear of death.

Riklin came closer to Ali and stared at him with a confused look. "Hello," he said with a cracked voice.

"Is everything all right, Riklin?" Bonhoeffer asked.

Riklin turned pale. Ali stood frozen, afraid to move while he was being discussed.

"You can go," Riklin told Bonhoeffer. He gave an indistinct order to his assistants and quickly walked away to get back to work.

The next day Bonhoeffer came to see if Ali was still alive, and to reassure himself; there was something strange about Riklin's behavior. Something strange that troubled his mind.

He met Ali dressed in an attractive suit. Riklin was not far away, though he never came too close.

Finally Riklin walked up to Bonhoeffer and admitted, "He looks exactly like my wife, may her memory be a blessing. Naomi, née Mussadof. The complexion, the eyes, the mouth, all hers. How can I forget her? How? Exactly the same. Exactly."

Riklin could not understand the feelings that flooded him. Fear and hatred and love and tenderness, and a fluttering of sorts, and feverish thoughts, and weakness and fear. Yes, fear. Riklin was afraid.

"He looks like her...but he is not her...she is dead."

He looked helpless, and Bonhoeffer liked him for it.

"Go with your heart," Bonhoeffer suggested.

"Excuse me?"

"*Nu*, your heart..."

When Bonhoeffer left the estate that day he told himself that without a doubt Riklin was a changed man: he had forgotten to demand that Bonhoeffer take away two extremely difficult temporary solutions, he had given no final warning, and he had not even noticed that a young man named Vladek had slipped out of the van and into the estate, and as long as Vladek did not drink himself silly over the next few days, his work skills would soon be appreciated.

A week after Ali came to the estate, word came that for the first time in twenty-five years, Dr. Meshulam Riklin was taking time off from work to take Ali on a three-day trip to Petach Tikva and Rosh Pina. There was no attempt to conceal the similarity to a long-ago honeymoon, one that took place in another world, when a happy young Dr. Riklin had whispered names of gemstones in his wife's ears and poetry on her neck.

When Riklin and Ali came back from their holiday they complained about the heat and the mosquitoes. But Riklin's face was glowing. He wore a new suit, custom-made by a tailor in Safed, which added a masculine splendor to his appearance.

A week later they went on holiday again. They drove to Jaffa to enjoy the fresh air. The respite was successful, and Riklin came back flushed and healthy. He announced that the next week they would go and visit the wineries of Rishon LeZion.

Shmuel's system was securely embedded beneath the grounds of the estate. Other experts continued to carry out Abramowitz's plans. From time to time another installation day would be declared, and another system would take its place. Abramowitz's side of the estate was emptying out. Everyone whose job was over had a conversation with

Riklin and was offered generous compensation to leave. Abramowitz's burning urge to be alone in his European garden, which turned golden and red and green with the changing seasons, was nearing realization. The barns, the pens and the stables were handed over to Rivka, including all the lands and inhabitants they comprised, and in return Rivka agreed to take in the workers. The small crop fields, the workshops, the repair-shops—all abandoned, given to Rivka or destroyed. Abramowitz's side, which had always been virtually self-sufficient, began to buy food in the nearby town.

Abramowitz strove for simplicity. He wished to retreat into himself. To withdraw. To compress.

Every day Riklin sniffed out his master's mood. Abramowitz said nothing, only dictated his desires and left Riklin to wonder about the main thing: how far would he go? Would there, eventually, come a time for Riklin himself to leave?

Riklin refused to believe it. He refused, yet he was overcome with anxiety. It seemed impossible. But what would happen if he were asked?

By the time Bonhoeffer brought Ali to the estate, Riklin's anxieties had all but destroyed him. He wanted to kneel before his master and ask, Will I be asked to leave? He wanted to ask: *What will become of me?*

But since Ali's arrival, Riklin's nights were filled with new dreams. In the mornings he would awake and not know whether Ali had given him new happiness or merely squeezed out his last remaining yearnings. What was he deriving from Ali? He was a silent figure. The outer shell of Riklin's dead wife. Other than that, nothing. Why did he need Ali? It was a joke. But from the day he saw Ali he was suddenly able to imagine Abramowitz asking him to leave without fear. He would take Ali with him and go. Every time he imagined such a possibility, Riklin felt a shiver of fear. He would never leave Abramowitz, never. And for a false life with Ali? A joke. But it was good to be with Ali. Good to want to do things. To go on trips. To eat together. It was good with Ali. And less frightening.

Riklin calculated the day when Abramowitz would ask him to leave. Abramowitz had never so much as hinted at such a possibility, but Riklin kept coming back to it, unable to abandon the notion. Over and over again he imagined the moment.

Ali was living in his room now, and his feminine beauty flooded Riklin with terrible pain. Why had Naomi not stayed with him? What sort of a painful, wasted life had she sentenced him to? They could have pleased one another. Had she not seen, as he had, that their love was stronger than anything? But then again, what chance had there ever been? Her sorrowful face had heightened her beauty but portended the risk she posed to herself. Even that sorrow, a feature that had only half-existed, was in the gentle face of Ali. How could it be? Perhaps Riklin's memory was misleading him?

A new thought suddenly breezed into his mind. Perhaps…perhaps even if Abramowitz was not planning to ask him to go, perhaps he would ask to leave?

He experimented with being absent. He went on an unannounced trip with Ali, a long meandering walk through the nearby town. When he got back, he found the estate full of questions. Questions, but not disorder. He left with Ali the next day too, returning in the evening. Riklin wondered if Abramowitz would say anything. And as if compelled by the devil, he took Ali on a quick trip to Haifa, to see the Carmel and its beautiful houses. Ali, possessed by a bashful impudence, asked Riklin to buy him clothes, jewelry, and perfumes. And Riklin bought him everything he wanted.

Shortly before autumn, Riklin announced that he was taking Ali on an indulgent trip to the Galilee. They would visit their favorite places. Stay in villages. Taste the mountain air.

A torrid lightning storm lingered on the horizon all day long, with no rain, only dry arms reaching out across the sky again and again. At sunset the lightning came closer to the estate and the people grew afraid.

Chaim Abramowitz went out into his garden, protected by German, American and British lightning rods. He sat down and looked out at Rivka's territories.

I have tired of it all.

The storm seemed to be waning, rambling elsewhere, but then a huge bolt of lightning cleaved the sky, lighting up the entire estate for a second and striking right in the middle of Meir Glop's garden.

For one instant the garden looked like an X-ray image. Then the lightning died down, but not before giving a command to Shmuel's system.

Not a legal command.

Not one the ignition system could refuse.

Abramowitz jumped up.

He was trapped between three focal points of fire.

Flames appeared all over the estate, leaping from the ground, the trees, diving behind bushes. People ran out of their rooms and their offices, scurrying every which way. Someone yelled, "He's there!" Someone shouted, "God!" They came rushing from both sides of the estate and tried to put out the fire, but the flames climbed the walls, and the people below them looked as though they were bowing and shrinking, until they dispersed. A new commotion began. People fled, scattered down the paths, bumped into one another. They grabbed belongings from their homes and fled with arms full. Someone carried an iron safe. Another man dragged a calf. From somewhere in the distance Dr. Riklin appeared, alone, but no one paid any attention to him. He could only stand and watch Shmuel's work in astonishment, his eyes reflecting the mass of fire that now covered the land.

Chaim Abramowitz stood in the center of his garden. He looked left, right, straight ahead and behind. In every direction the blazing trees puffed out their chests as fire darted from branch to branch, but here and there an escape path was still discernible.

He looked at the flames. The black-red tones inflated people's figures, their faces rose up and were swallowed back.

One side of the fire seemed sparser, and Abramowitz watched it. Beyond the thick wall of trees and fire, the edge of the estate was visible, the other side, the border and the land beyond it.

I have tired of it all.

He looked at the flames. At the sky.

He looked at his hands.

And he sat down on his chair.

Chapter thirty-two

Not Everyone Goes Down in History   1978

Here, over here. Talk with her first."

Gently but firmly prodded by Rivka Abramowitz's people, the young man walks up to her front door. He stands there awkwardly with a folder in his hand, while in the dry sky behind him, lightning flickers.

"Come in," a female voice replies.

He walks inside. "I've come to interview Mr. Chaim Abramowitz. Is this the right place?"

The woman inside is not young. But she is beautiful. Bewitching.

"To interview Abramowitz?"

"And they made me come in here…"

"Don't worry. I'm Rivka Abramowitz. I just made some nice soup, would you like some?"

She sits him down in the kitchen and puts a bowl of soup in front of him—lentils and tiny shreds of something peppery-red float

477

in the broth. She lays down a spoon and a knife, a little bowl with lemon wedges, slices of bread, a small mound of salt on a dish. "Eat in good health."

He looks around.

He used to know houses like this once, when he was a policeman. He knew them well. He was a star in the police until they kicked him out, the bastards. He feels the old desire to put his police hat on the table and take down a statement. Distressed women recount what they saw. There was a crime here. Men broke in to her house. She saw a fight through the window. The neighbors were so quiet she can't believe it. No, she didn't have time to write down the license plates, and anyway, she was watching the boy, hard to believe that kind of human scum exists, running over a kid and driving off like that. She just happened to be looking out the window. The tranquil homes he was invited into, to listen, and always the sense of a soft, comfortable home where something had been desecrated. The father who sits opposite him with a boy on his lap, speaking quietly, reporting, but in his eyes he is tormented, *I did not protect my family.* An affliction that will not relinquish, that will stay with him, because anything that does not come out in the conversation with the officer will never come out. And here, too, this quiet, the calm, the lemons. A house with an atrocious crime committed between its walls. He will listen now too. A statement will be taken.

But first the official details.

"The soup is delicious."

What happened in this house?

She goes about her business, leaves him to sip his soup and think, and his heart beats like a clock. Lightning flashes outside, all day, lightning but no rain.

Another sip. The memories gallop in his mind. Once he was in Paris and he took the Metro. Amazed at the crowded trains carrying people along endlessly. For several days after he got back to Israel he kept thinking about the motion continuing without him, doors opening, closing, people transferred from one place to another. Endless motion. One moment he was a part of it, the next—no more. He has that same feeling now. Exactly the same feeling. He will finish the soup and leave, and everything will go on just fine without him.

Right after he got back from Paris his mother died. He thought to himself then, You're thirty years old, you can hardly be called an orphan. Thirty years old. He loved her so much. But at thirty you can't behave like a child. She had wanted him to marry. Grandchildren. As if there were any use in all that. Once someone had loved him but he wasn't interested. Two years later they met on the street and she had a baby in a carriage. He was so sorry. To this day, he is sorry…

"Seconds?"

She is in the room again. He nods. She ladles soup into his bowl and reconstructs the layout of the dishes. New slices of bread, lemon wedges, a mound of salt. The whole meal all over again. Pleasing to look at.

"Afterwards you'll try some jam."

Afterwards he'll try some jam. Commands spoken in her soft voice.

And her eyes—what color are they? Her shoulders are thin and dark brown. He likes shoulders like that, but these ones are a little too thin. Just a little.

After the soup and the jam, a cup of coffee is placed on the table.

He feels he has to explain. And ask for explanations. What is he doing here? And where is Chaim Abramowitz? He was invited not to see her, but Mr. Abramowitz. The meeting was arranged with him. Or rather, not with him but with assistants, lots of assistants. So many letters and phone calls, people who set dates and canceled them, and set new dates, other people who canceled things that had already been confirmed, and people who just called for no reason, giggled, cursed, complained. Now he is here, finally, for the meeting, and he must have made a mistake, they told him he was on the other side. What is the other side?

"What do you do for Mr. Abramowitz?"

"I…no…he's doing something for me. I'm writing a research paper, I'm a student. 'Losses in the War of Independence.' It might turn into a doctoral dissertation, the professor hasn't decided yet. I heard Mr. Abramowitz has an important perspective…new…different…" He feels agitated, and so does the sky, as lightning melts away the light for an instant.

"That was a close one," Rivka says with a smile. "It's been like that all day, and no rain. Dry."

"That kind of lightning causes fires," he mumbles.

"Fires?" Rivka looks out the window.

"So where exactly is Mr. Abramowitz?"

"I'll show you how to get to him in a minute."

"So I did come to the right place?"

"The place is right, the side isn't. I'm Rivka. I was Mr. Abramowitz's wife, and his step-daughter. You came in through the wrong gate, and you got to me."

His wife, his daughter…

"Don't be frightened."

"Me? Frightened?" He titters and clutches his folder. "And all those people who found me on the path, who insisted that I come to you…"

She smiles. "My people."

"I submitted a request to interview him, but every time I arranged a meeting someone called to cancel at the last minute. Then yesterday, out of the blue, they called and told me to come."

"Why are you writing about losses in the War of Independence? I mean, we won."

He lights up, wanting to explain, still dwelling on what she said, how strange, *I was his wife and his step-daughter*, and he fills with a great desire to explain, to interpret everything, perhaps it's the soup, his stomach is full, and he suddenly has an urge to tell her about his dismissal, how they fabricated false testimonies, how he swore he would fight back…win…return to the service, and agreed to take a university course "meanwhile," so he wouldn't go crazy without anything to do, and "meanwhile" turned into the real thing, it was all so interesting, and he no longer cared about his career. He could have gone far, he was a decorated officer. Then he remembers he is not here to talk with her, but with Mr. Abramowitz. And what is going on in this place? What is "the other side"?

Two bolts of lightning strike the estate, one after the other.

"If you wouldn't mind explaining…How is it that you were both his wife and his step-daughter?" He is curious. His professor always teases him, saying, "You're still a detective, it's good for research."

"My father was a hero of Hashomer. He was defeated only by illness. My mother was pregnant when she met Chaim Abramowitz, and all my life I've known only him, he was always my father."

"And how…how after that?"

"Then my mother was killed, and I married him. I was nineteen."

"But…"

"You came to interview Chaim. You can ask him about that too."

He chuckles. "Well, I'm not sure about that."

"Mr. Abramowitz, if he agreed to talk with you, will talk about everything. About me too. Trust me, I know. I was married to him for many years."

She laughs. He laughs too. But she still hasn't explained, hasn't satisfied his curiosity.

"And how—"

"—and how, and how. And how did you get an interview? He doesn't see anybody anymore."

"I asked…they said yes…"

"He's not a young man anymore. Old, even. But strong. You couldn't get a knife out of his hand. Back in those days, every woman wanted to be his wife. Every woman!"

"Yes…"

"I had lots of men in love with me. I wanted to fall in love too…"

"I understand."

"No, you don't. You can't understand. Don't talk, just listen. I'm telling you things I haven't told anyone." She is practically yelling now, and for a moment he thinks she is about to cry. Why is she telling him things she hasn't told anyone? Then her voice softens, forgiving. "Abramowitz was always good to me."

A flash lights up the window, almost bursting into the house.

"Do you think it will rain?" she asks. "I was nineteen."

"You were nineteen," he recites.

"When you go to interview Chaim, you can tell him you talked with me. And tell him I was angry at him."

"Angry?"

"Yes. I was angry. And now, tell me something yourself, before you leave. Why are you really writing about losses in the war?"

He wants to explain, thinks excitedly of how he might tell her about his dismissal, even though he doesn't care about that anymore. And he starts talking.

Her eyes grow large. As he talks, her expression becomes childish, sweet. She is a beautiful woman, not young, and he wonders what is so interesting about his story, it all seems so trivial to him, the arguments, the appeal. She listens, her lips slightly parted, entirely focused on his words, which to him become blander by the minute, so bland. His thoughts drift away. Something flickers. She is no longer Chaim Abramowitz's wife. She herself said she *was* his wife, but she didn't say anything about the separation.

He stops talking abruptly. Enough with the old trivialities. "So in the end you separated, I gather," he says boldly.

She does not protest at his abandoning the story—proof of how boring it was, and how long he had gone on with it.

"I was the one who decided to split up. To live separately. Alone."

"You wanted to turn back the clock."

"What?"

Lightning again. Three bolts. Lightning, lightning, lightning.

"I mean, to separate is to take a step backwards. When you were nineteen...," he begins.

"I think perhaps you should go. Before it starts raining. Go to Abramowitz and tell him Rivka loves him. Don't be shy. Tell him

Rivka still loves him and always will, but she will not come back to him. She wants to go on..."

"I hope I'll remember," he says obligingly.

"You will."

Rivka calls out, and two assistants appear.

"Take this nice man over to Chaim, so he doesn't take a wrong turn again."

He shakes her hand and briefly considers kissing it. But he is taken aback by his own thought. He turns around and leaves.

*

How long has she been sitting in her home with her face buried in her hands?

Suddenly she feels a blinding light. A massive bolt of lightning. Within seconds, the window fills with shadows of fire.

Shouts from outside, people running.

Her men burst into the house, shouting—a huge fire on the other side. The fire is getting closer. Firefighters are on their way, but the fire is getting closer. They have to run.

She stands up.

What about him?

They look away—they must hurry. Over there, on the other side, everyone who can run has left.

And what about him?

They hold her.

What about him? she screams, fighting them off.

He was there, in the garden, in the middle of the flames. His men took off. Someone saw the student too...he was saved. But Abramowitz...the fire started precisely where he was sitting. She must leave now too.

"Chaim..."

She lets them take her away.

Chapter thirty-three

Essay

Class: Writing
By: Yossi Chen
Title: Pioneer Heroes of Our Country

Draft

In honor of the thirtieth Independence Day of our State of Israel, we, the students of the Seventh Grade at Urim State School, went to meet the pioneers of our country. I was supposed to meet the pioneer Chaim Abramowitz, who was a very brave man and built lots of things in the Land of Israel. But the meeting did not happen, because on the day I came to see him the pioneer was burned.

I was very sorry that he died, but I have to improve my grades, because of the report card from Chanukah, and in the place where the fire happened I found a man who told me that he was also a pioneer sometimes, and his name is David Bonhoeffer.

The pioneer David Bonhoeffer told me that a terrible tragedy happened in Israel, that he wasn't crying because all his tears ran out when he was young, and if I wanted, he would tell me all sorts of things afterwards, but we have to cry because the pioneer Abramowitz is dead. I asked him how to spell Abramowitz, and he took my notebook and wrote in very big letters, and told me to write it too, so that I could feel the name with my fingers.

My notebook got dirty from his hands, and he said he was sorry, he was helping the firefighters all day, until they got angry and kicked him out. He was there since yesterday, near where Abramowitz's house was, and he couldn't leave. He came to the Abramowitz Estate by chance, with some things to sell in his van, and suddenly there was no Abramowitz.

I asked him to tell me about the pioneer Chaim Abramowitz, and he said, write this, and then he told me that the pioneer Chaim Abramowitz came to the Land of Israel in difficult and dangerous times, and thanks to him, people built houses and plowed furrows and watered soil and prayed to God and did *mitzvahs*, and helped poor homeless people, and gave them money or built houses for them. Then there was the War of Independence and the pioneers turned into fighters, and the State of Israel, our country, was started. In the days when Chaim Abramowitz fought for his state, even the easiest thing wasn't easy.

That was all he had to say.

I told him my essay had to have one-thousand words, and what he told me wasn't even half. He told me to write that in the terrible tragedy not only the important pioneer Abramowitz died, but also Dr. Meshulam Riklin, who came back from his vacation early, and when he saw the flames and found out that Mr. Chaim Abramowitz was inside them, he marched into the fire and died, and apart from the two of them also the tree-planting pioneer died, his name was Meir Glop. May their memory be a blessing. Bonhoeffer took my notebook again and counted the words, and he kept getting mixed up and said it couldn't be that we hadn't got to a thousand, and if they asked him how many words you could write about Abramowitz he would guess that as much as all the letters in Psalms, but he never thought anyone would ask him, and he wasn't good at telling stories. He said that if only I could meet Chaim Abramowitz myself, then I might understand. Then he said that he only just realized that he never said all the kind words to Abramowitz, and now all he could say for him was the *kaddish*, and he would like to say more, but it was too late. He took my notebook and wrote: young men like you can't understand how difficult and bad it was here, in *Eretz Yisrael*, when the pioneer Abramowitz came. Then he said that not everyone who made *aliyah* was lucky enough to be near people like Chaim Abramowitz, who helped them live without being afraid. That people heard about Zionism when they were young, in the Diaspora, and had Zionist arguments in the cafés and in the youth movements, and decided to come to *Eretz Yisrael* with a lot of enthusiasm, and what they found here is a bit difficult to describe, not something similar to the way they imagined it when they sang songs in Europe about a land of wilderness and a land of desert.

Then he counted the words again, and stopped in the middle because he remembered something else, and he gave me the notebook to write: many people went back to their countries, because life was too difficult. And there were good people who insisted on staying here, and in the end they couldn't make it and they hanged themselves. Those poor people ran away too, really. But the state was built by people who didn't run away, people who always had a part of them that wanted to run away but they insisted on staying anyway. Bonhoeffer said they are the heroes, heroes that no one writes about, and that I, as a young boy, can see these people managing shops and working in offices and farming fields. He said that sometimes there were pioneers who ran away because they couldn't survive, but they came back, for example in the War of Independence, and with God's help they are still alive now, thanks to faith, and this is where we have to stay, and I am a young boy, and he can't explain to me with words how difficult it was to survive, first I have to grow up and live for many years, and then I'll understand on my own that it's hard to survive, even in a modern country like we have today, but what a tragedy happened now, what a tragedy.

487

I asked, what tragedy?

And Bonhoeffer said, Chaim Abramowitz. Then he didn't say anything for a long time.

Then he told me that the pioneers who came back, to this day they sometimes miss even the tiniest flavor of their fathers' homes. And that if for a minute the faith in their hearts weakens, their faith that Zionism is the solution, then their entire soul suddenly wants to go home. But I should know that Zionism is the solution, only Zionism.

He took the notebook, then gave it back, and said: You count, I get mixed up.

I had enough words, and I wanted to leave, but he asked me to stay because he had something else to say, and it could be a conclusion, in honor of Chaim Abramowitz. He said that on this day I had to put something in my essay about the future of the country, and I was happy because the teacher says you always have to have a conclusion.

He asked me if I'd heard about the Six Day War, and I said yes. He asked me if I'd heard about the Yom Kippur War, and I said of course, and that I even sat in the bomb shelters, because I was already eight.

He took my notebook again, and showed me where to write so it would stand out, and he dictated very slowly:

We won the Six Day War, and we learned that Auschwitz would not happen again. In the Yom Kippur War we learned that the Kingdom of David would not happen again. Maybe now the State of Israel will start to have an ordinary history.

Then he asked me if we have any spare rooms at home, but he said that didn't have anything to do with the essay.

When I grow up I want to be like the pioneers.

Chapter thirty-four

That We May be Forgotten

1920

> *"All of us knew we had come from an inhabited land to a desolate land, that this was a wilderness and that we would face hunger and malaria, yet nevertheless—faith we had."*
> *(Avraham Shlonsky)*

In the the pioneering days of 1920, as the road from Tiberias to Tzemach was slowly being paved, the figure of the journalist Leon Abramowitz can be seen supporting a limping pioneer. Dov is the pioneer's name, a giant creature who has only recently been waving railroad beams in his hands, shattering mountain rocks, and chopping down evergreens. He has injured his leg in an unfortunate accident, and since he refuses to rest and be as one of the weak, his injury is worsening. A thick white bandage is wrapped around Dov's thigh, and as the two men lag behind the workers and stop to rest, Dov unbandages his wound for Leon Abramowitz to give his expert opinion.

The flesh beneath the bandage is infected, and Leon detaches his words from his thoughts. "Rest your leg and it will heal," he promises. He makes a note to himself to consult a physician.

There is one good thing about the injury, which is that it positions Dov and Leon at an equal pace, enabling a dialogue between the journalist-delegate and the almighty-pioneer, a truly momentous opportunity.

Abramowitz has been drawn to Dov before, but the pioneer was not interested in talk. He wishes only to pave, chop, hew, level. With the strength of giants, with the roar of lions. But now, since his health has deteriorated, a profound wisdom seems to have entered his body. His expression remains artless, but there is a thoughtfulness to his words. In the evenings, when he takes out his harmonica, the instrument seems to be playing Dov, rather than the other way around. Sad tunes, perhaps ones better not played.

Once in a while a sharp pain seizes Dov and he can barely hold his jaw shut to smother a scream. When the pain passes, he sits down next to Leon, glistening with sweat, and asks fearfully, "Are you sure I'll get well?"

"Of course you will get well. Why wouldn't you get well? We all get well!"

Dov lowers his head. "Sometimes I feel that I won't get well. That this is the end."

"No, no," Leon Abramowitz protests, considering a new thought: the injury is in Dov's body, but the gnawing—in his soul. He must be encouraged and provided with a broad, historical, cultural perspective on his temporary situation.

"I have already told you what Yosef Chaim Brenner said on the topic of revival."

"You also told me that he said, 'This is the final station.' Maybe it is…maybe I won't get well."

"Look here, Brenner's words must be approached with erudition, Dov, for he said many things, and one must select carefully. It was not you that he was speaking of, Dov, not simple wounds in one's leg. It was the people's condition that he spoke of, in a generalized way, an impression. A slightly overreaching impression, if I may…"

"I feel that he was talking about me as well. That is how I feel."

Leon Abramowitz examines this giant young lion. There is sorrow in his words. A primordial brain sits on his Samson-like shoulders. How touching he is.

"Look, Dov, the words of Yosef Chaim Brenner are the water that quenches our thirst. But you must be cautious of accepting them at face value. For there was a man no less monumental, A.D. Gordon, who objected to Brenner's worldview: 'A nightmarish image with no human form whatsoever is what Brenner has made out of the People of Israel…from his inner sin of self-deprecation before European culture.' Now, you should adopt the ideas of this great man, whose vision you yourself have fulfilled with your massive strength. For I have seen how hungry your hands are for work—you were derived from the Gordon dogma."

Dov shakes his head. "Why are there so many leaders here? Each one speaking against the other. Once I was at a congress where the movement leaders spoke against other leaders, and I thought, We must be united."

"Do not worry, Dov. Everyone is united. Things may be spoken in different ways, but they all point to the same idea. You should feel blessed to have lived in a generation of love across all the divides of Israel. Rejoice, Dov, for historically speaking, these are days of love. Love, Dov, love!"

Dov blushes. Perhaps the words have touched the depths of his soul. Perhaps he is thinking about a certain woman from his group.

"Let's get up!" Dov says, rousing himself. With stubborn force he stands up on his feet and forces his injured leg to walk. Leon struggles to keep up with the giant.

"See, I would never have guessed that a wound is hiding there under the bandages. Your name means *bear*, and you are just as strong as one," Leon says, out of breath.

Dov tries to catch up with the group of workers. He has rested enough. It is not good for a man to be idle. But after twenty paces he stops. His lips part. He practically has tears in his eyes.

He looks at the mountains around him, then looks down. He reaches into his pocket for his harmonica, the one that produces such sorrowful sounds. He grasps it but does not hold it up to his lips. He ponders.

Leon watches him—what is in his mind? Perhaps nostalgia for the life he left behind in the Diaspora.

"Let's go," Dov announces, and starts walking again, with Leon at his side. The two men are silent, and the mountains around them seem to Leon to be closing in.

"Why did we come here?" Dov asks suddenly.

"Why…" Leon feels anxious.

"They didn't love us there, and they don't love us here. They killed us there, and they'll kill us here. It's all for nothing."

The wound is making him sad, Leon Abramowitz senses. "Perhaps we should rest?"

Dov ignores him. "There the *goyim* hated us, and here everyone hates us. What's the difference?"

But Leon hurls himself into the battle now. "No, no, Dov. No, no!"

Dov persists. The sadness pools in his eyes. "What are we doing here, really?"

"What…?" Leon is taken aback.

"We work and work…nothing changes. Look, a road. Our backs are broken. What for? What's changed in the world?"

"Oh, Dov. Do not worry. Things are changing, everything is changing. Constantly. Do not let the present hamper your imagination. Close your eyes for a moment and imagine: here is the world… and here is the world a moment later. Don't you see? Palaces and roads and fields of wheat as far as the eye can see. Our purpose in life is just as it always has been."

And finally, like the crack of a nutshell, an idea that has been forming inside him for many days is born and finds words.

"Look, Dov. Look. We are here to work hard. We are here for the purpose, the ultimate purpose!"

How good it is to say things, and at the very moment of their utterance, to understand them for the very first time.

"Do you know, Dov, what the purpose of Zionism is?"

"What?"

"That we may be forgotten!"

"Forgotten?"

"Yes, Dov. Yes, yes. Here, this is the purpose of Zionism: that we may be forgotten. That there will be no lovers of Jews and no haters of Jews in the world. No anti-Semites and no philo-Semites. That we may be a nation, just an ordinary nation, without lovers, without haters. That we may be, in short, a nation in its own land."

Dov nods. He has certainly comprehended at least half of it.

Leon Abramowitz grows excited. He has tried to formulate the notion before, but now he finds the most accurate words.

"That is why we came here, Dov. Do not let the wasteland and the enemies worry you. The diseases and the ravages. The conflicts and the desperation. That is the labor of Zionism and this is its reward— that we may be an ordinary people, living in its land, forgotten."

He knows now that the idea can be phrased even better, and the new words are on the tip of his tongue. He knows that an article can be written.

Dov limps on in pain, and Leon rushes to catch up with him.

"Do not worry, Dov. Do not worry."

Sources

The epigraphs are taken from:

Michael Bar Zohar, *David Ben-Gurion*. Zmora Bitan, 1987. [In English: Michael Bar Zohar, *Ben-Gurion: A Biography*. NY: Delacorte, 1979.]

Yosef Chaim Brenner, *In Winter* [*Bahoref*]; *Around the Point* [*Misaviv Lanekuda*]. Dvir, 1988.

Yosef Chaim Brenner, *From Here and There* [*Mikan Umikan*]. Warsaw: Sifrut, 1911.

A.D. Gordon, *Man and Nature* [*HaʾAdam Vehateva*]. Jerusalem: Hasifriya Hatziyonit Al Yad Hanhalat Hahistadrut Hatziyonit, 5711.

A.D. Gordon, *Writings* [*Kitvei A.D. Gordon*]. Tel Aviv: Havaʾad Hamerkazi Shel Mifleget "Hapoel Hatzair," 5685–5689.

A.D. Gordon, *Letters and Essays* [*Mikhtavim uReshimot*]. Haifa: Moetzet Poalei Haifa, Hasifriya Hatzionit, 5717.

Edna Meir Meril, "Alexander Levy, Designer of the Pagoda House in Tel Aviv—Forgotten Architect" [*"Alexander Levi, Metachnen Beit HaPagoda BeTel Aviv—Architect Nishkach"*] *Katedra* No. 71, Yad Ben Zvi, March 1994.

Benny Peled, *Days of Reckoning* [*Yamim Shel Cheshbon*]. Tel Aviv: Modan, 2004.

David Rap, "In the Fresh Air of the Forest in Palestine" ["*Baavir Hatzach Shel Hayaar Befalestina*"]. *Haaretz*, 25 October 2002.

Moshe Sharett, *Personal Diary* [*Yoman Ishi*]. Tel Aviv: Sifriat Maariv, 1978.

Avraham Shlonsky, "Marching Song" ["*Shir Lechet*"], in *Poems* [*Shirim*], Second Vol. Tel Aviv: Sifriyat Poalim, 1971.

Mark Twain, *The Innocents Abroad, or The New Pilgrims' Progress*. American Publishing Company, 1869.

Meir Yaari, *Portrait of a Leader as a Young Man* [*Dyuknao Shel Manhig Ke'Adam Tzair*]. Tel Aviv: Sifriat Poalim, 1992.

Acknowledgments

To Professor Judy Baumel, Anat Elhalal, Asaf Heller and Yoram Shamir for their helpful comments.

To Ronit Sneh who gave me access to her private archives.

To Mischa Katz who described the assassination attempts against Stalin better than Stalin himself could have.

To Ami Nahari who conducted research for me and collated useful Yemenite phrases and curses.

About the Author

Amir Gutfreund was born in Haifa in 1963. After studying applied mathematics at the Technion, he joined the Israeli Air Force. Gutfreund was awarded the Sapir Prize in 2003, and in 2007, his first book to be translated into English, *Our Holocaust*, also published by *The* Toby Press, was the 2007 Sami Rohr Prize for Jewish Literature Choice Award winner, as well as a Barnes & Noble Discover Program choice.

Gutfreund lives in the Galilee with his wife, a clinical psychologist, and their three children.

The fonts used in this book are from the Garamond family

Other works by Amir Gutfreund
available from *The* Toby Press

Our Holocaust

The Toby Press publishes fine writing,
available at leading bookstores everywhere. For more
information, please visit www.tobypress.com